RADIO HONEY

Tara Arkle

ISBN – 978-1-949802-13-9

Published by Black Pawn Press

FIRST EDITION

To anyone who has learned

to trust their own voice and

sing their own song regardless

of the radio interference.

Chapter 1

To the Sounds of 'Ordinary World'
by Duran Duran

London 1994

There's no point working in a radio station unless you *love* music. *Real* music. And yeah, sure, you'll have to play the station shit, but every now and then you'll be able to sneak one in that you genuinely like. Something that makes you feel good to be alive — pure musical gold — a little Billie Holliday or Marvin Gaye; an old Deee-Lite hit, or maybe, my old fave — the Shaft Theme Tune. I've been cautioned for less.

Then there's what you can do with the play list: you can move the tunes around to suit your own show-specific running order, depending on the way you're feeling that day; to accommodate an interview which ran long, insert a breaking news item, or just because you had to high tail it to the little girl's room and back: in which case an extra-long song is called for.

It could be a start it light, and build up kind of day, or a hit-them-with-the-big-tune-in-the-intro-and-keep-building-till-you-hit-the-end-of-your-coffee-rush-affair.

Then again it could be the kind of day where you're trying to forget a certain someone in which case you'll play every love 'em and leave 'em song in the 'I've been dumped' catalogue. Of which there are many.

And today is one of those days.

His name is Jack (or 'bastard'), although it could be Steve, John, Bob, or Adam — there have been so many that never got past the first shag. Followed by my cringing attempts to keep what modicum of original interest they had in me alive only to see them retreat further; at a giddy pace. Is the word 'desperate' now so clearly emblazoned on my forehead that no male in their right mind would engage me for more than an evening's 'friendly' without a matrimonial lawyer, and a good pre-nup?

And when you bump into these passing lovers months or years down the line, they are invariably with Jessica, Annabel, Lisa or Sarah, and she is so much more beautiful than your own reflection looking back at you in the mirror — 20's, 5'6", dyed blonde hair, great tits, great ass — suddenly you understand why Steve, John, Bob, Adam, *et al* dumped you. Or she is so plain Jane you wonder how Steve, John, Bob, or Adam dumped you, and plumped for her?

In your mind you imagine sexual acts she must perform with one hand tied behind her back; gymnastic like manoeuvres that make her indispensable. In reality it's probably something a lot simpler — something like good old-fashioned chemistry. I mean they say there's someone out there for everyone, but is that statistically and evolutionarily possible? I can hear my father spouting his statistical non-entities as I ponder this; he is very fond of a social statistic, the latest scientific data, or a cringingly data-driven chart analysis. But isn't it just as reasonable to assume that there is no logic, no rhyme or reason and we all simply clamour about just trying to get the best we can? Like a game of musical chairs where the music stops, and you, having missed all the other chairs, simply jump for the last available place to rest your rump?

Perhaps *now* when you see Steve, John, Bob, or Adam with this other woman you can rationalize that it wasn't that you weren't pretty enough or cool enough, but that he simply decided to sit down at a pause in the music? That somehow the music had been playing so loudly when you two were together with the swelling of violins and heart strings that there wasn't a moment to sit down and take stock? Propelled along by the beauty of the dance, you both twirled yourselves out of the ring?

Nah.

Face it, you weren't the one for any of them, and you wonder if you will be 'the one' for anyone and if not, whether that will be ok? Will living alone with some four legged be enough? Or will the horror of more heart-rending love affairs outweigh the need to get embroiled again and again until one day you wake up and realize that love is simply not meant to be a part of your life, and that you are lucky to have a loving pet, and a rabbit full of batteries?

These are the kind of thoughts that go through my head between CDs, as I play songs that more often than not I have risked the ground shaking wrath of my boss, Clare, or *Psycho-Tetris*, as she is affectionately called, due to her being as boring as this tile-matching video puzzle game — and psycho because she lacks the warmth of your average sociopath. I am happy, however, to get a good thrashing for deviating from the playlist simply because I believe that I, and my listening faithful, deserve the very *best* to express the very *worst* — this stream of broken hearts that could replace the Thames with its tears.

For example, the other day I got a letter from someone called Tina, and she said, "Dear Cass, Every time I feel low you seem to know and play some great tune that puts me back on track, and makes me feel like life is worth living..." etc. You see, it's not just me alone in some booth in the middle of

London — I'm plugged into the mains! I'm a beacon beaming out positive energy to those that need it and feeding my own soul in the process. It's not just a job, it's a mission!

People are always saying how God is love, and that's fine if you believe in Him, but closer to home I believe music is love. My job is about choosing the best messages to send out. When you mix the tunes up just right you form a powerful stream of energy that builds up in intensity pushing those good vibrations out into the world.

My Dad, who is a *major* science nerd, says that all the sound carried by radio gets projected into space and travels on and on, surfing the milky way and out into the universe: forever. To think that some alien species may be listening to my show out there, or quite simply that my words travel into that awesome nothingness, the quiet of the cosmos; that somewhere out there you may happen to fall upon an abstract voice, song, radio show, all suspended in space. It gives me the spins just thinking about it, but then maybe I shouldn't have had that blunt before coming into work this morning?

Anyway, down here in London town you'll be lucky to hear us at all. You see Ofcom found us some unknown frequency, out in the middle of radio-no-man's-land, threw up a few masts in silly places, and voilà, a station that only 25%

of Londoners can actually receive. Although out in the hinterlands of Greater London they can hear us just fine.

If you were to ask me, "Cass, why do you bother? What's in it for you?" I'd tell you, and it's the God's truth, or *my* truth — I do it for the people. To add my bit to the healing of the cosmos and the broken hearted, but I also do it for myself. I do it because I'm a frustrated singer, and these are all my songs.

Here in this radio booth, for those couple of hours, I own them all. I can sing along and feel like I'm a part of the music that's being played. These songs are my life's play list; my compilation tape to an unnamed somebody. Or maybe it's just an endless song I sing to myself to keep up morale?

You see, even though I make it down to Blink's club every Friday night, and get up and sing one of my own every now and then, I haven't gotten up the courage to go for the big time. The rejection would probably kill me. So, I play it safe, I play the songs that I know people want to hear, the ones they ask me to play. That way I stave off disappointment. And that's OK, for now; at least it was before Jack turned up the volume on the soundtrack of my life.

Clare is suddenly in the studio. I was too deep in thought to notice the change in atmosphere that usually accompanies her surprise appearances. Hel (Helen), my seemingly underage producer, is in the studio in front of me, and through the glass, unbeknownst to Clare, is working herself up into a frenzy, mouthing the words to 'Girls Just Wanna Have Fun' by Cyndi Lauper whilst simulating breast massage, and overall body pleasuring. This type of tomfoolery seems to be particularly prolific in an organization made up mostly of women, pre or post menstrual. However, as an all-female radio station, we pack a potent hormonal punch no matter the time of month.

Clare obliterates this disturbing show with her equally disturbing presence.

"Cass — I don't recall this being on the play list?" She looks me straight in the eye; straight down the invisible cue stick she wields my way; knowing she has every right to sink me in the corner pocket for playing unlisted songs. To say she gets upset when a presenter dares to play music not listed on the show running order is an understatement. Even hearing a presenter change the order in which the tracks were listed each hour could shut down her thinking processes faster than a protest rally at Tiananmen Square.

The station playlist, in itself, is a prime example of what happens when you allow too many people to load too many obscure tracks into Selector software. A package which has already been loaded with an off- the-shelf AC (adult contemporary) format CD package, with a rotation of one hundred songs that stifle the life out of personality and free speech. Then fail to apply artist separation notes which means you could be playing The Eagles into Don Henley, into Joe Walsh, into Glenn Frey; sounding like a catalogue show for one band's solo albums. And then ignore 'daypart rules' so that at eleven forty at night when you're just about to sip your cocoa and go sleepy time you get blasted with Jimi Hendrix and 'Purple Haze' when they should be playing 'Sweet Dreams' by The Eurythmics. Not to mention a basic failure to grasp popular music in the 20th century. Couple that with a major label bias, and we are fighting a battle not of the Somme but of the Song!

My heart recently harpooned, I'm in no mood to argue; my brazen balls are tarnished, and I let it slide:

"Clare — I'm sorry. It just kinda jumped out of the library at me this morning when I was looking for the new number one. I promise it won't happen again..."

Hel, now witnessing this surprise appearance, has quickly stopped her erotic show, and is high tailing it out of the adjoining studio. Knowing her, she will now thrust herself in Clare's outgoing path in an attempt to give the impression that she is an oh-so-busy-producer-with-vast-amounts-of-talent-and-expertise-which-are-seriously-underplayed-at-Radio-Honey.

"It better not." Clare delivers with a lack of emotion that suggests a life unfamiliar with the simplest joys, or a face unknown to expressions of the slightest good humour. An underlying impression, like a dropped shadow, implies dark, soiled childhood trauma that even the most seasoned psychiatrist would grapple with. She turns her unremarkable body around in its lacklustre attire, and gives me a back view of that lifeless, mousy brown hair. Hair that would find a new head if it could. The door thuds closed, mercifully.

From the studio window behind me, which faces the action-packed offices of Radio Honey, I see Hel come face to face with Clare who it seems has a spot of advice to pass on. Hel doesn't appear to be getting a pasting so much as some instructions. It's swift and looks relatively painless. As Clare leaves, Hel turns to me and wipes mock sweat from her brow.

I grab the mike and start to wind up to the next song as Hel comes in trying to be quiet, but even with her own volume turned down she is the noisiest little bitch I know. I track out and pull the fader down.

"What on God's earth are you playing at? I'm in enough trouble as it is without you playing Mata Hari whilst I'm trying to work!"

"Work — *schmirk* — have you heard the show today?"

"Yeah, I've *heard* it, but have you *worked* on it? Don't think so!"

I watch a tide of red rise up over Hel's face, and her mouth move, but no words gurgle out; it could be some time till I get any response. Still desperately trying to think of a comeback, she turns, and leaves the room, literally in a huff: you can hear the little 'huff, huff' sounds she makes as she goes, like a toy train; a combination of rough quality synthetic pants too tight for her abundant ass, and her internal steam exhaling in tiny gasps.

Hands down she holds the award for most likely to remain under the age of five amongst all the staff at Radio Honey. This isn't helped by the fact that all 4'9" of her has the girth of a Womble, and with dark hair, cherub round face, and big brown eyes she could pass for one of the 'Lost Boys.' Her enormous breasts, however, reassure us she is most definitely female, and these, counteracted by her enormous bottom, and her thankfully wide feet, accommodate the entire load with flat-footed self-assurance. Or as much as is possible in an environment where dignity must be fought for tooth and manicured nail.

Decibels and speed of verbal delivery mean that she is never normally dismissed due to size, and her heart is most definitely in the right place, although being somewhere south of where it should be due to the enormous amount of jiggling she does in the name of being herself.

It's coming up to the hour which means it's time for news, ads, and traffic. I check through the glass behind me to find out where our traffic girl, Gail, is and hope that Hel, despite her animosity, is ready with the latest celebrity gossip inserts. What I see, however, is Courtney, our resident Yank, and my preferred side kick, nay accomplice, working the room with her usual hocus pocus; walking amongst the many scattered tables of the Radio Honey production area like a honey bee amongst flowers.

She must be working on a scoop — I can smell it on her, but she just smiles at me through the glass when I give her the quizzed look; she even emboldens her movements with a nonchalant shimmy of her shoulder length, blonde hair.

Not a natural blonde, she has the high cheekbones of a Cherokee, coming from her Grandma's side twice removed, and is stocky in the kind of way that country gals can be, with an apple pie smile to match. Our token hillbilly, all the way from Kansas, she has decided, for some unknown reason, to invest her love and energy into this God-forsaken station, with more oestrogen than sense. She could be anywhere. With the personality of a Baptist preacher and the business acumen of a Wall Street trader she should have been running the station not 'jocking' in it.

Dressed almost entirely in sheepskin derivatives, she holds her own as only an American can in a hot bed of fashion bitchiness. In the quagmire of London's working girl chic, she ignores it, and goes her own way. It's quirky, but it works.

Today Courtney is somehow enduring the chaffing of leather trousers (unusual even for her, but then she *is* going straight on to the club later), and a cotton smock that owes more to Woodstock than it does to the West End. This is finished off with sheepskin lined boots, and a sheepskin vest.

We are all victims of the fashion conspiracy whether we are on the street or hidden away in a radio booth, allowed all the bad hair days that a disc jockey can manage. I, for one, am wearing the latest in Top Shop accessories, a sports wrist band that holds more water in a hot tennis match than it does in a dry, air-conditioned radio booth; a bad peroxide, with an inch of dark root; a t-shirt that inhaled too much tie dye; a sports jacket owing more to Oasis than Blur, and jeans that might once have belonged to Ziggy Stardust for their Perspex sheen. The shoes are sporty but platformed, a nod to the club scene that birthed them.

I beckon her into the studio, but she holds up her index, 'one minute' finger. She's off the hook for now because my trail is ending, and I still haven't decided what track I'm going to put on next.

I grab a CD off the top of the pile I'd stacked earlier, and slip it in.

"OK, let's get you home in style, it's 5.35, and you can just imagine how good it's going to feel slipping off those heels when you get home." I hit the play button, and Madonna will soon be singing about moist love, and hot holidays." Congratulations, we've made it to the Madonna hour." Fader down.

Hel, who has slipped in whilst I was doing my trail, starts talking the second the red light goes off. She has decided to forget our recent episode.

"I just wanted to make sure that you remember — you crazy gal," she gives me that comedy wink of hers, under the false impression that peppering her language with quaint euphemisms will ease her onslaught, "that you don't forget to *forget* to talk about that sensitive issue we discussed with Greg Donahue? He's real touchy. This is drive time, not the late show, so cool your militant heels, OK sweetie?" The comedy wink is back, and then just as I think the Lilliputian torture is over, she turns at the door, "Oh, and your Dad called for like the tenth time." And then she's gone.

The studio door pivots back open and Courtney rumbles in all smiles. She packs a presence on the best of days, but today, leathers aside, she is carrying a large box, and an extra-large smile.

"Howdy," she beams.

"Howdy yourself, partner...what's in the box?"

"Just thought I'd cheer the place up a bit. You know Christmas, and all...that festival we practice at the end of every year with as much Christian pathos as Judas Escariot?"

She is pulling brightly coloured strands of tinsel from the box and draping them in clumps over speakers, and CD racks.

"Damn right. Go sister! I like your festive skills. It's just what the place needs. A little tinsel, a few more balls...Do we get a Virgin, and a baby Jesus?"

"You don't deserve the full Pietà — yet, but I still have hopes for you, girly." And with that she smiles and is gone with her box to spread pixie cheer elsewhere, somewhere down the hall.

Through the glass partition, I see her enter the next studio along as I line up the next song. How does she do it? Are they all like her in the mid-West? Mental note: must visit mid-West to discover whether they are all pie-eyed and fan-fucking-tastic.

She's talking to Clive, our Australian technician and resident hunk. It would appear that the all-female radio station concept did not extend to female technicians. This, it would seem, was a step too far. And Heaven forfend we should actually be able to handle the breakfast show on our own: on the launch day, and thereafter, the breakfast show was hosted by a male and female team. So, one of the first voices ever to grace the all-female radio airwaves of Radio Honey was male.

I've got nothing against Gary: he's a good DJ, and a nice guy, but these are the kind of fuck ups that marketing and management should have gotten their heads around instead of fannying about in the no-man's land of their own sexual orientation. Or, in Anne Bleasdale's case — the station's PR guru, fresh back from her own self exploration in the California hills where she discovered peyote but not much more — a good, swift kick up the arse might have dislodged some of the remaining brain cells long enough to enlist some good ideas. The whole fucking station was a great idea that got lodged in someone's oesophagus. Sure, give women a platform of their own, nice idea. It doesn't have to be all tampon ads, and skinny lattes. It can even have a male DJ, but shouldn't he at least be gay? Shouldn't he be the gay best friend that every girl needs and wants? Especially to get her out of bed in the morning when her bed is decidedly empty?

Festooning Clive's roguish hair with tinsel, Courtney is enjoying herself. If I didn't know her better I'd say she was flirting...Hell, wait a minute....I scootch down in my chair so that I can watch them without appearing so obvious and read the body language through the glass — *her* body language. We know *he's* taken. He has the G-word. A girlfriend. Famous in her anonymity. The fact that we never see her makes her grow in unusual proportion. We, the girls at Radio Honey, have decided that she must be beautiful and buxom; a perfect female specimen to have hooked such a hunky bloke. But then, you know, it could just as easily have been a case of the music stopped, and he sat down.

Courtney is making her leather trousers go the distance, bending and shaking it. I can almost hear the leather straining from here. He's smiling, but it looks like amusement from where I'm sitting, not lust. Damn, if we could only get some lust out of him; some glimmer of hope, but he's one of those rare, good guys. That damn girlfriend of his did well. Most of us Radio Honey girls are still on the pull. This makes us horny and bad tempered which is not a great combination for a station full of females trying to put together a new concept in radio.

Finished with festooning and flouncing, Courtney pokes her head back in through the studio door.

"I'm goin' over to the cafe. Do you want anythin'? Beer? Whiskey? Heroin? A new producer?"

"Get your butt in here a minute." I take the cans off my head and turn down the volume on Prince.

"So, what's with the leather pants, you hotty?"

"Aww, just figured I'd give 'em an airin'— you know...?"

"What — the trousers or your fanny crack?"

"Aw, come on! They 'ain't that tight!"

"I can see New England from here! Who you wearing them for then — Clare?"

"Get out wid' cha! I'm no fan of escargot — No Mam! Gimme a big dick any day. Speakin' of which...." She moves closer and nods her head back over her shoulder in the direction of Clive's studio, "Have you seen the bulge in those 501's?! Damn near took my eye out!"

"Yeah, but he's taken, girlfriend. You're wasting good tears."

"Well, hell, my rabbit has a fantasy attachment now..." she winks slipping back out of the studio.

Chapter 2

To the Sounds of 'Smells Like Teen Spirit'
by Nirvana

Tonight, foretold by Courtney's leathers, is gig night. Out on the street a swill of spit-tossed rain bales in the lamplight, cross hatching the blackness of cars and pavement. I toss my guitar, in its beaten-up case, in the back of my shit-coloured mini. She grinds her gears at me, and we pull out into the lane. Soon the lampposts are trading one light at a time for the open road; swinging from the safety harness of their glare, each to each.

When I was a child, I used to imagine cats singing on top of the lampposts. One each. Heads held high, yowling a feline song, passed down the line, part of a melodious chain. It comforted me, especially on those long, motorway trips: my Dad and I, in the beat-up Citroen he had back then, to Grandma's and back. Down the A303, winding past Stonehenge, seaward. What mysteries is it sitting on, stone on stone? Maybe I was hoping those imaginary cats would sing the secrets of those hidden places where the monoliths had been, where all the secrets lived, where my mother was; leading us pillar by pillar to each hidden treasure.

Blink never got over Bonnie Raitt. Her hair is hennaed bright red and hangs down her diminutive back to where her non-existent arse pouts. She is the creator of 'Blinks' Club', and the compere. Sometimes she even gets her own guitar out and plays us something from her up and coming album, which has been coming for some time now. Every night at Blink's has a theme, it could be 'The Wizard of Oz' or 'Starsky and Hutch,' but tonight it's 'Gone with the Wind'.

Blink is dressed as Scarlett, of course. God knows where she found the oversized umbrella which juts out around her miniscule waist. The dress is made of red brocade and seamed with black. Her hair is tied up in red ribbons and falling with pendulous ringlets. A dash of bright, red lipstick lights up her pale, slightly demonic face.

She is introducing the first act as I creep in past Mack 'the knife' on the door; big, street cool, and cuddly. I tell him I'm playing tonight, and he waves me in. Normally, it's three quid to get in, but if you play you don't pay.

A few friendly faces nod hello from the blackness. Candles in bottles splutter on the tables; benches, chairs and crates are scattered for the seated. The room is small, the ceiling low in this basement dive, but the feeling is cosy, and the crowd are more family than friends.

I make my way to the back of the room and prop my sorry excuse for a guitar case up against the bar.

"Rum and coke, barman!" Riley is always amused by my rudeness. He smiles lazily and grabs me a glass.

"Playing tonight?"

"Yeah, I thought I'd better whip it out before I forget how to use it."

"If you ever forget, I'd like to try helping you remember..."

"Get out of it! You're too wasted to remember yourself!"

"Hey! Watch it girlie or I'll show you here and now!"

"Give me my drink before I start laughing so hard I can't fucking drink it!"

Thankfully I get my drink, he gets his change, and Tony is still wading through his first Blues number. He's got the bass to my 'Peach', and by that I mean I've got a Fender Verithin in Red, and he has the Bass equivalent, in matching red. He keeps saying we need to get them together, and make some music, but I know he doesn't mean our guitars.

He looks kind of nerdy with that hat, his wild dark hair, and those old, moth balled suits. Not very tall, and not very thin, the chip on his shoulder makes him look a lot bigger.

Holding his own on the makeshift stage he's singing his little heart out and all that inner angst marries well with the tune. It's called, "I Left My Heart on Your Settee," and although the title is a bit long, the song itself is short and sweet, and carries a giddy tune.

As I make my way through the tables to Courtney who has beckoned me over, showing me the empty seat she's saved me, his voice is rising to a painful pitch; the song breathing its last.

"You're just in time to see 'Happy Man' perform 'As I Lay Dyin'..." Courtney snorts in my ear.

"I'm still trying to decide whether he's cute or not," I whisper. Courtney shoots me one of those looks, and then tops it off by putting her fingers down her throat.

Tony acknowledges my arrival with a little nod, and a tip of his hat. Shit, you see those are the little things a girl loves. That old-fashioned stuff that they used to do back in the day, and in the golden era of Hollywood movies. I will never understand women who complain about a man holding the door open for them, I mean, who killed chivalry? It wasn't me. I'm still waiting for a man to throw his coat over a puddle to spare my stockings — *then* I can die happy. If you want a door to hit you in the face that's your affair, but don't go ruining it for the rest of us.

I have changed into an off-one-shoulder dress that I found in the Portobello market last weekend. It was in one of the bargain bins, and I fell in love with it. Of course, next season it will be all the rage; I have an annoying knack of being one season ahead which always makes me look out of place in the present — all talents are curses in disguise. It's a strange concoction of polyester and flowers, and owes its shape, I like to think, to a one-armed Greek sculpture. My modest bosom is holding it aloft, and I'm feeling sufficiently confident to carry it off. Another rum and coke and I'll be practically taking it off.

Then the club door swings open, and Cage makes his entrance.

Cage cannot enter a room without heads turning. He attracts attention like a musky ferret. I will never forget the first time I laid eyes on his luminous, big blues. He wears the combination of Chinese and Caribbean well. Femininely long lashes frame naturally kohl outlined eyes, which are large and moist as a deer. Lacking height, he makes up for it in chiselled features, dark hair, and an easy swagger that belies girlish hips. You could hear the collective sigh of the females present as his scent entered the room. The scent was primarily alcohol and marijuana, but what was left was decidedly male.

Even Tony's eyes momentarily flitted up from his fret board to clock the entrance of this bony, mixed race whirlwind.

Courtney kicked my leg under the table, but I was one step ahead of her, and was already returning his smile. He made a beeline for our table, and with Tony now eyeing the whole proceedings from the stage, made himself comfortable in a chair that I pulled out for him with my leg in one effortless motion.

I like it when I don't have to explain everything to someone, but rather our movements are a dance of synchronicity. Cage and I didn't have to look at each other or talk but could get along just fine knowing where the next move would land from either one of us.

He leans over, planting one on the cheek I offer him. The tiny candle, fighting the smoke, incense and lack of oxygen in this downstairs dive, flickers and gasps, sending little missiles of candlewick fireworks in front of his face. We'd had the affair, now we just lived side by side with the lust like horny cousins. I'd broken up with him on his birthday, which he always jokes about in an 'I'm-never-going to-forgive-you' kind of way, but jokes are only funny because they rely on some uncomfortable truth. I study his profile, and catch Tony watching me watching Cage.

"How ya doing Cage, you old dog?" Courtney is nothing if not friendly. Tony is howling like a mutt in summer time now, coming to the crux of his last song.

Cage rasps his reply, "Fair to middlin' my dear, fair to middlin'." He turns his face from Courtney to me. "What happened to your dress?"

"Ha-bloody-ha. Don't you know it will be all the fashion come next spring." I resort to my poshest retort.

"I can't wait. Can I get you girls some drinks?"

"I'll have a bottle of their finest Stella, many thanks," drawls Courtney.

"A rum and coke, barman, and make it a dark rum...like my men..." I give him a wink, and Courtney kicks me under the table again. As Cage lopes off, Courtney looks as if she's about to tell me off but is interrupted by Tony who is making his way over. He isn't looking too cheerful, but then when you spend your life playing the Blues some of it's bound to rub off.

"Is there room for one more?" Tony has already put his guitar case down by my chair and is easing into the one next to mine.

"Well, Cage was sitting there, he's just gone to get us some drinks," Courtney says loudly, looking to Cage at the bar.

"I won't be a moment," Tony looks like the last hound dog on earth, and I can't help feeling sorry for him.

"So, how've you been?" He turns his full attention to me. Can you feel sorry enough for somebody, share enough of their angst to want to help them with the only love you know how? Some dry hump of the mind? Or more?

"Good," I smile trying not to look at Courtney who is glaring daggers at me. "Good, yeah..." I tail off unsure what to say with the thought police sitting so close by.

"So, when are we going to get our guitars together?" He smiles for the first time, showing teeth that have seen straighter days.

"When hell freezes over..." Courtney seethes under her breath. I kick *her* under the table.

"Well, Tony, I'm not really sure... I'm, uh, not really a Blues player..."

"I don't just play the Blues...we could jam a little — I like that song of yours, 'Helium' — I've got a few chords I'd like to show you..."

"I bet you do," Courtney is having a conversation of her own.

"We could..." Tony continues unabashed

"Make sweet music..." Courtney muses quietly.

"...forget the Blues altogether — Hell, it's about time I lightened my tone! At least for an evening, and who knows..." Tony tries to be coy, but it really doesn't suit him; he just looks lecherous. I look over searchingly to where Cage is struggling with one too many drinks.

"Well, that sounds..." I try to think of something to say.

"Appalling," offers Courtney.

"But..." I try to carry on.

"I'm washing my hair, doing the ironing, feeding the cats..." Courtney's on a roll now.

"I'm really busy at the station at the moment; the only free time I get is here..." I'm talking to fill space without knowing where I'm going.

"My new album comes out next week," Tony offers, "Maybe you could get me on your show to play a few numbers..."

"Yeah, you should speak to my producer, Helena. I'll get you her number."

"Well, this is cosy," Cage is back with the drinks, saving me further humiliation and regret. Tony gets up and offers the chair to Cage who doesn't need cajoling. It's all feeling remarkably white horse and rider — not at all the usual heathen vibe. Cage breaks the atmosphere by dumping himself down unceremoniously and dolling out the drinks.

"That was a happy little number you were playing, my man," smiles Cage, his warmth and ease a panacea to any environmental chill.

"Yeah, well you know, a man's gotta stay true to the Blues if he's got it in him." Tony picks up his guitar case, and damn it if he doesn't tip his hat again, this time at the whole table. His eyes, however, land last on me before he spins around, making it clear who he was taking the time for.

"So, what shall we drink to?" asks Cage, as Tony moves off, "Wine, women, and song?"

"Aw, fuck it — let's just drink!" Courtney is so relieved to see the back of Tony that she'd have drunk to anything. We knock back our drinks in unison, and slam them down at the same time, just as the door to Blinks' opens once more, this time to reveal the subject of my woes: Jack.

Bending over to make it through the aperture of Blinks' now seemingly petite entrance, he straightens up, and adjusts his jaunty flat cap, smiling to no one in particular.

I hadn't taken much notice of him in the beginning, but he seemed to hone in on me, and it was then that I squared up to his broad shoulders and Jack-the-lad roguery and found myself wanting: him.

His compering talents were in demand; he had his own club across town, but he liked to drop in because he knew the crowd, and appreciated the company, something which was never in dispute.

I don't remember what I was wearing the night things took a distinctly sweaty turn between us, but I do remember that it came off quite easily. He was older than the going crowd; he had a certain mystique that, for the younger amongst us, pushed the intrigue to a level of genuine interest. And he wasn't one of those guys that never took you out; just came round for shag, and if you were lucky, brought a bottle. He would bring flowers — roses even! Lord, I nearly fell off my perch the first time it happened; he even took me away for the week-end: albeit a dirty one. The most I usually got in return for a night of shared bodily juices was a hickey.

It was one of those fabulous big hotels on the sea front in Brighton; the kind that would have flashed their lights to all the great names that passed through in its heyday. You could imagine them, waist coated and shiny shoed, tapping their heels like Fred Astaire up the white, marble steps. Turning to face the lady in question, a hand held out deferentially, tipping their hat, and the pair of them waltzing up and down in two-tone cinematised grandeur. The ladies cinched into their twinsets and girdles like tender truffles. Floating elves with gossamer wings whose tiny toes turned in patented heels; their waists disappearing into the tiniest pinch like the space between an ant's thorax and abdomen.

My father, with his love of all things scientific, was very insistent that ants, despite their miniscule proportions, had one of the widest ranges of reproductive strategies. He was fond of telling me, from perhaps a too youthful age, about what he would call "the absolutely fascinating mating rituals of these wee beasties." He liked to put on an accent when the mood took him; he could be whimsical and scientific within the same sentence.

According to Dad, female ants, through a process rare amongst animals, could reproduce asexually from unfertilised eggs. Here he would insert some horrendously scientific term which I will not pretend to remember. This tactic, from what I understand, was perhaps evolutionarily necessary when you consider that the male has an 'accessory gland' from which he can use his secretions to plug up the genital opening of the female and prevent her from re-mating!

My father's views on the world can inspire fear and dread of the simplest in human mechanics, not to mention that of the animal world. It is not unbelievable to me that mum, equally, did not fall for this line in conversation, and did not hang around for the full A to Z of the animal kingdom's mating rituals.

In hindsight, however, I realise that a secretory plug would not have gone amiss that Winter.

As Jack led me up those pearly stairs, the wind playing havoc with what attempts I had made to hair of a certain fashion, I felt like the greatest of all heroines in a tale of my own making. White arches framed the double doorways, which were accessorized by a swinging central access, for those who were feeling particularly euphoric. I felt like riding it round and round all afternoon, but Jack, being more of an adult, would perhaps have looked darkly on such behaviour. I was, after all, representing us both that week end. The façade stretched up interminably, stopping only to accent the delicate wrought iron rails of windows, jutting out like chocolate swirls on a milk tray assortment. This enormous cake of a building brought wonder to my eyes and heart as we passed through its gilded aperture and entered the grand foyer.

My stilettoes brought a cold clip-clop to the sumptuous, marble floor. I tried to walk more quietly, but only succeeded in dragging behind. Jack, already at the desk, turned to look for me, a passing hint of disappointment visible under his peaked cap.

"Mr. Wade, I've booked a double room." The concierge looked to his computer screen, but not without casting a cursory glance at me; his eyes said it all — hotel rooky.

When the elevator doors closed behind us Jack stood quietly eyeing the numbers. I tried to hold my excitement in, tempted to take his hand but knowing this was not where we were on the level of boyfriend/girlfriend. He wasn't your hand-holding type. He was more of your 'say the words you want to hear' type of guy. Putting it all on a top shelf so you had to stand on tip toes, hoping it would be accessible one day when you had grown those extra few inches.

Our room was white with dark blue accents: the pelmet and curtains, the bedspread. The room brimming with light, you could almost feel the sea air; the ceiling high and corniced, the cherry on this cake of a building. He pulled me onto the bed, and in the starkest daylight fucked me till the condom split.

Chapter 3

To the Sounds of 'Losing my Religion' by R.E.M

I don't believe it. Is she really doing that again? Clare is editing right behind me, through the glass partition. My theory is she likes to watch my arse while I work. It occurs to me that she may be in such deep denial that she has no idea why she is staring at my arse. She was born in an era when you had to sometimes pretend, teeth clenched, staring at the ceiling; wondering why you kept imagining Jane's tight sweater, or Jim's gorgeous arse. Perhaps she still feels she hasn't met the right man yet?

Surely her penchant for the brownest of shoe wear, and the absence of all feminine paraphernalia, not to mention even a whiff of soap, should have told her that hers was a boyhood of sorts?

Her inbred hostility towards her own sexuality puts a strain on the station, and everyone in it. We could be celebrating feminism, female-ism, lesbianism, everything-ism, but instead we are hitched to the wagon of an uptight femme-male with more issues than Seinfeld. And she's taking us all down with her.

If she could just admit that she is not what Mum and Dad, products of a post war, semi-detached upbringing had hoped for, she would be doing us all a huge service. But, no, she's staring at my arse whilst trying to convince herself she is doing a nice bit of editing. Simone de Beavoir declared in the 1950's that "One is not born but rather becomes a woman." If this is true, then Clare still has a long way to go.

I read somewhere, or perhaps it was another of Dad's Psychology Today magazines, that nothing inspires murderous mayhem in human beings more reliably than sexual repression. If human sexuality is denied or suppressed, the human psyche tends to grow twisted and perverse, and this rage rarely takes the form of rebellion against the people or institutions behind the repression but gets directed towards other helpless victims who are sacrificed to this guilt and shame. My bum and I were beginning to feel a bit vulnerable.

I tend to stand up when I do the show. Courtney taught me this one; it comes from the mid-west school of radio. She says it gives you more punch, and you're less likely to fall asleep on the job, which after last night, is not a bad idea.

I think I had a few too many before going on, and then a few more after to celebrate the fact that I had somehow remembered all the words. By the time Rhett Butler, otherwise known as Cage, hit the stage to do his rap impersonation of

"Frankly My Dear, I don't give a damn" set to Michael Jackson's 'Billie Jean', I was in no fit state to sing along on the chorus. Tony had just bought another round of drinks when Courtney hissed in my ear, "I'm getting you home before you do something you regret! Now come on, make your excuses and goodbyes."

"Frankly my dear!" I tried to intone in my defence, but the words suddenly sounded very far away. Inebriation not impeding the flow of any force stronger than my drinking arm, Courtney was able to lift me up, and push me in the direction of the door. But it was too late, I had already given Tony my number, and told him to call me about setting up a time to come into the studio, and perhaps play a few songs from his upcoming album. Not to mention, get our guitars together.

I turn to look behind me whilst Blondie sings, 'Heart of Glass', and find Clare still lost in a trancelike stare that takes in the entirety of my behind. I turn right around, trying not to strangle myself with my cans, so that she is now staring straight at my crotch. She wakes up from her butt-daze and smiles innocently up at me. My eyebrows tell her I'm not amused, and I turn my pert butt back at her just as Hel is spinning into the room with a sheath of papers in her hands.

"Honey, I need you to read through these before The Buttnicks come in..."

"The who?"

"No, Honey, not The Who, The Buttnicks. Get it right on the night won't you?"

"Get out of here before I throw hot tea on you. Oh yeah, I can't do that because I have *no hot* tea and haven't had a fucking hot tea all day! Now stop twatting around, give me those papers, and get me a fucking hot tea! Please!"

"Ooooo, Miss Grumpy Pants, didn't get your chicken vindalooed last night?"

"Hel! Do I have to come round this console and kick your scrawny, white arse?"

"OK, OK I'm going! You're so bad tempered when you're horny..." She manages to escape before the end of her sentence, and the end of her life.

Clive has just poked his head up from underneath the console next door. Courtney really went to town with the tinsel in there yesterday. The place looks like a hooker's paradise. Clive is looking mighty fine today. He's got on a white shirt, slightly open, just the right amount of buttons — two — and his dark hair is looking just the right amount of dishevelled. Very Colin Firth from the waist up. From the waist down more Leonardo DiCaprio; wholesome in a boyish, still holding onto some baby fat kind of way.

Blondie is peaking, I break in over the top, "'Heart of Glass' by Blondie. I think we've all been there — you 'had a love, it was a gas, soon turns out you have a heart of glass'. On the album version she sings 'soon turns out to be a pain in the bleep — rhymes with 'glass'. Anyhow, that was the radio version. We're getting you home here in style on four-sixty-three a.m., Radio Honey. Coming up we have that traffic report for you, with our gal from the val, Gail, after these important messages from our sponsors," and out.

Gail wheels in, all punk hair, and nose rings. What she lacks in stature she makes up for in piercings.

"Hey, Gail."

"Hey."

"Got any really gory pile ups for us?"

"No, just the usual pump and grind."

"When are we going to get you out in a helicopter to do proper reports like the other traffic gals?"

"I'm scared of heights." She deadpans. Gail is not one of many words, which makes her perfectly suited to Travel. Travel is a bit like the Shipping Report. Gail does a good, straightforward job; she is capable of surprising you with the odd joke, now and then, but don't hold the fader.

"You going anywhere nice for Christmas?" I try again.

"No, I'll be here, working."

"Oh, where are your family then?" Still searching for that illusive 'in'.

"Abergavenny." This seems like as good a place as any to give up.

Gail snails unenthusiastically through the traffic report, and then, gathering her papers together without looking up, nods in my direction and is gone. At least for another hour.

My living Hel makes her way in carrying a large mug of tea. I glare at her as she travels all the way around the console, seeming to take forever, and places it gingerly on top of the sheath of papers she had brought me earlier, making a large, brown ring. She looks up and flutters those baby seal eyes at me.

"There you go! One lovely, big cup of tea for my favourite DJ! Don't say I never do anything for you — now hurry up and read those bloody reviews of The Buttnicks!"

"I will! I will! Of course, it would have been easier if I'd had them to read *before* the show like other presenters do when their producers are *organised*!"

"Sweetie, no point mincing your knickers with me. You can't have tea *and* sympathy — this station can't afford it!" And she minces out. I can feel the nervous tension extend from a twitch in my eye all the way down to my backside. I turn, half expecting to find Clare there still admiring my arse, but she must finally have found something else to do. I almost feel rejected.

The Buttnicks, all five of them, are wheeled in as I read their annoyingly boring biog. I have put on an extra-long track to cover me whilst I wade through their discography and other drivel. I let the pages flutter to the floor as I make a silent finger to lip gesture and get myself out of the end of the track and into the ads as the door pivots open to let in "Cardiff's answer to The Pogues":

"The Buttnicks will be entertaining us in the studio after the break, so stay with us, and you won't miss out on your chance to win tickets to see them live." Where do they find these guys? I muse to myself.

The Buttnicks, who are noisily filing into my studio, take this opportunity to applaud themselves rather loudly to which they receive my well-honed demon stare. Once the fader is down, I make a few fiddling adjustments to my commercials rack — not to let them feel too important — and rummage through a few potential CDs before I fix them with my very important DJ-at-work-smile and greet them into my studio.

"Well, hullo, gentlemen, I trust you had a good journey here from...where have you lads travelled from?"

"Cardiff," drawls the one without front teeth.

"Cardiff..." I repeat fighting for something to say about Cardiff. Finding nothing, I move swiftly along. "Well lads, thanks for coming in today. This is what we were hoping to do: I'm going to introduce you and have a little chat about your new album; then we'll go to a break where we can take some level for the live performance, and then we'll come back with our competition, OK?"

"Could we get some tea or somethin'?" This time the one in the flat cap and greasy hair is giving it up for his crew.

"Of course, I'm sorry you didn't get one earlier, let me just call my slave..." I turn and glare at Hel through the glass who just happens to be turning around to face me from her desk in perfect time to my request. I make the sign for 'Get your arse in here pronto' which is a snarl attached to a come-hither movement with my right arm.

Hel is soon winging her way in through the heavy swing door of the studio, all grins, and innocence.

"Can we get some refreshments for The Buttnicks?"

"Of course!" Hel enthuses all too gushingly, "What'll it be boys?" she asks with a well-turned twinkle in her eye. The lads, unsure of how to take her warmth, decide to ignore it, and order a very lengthy, and painful to watch series of teas and coffees with assorted sugars. Half way through, Hel has to stop them, and tearing off a bit of paper from their biography, which is strewn under my desk, asks them to repeat it again so that this time she can write it down.

Whilst this painful process is going on, I get out the mike stands and start to set each seated Buttnick up to a microphone. Whatever their instrument, each microphone has to be fed back into my desk and checked for level.

I rush back round my desk as my least favourite commercial about haemorrhoids is concluding, lift the fader up to chat us into the next song, and buy me some more time to get The Buttnicks up and running. "We've got The Buttnicks live in the studio, fresh from their tour of the M4 corridor, after Right Said Fred tells us how sexy he is," and press play.

The boys are still trying to figure me out; find a gap in my armour. I get on with wiring them up. It's not easy being a 'girl' in this job; lots of guys don't love you for it. As I kneel down at the vocalist's feet to adjust the mike stand he says with apparent glee, which is picked up by his accomplices:

"Whilst yer' down there darlin'..." They all break apart laughing.

I stand up, extending the mike stand so that the knobbly mike grip hits the vocalist in his aforementioned privates, which are positioned conveniently towards the edge of his seat. He doubles over.

"Oh, God! I *am* sorry! These blasted mike stands are too much for a delicate thing like me..."

The rest of the crew clock my sarcasm, and toothless says, "You oughta be more careful."

"My dear man, there are many things I ought to have been and done, but I'm just a no good, fucking radio DJ with more caffeine than sense." I say in my best posh accent with overtones of wise-ass. "Now what are you playing and where are you sitting 'cause Right Said Fred are only going to be shouting about their dicks for another..." I check the LED display on the CD player, "... one minute and forty seconds and then you guys are going to have to be ready for your interview, and ultimately to play your latest single to the nation." Realising I mean business, Toothless gets out a guitar case propped behind the door and pulls out a Fender Stratocaster.

"Nice Strat," I offer, as I unwind a new cable and plug it into his guitar without as much as a *howdyoudo*. He finds a seat, and says, "Thanks, it used to be me Dad's." And the war of the sexes is over — for the moment.

"I might ask you about that in the interview if that's OK?" Building the friendship back.

"Yeah, that 'ud be cool". He fiddles with the knobs on the Strat, and I plug the other side into the socket on my console.

"Right, who's next?" I say brandishing a jack cable.

After The Buttnicks had annoyed me to the point of self-harming, I needed a break. Courtney was rehearsing lines for a new trail in the next-door studio. The red light wasn't on so I barged in.

"To what do I owe the pleasure?" she purrs.

"Just the simple pleasure of your company." I throw myself down on the swivel chair opposite which takes me on a little voyage across the room. My accompanying deep sigh lets her know what my short passage across the carpet has not.

"What's up poppet? Nasty radio station getting you down?"

"Yes, horribly. And I want my Mummy!" This sentence hangs in the air above my head; I hadn't planned to invoke the goddess of my unrest.

"Ahhh, come rest your weary sling backs on my console." I sling my kitten heals up on the desk, and she leans back in her chair.

"Why are men so threatened by a strong woman?"

"It's because we have bigger balls — they're just further up."

"But why can't a man let us have balls, and be happy for us?"

"Every man wants to beat his chest and shake his balls *and* have the loudest and biggest. It's the law of the jungle, honey."

"So how does a strong woman attract a strong man, and should she even try? I mean should we be with a weak man or hold out for a man not threatened by a strong woman, and if so, does such a man exist?"

"Ah, that is the eternal question. Eve was the first strong woman and look what happened to her..."

Out amongst the scattered desks of Radio Honey's production centre, everyone looks busy. This is a worrying sight; not an idle one amongst them. I catch Jezebel look up from her work. Gotcha!

A dark horse, she radiates a silky self-assurance; she gets on with her work and doesn't make too much conversation. Not to mention the fact that she and her producer never seem to exchange a cross word; now that's just not normal! I decide to stop by her desk for 'a friendly'.

She seems to anticipate my beeline for her desk and tries to look busier than ever. With her long, wavy dark hair waxed to a beautiful sheen, and her burnt umber, flawless skin, she is black powers answer to 20th century radio. I marvel at her placement in the fold, like a quiet jewel in the crown. But there's something more, something indefinable, like a hidden secret that she sits on. I would give my complete works of Oscar Wilde to know what is going on in that head of hers.

"How's it going?"

"Yeah…it's good," then realizing etiquette required a return volley she asks, "and you?"

"OK, I guess. I just had this awful band in — The Buttnicks…"

"Yeah, I heard…over the tannoy…"

"God, talk about misogynists."

"Yeah, certainly not Radio Honey material."

"I have no idea why they were booked. Sometimes I think Hel does it just to annoy me. I mean let's get in the most horrible, toothless little men we can find, and make Cass fight for her life to get a decent sentence out of them…do you get any shit from your producer?"

"No, she's pretty good."

"Fancy swapping?"

"No", she laughs; a beautiful laugh.

"I'll throw in a few bottles of wine?" Jezebel just giggles. As if sensing my disloyalty, I spy Hel making her way across the room towards me.

"Oh-oh, here comes trouble — catch you later." I meet Hel half way across the room, and she is already mid-sentence.

"—are you trying to escape? Because you know, you haven't taken your homework, you naughty thing." She hands me what feels like a three-hundred-page novel judging by the weight. "She's coming in tomorrow — Jessica something or other and you need to read the book and write some fabulously witty questions..."

"I thought that was *your* job?"

"I have to go and interview what's-his-blob for the food item over in Soho, and then watch and review three films because our film critic has the flu or has fallen off the edge of the earth—Heaven only knows! So, you see you really have gotten off light."

"Gee, thanks..."

"Don't mention it." She twirls on her childishly small trainers and is gone. With nothing left to do I head for the door. But it was too good to be true. The pitter-patter of flat-footed feet is getting louder not softer:

"Cass, your Pa-Pa is on the line, and I can't hold him off with more cods-wallop another moment. Come on, chop-chop." Turning back to face the maelstrom of office haberdashery, I throw myself into my office chair, and push line one.

"Dad!" I try to sound like I have more energy than I do. "No, I am, I'm sorry...Yes, I will. No, I haven't — yet! I'm going home...yes...no...I will. Yes. OK. Yes, love you too. I will. OK, bye. Yes, bye. Bye."

"That was a lesson in exotic vocabulary options."

"Shut up."

"Did he tell you to eat properly, and brush your teeth?"

"Have you ever had a phone jammed up your arse?"

"Does Mama Bear give you a hard time too?" My look stops her onslaught. The silence between us takes on a new energy; not one we have shared before. I grab my bag off the desk, and head for the door.

"Sorry?" Her words sound pale and confused. It's not her fault. How was she to know my grim little past? It's not something you share around the coffee machine. It's not something you share, generally. But there it was; out in the open. Breathing like a fish up at the surface, all big O's and Ah's. I never knew my mum. They say you don't miss what you never had, but the people who say things like that didn't have anything worth missing.

Passing the grizzled remains of potted plants that only a few months ago had been fulsome with foliage, I head purposefully for the exit. You'd think a radio station full of females would have green, caring thumbs, but this lot just don't give a shit.

Jeff is the lithe, sixty-five-year-old ladies' man who is in charge of security at the main reception. Nobody gets past his wily nose, and that includes the inmates of next doors radio station, Head Banger FM.

This is home to the hairiest bunch of heavy metal enthusiasts this side of Maidenhead. They make the women at radio honey look virtually hairless. If you include their facial hair, they could probably provide wigs for most of Soho's transvestite population. We have been known to exchange grunts with them, but Courtney, in true pioneer spirit, has even spent a couple of hours with them whilst they do their shows. She tells me it's pure metal madness. I might just have a little peak myself one of these days. I mean I like a little Led Zep as much as the next hirsute loving female.

"Goodnight Jeff," I say unable to hide the weariness in my voice.

"Eh, Goodnight, then. What's with the long face?"

"The long and the short of it, Jeff, is I'm tired and I wanna go home."

"Well I hope you've got something to snuggle up to — it's going to be minus one tonight."

"Your kind thoughts will keep me warm, Jeff — goodnight!"

"Goodnight love!"

As the door thwacks closed, and the fresh air of the street rushes to meet me, I breathe a bellyful of relief. It's time to go home. I can turn off Miss Personality, and just be.

But then I hear it — the demonic hail of tiny feet, and that unmistakeable voice:

"Wait up! Cass!" I turn to see my gnome of a producer running with arms hitched at her midriff as she tries to protect herself from her own animated breasts. She reaches me, having crossed only an expanse of one road, and a few paving stones, out of breath.

"Forgot to mention," she pauses for a large inhale, "you need to be at the Elle Fashion Awards tomorrow. Well, *we* do. So, we need to be there for twelve o'clock kick off, and then come straight back in to work. Don't forget to wear something fabulous! Tres décolleté—Oo la la! Here's some gumpf on the event." She tosses me a sheaf of papers. I don't even have the energy to object.

"See you tomorrow!" She trills as she turns to leave. "I'll remember to bring the recording machine thingy this time!" she yells. I raise a thumb in the air and keep walking.

Fashion awards. Great. I'd almost forgotten. Another year of whose who and being eyed up and down by demented cockroaches for not wearing this season's must haves. Perfect. Will have to dust off my Manolos and iron my Westwood at the very least.

When I get in the door of my apartment there are five messages, four from my Dad, and one from Tony.

Chapter 4

To the Sounds of 'Black Hole Sun' by Soundgarden

Pyewacket winds his way around my legs like Indians circling covered wagons. He was named after the witch's cat in the movie, 'Bell, Book, and Candle' starring James Stewart and Kim Novak. Fresh from Hitchcock's 'Vertigo', Novak's white blonde hair seemed unconvincingly witchy; her cat had more meow in him than she did. And yet the story is a good one. I love Stewart; his gravely, unusual voice, his worn in maturity. Maybe I should develop a Daddy complex?

According to the film, if a witch falls in love, she loses her powers. The sign that Novak has lost hers comes in the form of tears when she thinks she has lost Stewart forever; this signals the end of her relationship with her familiar, as it high tails it out of her life. I'd like to be able to magic up enough hocus pocus to meet Mr. Right Now, or Mr. Now and Again, never mind Mr. Right.

I envy that voodoo that you do so well, my sisters. You who have found the one; the man who will stand by you through thick and thin, through rain and shine, through bad hair days, and unshaved legs days. You are the winners in this game of life, although you probably don't even know it. You probably complain about him in that dismissive way that women talk about men by the coffee machine in the office or over one too many glasses of dry, white wine after work at the local, naff wine bar. This man has become so accommodating, so understated, that it is easy to pass him off with comments about his annoying habits; those petty annoyances that I would give my right arm to 'suffer'.

How many times have I questioned my own accommodating nature, my easy virtue, when I hear how these self-same women complain about 'swallowing?' I mean surely, it's in bad taste to spit? I don't understand how these self-same women, who claim never to entertain a cock in their mouths, keep their men when ask any man, and he will tell you that his number one favourite thing in the whole goddamned world is to have his cock well and truly sucked.

And yet, there they are, these women of marvellous, true men. Nonchalant in their happiness; their men tethered to their mast. And not a cocksucker amongst them. My only theory is that these men chose to put the ring on these women because they know for goddamned sure that if they won't suck *their* cock they won't suck anyone else's.

Furthermore, I can only imagine that these men get their cocks so well and truly sucked by women such as myself, that it lasts them a lifetime with their good wives.

I press play on the answering machine.

"Cass, it's Dad…hope everything is OK…."

My father is a closet scientist, slash theoretician, slash physicist, slash nut-job.

"Just wanted to talk to you really. Been reading this really great book; I want to send you a copy…"

The last book he sent me was 'The Selfish Gene,' a big hit with the hip kids of the seventies.

"It's the gene that chooses us, not us the gene", he had laboured, trying to impart some wisdom into the higgledy-piggledy no man's land of my brain. "You are the receptacle, he is the donor. The gene is using you to try out its options." After my blank stare, he continued: "It's those miniscule genes in our bodies that ride *us* not *we* them. *They* decide what kind of mate they need to copulate with to get the kind of genus they are after in their progression towards some utopia of their own invention. We are just the receptacle for this trial and error evolution." My father is a good man, but he reads far too much for an IT consultant.

"No, Dad, *I* choose the mates I want," I counter.

"No, you choose the mate the gene wants. Their smell, their looks are all a series of genetic numbers, or pheromones that you interpret without even knowing it. The smell of his sweat tells you if his gene pool would make a good match with your own."

"That's disgusting. I do not go around smelling guys' armpits".

"You don't have to. You unconsciously take in this data without even knowing it".

"It's still disgusting..." My Dad would eventually tire of trying to educate me, and my unconscious choices would remain unconscious.

"Cass," the tape squeaks as it plays over the two thousandth message from him — I should probably get a new answering machine? A new phone number? Train my father not to leave such long messages? Doubtful this would work; he has always loved the sound of his own voice: voice-mail is his ideal setting — no objections, interruptions, questions, quizzical looks — this was a medium made for him, "it's based on some relatively new research, but I think its relevance will be proved in the fullness of time. It sets out how young women today are throwing their lives away on careers, ignoring their biological clocks, and creating an industry of workers who, once they take maternity leave, often fail to re-establish any viable career. So, in essence, it proves the ridiculousness of women entertaining a career and motherhood, and that the two are diametrically opposed. It's a very interesting book. I think you should read it. I think you need to decide between motherhood and a career because attempting to do both is simply not a viable option. You are in essence fooling yourself. The choice really needs to be made sooner rather than later so that you don't end up wasting your time and energies. And we know that energy is finite. So, use it well! OK chipmunk?" — This moniker because I had missing teeth as a child for far longer than most kids — "Call me back when you get this message — OK? Yes? Call me, your father." He always signs off as if I would have no idea who has left this long and rambling message. Surely, I would have gathered that this was the man who raised me? The voice of my childhood? The voice in my head? - Most of the voices in my head; indelible and presupposing. *His* is the soundtrack to my life, if truth be known. The inventory of my life stretched out like one inescapable song; longer than *Stairway to Heaven, Bohemian Rhapsody,* or the twenty-six minutes of Pink Floyd's *Shine on you Crazy Diamond.* Filled with equal passion, but longer; much longer.

Pyewacket jumps up onto the bed, and after circling uncomfortably on my lap a few times and showing me his bum hole, which I could do without, makes himself into a furry ball in my lap; his tail the last part to complete the circle.

It was Cage who found Pyewacket: one of four tiny, mewling fur balls in a house down the road from where he still lives with his Dad. It's been just the two of them since his Mum upped sticks and moved to New Jersey with another man. Cage's Dad remained adamant that his x-wife was a Capitalist Bitch, only capable of sustaining a relationship if there was material wealth to be gained from the union, or as he put it: "the transaction." (This evaluation seemed to exclude his penniless self). Cage's Dad, as you may have gathered, was not a huge fan of capitalism, or the Conservative Party. In fact, he had made it his life's work to develop a thesis on the detrimental effects of Capitalism on Labour's burgeoning power base whilst working for the GLC, before its demise. Which he will tell you was another Capitalist manoeuvre to undermine the solidarity of societal structure through devolution and the quango of its replacement, the GLA. He joined the local Labour council, and has been there ever since, extolling the virtues of Neil Kinnock to anyone who will listen, often down the local pub where he is a fixture.

Their bachelor pad is a quagmire of minimalist Marxism. The smell of sweet and sour sauce is the first thing that hits you as you enter, then the darkness envelops as you climb the stairs (the smell of condiments becoming more pungent with every step) towards another smell: this one more human. Cage doesn't actually have his own room. He sleeps in the living room, along with objects and clothes imbued with a life of their own. Even dust dare not live here for fear of being lost forever in a morass of existential gloom. Cage occupies a space between the sofa and the door; this is his kingdom. CD's spread the territorial marker across the carpet towards the faint glow of the window on the opposite side of the room, which is usually covered in a blind that may once have been white.

Here he sits rolling what will be the first spliff of the day should you wake him about noon and wish to stir him from the overpowering odour of his habitat. Here he will pull a CD from a pile, and lock it into its electrical pocket, and press play. His nascent ability to mimic the effects of helicopters, drum machines, and most man-made objects, including man, a gift that is fast making him a local legend.

It was a near perfect spring day, and we had been dating for only a short while. His moustache made an itchy kiss as he came in the door, but I didn't mind, and never did even when said moustache was the stopper to the refill bottle of alcohol in his stomach. Sometimes he smelled so much of booze that I wondered whether he was simply pickled, and he was the bottle for the booze, not the booze his bottle; the alcohol using him to expand its liquid consciousness.

He calmly dropped the kitten-covered-bomb-shell that there was a litter down the road from him looking for homes. It didn't take me long to find my coat. I think he sensed my need to have a baby of some kind, even a cat baby. I should note here that this was not something I myself was aware of; my denial ran Hades deep.

We knocked and were shown into a tiny room overlooking the snaking, grey railway lines housing a washing machine, a sink, and clothes-covered counter, under which little Pye was playing with his brothers and sisters. With that bandy-legged innocence of new-borns, they pranced, and pounced and showed off their new-found appendages. Batting each other with one paw, and already sure footing it away with the other. Pye was simply the bravest and the silliest; his daring feats audacious acts of misplaced valour. In his skittish brain he would always think he was capable of the impossible, like some deluded, furry caped crusader. I don't think he had lives so much as guts and stupidity, but he was the boy for me; all black and white of him. Both of us fuelled by intoxicating amounts of self-deception had found each other. I took him home wrapped in my coat.

Pye vibrates; warm and self-assuring. "If it vibrates you can count on it" should be my new motto. Pouring myself the remains of a bottle of wine, decanted, but still drinkable, and re-lighting the spliff in the ashtray, I reach over Pye for the phone. It doesn't take long to answer:

"Tony, it's Cass."

Chapter 5

To the Sounds of 'Cigarettes and Alcohol' by Oasis

I'm running, but it feels like my legs aren't moving, just dancing in jelly mould. I have one arm raised and the strangulated, half-woman, half-banshee wail that emanates attempts to slow the black behemoth rounding the corner.

I'm late. Of course, I'm late. I'd numbed myself into obscurity last night. Somewhere in the back of my mind I'm being told, "Cassandra", because my mind always addresses me by my first name, in its fullness, like an angry parent, "You are avoiding the natural pain and frustration of life by inebriating yourself! All these momentary escapes will catch up with you in one big bang, and you will not be prepared for real life, lived sober, and for the brave!" My mind is not afraid to be longwinded and right. But right won't get me through today.

"The Savoy, please!" Hurling myself into the cab, Manolos first, I catch the hem of my Vivienne Westwood skirt, and hear a sad little rip. My frustration is short lived as I am too used to the ineptness of my life to be bothered by remorse. This and more I obviously deserve. Onwards chariot of the inept!

"I said twelve 'o'clock not twelve thirty you terrible girl!" greets Hel. "What happened to your skirt?"

"The same thing that will happen to you if you do not shut up! Now, walk! Take me where we have to go and let's get on with it."

There are lots of important and glamorous looking people milling around in the inner sanctum of The Savoy looking at everyone else is if they were vermin. One huge chandelier hangs above them all, and images of Del Boy mistakenly unhinging one and its contents falling with grace and magnificence, taking out this fashionable mob in one fell swoop, plays in my mind's eye.

We arrive at what appears to be a hastily put together table, out of place in its surroundings, being all steel and compressed wood, hastily covered with a red cloth. It is obscured by a sea of small badges. A young woman sitting behind all of this as if in charge of the gates to Heaven, bears down on the proceedings with so sanctimonious a tone that it warrants the snarl of recrimination I give her which amounts to my name:

"Cassandra Bates," at which Hel looks up at me from her lowly position without heels or height, "Plus one." I add for her measure. The sanctimonious one searches her all-important list, and drawls:

"Here you are," handing me two name tags. I throw mine in my open handbag; there is no way I am pinning anything to my top unless it is an award from the Queen herself.

"Aren't you going to put it on," wines Hel half-way through stabbing herself with her own.

"It's all so High School Reunion pinning tags to yourself. 'Hi, my name is so-and-so, and didn't we exchange air back in nineteen seventy-nine?' Spare me the high school nightmares, being unpopular is something I never want to have to go through again. "

"A psychiatrist would have a field day with your inner child," Hel says tightly.

I hang onto the only lifeline I can be sure of: my underwear; my buttocks tightly clenched as if for war of any kind: physical, emotional, fashionable. As any Frenchwoman will testify, matching underwear is the essence of feminine perfection. I read somewhere that a Frenchwoman wouldn't dream of leaving home, as we British so frequently do, in mismatched underwear. They shudder at the thought. A French woman exudes the certainty of perfection from the inside out; she breathes a supreme air, made of quite surreal and sanctimonious ingredients that the British female will never possess. She is cool, calm, collected, and wearing the sheerest, silk undies imaginable. They have every right to look down their noses at our M & S five-pack of smalls.

My La Perla twin set in place, head held high, and my own small dwarf in hot pursuit, we find a table near the stage with our names on it. I quickly scan the other name cards to see what God-awful people we will be sharing a pew with.

"Psst," hisses Hel maturely, "that horrid woman — Harrison is sitting with us!"

"Oh, this should be fun..." I can feel my sphincter muscle tightening at the thought of her.

"Don't know any of the others..." she meanders, making a full circle of the round table to take in all the little cards.

"Be a good producer and get me a drink would you?"

"Only because I have to go to the loo. I'll make a special pit stop for you on my return. Be good..." I watch her jostle with the high-class riff-raff and disappear as those taller than her — everyone — pulls in around her.

An all-encompassing yawn forces its way out of my mouth, when I hear an unsettling voice: "Tired already? It's only just gone noon!" Harrison has arrived. The Observer's answer to Candice Bushnell, but without the love life; her Female Life Style Column has been the bane of my existence for as long as I can remember.

As a young student, I discovered her *oeuvre,* and was astounded to read the voice of a woman who didn't seem to like anything or anyone at all, least of all women. The ones she did talk up were either emaciated stick figures with pedigree and no talent; or members of parliament who wore skirts but acted like they wore the trousers in their constituency. She was gung-ho in all the wrong places as far as I was concerned, and when the station launched, she was the first to put a death nail in our coffin. I think one particular excerpt I remember went something like, "...and should any female over five and under ninety-five find the time to turn on their radio and search out this ramshackle excuse for bra burning the first voice they will find is that of male breakfast co-host Gary Standen, who, had he been born a woman, would have had the good sense to turn down the job..."

This was perhaps the only fact with which I would ever agree with her; this humiliation was not lost on the other members of Radio Honey. We often questioned what on earth was going on in the minds of management when they decided to elect this gruesome twosome — Gary, and his side-kick, the very un-angelic, Angel? I believed in this concept, signed up with conviction in my heart and soul. Then, launch day, the first voice the nation actually heard on *the first all-female radio station* was that of a man...

Joe McGrae, the Texas mid-fielder from company headquarters, no doubt thought it would be a good idea to straddle the feminine line with a little testosterone, spread a little male pixie dust over the proceedings. He might as well have sent us a twelve pack of gonorrhoea.

"Jane...how are you?" I manage.

"Fabulous, darling, simply fabulous. How is our little pantheon of feminine brow beating — Radio Femme?"

"Honey." I correct.

"Don't get personal — it doesn't suit you. So how is it?"

"Not bad, thanks." I give up.

"Hmmm," she eyes me suspiciously, and takes her seat, unconvinced.

"Have you had your stats yet?"

"Um, yeah, but they were complicated by poor reception due to problems with the placement of our initial masts."

"You mean nobody can bloody hear you."

"Something like that..."

"Well, darling, I'm sorry, but you know my feelings: I think making a station for women is acknowledging that we are a less heard minority and your poor reception simply proves it. One should never draw attention to one's flaws. Women have been camouflaging successfully for generations with lipstick and lies — why should we come out now? It just won't work, sorry dear."

"No, you're entitled to your opinion, Jane, but there are some of us who, like Ms Pankhurst herself, believe in action over non-action."

"Yes, and look where it got her, dear, pummelled flat under the hooves of a man's horse. Very unflattering."

"That was the suffragette, Emily Wilding Davison."

"Same difference."

At this point I am 'saved' by Hel's appearance with my drink which she hands me at eye level —between mine and Jane's.

"One red wine. Don't drink it all at once."

"Things must be bad, darling, if you're drinking in the middle of the day." Fortunately, I cannot see her face, but I can feel her cynicism behind the ruby liquid. I take the glass and have a healthy gulp. Without a retort I resort to introductions: Hel to Jane. This goes down like a hooker with osteoporosis; Jane eyes her with even more distaste than she did me, but it would seem I am far more fun to tease:

"What happened to your skirt darling?"

"I had a little accident getting into my cab...."

"You should take more care. It must be all the drinking." I can feel the blood rising up my neck, charging the pathways to the primal seat of our basest instincts — such as violence — the *subcortical basal ganglia*. Blame my father for my grasp of Grey's Anatomy.

Interestingly enough, recent studies have found that whereas we had always assumed that our modern brain, the *neo-cortex*, was responsible for learned responses, we now know that the pathways to the more primitive parts of our brain receive the information quicker. In fact, in 'fight or flight' situations, we respond to this danger signal first, instinctively, and then emotionally, with the newer parts of our brain. Like slamming our foot on the brakes when a threatening situation arises, and then feeling the emotional fall out from that response; or punching someone first, and then realizing we could go to prison. Which seems like a fair response at this point.

I take another gulp of wine, dampening the inflamed pathways with the oldest medicine — the humble grape. The chairs at our table are being hastily filled whilst up on stage inactivity has suddenly turned to high octane action.

Devla Havell is mincing in the side-lines, obviously waiting to be introduced. Before that, however, we have to endure the painful speech of the magazines' publicity department telling us how wonderful this event is, and why we had all taken time from our busy schedules to be here. I, for one, was beginning to question my own existence, never mind my presence at this event.

Jane was exchanging insider gossip in hushed tones with Hannah Mayhugh, the director of Bel and Dio, the new fuller figure fashion wear catalogue. They both managed to turn at the same time, mid conversation and eye me, as if measuring me up for the new line. Hel was fidgeting with the recording device, trying to remember how it worked no doubt. Our job would be to survive this nightmare, and then interview those winners whose awards symbolized their overwhelming contribution to the force of womanhood.

Needless to say, we had to endure Jane going up to receive her prize for best female columnist. The flouncing and fanfare accompanying this farcical journey up to the stage, jaw numbing banality of her speech, and painful posturing once back at our table, was considerably more than I could bear. Thank God, therefore, for the wine. It was bad enough that I had to endure the sight of her twinkly award sat between us on the table. I, who had never won a fucking thing in my life. Not a thing. Not one prize at school, and not one since. Not a raffle or lollipop. Nothing. Was it any wonder I deeply hankered for some sense of acknowledgement now? Anything? Even an unplanned pregnancy?

Bambi Davis wins for best female singer/songwriter, and I bump into her in the women's toilet, where I go to escape Jane, her trophy, and Hel generally, and metaphysically. Only to find Bambi throwing up in the sink.

There are several emaciated and designer clad women tottering in and out on their high heels, but they take one look at a figure huddled and vomiting and act as if it is part of the dining ritual.

After the worst of it, I offer Bambi a towel; half wondering if I should dash back to the table and grab the recording device? This could, after all, be a rather candid interview? Sadly, valour gets the better part of me.

"Thanks," she manages through her puke and lipstick covered mouth. With one good wipe she takes both off.

"Can I get you anything?"

"Nah...I'll be ok", and with this she looks a little unsteady on her feet. I grab her arm and manoeuvre her towards a chair. She feels frail, as if all her flesh had decided to tender its resignation. Leaning over on her legs, teetering on bony elbows, she gives me the first look of the evening.

Her green eyes swamp me; so much more luminous than the cover shot of her on the 'Goin' South' album which has made her a household name. I think I played her single once, and got a trouncing from Clare, but it was worth it. The song, "Hog Tied" was a priceless tale of being dumped and tying up the offender. Sterling stuff.

Bambi leans in close, for what I imagine might be an exclusive insight...

Back at the table, I make my hurried excuses:

"Hel — I've got to go. You will have to do the interviews."

"But *you* can't! *I* can't! Why?"

"So soon?" pipes in Jane, and then catching a whiff of me reels back, eyes large as soup plates, in disgust. "Good Lord! You stink!"

The taxi driver who takes me home isn't impressed either; he makes me sit on the end of the fold out chair all the way to my house. Accepting my ten pound note gingerly, he literally tosses the change out the window; which he wound down, along with all the others throughout the journey, so that not only do I have to hold my own on the edge of my seat, but I have to balance whilst buffeted by winds from all directions. Still, I suppose I should be grateful for the lift?

Hel is just falling in through the door, looking haggard, when I get back to the office, washed, scrubbed, perfumed, and changed. Not to mention a quick joint to cheer myself up.

"Well thanks very much..." She manages.

"I'm hardly going to stand there, covered in vomit one more minute than I have to, Hel. Fucking Bambi Davis puked up on me in the toilets! *After* I tried to help her clean herself up! That woman's got more puke in her than Linda Blair in 'The Exorcist'!"

"Oh, Lord..."

"Yes, 'Oh Lord'...needless to say, I had to go home and change. The one silver lining is she has promised us an exclusive. So, how'd you make out?" Hel relaxes her angry caterpillar eyebrows, and heaves the recording device on to her desk:

"Abysmal. Terry Cline refused to be interviewed, Jane was always too busy when I tried to interview her, Charlie William's breasts were more eager to give me an interview than she was, and Clair Beauford just looked right over my head..."

"Well, that I can understand...you are unbelievably short..." Hel is too tired to give me a scathing look, or a response.

"But I did get an interview with Jennifer Soldat about her one woman show at The Troubadour in the Old Brompton Road." Hel looks suddenly pleased with herself. She obviously has never been to The Troubadour on the Old Brompton Road.

"Hel, that is not even worth a listing, never mind a mention. So, great, we have fuck all!"

"Well, it's not my fault! You left me! All alone!" She was doing her little girl lost, complete with trembling lower lip.

"Oh, grow up!" And those were the last words we exchanged until show time. I sat at my desk and threw together my show notes with all the enthusiasm of a check out girl at Freezer Foods. By the time Tony walked in, earlier than scheduled, I had been scratching the underbelly of the empty barrel of fun for some time. His smile reached me before he did. Sloping low from his shoulders, his guitar case nearly scraping the floor, his mothballed suit looked like it hadn't been washed since the moths died.

"Hey!"

"Tony...hey," I was suddenly feeling way out of my depth. This I usually covered up with bull shit and bravado, but I wasn't feeling either. I knew that this situation could have been avoided, plus I was mixing business with pleasure, and there wasn't much pleasure in it.

Of course, it is at this moment that Courtney also chooses to show up, and taking one look at Tony, and then me, throws a dirty look my way; giving us both a wide berth. A berth she kept for the rest of the day which was probably just as well as I couldn't explain this to myself let alone anyone else.

Hel appears, trying to look as if she hadn't come from the direction of Clare's offices, and I introduce her to Tony. I note, with additional dismay, that they are nearly the same height.

"Hel, this is Tony. Tony—Hel" They shake hands awkwardly. "Can you see if Clive can squeeze him in to record the audio of two of his songs to be played in at a later date?" Hel's eyebrows tell me what she cannot in front of Tony. Tony and I watch as she lets out an inaudible sigh and flat foots her way out of the room.

"So..." Tony attempts a seductive look which just makes me feel slightly nauseous.

"So..." I was even boring myself.

"What are you doing after?"

"Nothing," I hate myself for my answer and the assured knowledge of where all this was leading.

"Yes, he can squeeze you in now," announces Hel, from the doorway.

"Great", I sounded as relieved as I felt, "I'll see you afterwards". I manage to smile at Tony, and he smiles back, hoisting his huge guitar case up and out of the room. He turns at the door:

"Maybe I can take you out to say thank-you after your work?"

"Yeah, OK."

I watch him walk out, assessing his arse as he goes; it is lost in the bagginess of his jeans. There is literally nothing to excuse my behaviour.

"Who's that?" It's Jezebel; or just her head above my computer. The last person I would expect to talk to me, or break into my personal, shit-shaped life at this point in time.

"Oh, he's a Blues man. A friend."

"Looks like more than a friend to me." She winks and keeps walking.

Then as if I needed one more reason to hate my life, Clare is suddenly blocking my thoughts of self-mutilation with her body.

"Cass, can I have a word?" Without waiting for a response, she starts walking towards her office, and when she doesn't turn around I realize it is my duty to follow.

"Shut the door," she tells me once we are both in the inner sanctum.

"Take a seat". I don't dare ask what this is all about. It was coming just as sure as taxes. All I had to do was wait.

"There have been some complaints..."

"Complaints?" My voice rises and breaks. I suddenly feel as small as Hel.

"Complaints". Clare clarifies.

"What about?"

"Let's just say that not only have there been unlisted songs on your show, but some of your views have not been shared by your public, and your own team members have had a few things to say about your behaviour. i.e.," and here she pauses, having made a particular flourish of the 'i' and the 'e', "in and out of the studio, and in regard to normal, civilized office behaviour." She stops to gauge my reaction. I am tight lipped, so she continues. "I am also considering changing your producer." Now my mouth is open.

Despite my often hate-filled moments with Hel, we are a team, a unit, and we rise and fall as a whole. At least that was how I felt at the moment at which it was all seemingly being taken from me.

"But we work well together," I manage.

"Do you think Helen would say the same?"

"Yes, I do," I say with an unusual surge of passion and enthusiasm.

"Well, I will be keeping a close eye on things, and am making you aware that changes may be swift, and sudden should I see fit." She unfolds her hands on the desk, and I take this as a sign that the meeting is over. I stand up.

"Cass…" I was nearly to the door.

"Yes"

"When was your last day off?"

"I don't know, why?"

"Maybe you should consider taking next Monday off — have a long week-end."

"But I don't want a long week-end!"

"I think you could do with a break." She had decided. "I'll see you back on Tuesday." Disbelief courses through my body. I shut her door, bypassing the *neo cortex*, and going straight to the *subcortical basal ganglia* where graphic images of what I would like to do to her flash before my eyes, like a dying man's last ecstatic visions.

Hel was the first person I chanced upon.

"What did you say to Clare?!"

"What? Nothing!" She simpers; too impassioned to be plausible.

"You've been speaking to her haven't you? Wielding your little way into her good books by dumping on me! You told her about the awards didn't you?!"

"I didn't say anything!"

"I stand there defending us, and you stand there tearing us down! I thought we were a team?!"

I'm suddenly aware that the whole office is looking at us. I storm out of the room, leaving Hel standing by our desks, her tiny, plasticine hands wringing themselves together.

When things go wrong you don't often see it until it is too late. You sort of soldier on thinking things are just normally shit, not abnormally crap. You imagine that this is the way of things. No biggie. Whereas underneath this seeming mediocrity the wheels of misfortune are quietly turning, building up in intensity, the grains of sand slowly accumulating until the latch is pushed up by the weight of judgement against you, and the shit hits the fan full force.

"Jessica Stone is here with her new book, 'Grrrirl Power' — welcome."

"Thank you," Jessica shifts uncomfortably in her seat.

"I read your book," I lied, I had read the sheet notes, "and it occurs to me, Jessica, that the rise of the 'gggirl', as you put it, is not as powerful as the girl bands and tabloids would have us believe…"

"I disagree, I think the empowerment of girl bands in pop music, and their success is a real indication that we are moving forward with feminism in strong, self-controlling ways…"

"You cite bands like 'Girlie Show' and 'FemmeBots' as examples of this rising tide of girl power, but surely these are just pubescent girls? I mean dressed up in stockings and suspenders —which frankly is not what most women want to see — it's what men want to see. So, aren't we just playing into the old patterns of male dominated society?"

"These women aren't puppets, they're speaking a strong message about self-empowerment which goes above and beyond what they're wearing; these are choices *they* are making — nobody else," and here she emphasized her book title to good effect, "it's all about Grrrrl Power." She sits back satisfied with her answer, but I'm not.

"But surely it should be 'Woman Power' as girls are simply underage, and not grown up enough to know what empowerment is?"

"I disagree; there are many young girls who understand about women's issues."

"I just think that continuing to refer to women as girls, in that diminutive way that we have since the beginning of time, treating them as too simple to be able to vote, or not worthy enough or smart enough for equal pay — all these references that continue to play to women as girls sends the wrong message — plays into the hands of the patriarchy?"

"I disagree, I think young women can have fun and still be taken seriously."

"Don't get me wrong, I enjoyed the book, and the message you are trying to send," I lied, but needed to butter her up for further abuse, "however, these pop singers are signed to male dominated labels, told what songs to sing by male producers, and the members of the band are usually chosen by some bloke in a Guns and Roses T-shirt and trainers who thinks he has his finger on the pulse of contemporary music, but lives alone in a basement with his sound system and a half dead goldfish."

Jessica tries to laugh this one off, but listeners could not see my deadly serious poker face; the one I reserve for my political moments; the one's Hel hates, and Clare for that matter, but I had been given 'the day off' Monday so I might as well make this afternoon count.

"I think they've got more sense than you make out...." Jessica was no longer sure how to handle the interview.

"So, should we really be jumping up and down and saying that feminism has not been in vain?"

"Well I wouldn't go that far..." Jessica is beginning to look slightly broken and a wave of sympathy rolls over me, despite my better judgement.

"Tell me, when did you fall in love with 'gggirl power'?" I tried to emulate her enthusiasm for the word of the moment, but it felt, and must have sounded, hollow.

As she began to tell me about her early love of pop bands, and a burgeoning sense of women in music I drifted off, imagining the Britney Spears posters on her bedroom wall, the pink bedspread, and furry heart shaped pillow. And I realized, young as she was, she had probably been commissioned to write the book by a male publisher, eager to get in on a rising trend. I was almost grateful when it was time for Hel to come in and cover for our ailing Film and TV critic.

"We are lucky now to have my very own producer, the inimitable Helen of Troy — Hel to you and I — to cover for our Film Critic who is at death's door, or at least he better be for missing today. Get well soon Jeremy!" Hel is so excited to have a microphone, and headphones that she is literally panting on air; she realizes this is a once in a lifetime opportunity; it's just not done for producers to become contributors. Our budget, however, means that this is an opportunity that is led by circumstance not talent.

"It's good to be here!"

"So, what's the first film you have for us today, Hel?" I want to giggle. Her apple plumb cheeks are rosy as the inside of a beef tenderloin.

"Well," Hel gathers her papers together, nervously fingering the edge of the page, and continuing in an affected voice, "our first film, Cass, is a remake of Alfred Hitchcock's 'Vertigo' starring Bill Haley and Jessy May Hewitt," she is reading verbatim from her sheet of paper, and it sounds like it: "they play the parts of these star-crossed lovers in this psychological thriller about a retired police officer who gets hired as a private detective by an acquaintance to follow his wife, and —"

"Wait a minute, Hel," I interrupt, "did you see the comedy version 'High Anxiety' that Mel Brooks made?"

"No," she is stumped without her script, and of course I realise the cruelty of butting into her carefully rehearsed play sheet.

"You have to see it! — it even has songs! Classic Mel Brooks at his best!" My enthusiasm is lost on Hel, and I let her snail through the rest of her required reading.

"So, what else have you seen this week for us?" Trying to keep things moving.

"Blockbuster 'Hell's Gate' with tough guy, Jez Baker is a great sequel to 'Hell's Mouth'!"

"Any relation?"

"Shut up!" She breaks out of character, and then embarrassed, slips back in:

"Jez plays the hero of the last tribe of survivors on Planet Earth, being slowly destroyed by the underworld monsters who come alive after the last movie where we saw them fill in the void in time that brought them hurtling through space, and prey to all the worst demons imaginable in the black holes of the cosmos..." she takes a breath, and continues, "in this one he hooks up with Gemma Steel —"

"I've seen the posters — it looks like she's had her boobs done..." Hel doesn't know how to talk about boobs on air, and so sweeps over it:

"I don't know, but she sure can do Kung Fu!" Her eyes sparkle with the memory.

"That's good to know, but I want to know if she's had a boob job — this is the kind of info we need to know on the film feature. We need the inside leg measurements on the celebrities as well as the shows..." I'm pushing her out into unknown territory, teasing her.

"I'll find out for you, and you can announce it in your celebrity sleaze item..." she looks up at me, her eyes bored, knowing I will not allow her to have a clean sweep of this one. She will have to suffer like all my contributors. I am the boss, and these are the perks that come with the job.

"Great — thanks."

"As I was saying," said with audible constricting of her epiglottis, "this blockbuster sequel…" About this time, I went off into a dreamy reverie about Jez Baker, and I had Gemma Steel's new boobs, and they looked grrrreat.

Tony was waiting for me when I finished. Why is it so difficult to say, "I changed my mind — I really don't want to spend the evening with you? I would rather tether myself to the number seven bus, and be dragged down the length of the Edgeware Road?" Needless to say, for all my internal effrontery, I did not manage to say this. Instead, that evening, we lay down in my room, on the flower print bed spread that had once been my mother's, and I let him do what he had been wanting to do to me for a long time. I even put aside my usual caution when he told me not to worry about contraception because his swimmers were incapable of inception. Did I enjoy it? Feeling needed is sometimes all that is required. Pyewacket watched from the corner of the room, and with a distasteful turn of his head, suddenly emitted a small, violent cat sneeze, and sauntered out of the room.

It occurs to me, in the guise of measured scientific enquiry, that were inception a woman's job, would we be happy to take the necessary measures, or claim they just undermined our pleasure? Would we buy 'extra small' even when our vaginas were clearly Grand Canyon sized? Would we make the simple idea of having to wear a contraceptive such a song and dance? Would we look at our partner with disappointment, and tell them it was *their* job to make themselves sex-ready?

A sexual health expert recently told the New York Times that the real reason men don't like to wear condoms is all to do with size...apparently the average erect penis is just over an inch shorter than standard condoms, which are normally at least 6.69 inches long. So that extra length could be making men feel inferior? Who wants to be shown up in the bedroom by an invisible competitor?

When I get to the club that Friday night, and find myself at a table with Tony, Cage, and a recalcitrant Courtney, I'm enjoying myself; surrounded by my friends, and the added 'bonus' of someone who gave me the attention my poor excuse for an ego craved. Tony, spurred on by his recent ejaculation, is sitting taller than usual.

As the door pivots open, letting in oxygen that was badly needed in this underground hole, Jack's presence seemed like the most unspoken, but inevitable of occurrences.

I could feel him watching me that evening, as the 'Starsky and Hutch' theme got well underway. Dressed up as Hutch to Courtney's Starsky, we did a winning performance of 'I've got you Babe' by Sonny Bono and Cher. Then Cage, dressed as Huggy Bear in a yellow shirt open to his waist, showing his scrawny rib cage with its lack of hair, and purple bell bottoms, performed a new song he'd been working on, "The Rich List." He tore a strip off the famous, naming and shaming in a rap that lay waste the modern culture of greed and gluttony. It was positively life affirming for the under privileged.

Skatch was 'scratching' up the decks in the corner, in front of a poster of the red and white Ford Torino that was the Starsky and Hutch mobile. Removing his afro wig at the end of the song, Cage takes his applause, and jumps down off the stage. He arrives at our table sweating.

"Wow, it's hot in there!"

"You were brilliant!" I enthuse.

"You make me wanna be black...can I borrow y'ar wig?" Cage chucks the wig at Courtney, and flops into his chair:

"Enjoy!" He runs his hands through his mop of hair, making it stand up with sweat.

"Good going, my man," Tony manages. They exchange manly fist punches. Courtney is wearing the afro:

"How'd I look? I might finally get me some rhythm; I can't dance worth shit, anyhow; you got more chance of a hog dancin' the two step than me doin' a goose step."

"You can't be that bad?" Cage is intrigued.

"Get y'ar ass up and I'll step on y'ar toes some."

"I'll take a rain check…"

"I can't dance either," Tony makes an attempt at joining the group. Courtney shoots him a look, and I can read her mind, it goes something like: "And you don't move right either." I try to smooth over the cracks:

"Anyone want a drink?" George is up on stage reading one of his poems. He's pushing sixty, and can be found wandering the streets, looking like Shelley's lost relative, the muse riding roughshod through his tangled hair, his lips moving to some couplet he is rehearsing. You might find him sitting outside in the cafes, accosting people with verse, eyes shining. Tonight, he performs, 'She Walks Devine'. Spittle gathers in the corners of his mouth, passion taking more than words hostage. His grey hair rattles; his clothes hang like an artistic afterthought.

I remove my moustache and walk up to the bar. Suddenly Jack is there beside me. I almost jump out of my 70's cop skin.

"I'm not saying facial hair suits you, but you're looking good…" I give him my best withering look before responding:

"Maybe you really have a deep need for men with facial hair, but have been unable until now to admit it?"

"You could make a new man out of me…"

"I could have made a man of you, but I've been there, done that, thrown away the T-shirt". The silly bastard actually looks wounded, as if he hadn't harpooned my heart more roughly than a Japanese whaling ship.

Chapter 6

To the Sounds of 'Can't Help Falling in Love' by UB40

Sitting on the corner of the bed, rolling my tights back up the winding road of my legs, I can feel his eyes on my back. Monday morning is sneaking through the crevasses of his crappy canvass roller blinds, more useless than my now laddered tights. My mind is a winning blank; no remembrance of a jobless day. No, I have fried my brain with weed and alcohol, and thrown myself into the human frying pan in an attempt to forget. For the first few moments of this morning, performing the rolling of the tights, my mind is a wonderful, quiet creature with nothing to berate me for, but then a horrible show reel of the last twenty-four hours begins to run behind my eyes.

My father, fresh from his more whimsical, Buddhist period, quoting Alan Watts, would tell me that the mind is a 'drunken monkey': always bringing up those things you would rather forget, always poking you in the side, and laughing at you; reminding you of those embarrassing things you did, those inappropriate fuck ups. Why is it that this brain that is supposed to belong to us, and be on our side, seems to be the enemy within? Who's paying it to wind me up? Who's controlling it? It doesn't seem to be me. Sometimes I wish my Dad would just do his job and stop reading books with big philosophical meanings that he then has to bend my mind with. I mean, I have a right to a blameless existence, a non-existential life, right? Ignorance is bliss. That's what I want on my tombstone.

But what's actually happening in the brain to make it bring up these things we would rather forget? And why? Oh Why?! If you look up the science, or speak to my Dad, he will tell you that it all has to do with the way our brains have developed; with evolution. If bad people or bad things happen to you it's important to remember them because it could form part of your survival in the future; it's part of the building blocks of your tool kit to stay alive. Identifying danger, whatever and whomever the shape it may take, is such an integral part of homo-sapiens' make-up that you can't take it out of the modern animal. Those people or instances that were good to you are not as memorable, and that's because they didn't threaten your existence, so remembering them doesn't rate up there on your Richter scale of emotional turmoil and therefore play-back.

A whiff of sperm and sex lifts off the sheets as Jack shifts down the bed to ruffle my hair.

"Don't you want some breakfast?"

I turn to look at him, surprise featuring despite my constant desire to appear the effortless coquette.

"Yeah…that would be nice." I watch his quite perfect body rise out of the white waves that buffet his body. A fully shaped man; all muscle rising and moulding to his chest, arms, legs; like a sculpture rising from the unhewn rock of the bed sheets. Sheets that probably haven't seen a detergent since I last soiled them with my lust juices, flowing as they voluminously do at his touch. Damn him. Why him? He's a fucking bastard. But God he has something. Something that makes me want to soak up the air around him and be grateful for this reprieve; for more moments like this.

The flowers I gave him all those weeks ago are still encased in their plastic, idly dying in a Coca Cola bottle on the bedside table; their water a study in microscopic life.

I rummage under the bed for one of my shoes. He's throwing a kimono over his wide shoulders, freckled light brown, and, as he leaves the room, I am left with the view of the dragon emblazoned on the back. Wishing I was born in the year of the dragon, and not year of the sheep, I fish my other shoe out of the tangle of bedcovers and follow him into the living room.

"So, who've you got in today? Anyone interesting?" He's breaking eggs into a bowl in the kitchenette. And there it is: the fruit of my failure. A simple question, so innocent, waiting like a cocked gun. I would rather take his hand and pull him back into that bed and suck his cocked gun than have to admit the sad facts.

"I've been given the day off." He turns, and the kimono falls away revealing a soft down over a firm chest. I eye the edge of the kimono begging it to give me one nipple, just a snippet, but he wants to talk about it. I find sex, in all its various guises, to be the best antidote to the drunken monkey.

"What do you mean?" My sigh says what I don't want to, and I look around the room as if for an exit. "One or two eggs?" he continues.

"Um, one will do thanks, not very hungry."

"You look like you could do with some feeding up."

"Thanks. I'll convey your confidence to the chef." I try a smile, but he's onto me. For somebody who professes a keen desire to stay away from commitment, he is perfectly capable of plumbing the depths of human emotion. As long as it doesn't lead to anything serious.

"What happened?" I sigh again, hoping to delay.

"Apparently I am in the dog house for various misdemeanours — don't ask me — and have been told to take a day off to consider my transgressions against society."

"Like what?" He turns with the bowl, briskly whisking the eggs.

"Ohhh...inciting bad behaviour amongst the staff, being offensive to the listeners, not bringing in the goods — all kinds of stuff..."

"Hmmm..." He is pouring the scrambled eggs into the waiting pan. "You could always do a bit of DJ'ing at my club...if you get stuck..." I could have hugged him.

"Really?"

"Yeah, really. See how you go, eh?" He pops some toast in the toaster, and as steam fills the little nook of kitchen land, he pours boiling water into two mugs.

"You've really made my day, my week..." I try not to look too grateful; as if he really were the last lifeline in my pathetic life. "Thanks."

"Hey...it's cool..." I watch him perform simple miracles with butter and bread, milk and mugs, and the low hum of background radio makes all the breakfast smells come together as one.

Jack pulls the door closed behind us on the street, and I look far up into his eyes, his cap reinstated on his scratchy mop of already receding hair; the only lapse in an otherwise practically perfect specimen of manliness. I wonder what I have done to deserve this. Should I be shouting from the rooftops, "He's mine!", or waiting for the guillotine to drop again?

"Well…" he offers, looking up the road to freedom.

"Well…" I counter, afraid to say more.

"I'll call you…" And the guillotine drops.

I feel like baby bear. Somebody has been sitting in my chair, and although it's not broke, I can feel the indentation of her bum. Her warm arse sat on *my* chair and did *my* show. Her warm arse swivelled around on *my* chair, barking orders at *my* producer, who might as well have jumped from *my* ship with the rats. She's even left a fucking coffee mug stain on the console.

Everyone looks at me when I walk in on Tuesday. With a look that says they feel sorry for me, but they don't want to associate with me least they catch the disease. I don't bother with trying to smile, or my usual easy banter. This is war. Every woman for herself. Even Hel seems to have cooled towards me. Maybe she preferred her time with whomever they got in to fill my shoes. I don't even want to know who they got in. I have a feeling it's some new girl that I've heard the odd snippet about but have never seen. She probably sucked up to Clare, and put 'lesbian' on her CV. I am full of such unbridled hate for everyone that I am seriously wondering how I will make it through the day.

Then, through the desert of tables and chairs an apparition appears, blurred and slowed around the edges, as if standing out in time and space from the crowd. It's Courtney, and she's smiling. All my hopes and dreams focus in on her as she moves through the chaff towards me, bending their heads to their desks with her goodness; her charity spearheading the air in front of her. In the next movement she has me in a bear hug embrace. It's all I can do not to cry.

"How was your day off? I hope you at least got some cock?" She searches for eye contact, pulling me away just enough to look into my baby blues.

"Yeah, I got cock," I smile, sheepishly, feeling like the baseball player who just scored a run for the team.

"Not Tony's I hope?" She looks genuinely worried.

"No." She looks even more worried.

"Not Jack?" I look around the room; heads have lifted through shame and into curiosity. We move automatically out of ear shot.

"Well, I kind of had both in the space of a week end..." I'm not sure if it is pride or fear on her face. She says nothing, which for Courtney, is truly spooky. She steers me out of the office, and out into the smoking courtyard. The hulking door that separates outer and inner sanctum is pushed closed with a loud, subterranean clunk.

"What's goin' on?" Now she's back. "Have you lost total control of your senses? I mean mother-of-God-and-tiny-baby-Jesus, what is the mother fuckin' deal?" I can only look at her winsomely hoping she will stop for air. "So, who had the bigger cock?" She smiles a little. I rally to our usual game, relieved to have something familiar to cling to. "Well?" Courtney is waiting for details.

"Well, I guess..." My eyes search the heavens trying to remember. I think I kept my eyes closed throughout most of my encounter with Tony because I just can't seem to get a visual handle on his appendage. "I'd say Jack had the bigger dick, but long, you know?" She nods understanding phallus comparisons intuitively, and also having had a lot of cocks herself. "I'd say Tony's was probably thicker, kind of short and fat, but you didn't miss the length — you know?"

"Girl, you've got a nerve slippin' an extra length in there without me even knowin'!" She laughs, and flicks back her lovely golden hair.

"You know I'd have called you, but it all happened so fast; it was all I could do to dislocate my jaw from the floor when he called me."

"Who?"

"Jack"

"When?"

"Sunday"

"What'd he say? He's got some grovellin' ta do? He damn near poked yer' heart out with his dick last time."

"Yeah, well, I let him have it at the club Friday night, remember?"

"Yeah, he looked like a bona fide hound dowg that night, his tail so far between his legs he could a been a lady man from Thailand."

"Well, I think he thought about it...and..."

"I just hope he means it this time and isn't just hard up for a screw."

"You and me both, but he did say I could DJ at his club if times got rough over here." Courtney looks me square in the eyes, and I can see the wheels turning in her head.

"Well that's not somethin' ya hear every day. Damn, if a man actually comes up with the rent, and not just the sperm then you're onto somethin', and it don't matter what the gig is; rent's rent. You can get any poor fucker ta give ya an orgasm, provided he can find your clit with a dictionary and The Joy of Sex for back up, but rent as well?! You got the pay load right there." She had a point.

"It's good to see you," I manage as the tears start to well up in my eyes before I even knew they were standing in the wings.

"Hey..." she puts an arm around me, "why the tears? You got two dicks in one week-end; you should be walkin' funny and talkin' proud!" I brush them away before they can roll. Inside I am waiting for the ones in the wings to get on the blower and call the whole fleet down.

"What you say we have ourselves a damn nice meal tonight? Go out on the town and treat ourselves to some fine wine and finger food, and I'm not talkin' a lesbians last supper — how 'bout it?" You can't help being drawn in by her smile that seems to stretch ear to shinning ear, bejewelled as they are with more rhinestones than a cowboy.

Lifting an overloaded sandwich to her lips, I watch Hel at her desk, lettuce leaves and mayonnaise threatening to jump ship. Blissfully unaware of the world around her, she seems to be talking to herself before she pushes this symphony of sandwich fillings into the cavern of her mouth. The phone interrupts her, and with a mouthful she lifts the phone, and jabbers away, yanking off a segment of lettuce, and nibbling on it while she talks. Too tired by the predictability to complain about the fact that she has not given me any of today's notes, I simply watch this study in human behaviour. Mired in her juvenility like a sand crab, her unshockable youthfulness righteous armour, she soldiers on; losing herself in the details of the sandwich. I quietly envy her.

Lacking energy and confidence, the switch flicked on omnipotent DJ mode, I segue through two songs back to back, idly watching the hive behind me. Those busy little Radio Honey bees, making their matriarchal honey. And where is the queen bitch, I mean bee? She has been keeping well away from me today. I wonder when I'll be thrust back in her presence, to find out what latest fuck ups I've managed to inveigle in the name of Judas Iscariot.

Hel seems to have suddenly remembered that she is my producer: she spins round in her chair and stares open mouthed at me through the glass. Calmly returning the swivel in my own chair, I return her gaze as calmly as one awaiting death. The laboured path she weaves on her way from her desk to my door fills me with a strange warmth. I feel I'm watching all the activities around me as if floating from above, as if nothing and no one can harm me any longer. I smile inwardly and outwardly, and she is there, in front of me. And I haven't even had a blunt this morning. It occurs to me that perhaps I simply don't care about this whole sorry excuse for a station anymore. Maybe my day off really did knock some sense into me? But I'm not convinced.

Hel moves around the studio, talking, and moving things idly from one place to another. She can't fool me with her apparent busy-ness. The attention to detail. I know somewhere inside me that she's no longer on my team. That she and I no longer hold hands on this. I am the sound of one hand clapping. She is keeping busy to forget the knife she has put in my back. She is treating me like a book cover instead of a novel she has read, page by page. But when I watch her, I can only love her. Her silliness. Her innocence. One day she will understand what she has done, and she will be sorry, but I don't want her forgiveness now. I like to see her strong and independent, doing what she thinks is right, even if she has left a knife wound in my back. I smile knowing I will be sacrificed, knowing I am the alter god's favourite. So be it.

"There won't be any live travel, as Gail is off sick..." she is mulching the papers on the console into one pile, "probably got her nose ring stuck in her stockings," she smiles at her own joke and moves on, "so you'll have to go to the prerecord travel — got it?" She smiles her new mechanical smile, and I smile my new Buddha-in-a-trance smile and finished posturing we both continue with our day.

"Cheers! To two cocks in two days! That's a week-end's work well done!"

It seems like the whole restaurant looks round at the mention of 'cocks.' I shrink slightly in the shoulder region, but still manage to meet Courtney's glass in the middle. Clink: the sorry sound of a modern woman's hollow success.

Somewhere deep inside, where my father's self-help books really come into their own, I know this is nothing to write home about, nothing to drink sparkling wine over.

"So are ya' gonna juggle all four balls, girl, or let a couple drop?"

"I have no idea what I'm going do. I think I might just do nothing cause I'm kind of tired of thinking…"

"Hell, I'd be grateful for a dog to shag my leg at this juncture!"

"You know, I knew this marriage guidance councillor who told me that after all her years in the business, she'd discovered that a lot of women had learnt how to enjoy cunnilingus by letting their lap dogs lick them to climax, and that's how they learned how to get back in the saddle with their own husbands…"

"Get out wid' cha!"

"No, serious!"

"Gives new meaning to the term 'lap dog' though — dunnit?!"

"It certainly does!" We smile at the contents of our wine glasses.

"That is goddamned gross!" Courtney has let the images filter down, "God strike me down, and flail my insides if I should ever fall so low."

"Well, it takes all kinds...of dogs..."

"Aww," Courtney is still trying to get the image out of her head, then she seems to sober up fast, and fixes me with her serious look; a look which I only usually get when I have bypassed the laws of alcohol to body ratios.

"Cass, I've got somethin' to tell you, and I don't really know how to begin it..." I'm not sure I want any more bad news, but would rather it were quick as a virgin's first dip at the vagina fair.

"It can't be that bad, we're both still drinking!"

"Cass...I was the one that filled in for your show Monday..."

Chapter 7
To the Sounds of 'Fools Gold'
by The Stone Roses

My Dad named me Cassandra after some misplaced romantic notion that it encapsulated everything sweetly poignant about womankind. He had read a poem where the woman, Cassandra, is magnificently loved and lost, wooed and tortured with sorrows, and surviving them then suffers some more. My namesake, however, stayed stoic to the end, and somehow bore her misfortune with a feminine strength and mystique that my Dad admired. I was lumbered with this imagery and heroism from a young age when he would blithely inform me that my name was something of a talisman. Moreover, that my second name, Lilly, coming so soon after the first, commemorated his grandmother who had been a suffragette, and suffered a similar grisly fate to Emily Wilding Davison except at the hands of her own husband, not a race horse. It was with this heady brew of family mystique and tragedy that I gamely fought on and shortened it to Cass, perhaps to limit the growing up and into that I was expected to do.

Mum walked out on us when I was five, as Dad tells it. She too had a lot of growing up to do, and the constraints of diaper duty and late-night squalls meant that she listened more and more to the call, sylph like on the wind, of freedom. Ever the gypsy, she caught a moving train one day, and hasn't returned on any tide. I do wonder about her a lot. I'd be lying if I said I didn't. Dad always says that she did what she had to do, and neither of us should begrudge her that as she would have been miserable if she'd stayed. But when I ask him if she wanted a child, he just says that it wasn't a question of wanting. Mum was such a free spirit that she looked on it as another one of her adventures, as another part she might play, but usually there's an end to the run, and she would move on to the next part. With me, it was just more of the same part — Mum — exit stage left changing nappy, and enter stage right changing another. My gift to her was amateur dramatics of the worst kind.

Dad is married to his work. It's safer that way, or at least that's what I think he thinks. He did have a girlfriend once, and all they seemed to do was give each other stuffed toys. In the end, you couldn't see his bed. I knew it was over when I could see the quilt again; the quilt I associate with Mum because each hexagon is a different piece of fabric, just like all the parts she longed to play. It's a hand-me-down from my mothers' mother, and one of these days, when I get up the nerve, I shall ask Dad for it, and it will lay on *my* bed where I will trace my finger around all the hexagonals; each one a life I imagine her living somewhere.

Courtney is nowhere to be seen when I come in to the office. She probably knows better than to cross my path so soon after her recent revelation. I still don't understand why she agreed to do it? I mean, aren't sisters supposed to support each other? Her lame excuse that it was far better she did it than someone who might genuinely try to sabotage my position and take my post just didn't leave a good taste in my mouth, or a happy voice in my head.

"Cass," Hel is trying to look efficient, she even appears to be sporting what looks like a trendy little tie, but it clashes with the equally pin striped shirt. This is the school girl look trying to be city. The lunatics are slowly taking over the asylum under the guise of management. "I've got your blues man's edit to run into the show today to fill in for the fact that, Joe Parsons has pulled out at the last minute — not sure we'll miss his dulcet tones — and your first up, is the club guide, but I don't have the inserts ready yet so I've just got to dash off and finish them now…" Her and the tie swish efficiently past, and I don't make any comment to stop them. I imagine this means I shall just have to play songs until she tells me what is going on. It can always be worse?

That's when I see Courtney, walking across the back of the offices with Fay. They look deep in conversation. Fay does the nine to midnight slot, which could explain how she got in all that trouble with the heavy metal boys next door. They only wake up after the pubs close, and you can't help bumping into them when you leave the studio late at night as they spill out into the reception area that both radio stations share.

Fay is in her mid-40's and her voice is her ticket. That sexed up throatiness is like listening to a female Barry White, and she's not unattractive. Her long, dark hair frames a slender, almost beautiful face, and a well-proportioned bod. So why do I feel sorry for her? Almost motherly? There's something about her that's fragile and makes me want to throw a protective arm around her. I know she's been around long enough to have suffered more 'slings and arrows' than I have, but I never imagined in a million years that she would put her marriage on the line for one of the young, head-banger bozos in the studio next door. For now, she's just quietly simmering in unhappiness, and yet giving what portion of the capitol we actually reach a female boner with her liquid voice.

They stop at the doors to the smoking pit, push them open, and disappear.

"Right, so got that?" It's Hel again.

"Got what?"

"Are you okay with the show today? — Oh, I rhymed!" She looks genuinely pleased with herself.

"I'll notify Poetry Weekly"

"Just notify your next of kin because if you don't get your skinny in the studio and start prepping for the show you'll be a goner."

"Is that what Clare told you?" Hel tries to look genuinely hurt.

"It's just a joke."

"You don't make me laugh anymore. I know what you're up to, and there's blood on your hands."

"What do you mean...blood?" I get up from my desk and walk to the studio without answering.

The added padding on the studio door makes its closing all the more pleasing; the quiet, and sense of solitude all the more effective.

Clive waves from the other studio. He always looks so happy. How do people do that? There are some that seem to coast through life without upsetting people or having domestics, and others, like me, that trip on every crack in the sidewalk, and piss off every person they pass. My karma must be seriously soaked in sin to attract such a bashing in this life.

I must have upset a lot of people in the last one because they are really sticking it to me in this one.

There's a box of 'Sorry' chocolates on my desk when I finish the show.

"Do you like them?" she'd come to seal the deal.

"Um, yeah, thanks…"

"I know I'm just about as popular as tits on a boar hog right now, but I want you to know…it's not personal, and I shouldn't have done it, and it was damn near worthy of a butt kickin', and I won't ever do it again, and I'm really sorry…" She looks so forlorn that I'm tempted to hug her there and then, but Hel spoils the moment.

"Ooohh, chocolates!"

"Keep your hands off — they're mine!"

"Fine, I won't offer you any of my fudge…" She knows I'm a sucker for fudge, and with that she yanks open her draw, pulls a square of fudge out of a packet, and pops it in her mouth with all the lip-smacking enthusiasm of an old Flake advert. Thankfully she turns and sashays off, leaving the image of her butt with us longer than the rest of her.

"That girl makes my skin crawl. She couldn't produce her way out of a lift."

"You should know — she was your producer for a day..." I goad.

"Yeah, and I hated every moment of it. You'd be better off with a freakin' bush baby for a producer — wait a minute — she is a goddamned bush baby!"

"Well, if Claire and Hel get their way I *will* be working with marsupials on Zoo FM."

"Whad'ya mean?"

"Clair pulled me into her office after the puking awards ceremony, and it seems Hel had complained about me that day, and she says she's thinking of splitting us up..."

"Well, that's no bad thing; you should have shook her hand right there and then!"

"Yeah, well at the time I was still fond of Hel. I mean, damn, we've been a team since the station started."

"Yeah, all of six months ago. I've got zits older than that! You should go back and complain on *her* ass! Get yourself someone of school leavin' age — someone you can look up to — and I don't just mean height wise!"

"I can't do it...I just can't. I'm not cut throat. Even though I'm really pissed off with her — I still like having her around. She's like a cold sore I've got used to."

"You need to nip that right in the bud!" Sensing that I'm willing to take most things lying down at the moment, not just my love life, she gives me her worried look.

"I know I didn't help none stickin' one in there with the rest of em'..." I didn't have to say anything. We both knew she was right.

The woman dumps the cage on the counter. Pye looks a sorry sight; the cone neck-brace an uncompromising adornment. If cats can look pissed off — and they can — then this was the look I was getting loud and clear right now.

"He'll need to keep this on for the next two weeks, and..."

"Two weeks!" I couldn't restrain my shock and horror. Pye didn't look happy with this additional news either. Some people don't read cats very well, but cats are just as capable of giving us their full regime of happiness and disappointment with their limited palette of eye, ear, and bum semaphores. Not to mention the meow alternatives. The plaintive, mostly hungry, and the other, slightly less persistent, in need of a door opener. Their language is nearly as simplistic as the male. I have always admired the male of the species for their basic on/off psychology. Women are such complicated animals; so prone to whimsical little moods. No wonder most men feel like they are walking on land mines. The switch can flick at any moment after a less thought out phrase from the male, something about what she is wearing perhaps? Or putting a question mark on the end of a sentence instead of a full stop. Men are so much more basic and this pleases me on a fundamental level: you always know where you stand with them. We women should really pay more attention because chances are if he doesn't call, chase, or smile in your direction he is *not* interested. Men are like lions in the jungle: if it means extra energy for something they don't really want they will yawn and put their heads back down onto their big paws.

Science backs me up on this too: According to Dr. Louann Brizandine, a member of the American Board of Psychiatry and Neurology, the biggest difference between the male and the female brain is that men have a sexual pursuit area that is 2.5 times larger than that of women. So, if they want to pursue you — believe me, they will. Whilst the female brain is driven to seek security and reliability in a potential mate before she has signed on the sexual line, a male brain is fuelled to mate again and again. Making him a less than stable alternative to your dildo. However, Dr Brizandine tells us that despite stereotypes to the contrary, the male brain can fall in love just as hard and fast as the female, and maybe even more so. When he meets and sets his sights on capturing "the one"

— as it will always be driven at a hormonal level, hence the animalistic bent — mating with her will become his prime directive. So, put away your book on psychology ladies, and get yourself a tiny skirt because if you can't get his attention with the red rag of your mini skirt chances are he just isn't interested.

"Yes, two weeks, and you may need to keep an eye on his feeding; it can get complicated trying to navigate the bowl with this thing on. You might have to hand feed him if it gets too difficult for him."

"Hand feed him?!" I almost screech, "Wet food?"

"Well, not literally your hand, but with a spoon or something." She looks at me hoping I am capable of assimilating and processing this information without further instruction.

"OK." She looks relieved.

"He's had his pain medication today, but you'll need to crush one of these up in his food twice a day." She produces a packet and pops it in a bag. "Plus, you need to put these eye drops in his eyes twice a day if they start to get weepy. His eye duct was damaged on the left side, and it could become clogged up with some of the waste particles being eliminated from his system." This too is dropped in the bag. "That'll be..." She consults her screen, "Two hundred and seventy pounds."

"What?!" This time the screech is fulsome.

"Yes, I'm afraid, that's one night at the hospital, plus the operation, plus the medication..."

"Jesus! Did he have any spa treatments while he was here?"

"I'm sorry, Ms Bates, but you should have asked about our prices if you were going to have any problems with payment."

"I don't have any problems with payment; I have problems with the amount of money I'm having to fork out for pet hospital and sanctuary prices. Can I take my next vacation here? Wow..." I hand the woman my card, and the transaction is completed in simmering silence.

"Here you go," she says handing me back what remains of my card with the minimum of eye contact.

"Yeah, thanks...sorry...thanks..."

"Right..." She offers a smile as a way of ending our encounter. I take it, swing Pye off the counter, and leave with *my* tail between my legs.

"You're a fucking cat — cat — not a bird!" Pye looks up at me, surrounded by his plastic fantastic big bow tie, the misery quite evident.

"Well, if you will leave the window…"

"I did *not* leave the window open, Cage! I don't know how the little bugger got there!" Cage is trying to finish the joint he is rolling more quickly than usual so as to placate me — or sedate me.

"And now, I have to get the little fucker to take these tablets…have you ever tried to give a cat tablets?"

"No…"

"No — I didn't think so. Well, they aren't stupid. They don't bloody like it." I'm crushing the pink tablets with a knife on the kitchen counter, and all the little bits are getting stuck in the grouting. I inadvertently lick my finger after scraping it into a dish.

"Shit!"

"What?"

"I've just taken cat pain killer!"

"Don't worry, it'll only put y'ar pussy to sleep…come here — ya won't feel a thing!"

"Fuck off!" We're both smiling. Kneeling down next to Pye's bowl I scrape the bits in and mix it around with the food. Pye pads over, trying to see over his vast collar, sniffs it, and walks away.

"You see! I told you! They know."

"What does 'e know?"

"He knows there are drugs in his food, and he won't touch it."

"He'll come round when he's hungry enough — now smoke this." I take the offering. "Come and sit down and relax. You're getting' all wound up. He's gonna be jus' fine." I slump down next to Cage, not feeling so sure, but glad to put my feet up.

"Look I'll even make ya a nice cuppa, OK?"

"OK." It was nice to be looked after. I pull on the joint, and watch Cage potter around my kitchen, searching in cupboards, and generally making a pig's ear of things. The only discomfort is watching Pye bang his head from one piece of furniture to the next in frustration.

"Where's ya mugs?"

"Over there....no — one up — that's it." He pulls down two mugs and pours out the steaming water. Pye tries to wind around his legs, but his head collar gets in the way.

"He's going to have to get used to his new headdress!"

"Haiwatha Pye!" Cage strikes a pose.

"He better not try to pull another stint like this."

"Are you sure he 'ain't been getting' high with you, and thinkin' he can fly?"

"I swear — I don't give our son drugs!"

"I hope not," Cage brings over the teas, and we both watch Pye as he tries to get comfortable. Eventually he gives up and lies with his head skewed off a pillow.

"So how are things with the lay-dees?"

"Oh, pretty crap. Leane is up the spout."

"Yeah, you told me..."

"Anyway, I told 'er I'd stand by 'er if she wanted me to, but she's not havin' any."

"That's really nice of you."

"Well, I don't mind. I like the idea of little 'uns." The image of me, Pye, Cage, and a baby in a pram, feeding the ducks, laughing and smiling jumps into my mind; I let it sit there, playfully.

"You reckon you'd be a good father, do you?"

"Yeah, I do...." I look over at him — he's serious. Then he starts choking and coughing on the hit from the spliff.

Chapter 8

To the Sounds of 'Linger'
by The Cranberries

As if further evidence was needed to promote coupling up, new research at the University of Massachusetts has found that male pheromones are instrumental in putting off the menopause in married and cohabiting women. Single women go into the menopause on average two years before those with partners. I call my Dad.

"Did you know that pheromones can put off a woman's menopause?"

"I told you, we smell out our partners: our sense of smell is a wonderful thing. It is the strongest of our senses, and the most memorable. People will often remember a time or place from revisiting a smell. Our other senses can't hold a candle to it."

"Yeah, but did you know that pheromones can speed up puberty, control women's menstrual cycles, and even influence sexual orientation?"

"Yes," there literally is *nothing* I can teach my Dad. He clears his throat, and I prepare for further unassailable facts; I begin to regret phoning, "These pheromones also affect who we have sex with, and how often; these odours which we are mainly unaware of influence so many of the things we do. Just like animals they can produce strong, primal reactions.

"It was thought that these senses had faded in humans, but now researchers believe that we can detect chemical signals from other human beings. Just behind your nostrils is a set of tiny holes known as the vomer nasal organ, and they believe that these contain the nerves that react to the pheromones and send signals to the brain, and that they work on the limbic system, one of the oldest parts of the brain." I made a grunting noise to let him know I was still on the phone.

"I told you about 'The Selfish Gene'?"

"Yes, yes, Dad, anyway, I just called to say 'Hi.' I've gotta go because I'm late for work," I lied.

"Have you got my brief on Deborah Harding?"

"I gave it to you yesterday."

"No, you didn't"

"I promise you I did."

"I didn't get it, Hel."

"Well I'm sure I gave it to you with all the stuff on the film critic's guide."

"I didn't get that either."

"Are you sure?"

"I'm sure."

"Hmm," Hel looks genuinely confused, and flounces back to her desk where she does a pointless display of moving bits of paper about in an attempt to find the irretrievable.

I sit down at my desk and look around the offices. The usual air of busyness punctuated by acts of sheer boredom. Jezebel looks my way, and then quickly returns her eyes to her computer. That united front of the all-female radio station just looks like an exercise in self-preservation punctuated by expressions of gloom.

"Here we are!" Hel holds up a sheet of paper victoriously.

"It's a bit late now."

"No, look, you have five minutes before show time; you can just have a quick read."

"Thanks a bunch, Hel. I just love being prepared."

"You'll be fine. You always do great."

"Are you serious?" Hoping I might actually get a compliment.

"No!" She laughs.

I punch in "Crazy" by Seal, and sit back in my chair, surveying the domain of the enormous desk with its dials, buttons, faders, and dancing LED display.

The smell of patchouli oil wafts in through the open door. Gail, resplendent in black, omits a metallic sound from her zips and straps chaffing together as she marches to her pew.

"Hey," she manages.

"Hey." I try to imagine her world: the torrid Goth melancholia, the scarves draped over lampshades casting a gloomy light, the meetings with others of her kind in dingy dives, the conversation a stunted mixture of grunts and hair tossed guitar riffs. Or maybe this was a cover for a deeper mystery where she harboured a love of strawberry ice cream, and her mum. Maybe she has a Take That poster and reads Vanity Fair. Maybe she watches reruns of 'Hart to Hart' and has a penchant for Cat Stevens?

"Doing anything fun this week end?" I venture.

"Nah, same ol'..."

"What'll that be then?"

"Might go to see a death metal band with my boyfriend."

"You've got a boyfriend?" I suddenly realize I sound surprised and try to tail off the end of the question.

"Yeah." The probing sadly has to stop — the travel has to begin.

"So, what's happening on the roads today, Gail?"

"Ruth's here, shall I bring her in?" Hel's head pops in through my otherwise impenetrable door, and I realise Gail has been gone for some moments.

"Yeah, why not…"

"Your first up after 'Theatre Guide' is the classical percussionist, but I didn't have time to write anything so I'll feed you some questions down the line…" I don't have time to complain about this latest shortfall: I'm trying to read the biog on the percussionist before Ruth blows in. Middle age has dealt Ruth a double blow; she is unusually grumpy, and her face has accepted this as a permanent decision and arranged her features accordingly.

"Hello." Delivered as deadpan as it is possible to emit this greeting, she makes her way from the door to the chair opposite.

"Afternoon, Ruth" Not raising my head from the biog.

"Have you seen any of today's pickings?" This is a loaded question because she knows I don't have time to go to the theatre which is why Hel is paid to go and view them, write the questions, and give them to me. How nice it would be to live in such a perfect world.

"Um, sorry, Ruth," I look up, and try to focus on her. She is wearing a vibrant scarf that seems to be riding up her face in an attempt to drown out her ruddy complexion. The tassels that accompany the nomadic design add to the mass of fashion hysteria, and what looks to be eczema. Her skin appears to be flaking in erubescent tones of angry.

"Nice scarf."

"Thanks." She's not fooled or side-lined "So, have you read about or seen any of today's offerings?"

"Ah...sorry Ruth, bit behind today — what are they?" I put down the biog — clearly it will have to wait.

"We've got a particularly bewitching version of Madam Butterfly — do you know the story?" Fortunately, the story lay the background for one of my families more poignant episodes. My grandfather, an American, had been posted out in Germany during the repatriation, and had fallen for Grandma Elena, or Oma as she is called in the Germanic vernacular. When she was heavy with my Dad, Grandpa went back to America, but not before taking her to see Madam Butterfly: their one official date that didn't involve a back room, and a lack of contraception (— sound familiar?).

Madam Butterfly became a byword for our family history, and Oma could often be heard humming a familiar aria as she did the dishes. The similarity to Oma's own storyline was not lost on her or Dad. The only differences being an abandoned German woman not Japanese, and Oma did not commit *hara-kiri* when he abandoned her; although on an emotional level I wonder what scars have been left. She never openly bad-mouths grandpa although my Dad does. When he managed to track him down, and discovered he had a new family, Dad wasn't just angry, but disappointed by the lack of feeling between them. He came home vowing never to bother with him again.

"Family is about whom you spend your life with, and grow up with, not necessarily flesh and blood," he would tell me afterwards. Not having had any family apart from him and Oma, I often wonder what it would be like to have a big family: brothers and sisters, aunties and uncles. What relatives we do have in Germany are remembered at Christmas with cards, or through old black and white photos that come out when we hear that one of them has passed. That's when Oma will pull out this sad old cigar box, and root around in the interior for faded photos of dimly remembered relatives. Last Christmas was no different from the rest, except there was no dead to remember. No photos to drag out and scrutinize for family resemblance. No need to hear stories about people I would probably never meet and had lost interest in ever tracking down. Oma decided that once she left Germany, heavily pregnant and in shame, she wouldn't look back, and she's been good to her word.

"Yes, I know the story."

"Great," looking relieved, "we can talk about that. Then there's a play: Osborne's 'Look Back in Anger.' Are you familiar with Osborne's work?"

"Can't say that I am, although I know everything by Joe Orton," I say trying to sound like I know something at least about theatre, "when will they do 'Entertaining Mr Sloan' again?"

"There are no plans at present," Ruth often looks discouraged that she has to discuss the magnificence of the theatre with a dunce.

"Right," I try to sound positive, "I'm just going to get us up and running, and I'll bring you in after the first ad break, OK?"

"Fine." Ruth looks busy with her paperwork and handbag, fixing her glasses on her nose in readiness.

Queuing up the trails, I slip on the headphones, and count us in off the back of the news.

"You're listening to Radio Honey with me, Cass Bates, and coming up on the show today we've got a real luvies moment with Ruth Gordon in the studio, and live music with blues man, Tony O'Leary, plus world renowned female percussionist, Deborah Harding joins us in the studio! Oh, and I can feel something, what is that, that — oh, oh, oh — feeling?" Dramatic pause, feeding the opening strains in:

"'Can you feel the love tonight'? It's Elton John." As I pull the fader down, Hel pokes her head round the studio door.

"Don't forget Deborah Harding is stone deaf."

"Really?"

"Didn't you read the biog?"

"Well, usually I would expect my question sheet to tell me what's going on, but it would seem that my producer has bigger fish to fry — or maybe other presenters." Hel sighs and leaves.

"All OK on the good ship lollypop?" Ruth asks coyly.

"Couldn't be more saccharin." I try to look busy reading the biog again, but I am so unsettled that I have to keep re-reading the same passage over and over. I can hear Ruth breathing, and it's not helping matters. Hel is in the studio in front with Colin, playing the coquette through the glass; I watch her smiling, and inadvertently fingering the bottom of her shirt, which is hanging out in an attempt to look cool and unkempt. Clive is smiling, but still busying himself with his work.

Behind me, through the studio glass, I see Courtney and Fay exchange a few words, and then go their separate ways. Elton is peaking.

"Ruth is here in the studio to give us the latest low down on the lights on Broadway, after these quite important messages…" I push on the ads, "So what shall we start with Ruth?"

"Let's start with Madam Butterfly, shall we?"

"You're the boss," I say attempting my usual light heartedness, but it doesn't wash today, and she knows it. My mind is still on the events of the past week.

"No, my love — you're the boss."

"Yeah, thanks for the reminder." Then the real boss walks into the studio next door with Clive, and my heart runs cold. Clive smiles his affable smile, and although Clare doesn't know how to smile, her body is relaxed in his presence; just boys chatting about *stuff*.

As Clare turns to leave Clive she can't resist a little glance into my studio. Her look is hard and blank. But I read it fair and square. I'm in the doghouse, I'm on borrowed time, and we both know it.

"Here we go, Ruth…" I bring up the fader, "Ruth is here! Welcome back Ruth! What have you got for us today; what wonders are making the lights sparkle in the West End?"

"Hi Cass, nice to be back. Well, I've been to see the new production of Madame Butterfly at The Royal Opera House in Covent Garden, directed by Jason Durnstable, and starring the inimitable Lara Blain fresh from her sparkling debut in

Australia where she wowed the audiences in 'Phantom of the Opera'. "

"Boy, not even a chance to get over the jet lag?"

"No, she went straight from one show into the other, but she's a relatively young performer so she'll take two shows a day in relative stride, jet lag or not."

"I can just about cope with this one! Or so I'm told..." Ruth ignores this comment, but I know somewhere Clare is listening.

"The wonderful thing about this version of Madame Butterfly is not just the modern nod to the present day in the use of sets, thanks to film impresario, Leonard Spademan, but the way in which Durrnstable allows his cast to relax their otherwise trite operatic body language. In particular, for our American to play the role of a modern-day soldier with more political might than in previous incarnations. We feel the weight of modern warfare come to bear with a nod to the political unrest in Mexico and the genocide in Rwanda that we saw earlier in the year — breathing down the neck of this version and imbuing it with a modernity that this opera hasn't had in many years."

"Do you think the director is trying to make a comment on war today?"

"I think he is definitely trying to convey the destructiveness of war not just for civilians and society but on the fragility of human relations on the human species."

"How does this version justify the American soldier's betrayal? Surely abandoning a pregnant woman in any strata or time line in society is viewed with derision?"

"The tragedy suited Puccini. It was the perfect background to play out the drama of his music, and I think it plays out in today's society just as succinctly."

"Is that life imitating art or art being used to dramatize life?"

"I think all artists believe that art can be used as a vehicle to tell a story and point the finger."

"Shouldn't Puccini, and any modern version, be pointing the finger more at the American soldier and spending less time on Madame Butterfly's dying words?"

"I don't think this is a modern soap opera — it is opera — pure and simple, and must be seen as a vehicle for music, not as a vehicle solely for modern polemic."

"But surely Art should educate?"

"Art for art's sake is no sin, this is an art in line with the Greek Tragedies of history where the story is an outline for human suffering, and the story is the thing. The social services are quite another." As I opened my mouth to reply, I could see

Clare in Colin's studio in front of me, her arms folded, looking straight at me.

Ruth was just leaving. We had exhausted our debate, and even Ruth looked weary and tired of talking theatre, on any level, philosophical or mundane.

Deborah Harding was being brought in along with her manager, who, thankfully Hel was re escorting back out to the offices to wait for his client and listen to the interview over the tannoy.

"Please, take a seat, Deborah; I'll be with you in a minute." Deborah smiles, and obediently sits down in one of the guest chairs. As we come out of "You are the Sunshine of my Life," by Stevie Wonder, one of my personal favourites, I quickly check Deborah for level, and then launch into one of the most disastrous interviews of my life.

"Deborah Harding, the world-renowned classical percussionist is in the studio with me, and she doesn't need to bang her own drum because I will be doing that for her — welcome Deborah!"

"Thank you."

"The work you do has been acclaimed by most all of your contemporaries in the classical world, but what I find amazing is that you are actually stone deaf…"

"Clare wants to see you." Hel daren't contaminate herself by stepping into my studio but hangs behind the studio door. The walk from the studio to Clare's office is like walking the plank, it is the longest gallows march I have ever undertaken, and I don't dare lift my eyes to view my fellow DJ's and their producers who are no doubt sniggering into their pink Radio Honey coffee mugs.

"How did 'tone deaf' become 'stone deaf'?" Clare is unnervingly calm.

"I...I...well — that's what Hel told me and she never gave me my questions and biog — not that this is unusual, it seems to be more and more the case, and I have not felt quite myself — I mean you replaced me for God's sake last week — I'm not feeling great as it is!"

"This is not about you, Cass. This is a question of professionalism. A professional Radio DJ should be able to perform to the proper standard no matter what. If you are not up to the job then we shall have to get someone to fill in for you again."

"For Christs' sake why don't you just tell me you want to get rid of me and stop all this pussy footing around!?" The force of my own words and the use of the word 'pussy' temporarily stun me into silence. Clare seems equally surprised, although by which part of my explosion I am still unsure.

"Let's call it a day shall we? We'll resume this conversation when you have calmed down, or hopefully will have no need to discuss this matter further should things smooth out of their own accord." I get up and leave without further comment from either of us.

Chapter 9

To the Sounds of 'Insane in the Brain' by Cypress Hill

"Ladies and Gentlemen, I am proud to present — for one night only, 'Space Oddity', and Bowie look-alike — Cage!" With his face painted silver and a huge star covering one eye, Cage takes to the stage like a seasoned professional. The applause, even as he walks to the make-shift platform, is deafening. He is a firm favourite at 'Blink's'; everybody loves him.

'Meat' and 'Veg' join him on drum and bass, respectfully. Cage pulls the mike out of the mike stand in one movement, and prowls up and down the stage, sideways, giving us all his one good, starburst eye.

Tonight's theme is 'Star Trek'. There are huge Styrofoam rocks — God knows where Blink found them, or if she made them — littering the stage, in pinks and baby blues. There is a cardboard cut-out of Captain Kirk with his stun gun poised; against a black, starry sky backdrop.

Cage drops his body down to an almost hunched, knuckle dragging scrape across the stage; his rap monologue taking on new proportions of demonic; his eyes fired up, the audience willing him on.

"He is fuckin' nailin' it!" Courtney yells in my ear, her take on futuristic earrings jangling. She is dressed in a black T-shirt with silver sequins, cut-off jeans hot pants, shiny, metallic tights, and thigh length boots that owe more than a passing nod to fetish wear with their plastic sheen. She can't take her eyes off the stage: off Cage.

The nearest I could come to a space inspired costume at such short notice is a pair of silver leggings, a black leotard, and a silver buckled belt. The red wig is a memento from a recent Halloween outfit. My fuck off high heels really have nothing to do with space, but their unusual chunkiness gives the outfit a futuristic edge.

"Speaking of nailing it, have you heard from Jack the lad?" Court leans in my ear.

"Nothing…" I had been using all the force left in me to avoid calling him. My index, dialling finger was practically tearing itself away from its other brothers and sisters to poke out his digits. It was taking all I had in me not to call him; lecturing myself on why women should never call, and why if I did it would only make me feel hollow and desperate, and worse: make me look needy. *Needy*, the worst word in the dating manual.

If you look at the evolution of the human species as a foundation for dating, it's easy to go along with the belief, eschewed by dating experts in the field, that a man needs to chase a woman. At heart a man is still a caveman. Just check out those knuckles. A man needs the chase; he likes to win his meal or his woman through a series of hard-won steps. To deprive him of this antediluvian process is to take away his reward and therefore his interest. The build up being tantamount to the success of this crude mating ritual. To set off in hot pursuit being the first step, spurred on by the 'scent of a woman' as the film world would have us believe, plus various multi-million-pound perfume ads; to be rebuffed, an important two; to be kept waiting, and therefore, the all-important stage of wanting what you can't have, and finally, when the reward is achieved, the sense of accomplishment that makes the man feel the trophy is worthy.

If you simply lie down at the first hurdle and give yourself over to the salivating Cro-Magnon, he will experience no sense of achievement, and will chew on you a while and move on to the next moving target. It's jungle ethics. Not that I have ever had the patience to try it. My libido and lack of self-worth leave me no time for such games.

My Dad has tried to school me in the ethics of the chase; the bare-back science behind the myth of primitive man dragging his female back to the cave. Researchers have performed their own experiments, showing blurry as opposed to clear images of females to sexually active males and found that the blurry image was more attractive because it was less attainable. Similarly, products on shelves that were harder to reach had more 'wow factor'. Proving that the average male needs to feel he has gone that extra mile to merit his reward. This 'relationship' between effort and value is so closely associated in the dating ritual that any outcome that relies on increased effort, even pointless effort, automatically results in increased preference. It would appear that love is not only outcome challenged, but statistically a moron. Even Leonardo daVinci, is purported to have said, "Love is something so ugly that the human race would die out if lovers could see what they were doing."

"He hasn't called?"

"No..." My whole body droops under the weight of this tired reality.

"Aw, honey, I tell ya — ya can't live with em', and ya can't keep 'em in a crawl space under the house." Her looking sorry for me makes me feel even worse. My looking like an extra from Pan's People isn't helping either.

"When will I learn?"

I can't hear her response because Jack has just walked through the door wearing some space age, silver wrap around glasses. He catches my eye; or rather I catch his directional beam. He makes the universal sign of 'want a drink' with an imaginary glass brought to his lips, framed by a question-mark face. My God, he's asking if I want a drink! I manage to nod. Courtney is too busy watching the stage to see this brief exchange.

"He's here!" I gasp as he turns to the bar.

"Who?"

"Jack!"

"Oh, great — more torture."

"No, he just asked if I wanted a drink!" My enthusiasm is not rubbing off on her; she's more interested in Cage's stage prowl. I have man eating butterflies in my stomach and feel I won't be able to open my mouth to talk to him — they will all flutter out.

"I got you a rum and coke — that's what you usually have isn't it?" Jack towers over us, the candlelight reflecting off his space goggles. I feel like a deer in the headlights.

"Yes....thanks." He helps himself to a seat beside us. One thing about Jack — he's not shy.

"Hi Courtney."

"Jack," she manages.

"I like the...costume...cute." He teases.

"And what are you? A Space Oddity?"

"Something like that," he looks like he's had a few drinks already; obviously in too good a mood to take offense from Courtney or anyone else, he turns his wrap-arounds on me:

"So..." everyone is singing around us, but they might as well have been whistling Dixie for all I care. He's here; he's bought me a drink; he's sitting next to me, and he has both eyes (or what I can intuit of them) locked on mine. My cheeks feel very hot.

Then he reaches out a hand and squeezes my knee — briefly, "What are you? — One of Pan's People?" He grins. In my mind I answer, "I'm whatever the fuck you want me to be!" But I force that one down and try to be coy: "I'm a hologram projected onto this space-time continuum." Suddenly regretting this as too theoretical and complex for this point in the evening or his level of inebriation.

"Well, fancy a space jump?" He wasn't messing with his metaphors.

"Does a spaceman shit in his suit?" We are back on planet earth. He clinks his glass to mine, and we drink whilst everyone is applauding Cage. He jumps down off the stage, and Blink introduces the next act.

"Thanks Cage! Now, we have George with a poem he's written for us about space..." George, the resident poet, doesn't need the space theme to bring out his inner cosmic side; he's high on life and other substances as a matter of course.

"Hey Cass..." It's Tony, and he's standing right behind Jack. I can feel Courtney beside me, dying to say something. I'm simply dying.

"Hey...Tony..."

"Can I get you a drink?"

"I'm good thanks."

"I'll have a bloody mary if ya're askin'," Courtney manages.

"Sure..." Tony sounds unsure but leaves anyway.

"You don't drink Bloody Marys," I turn to Courtney.

"I know, just gettin' into the spirit of things," she glares at me, and I get the message. I turn back to Jack, but before I can continue Cage is at the table.

"Hey!" He looks less pleased to see Jack. Courtney lights up.

"Hey! Come and sit down fellow space crusader!

"I need a fuckin' drink — anyone?" Jack and I shake our heads, raising our glasses.

"I'll have a beer, spaced man!"

"And you are?" Cage smiles at Courtney.

"The reason lunar landings were invented. I'm an alien from Mars."

"Well beam me up, Scottie!" He grins that sexy grin of his. No woman is safe when he turns that on. Poor Courtney. She could do with a good space jump, and all she was getting was atmosphere.

"So, how've you been?" I try to sound relaxed.

"Good, just busy with the new club," his leg leaning against mine, the warmth travelling through my body, spreading, I try to concentrate on his words which are just a front for what we both know is really going on: chemistry. I hate to admit that my father, with his ideas of hormonal biorhythms, might be onto something. DNA has a specific gene section that activates the synthesis of key proteins which in turn initiate the internal biorhythms; when these cycles overlap it's called a "desire curve". I'm experiencing one of those waves right now; I can feel an unspoken scintillation between us that I can't put my finger on. Or that I would like to put my whole body on. My genes are obviously of the opinion that his genes are — just right — his pheromones speaking a language my head can't hear, but my body can; responding wordlessly, invaded by his hormonal sequence, his essence. It is overpowering. I try to concentrate on what he is saying:

"And you? Been laid…off recently?" The corners of his lips turn up ever so slightly.

"No," I smile, "but I'm due a dressing down at any moment, sure as God made little green apples."

"What, you just can't do wrong for doing right?"

"Yeah, something like that." Tony arrives with Courtney's Bloody Mary at the same time as Cage puts down her beer: they both look at each other.

"Thirsty, are ya?" Cage is amused. Courtney, for once, embarrassed: her joke back firing.

"I can take it!" she rallies.

"I bet you can ya dirty space alien," Cage sits down, and takes a swig of his beer, eyeing me and Jack. Tony stands alone, no seats available, the circle closed.

"Well, I guess I'll see you guys…" Tony lopes off.

"Yeah, thanks for the bloody Mary!" Courtney yells after him.

"That wasn't very nice," I look accusingly at Courtney.

"I'm doin' ya a favour," she leans in: " — ya can't juggle four balls in one night," Courtney avoids looking at Jack who just catches the tail end of the conversation.

"What?" He pipes up.

"Nothing — um, I might need another one of these…" I drain my glass in one go and put it down on the table.

"You're going to be one spaced little alien," Jack sounds pleased; Cage is watching us.

Jack gets up, and turns to Cage and Courtney:

"Any more drinks?"

"I'll have a beer," Cage jumps in.

"I think I'll hang on awhile, thanks all the same," Courtney's chewing the inside of her mouth, dying to say something, and I don't have to wait long:

"Well, well, well, we all know how this is gonna end…" I watch Jack walking away.

"Whaaat?" I play the innocent.

"Don't bat your space hoppers at me!"

"What did I do?" Cage watches us, less amused than he would be ordinarily; like Courtney, he isn't a big fan of my boyfriends. George suddenly sits down in Jack's empty chair; it takes all my self-possession not to scream at him to get out.

"George — um, that seat is taken."

"Yes, yes, my dear, you know that charity begins at home?"

"Yes, but someone is sitting there!" Courtney is trying to suppress the giggles. Cage gets up:

"He can 'av my seat." Cage moves off, wordlessly.

"Great!" Now Courtney's pissed off with me. I turn my aggression on George:

"Was there something you wanted to say George?" You can't hurt George's feelings: he's too inebriated and thick skinned.

"My poem, 'She Walks Devine' is being published..." his eyes seem to glaze over for a moment. The opacity of his skin highlighted by the glow of broken capillaries in the candle light, "...in a Poetry Magazine..."

"That's great George, really great," I try to sound happy for him. Courtney shoots me a look and gets up from the table.

"I'll be at the bar if you need any help with y'ar menagerie," she clumps away in her space age boots, pulling the tights out of her ass as she goes.

Hazel Plastic, her stage name, is getting up to play. Blink is finding her a stool. Hazel is as synthetic as her name; everything she wears owes something to man-made fibres, and her music is more X-Ray Specs punk than 1990's dance swagger. Teetering on the border of a new age, we have so much to look back on, and so little to look forward to; good music owes more to the past than the future, and the further we get, the more we look back and see that our forbearers blazed a trail we can only whimper at.

Hazel starts to shake her tiny afro, her plastic bangles start to jangle, her dayglow lips open, and her high, exotic voice begins the refrain, "I want to be your conveyor belt, your radio frequency, your pizza box delivery..." She is in a world of her own; there are no imitators.

Jack is back, looking down at George, then seeing Courtney's empty seat he moves into that. George has zoned out anyway, I turn to Jack:

"Thanks."

"Get that down your neck." The ice cubes tickle my lips. His leg is back against mine; he leans his arm behind my chair, and whispers in my ear, over the shrill, Venusian voice of Hazel Plastic:

"I've got a bottle of rum back at my place..."

"What the fuck!" Jack jumps back. The white glow of Pye's neck collar startles us in the dark, moving towards us, as I fumble for the lights. We hadn't made it as far as his place. Mine was on the way, and I too had rum. Laughing, bent double, and needing to pee, I manage:

"It's just the cat!"

"Oh God, that frightened me!"

"What did you think it was? — A tiny ghost?" I flick on the lights.

"I don't know — Shit! What's with the thing on his head?"

"He fell off the balcony: he needs to keep it on till his jaw heals. I've gotta pee — back in a mo." I disappear into the toilet and sit grinning to myself as an admirable stream hits the porcelain. I am drunk; I put my hand out to steady myself. In the mirror, I smile at the reflection, and make a silly face; squealing quietly to myself. In the other room I can hear that he has put some music on, and when I come out find that he has dimmed the lights. He is leaning over my music collection.

"Do you think you have enough albums?"

"You can never have enough albums." I walk over to where he is leaning; now studying my CD collection. He pulls one out: Terence Trent D'Arby.

"Here's one I haven't heard in a while," he says.

"Sign your name across my heart..."

"What?"

"Sorry," I catch myself, "that's his famous song lyric."

"Oh..." He studies the back, "can we put it on?"

"Sure." He hands me the CD, and I click open the pocket and slide it in. Behind me now, his hands are on my hips, and I have to concentrate on what I am doing because my legs just want to buckle underneath me. Moving, slowly, his hands work around to the front of my body, up over my breasts, and I have to stifle a moan. He is biting my neck as I hurriedly press play and, turning around, take his tongue in my mouth.

Saturday morning, the sky grey, the rain falling, he is still there, in my bed.

I get up quietly and make two cups of tea. When I get back to the bedroom, he is sitting up in the bed, the covers folded under his arms, his face swollen from sleep.

"Oh!" Momentarily startled, I compose myself, and wind my way round to his side of the bed, putting the tea down, "Good morning!"

"Good morning," his voice sounds sticky with sleep; one side of his face bears the imprint of the pillow. I giggle nervously. He looks up at me.

"You OK?"

"Yeah, why wouldn't I be?" I climb back in bed, gingerly balancing my tea, and pulling my robe tight. We sit without words, sipping our tea, the rain the only comment.

"God, will it ever stop raining?" He says to no one in particular. Pye pads in, looks at me, and meows.

"That is one weird looking cat," says Jack.

"Don't be cruel; he'll be handsome again when he gets his neck brace off." Pye meows again, waiting. "I better just feed him." Getting up to leave the room, Jack speaks the words I never expected:

"Cass…?"

"Yes?" I turn at the door.

"Can I ask you something?"

"Sure…"

"Is your period late?" It's not every day that a man expresses an interest in your monthly cycle, so I think I can be forgiven the spluttering that preceded the response:

"I, um…I…er…I don't think so," and then, like a car that you've seen every day but paid scant attention to, watching it far off in the distance as it approaches, it suddenly hit me full force. "Actually, I *am* a bit late…" My legs feel weak, and I suddenly have to sit back down on the edge of the bed.

Chapter 10

To the Sounds of 'Ice Ice Baby'
by Vanilla Ice

My father's house is set slightly back from the road. A simple tarmac path leads all the way from the sidewalk to the door; the grass either side trimmed to a number two. An x-council house, it has all the charm of an egg box. With no attention to detail, it avoids the pitfalls of garden gnomes, potted plants and other efforts to otherwise polish a turd that has become standard.

Even a doorknocker or doorbell is missing. You need to knock as loudly as possible on the inlay of glass that makes up half the door being careful not to knock the glass out.

"Hello sweet child of mine!" Unsure of how to take this newest of endearments, I simply enter.

"If I'd have known you were coming I would have bought something special from the frozen food section." This is not a joke; this is my Dad's idea of special occasion food; a gateau that requires leaving out until it has achieved room temperature and a pleasing state. I think he likes the turgid sense of waiting.

"Just a sudden urge, Dad...not really sure how I got here to be honest..." Reading my features like a map he has always kept in his back pocket, he steers me to a chair wordlessly, and slaps the kettle on.

"Tell your old Dad everything," he says slipping into the chair opposite.

"Um, Dad, everything has gone to shit…"

"To − ?" He is fishing for the correct term.

"No, Dad. It really has. There is no other word for it."

"I'm sure with the wonders of the English language you can come up with a better adjective than that to describe your current state." There is no use. I will not get past the gate without using the right terminology.

"OK, um…" this game has worn itself thin over the years, "how about, to hell in a handbag?"

"Better, but still limited. You're using an expression not a real term."

"Argh!" Feeling more frustrated than when I arrived, "How about my life is deteriorating, fermenting…um… unpalatable?"

"OK, that will have to do. Go on…"

"I don't know where to start. I don't quite know what is happening, but my boss is doing everything to make me feel like I am Satan's answer to radio jokeying, my producer is bad mouthing me behind my back, my best friend took over my show the day my boss *made* me take the day off, and, and...." I couldn't tell him the rest: I still needed to be sure.

"Sounds like a bad case of 'everybody hates me.'" The kettle shudders to its climax, and he gets up and goes into the kitchen. I look around the room; empty without him. What little he has seems to take over the space, vying for attention. The sofa throw spreads itself across the expanse of cushions in an effort to absorb their small, plump shapes; displaced in a moment, expanding its fabric markers in a territorial advance. The small coffee table has given itself over to voracious magazines and newspapers. The few paintings on the wall seem to have grown in proportion since I was here last, the white borders where they aren't speaking volumes about where they are.

"One lump or two?"

"Two please, vicar."

This place was never my home, it's always been Dad's bachelor pad; the culmination of a life's lovelessness. He never remarried; he never really tried to meet anybody new. He seems happy with the simplicity of his life; free of the mental mayhem involved in loving another human being. He acknowledges that my mother was a complex example; however, I think he's too scared to try another variety. How can we ever be sure what we are letting ourselves in for?

Meeting new people seems the height of insanity. In the olden days people married through old friendships; you knew, to a degree, what you were getting yourself into. Today the spin cycle of romance is too fast or too casual; there is no courting ritual variable, unless you count meeting for coffee, or a drink addled grope.

"What about your personal life?" He's back with the teas. Trying to find a place amongst the magazines and newspapers, he gives up and just places them down where they begin at once to leave a watery, circular pool on The Sunday Telegraph.

"Don't ask. That is the biggest mess of all."

"Ah, please try not to take a leaf out of my book on this one. At least try to have a straight forward, even boring, relationship with the opposite sex; or the same sex if that's what floats your boat, but find someone nice, someone who will care for you."

"I'm trying, Dad, I really am, but I just can't seem to get it right. Is there some hidden formula? Is there something I should take as a good sign even? A man who enjoys a curry on a Saturday night? A dog lover? Or a cat lover? Someone who truly cares about world peace? Or just someone capable of holding down a day job, and not hating his life and everyone who ever played a minor role in it? Oh God, I just don't know anymore!" I am pushing the emotional boat out, but he's swimming with the tide. This is his kind of territory. He loves the opportunity to expound on life.

"According to Schopenhauer", and he's off: "emotional, physical, and sexual desires can never be fulfilled; he recommended a lifestyle that negated human desires, actually quite similar to Buddhist teachings..." I had turned off the moment he said Schopenhauer but let him continue out of politeness.

"According to The Rolling Stones, 'you can't always get what you want, but if you try sometimes you just might get what you need...'"

"Hmm, is that so, I think I'd be happy with getting just what I need." He looks contended with the idea too.

"Yeah but *want* is a powerful, primal scream!"

"It's the child, the Id expressing itself — nothing more — let it go. Nothing can be that important — surely?"

"But it is! I want love. I want the real deal — what I've been sold, told to expect with every book, commercial and franchise! This is my inheritance, and I deserve it!" Suddenly unsure: "Surely?" My Dad considers me for a moment; his long face spluttering in the light that moves across the room; its grey cloud-lets casting their shadows:

"Romantic love, as any science-based research will tell you, is broken down into three categories: lust, attraction, and attachment. Different chemicals like testosterone and oestrogen are responsible for their varying degrees of success which leads to the inexorable conclusion that happiness, my dear daughter, is chemical. Nothing more. You must decide, take control, and be the brain, not the hormone." Without the feel-good answer I was looking for, I watch the occasional glow shift its focus on the objects in the room, marking its passage, taking with it hope; wondering why my fate is wrapped up in theory, not emotion; why my wagon is hitched to this serious man with his clinical take on the squishier aspects of my world. These are the moments when a mother really would not go amiss.

"Dad, cut me some human slack. I just want to know why I can't find someone to truly love me?"

"Oh, come on, you're young yet; you have your life in front of you to find someone. You haven't exhausted the ol' gene pool yet. Have you been out there smelling all the armpits you can?"

"Dad!"

"Don't underestimate your pheromones. Seriously, you have plenty of time, and you're doing all the right things, asking all the right questions. You're right to realize that it isn't easy, that more often than not we make all kinds of mistakes, and very few of the right choices. But you get back up on that horse, and try again? Eh?"

"I just don't have the energy, Dad. I'm not sure I want to. I just feel so defeated, and, truth be told, I'm not sure I really give a damn anymore; I'm even wondering what I'm doing with my life — my whole life! There's not one corner I'm happy with. Oh, and my cat — I didn't tell you about Pye: he fell out the window, and he's in a neck brace…"

"I'm sorry to hear that…I really am. Bad things tend to converge all at once; you seem to be having an episode…"

"It doesn't feel like an episode, Dad, it feels like my whole life!"

"Now, now, let's not get all *Weltschmerz*."

"All what?"

"— It means a disillusioned ennui — it's a German word."

"Dad I don't want a lesson in German philosophy — I want help!"

"It's not actually a philosophic term, but…" My look of agitation cuts him short, "well, let's see…you know I'm not very good at living it, but I'm good at listening. So, talk, and I'll listen, and if I can help, you know I will." He was right, he was shit at living it; maybe I was shit at living it too?

"Dad, do you think I'm fated to a life of badly advised love affairs like you?"

"I certainly hope not — No — I'm sure you'll learn from your mother and I's mistakes, and be all right..."

"But we have no idea if she's happy now, if she's with someone, if she has a family, more children..." Dad looks down at the tea mug cradled in both his hands:

"No, we don't even know if she is alive, or living in Britain, you're right, but we do know that she's trying just as hard as the rest of us to get it right. That's all any of us can do. But in the spirit of trying to get it right, I try to read everything I can get my hands on, just in case somebody out there has a better idea than me what all this madness is about. What it really means for you and me at the end of the day..." I was looking at my tea mug now. Getting up, I put it down on the mark it had made earlier on The Sunday Telegraph.

"You're not going already?"

"I've got to Dad; I've got a show to do."

"That's my girl!" Turning to look at him he realizes that this is not a rally cry to round up the troupes and conquer the enemy, but simply an acknowledgement of time.

"You know where I am if you need me?"

"Yes."

"You'll call if you need anything?"

"Yes."

"Don't do anything hasty"

"No."

"Here, don't forget your scarf." Dad hands it out to me, it hangs like a ferret from his outstretched hand, a mass of fake fur, rain soaked and bedraggled; a worried look deepens the lines on his forehead. Somehow that helps: knowing he's concerned.

"Thanks." He looks at my outfit, as if handing me my scarf has made him consider if it truly accessorises. "You know, if you dressed more grown up you might attract somebody more grown up."

"Dad!"

"I'm just saying that to attract a mate you have to send out the right signals as well. A short skirt, laddered tights, and a leather jacket have all the hallmarks of trouble, not easy ride."

"How can you say that? This is how people dress these days!"

"Successful people? People with solid careers and marriages?"

"People." I try to accentuate without having to elucidate. "People who live in the here and now; and yes, people with jobs and relationships that work."

"Well," he says, looking at the ground, his bald spot eyeing me, "I just think you need to dress more maturely if you want a more grown-up life. Life imitating dress."

"That is not a thing."

"I'm making it a thing." He smiles.

"You cannot dress your way into happiness."

"You can. You can dress the part you want to play. You are sending out all the wrong signals in that attire."

"Ugh, here we go..."

"You know I'm right. You know that the way you present yourself is very important. When somebody goes for a job interview they put on their best suit. You are not dressing your best. You are not putting your best foot forward. It's no wonder things aren't working out for you. It really isn't."

"Goodbye Dad." I'm at the door. He's following and dishing out his last words of advice:

"And for goodness sakes call me every once in a while!"

"Yes, Dad."

"I spend more time talking to that crazy woman — what's she called?"

"Hel." I turn on the walkway. "Her name is Hel or Helen, but she is more Hel than Helen."

"I see."

"No, you don't see, Dad, or you wouldn't go on at me. You have no idea what I'm dealing with at the moment…" The tears are framing themselves.

"I'm just trying to help."

"Well you have one hell of a way of showing it." He calls after me, but I'm turning onto the road. I don't want to cry in front of him. He doesn't know what to do with tears. He never did.

Chapter 11

To the Sounds of 'U Can't Touch This'
by MC Hammer

The pen is see-sawing between her fingers; catching between index and thumb. Clare has us all poised in anticipation; caught in the cat's cradle of her pendulous swing of the pen; her eyes fixed on no particular point but taking in the whole room. The entire staff of Radio Honey is squeezed into the conference room. She clicks the nib in and out, and begins:

"The latest stats are in." Here she pauses for effect. "It's not good. Every show across the board is down. We have lost 40% of our starting figure. Accounting for fall off for novelty value we should still have kept the majority share. This means we are not meeting our targets, which means the shows are not meeting their audience. Which means each and every one of you needs to do better. And whatever you have to do, within the limitations of our remit, you must do it." She pauses, her jowls hanging in Churchillian seriousness. "You must and will find a way to achieve this. Otherwise heads will roll. I have no option. We must find the winning combination. This means in particular that drive time," she looks squarely at me, "and breakfast," she looks over at Angel and Gary, "must work the hardest. Your prime-time slots must be performing to their optimum to pull the listeners in and keep them across the schedule. Understood?" She swivels her entire body to face us, in its browns and greys; clothing of the saddest hues imaginable. Her trousers, in some synthetic that had been washed and pressed so many times that it no longer knows if it should hold to a pleat. The bobbles are taking over her sweater, and the jacket is stoically resisting the temptation to climb into its own pockets.

She surveys the room for any response, and when she gets none continues:

"There will be a review a week tomorrow, so I suggest you implement some new trails, get some down time with Clive," a collective sigh went up from the assembled masses at the thought of some down time with Clive, "and resuscitate those tired, worn out show trails. And, I suggest you jump start some new ideas." Some of us were imagining Clive giving us a jump start." She surveys the room, her eyes like lighthouse beacons looking for dissention or emotion of any kind. Masking our mass hysteria with feminine aplomb, she comes mercilessly to a close: "So, a review of stats in one week. Be warned. I will not be allowing this lull in ratings to go on, and you will survive or fall on next month's ratings. Let's not be off air by Christmas, eh?" She turns her back on us and busies herself with a pack of jelly babies on her desk.

Just when you think the air could not get any colder, Hel pipes up, "What about a Secret Santa?" The entire room looks at her as if she has just beamed down from the Enterprise.

"What about it?" Clare, clearly not enthused, is chewing on a jelly baby head, holding its tiny body in her pincers.

"Well," watching Hel splutter and stutter is the only fun the Radio Honey Crew are going to get all day so they sit back down, ready to enjoy: "Well, I just thought it might be nice if we did a Secret Santa this year..." You can literally see her mouth going dry as she ekes out the last words.

"I think you should be concentrating on your shows not some simplistic holiday fodder, don't you? Your survival depends on it." Packaged in the darkest of terms, Hel all but shrinks back into her shoulders, and peeps approval.

Gary, our resident male, gets straight up from his seat and goes to speak to Clare. His hairline looks more receding every time I see him. Working with an all-female team is no doubt having as much of an impact on him as the rest of us.

"She's set the bar pretty low," Courtney snorts as we file out.

"Yeah, I mean, how hard can it be to bring the ratings up when you can't be heard in the first place?"

"I'm gonna work on some scratch and sniff inserts for my show; make it totally interactive."

"I think I'll go for some live nudity. Nothing like cold extremities to warm up your listening public." We high five and go to our separate ends of the room and dig into our respective warrens.

Courtney's desk is buried under stacks of books and paper work so that it looks like a small urban village complete with high rises. Back at my own desk, I have two messages: both of them from Jack.

"Right," Hel has one hand on her hip, and is trying to look officious; an inch of chubbiness peeking over the waistband of her 501's, "any thoughts on how we can make you show fan-dabby-dooby?"

"Yes, you could start by not using phrases like 'fan-dabby-dooby' because that just makes me want to bludgeon you with a large instrument." I turn in my swivel chair to face her so that she can see the full extent of my distaste.

"Right, OK, so, any ideas?"

"No — you?"

"Well, I thought we could have the best quotes of the week from celebrities and the media, and then ask our listeners to call in with theirs?" Hel looks genuinely pleased with herself. My gunshot glare keeps her dancing:

"Or we could take that quote from that super model, what's-her-name, who said she wouldn't get out of bed for less than a million dollars, and ask the listeners to tell us what they wouldn't get out of bed for less than?"

"It was ten thousand dollars, not a million."

"Right," ignoring me. "Or we could swap our live music item for street artists from the underground?"

"Clare would bust a tit over that one, so 'No'." I put my feet up on the desk, trying to look like I'm thinking, and chew on my pencil.

"So, you like any of the ideas?"

"No."

"Well, what ideas do *you* have?" Hel gives me her best exasperated look.

"How about we get our listeners to call in with all the shitty break up lines their partners have ever given them, and have a genuine 'Love In' where we share our break up stories?"

"No, that would not be kosher."

"OK, what about we get a dog and a cat to fight it out in the studio, and the listeners lay bets on who will win. It won't be very visual, but the sound effects could be pretty exciting?"

"Seriously Cass!"

"OK, then what about we ask people to send in their names and addresses and we pick three out of a hat and do an interview on them and their lives? It could be called 'Not the Celebrity Interview'?"

"That would be seriously boring, and nobody would tune in."

"Their extended family sure would."

"Cass if you are not going to take this seriously…"

"I have given you three ideas already, and all you've given me is one — your turn!" I swing my legs off the desk and throw my half-chewed pencil on the desk. Isn't it poisonous to chew on lead, or is it more dangerous to listen to a poisoned dwarf?

"Right, well, just cool it, and let me think…" she tries to look deadly serious and starts doodling on a pad on her desk. Jezebel tries to walk past, and I stop her:

"Jez! What great ideas have you got for you show?" She turns, reluctantly:

"Well, let's see, we have a piece on the rise of black music from grassroots to the present day…"

"You see!" I turn accusingly to Hel, "That's topical *and* intelligent!"

Jezebel scurries away before she can be drawn in further to our feud.

"I can do topical and intelligent — just give me a moment." She continues scribbling. I get up and stand over her shoulder.

"You are just doodling!"

"I'm not — it helps me think!"

"I give up. I'm going to make some coffees — do you want one?"

"Yes, please." She continues doodling.

In the kitchen, the breakfast team, a mixture of borderline worry-wart meets full-blown anxiety, Gary, and Angel, who is a card-carrying wing man to his paranoia, are discussing the difference between input and output cables.

Angel carries herself with the kind of self-satisfied assurance that makes you want to spit in her tea. She's nice enough, but unapproachable. She's the sort of woman that would give botox a miss simply because she wants you to know when she's angry. One look at her permanent grimace is enough to make you change your mind about anything other than light-hearted chitchat or brash superlatives about it being good weather and hot coffee.

Her radio pedigree is undisputed, although any of us would be hard pressed to name a station we'd heard her on. Her radio persona is a mix of Delia Smith meets Edwina Curry. She is nothing if not officious and when in full stride across the offices you dare not intervene in her intended arc. As if we needed another incentive to toe the line or snort the line, it is the sight of Clare and Angel strolling amongst the scattered, lonely desks of Radio Honey, their shorn heads bobbing above the sea of tethered employees.

I try to look inconspicuous in the corner, sieving coffee granules into two cups.

"Cass," Angel spots me. "So, how are things on drive?"

"Mediocre, how are things on Breakfast?"

"Well, they would be a whole lot better if Gary's bowels weren't so fucking predictable." Gary lets out a knowing groan.

"Why, what's going on?" I take the opportunity to squeeze past her, take the kettle, and fill the two cups; trying to sound interested in Gary's bowels.

"Every goddamned morning, regular as clockwork, he has to do his morning dump — except it's right in the middle of the show!"

"I can't help it," Gary's piteous claim is ignored.

"Unfortunate — have you tried taking X-Lax before the show?" I offer.

"We've tried everything short of a bum-plug." Gary shifts uncomfortably at the thought. Angel isn't afraid to mix business with talk of pleasure.

"Well, good luck with that!" I scurry out of the kitchen with the two mugs.

"I've got it!" Hel is brandishing her doodled piece of paper at me.

"Go on," I encourage setting the coffee mugs down.

"We start with a throwback to the old days. We look at how women have come along in the work place, some of the first references to women on radio, and accompany the references with songs from that era. Except we don't play the whole song we use snippets to illustrate what we mean, like we start with how a woman's place was in the home, and play some song about a woman's place is in the home; and then say how her man would come home with 'lipstick on his collar' and play the Connie Francis song of the same name; and then we can have Aretha Franklin and 'R-E-S-P-E-C-T', and then move onto other stuff..."

"That would take one hell of an edit with Clive..."

"Yes, it would," we both take more than a moment to contemplate this...

"But we need more than a bunch of sound bites and old tracks, we need to hang it on something," I sit down thinking hard for the first time. "We could call it 'Women on Top' or 'The Rise of the Femme Bot'..."

"Umm, maybe something more..."

"But we need some more fun and games — some big names..."

"We could get a bunch of comedians in to have a funny look back at women's rise..."

"Good," my mind begins to whir, "that way they can do the leg work for us — come up with the jokes..."

"Exactly..." We both finally smile.

"Have you done it?" Courtney calls from my living room.

"Yes, but I pissed all over my hand!" I come out of my bathroom holding the test strip.

"How long does it say to wait?"

"Two minutes." Standing there, holding the white strip of plastic in my hands, staring at the little window display, I realize a lot is riding on the next two minutes.

"Shall I roll a joint?" Courtney says trying to sound useful.

"You better, whether it's to commiserate or celebrate."

"That's the great thing about drugs: no occasion is too big or too small!" She's trying to keep the situation light, but it couldn't be heavier.

I sit down on my couch; they say you should sit down to receive bad news, and I was ready. I can't take my eyes off the little window. As the little blue line becomes stronger, and then another bleeds through I suddenly forget what the instructions said. Was it one line for positive and two for negative; and if it's negative does that mean you're pregnant or not pregnant?

I go back to the bathroom and fish the instructions out of the bin. From her rolling position, Courtney calls out:

"What are ya doin'?"

"I've forgotten what two lines means..." my voice calls out from the echoing bathroom.

"It means y'ar pregnant..."

The idea of a biological clock is not just a quaint metaphor. There is actually a distinct region of the brain that is quite literally the designated time keeper. (How do I know this? I think you know how.) Situated in the brain, above the optic nerve, this little marvel of an area gets its cues from the light in the environment to help us keep time. It's called Circadian rhythm and it allows organisms such as ourselves to interpret, predict, and prepare for the many eventualities of our existence based on the twenty-four hour clock which is a misnomer as a woman's body is aligned more to the moon than the wrist-watch.

The notion that we have an invisible clock imbedded in our bodies that silently ticks off the childless minutes until a monumental bong, like Big Ben, signals the coming of the egg apocalypse is random at best; a moment when egg to insemination ratio meets critical mass, and worse still, when we risk the unspeakable possibility of not having any of our potential babies fertilised. Shock-horror hold the front page. Men don't have any such clock; seem to have a limitless supply of able-bodied sperm; swimmers impervious to the passing of time; only slowing slightly in their mobility. The image of the grey-haired dad with the younger model is not a stranger to media coverage (think Charlie Chaplin or Pablo Picasso); acceptable as images go, and not frowned upon as the childless woman so often is. Why did she go for that career rather than a cavalcade of shitty diapers? Such a senseless waste of her child-bearing machinery.

This gendered time bomb, with nuke heavy bias directed straight at the heart of the women just as they were beginning to take a larger chunk of the professional market in the 1950's, once again lay the responsibility squarely at the woman's door; the womb by another name. Interesting that the idea of the biological clock for women came into effect at the same time that women were beginning to clock on and off at the work place with greater regularity, meaning that their commitment to their first 'job' of creating the next generation, rather than furthering their own careers, was seen as a mismanagement of their time. Tick, tock...

It was time to bite the bullet. Jack was getting that threatening sound in his voice, and I didn't like it. Gathering myself together for the call I'd been avoiding, I settled down on the sofa, and pressed the phone to my ear.

"Cass—where've you been? I've been calling all week?!"

"I know, I'm sorry, it's just been a really difficult, shit week..." There was that truly useful word again. In the back of my head, where my father has permanent residence, I could hear him berate me for my lack of vocabulary and was not really concentrating on what Jack was saying. I was pulled back into the conversation.

"Cass?"

"Yes, sorry..."

"Did you do a test?" His voice cracked; the truth caught in my throat.

"Yes."

"Well?" You could have hung laundry on the damp pause.

"I'm pregnant." His intake of breath, and subsequent exhalation sounded like clouds gathering for the Apocalypse.

"Oh God! Shit..." There was that useful word again. "Shit, shit, shit." My Dad would have a field-day with his vocabulary.

"Well, I'm not surprised you're feeling shit — with this… with this situation on your plate."

"This situation?" The woman or wordsmith in me is suddenly sitting up and taking notice. I blame my father, and his attention to language; perhaps more.

"Yeah, an unwanted pregnancy." So that was how he wanted to play it. A non-starter from the word go.

"Right. Yeah…"

"Well, I mean, we're — neither of us — in any position to…I mean this is not what either of us had planned, and, certainly, we've just started seeing each other again, I mean…"

"You had no intentions of starting up with me again did you, Jack? You just wanted a shag." There it was. I didn't even realize I was capable of saying it.

"What do you mean?" Have you noticed how people say 'What do you mean?' when they know damn well what you mean, but are just buying time?

"I mean, unplanned or not, you had no intentions of getting back with me. You just didn't like the idea of me with anyone else."

"What — are you seeing someone else?"

"What if I am, it's none of your business. You broke up with me, remember?"

"But are you seeing someone else because it could be theirs..." the note of hope in his voice made me sick.

"I have not been seeing anyone else." Unsure of why I was lying, and lying to myself the most, I realised I had no intention of this baby being Tony's. I had convinced myself from the offset that it was Jack's although, theoretically, it could have been either of theirs. This realization was only slowly dawning as I spoke; a background hum to our conversation, and the parallel thought regarding the science of fecundity (thanks again, Dad): whether it would hold true here: in humans, and some primates, after ejaculation some of the semen hangs back, so to speak, to form a copulatory plug; a barrier against future sperm, unlike those ants, where the plug prevents mating of any kind, here the womb closes its doors for up to an hour to give the first in a head start, so to speak.

"What about Tony?"

"What *about* Tony?"

"He seems pretty keen..."

"He is keen. Period."

"Yeah, well one of those would be nice..." His smirk was audible.

"Ha bloody Ha. I know why you've called Jack. You want me to get rid of it — am I right?" Emotion was fighting logic, and neither had a hold.

"Well…"

"Be a man and say it!"

"Well, Cass, be realistic! Do you really want to put your career on hold now — for a baby?" The force of his words created a heavy pause that filtered down the line in static.

"What career? Have you been listening to me at all?"

"You have a good job at the radio station."

"That job is going down the pan fast."

"How would you support yourself?"

"The state loves single mothers."

"You're crazy — you're not really considering this are you?"

"I'm not seriously considering anything at the moment, Jack, but one thing is certain — I don't need your sorry ass to help me make up my mind. It's obvious you have no interest in me and this baby, so why don't we just end this conversation now, and save both of us some valuable time, eh?" That's when he hung up.

In the last one hundred years mankind has walked on the moon, driven the motorcar, sunk the Titanic, discovered the universe is expanding, invented the telephone, the computer, the personal stereo, the dishwasher/dryer, cured diseases, detonated the atomic bomb, designed robots, split the atom, created moving pictures, made instant coffee, and yet we haven't got a cure for love.

There are 6.2 billion humans on the planet, and I can't find one of them to love me. Lightning strikes the earth one hundred times a second — why can't love strike me? Eleven thousand bunches of flowers are bought every day in the United Kingdom: somebody is getting wooed. One hundred Americans commit suicide every day — probably due to broken hearts. Two hundred and twenty humans are born each day, mostly to live loveless, unfulfilled lives.

Anyhow, we shall probably suffocate in our landfills of disposable products, proving that, yes; everything can be disposable if you want it to be: razors, tyres, even love.

Chapter 12

To the Sounds of 'Heart of Glass'
by Blondie

"Bambi's here!" Hel's excitement leaks out of her like petrol; oily rainbows trail her erratic fidgeting around the desk. It's not every day we have a B list celebrity on the premises.

"Good, take her into the studio. I'll be there in a minute." Bambi Gresham had been good to her word. She may have puked all over me, but she remembered her promise, and is giving me that exclusive — her new single, "Take Me as I Am." Yeah, covered in vomit, I thought, nearly heaving at the reminder.

She smiles, and even stands up to shake my hand as I enter the studio, "Good to see you again."

"Likewise, although, nicer to see you without puke in my hair." She laughs girlishly.

"My thoughts exactly." I take my place behind the desk. "How've you been?"

"Oh, better, but this tour is going to kill me." She looks genuinely pale at the thought, despite fighting to smile. "They've got me going to 10 countries in 12 days. They're slave drivers these record people."

"Hey, you know, they get you wherever you are. Earning a living isn't what it used to be. Believe me." I press up the ads out of the news feed.

"I hear you!" I *had* to be earning brownie points with this one. Clare couldn't help but love me for this exclusive; although she hadn't said a word, and I'd sent Hel up to her office specially to leak the news. Hel came back saying she had received the information with a calm faced, "Good." That's what we call progress in these parts.

I'd been talking up Bambi's appearance on the show all week. If I mentioned her name one more time people would start to say I was losing my vocabulary:

"I promised you Bambi! And I've got her in the studio, but you'll just have to wait whilst Boys II Men sing 'I'll Make Love to You'— that's a bit forward! I hardly know them!" I pull the cans off one ear, and find Bambi bent over her handbag.

"You alright down there?" She comes up suddenly, looking surprised.

"Ah, yeah, how long till we go on?"

"Oh," I look at the digital counter, "about three minutes." I smile at her, but she suddenly looks concerned.

"Is there a loo?"

"Uh, yeah, but you'll need to be quick, it's just across the hall."

"Great," and she's gone. Hel pokes her head in the door.

"I forgot to tell you, your boyfriend has left several messages," she sticks her tongue in her cheek, trying to look saucy, but it makes her look like a kid with a gobstopper.

"What boyfriend?"

"Mr Blues Man."

"Oh, God, he's not my boyfriend. Now get!"

"Oh, and your Dad called."

"Leave!" She smirks and closes the door. I study the console seconds ticking off, and try not to think about the baby growing, with every second, in my womb. How can it be happening when I am so unaware of anything unusual about my body? There are no outward signs; inward even. I feel just the same as I ever did, and yet there is another human being dividing and dividing into more and more cells; wordlessly creating itself from some original DNA. The ball has been sent spinning, and all I have to do is keep breathing. And then eventually, pant and push like hell. I am suddenly aware that we are coming to the end of the track, and Bambi still isn't back. That unsettled feeling starts to rise up in me as I watch the digital counter click its way through the song. I have to make a decision, and quick. I bolt out of the studio, looking for Hel. She is not at her desk. I grab Jezebel's producer instead.

"Jane — I need help — my guest — Bambi is missing — get Hel to get into me ASAP!" I leave her open mouthed, and dash back into the studio just as Boys II Men deliver the end of their swoon song and slip us straight into an ad break.

"Shit, shit, shit, shit..." behind me, through the studio glass, Hel suddenly appears, and Jane is on her. Hel turns to look at me through the glass as Jane is speaking to her. I make the sign of one who is seriously on the edge — an unattractive grimace with my two arms flailing in the air. She gets the message. She is soon swinging in through the door.

"What's going on?"

"I don't know! She went to the loo, and she hasn't been back. I've got a bad feeling about this. Can you go and find out what's keeping her?"

"Yeah." Hel turns to leave.

"Did she come with a record rep or someone?"

"No, I don't think so."

"If you can't get her out of the bog, get on the phone to the record company, and find out if this happens a lot."

"Will do." Hel actually looks officious; she works better in a crisis.

I come out of ads and bullshit my way into another track, and around the houses. This is all beginning to feel strangely familiar.

Clare has her head buried in her computer screen when I walk in. I simply close the door, sit down, and wait for the slam dunk. Finally, she presses a button on her computer that makes a closing operations sound, or is it the sound of the final frontier I just crossed? — And turns to me:

"Well…that didn't go quite as planned did it?"

"No."

"Maybe, in future, when you know somebody has a drug and alcohol problem to start with, you might consider the fact that they aren't perhaps the most suitable and reliable of studio guests."

"It was an exclusive!"

"It *would* have been an exclusive if she hadn't been carted out of here in an ambulance, a syringe still sticking out of her arm."

"I had no way of knowing this would happen, Clare — for goodness sake — you've got to cut me some slack on this one."

"I'm getting just a little tired of cutting you some slack, Cass. Now, in future, if you have an exclusive, could you also please pass it by me first?"

"Yes."

"Ok. Let's say nothing more about it."

"At least you got the exclusive on her being carted out of here in an ambulance," Courtney, God love her, always looks on the bright side. That is why, I'm convinced, she never seems to have a bad day.

"Clare didn't quite see it that way."

"Well that's just because she's a dried up ol' misery. Her pussy hasn't seen any action since she broke her hymen on her first pony ride."

"Yeah..."

"C'mon, don't look so glum. We're gonna have a good night at the club tonight, it's the week end. We'll put this all behind us, and next week it'll all be better." I was almost inclined to believe her.

The streets are festooned with Christmas fodder; the mad pressed expression of the religiously damned hell-bent on acquiring the maximum amount of salvation for the minimum amount of fuss was perambulating down the Edgware Road. Music stores pushed their grands closer to the glass, their pearly teeth smiling onto the street; pimped and wrapped presents teetered on shelves, presupposing your wealth and aptitude for the invisible within: the hidden gems you too would wrap and give, in the hope of receiving; the gift that keeps on covering for misgivings was dancing out its wares and spangling in so much neon and gaudy glitter that nobody dare expel the myth with a word of warning. Likewise, nobody seemed particularly full of the Holy Spirit. Babies, wrapped up like monks in their tiny pushcarts, were wheeled with increasing speed across junctions and in and out of cues of people all going somewhere and nowhere with the utmost speed.

His birthday was coming. Would my baby have a birth day? This was certainly no virgin birth, there would be no wise men following this star-crossed misdemeanour. No celebration; just recrimination. How does one proceed, if at all? Do you just chalk it up to experience, or hold the line on some kind of truth that you may not understand, but which just might underpin the fabric of the universe? Was this meant to happen? Or was it just an example of idiocy (mine) or a badly made condom (somebody else's fuck up). In the giant scheme of things was this all just God's little joke, or does he even have a sense of humour?

Scientific truths are based on facts, but the realm of the unseen configures itself exponentially out into the vast unknown. Travelling with its own velocity, measured only by faith. If I had faith what shape would it take? Buddhism? Catholicism? Judaism? Sikhism? Muslimism? Naturism?

Nihilism? Could I put my faith in some other construct? Believe that everything is meant to be, like a river that has no presupposed bent to its course, but flows with complete *ism*? Would faith be enough to sustain me? — In the darkest times? Was this baby a gift or a judgement? Was I simply a very bad girl or in the wrong place at the wrong time? Would a couple of Hail Mary's do the trick? What would Mary say? What would Mum say?

I tried to remember a Christmas with Mum. As if squinting my eyes, and brain to squeeze out a memory would deliver her like a present under the tree. There just isn't a log of one winkled away; if it happened it happened in some no man's land where my memory ceases; maybe I have erased it to increase my chances of surviving her loss? That warm image would haunt me; perhaps she loves Christmas: is one of those people who have baubles up all year round, or physically respond to the rush and the colour, the dash and celebration, the hail and fayre of it with a true religious zeal? Perhaps she was the spirit of my Christmas, and when she left, so did my love of the holiday?

If memories can be hidden from us, to spare us, then I believe her memory hides in the recesses of my grey matter; winsome and adorable as she would have to be; smiling, smiling, smiling.

What would she say of this life growing inside me? Would she be happy? Would she frown her perfect brow at me, and gently remind me that I had more living to do before I tackled that particular hob-goblin? Or would she be there: suckered close and personal; ready for any of the many difficult moments yet to come, excited; ready to go out buying the pram and the cot, the tiny clothes, the bottles, the bibs?

She'd tell me about my birth; centre me in the world of women; join me to the sisterhood with her own milk of mothering. My child would be the next generation; we would be three generations, like Russian dolls: together, fitting into each other with the cosy familiarity of genealogy.

The lights from the cars melt into the coloured lights from the stores as the tears come. Merry Christmas every one.

Chapter 13

To the Sounds of "All I Want for Christmas is You" by Mariah Carey

The Christmas party at Blinks is always a big affair. Last year Blink dressed up as a Christmas tree, this year she has gone one better and is dressed as Santa Claus. She is the scariest Santa I have ever seen.

"Ho, ho, ho!" She welcomes, handing us each a tiny wrapped present from her sack, which is bigger than she is. Her maroon Santa-suit is cinched in at the waist, and her tiny, cat-yellow eyes peep menacingly over her moustache.

"Maybe it's a copy of her new album," Courtney cynically suggests once we are out of ear shot. Hurriedly unwrapping them, our cynicism now turned to excitement, we are brought back to disbelief:

"It bloody is!"

"Hells bells! She is the best self-publicist I know! I take my hat off to her!" Courtney sits down with a flourish, and puts her reindeer hoofs up on the chair in front of her.

"You know I think you look very sexy as a reindeer…"

"Are ya gettin' moist?"

"I could be," I wink, shaking the bells on my hat.

"Well, you've never been a cuter elf."

"Thank you. I feel elfin frisky." I have cinched my belt in an extra hole just to be sure that what must be two months-worth of pregnancy isn't showing.

"When don'tcha? And anyway, elves aren't frisky: they're too small to frisk."

"How do you know? Are you a friend of Tinkerbell's?" George goes by with a big Santa hat on his head, sucking a candy cane. He waves at us.

"I'm a friend of any small creature that's gettin' as little sex as I am." Courtney looks around the room as it fills with Christmas cheer, hoping to spy a promising male. "I hope I'm not the only reindeer here; I mean where's Donner and Blitzen — we've got Vixen," she raises her eyes at me.

Cage is coming through the door with a pair of antlers on his head that are lit up with tiny red lights; his presence alone is festive, and cause for celebration.

"Oh, thank God — another reindeer!" Courtney exhales. Then she actually stands up and waves. Courtney *never* waves. He is busy talking to 'Meat' and 'Veg' who have covered their bodies in tinsel and Christmas lights. I watch as they climb up on stage and plug themselves in; lighting up. Meat sits down behind the drum kit and Veg hooks on his bass. Blink and Cage join them up on the stage.

"Well, Merry Christmas everyone!"

"Jingle bells," Cage leans into the mike.

"We've got another packed show for you tonight, but to kick things off..." They launch into a rap rendition of 'Fairytale of New York' by The Pogues with Blink singing Kirsty MacColl's part. Everyone is singing along. It usually takes half the evening to warm the audience up, but tonight everyone is up for it from the start. Despite the inviting atmosphere, my stomach is in knots because I know that it's only a matter of time before my nemeses walk in — both of them. I steel myself for the inevitable but am resolute about my attendance tonight. After all, this is my place, my friends; I'm not going to let either of them push me off my turf. Tony, to be fair, hadn't followed up his phone calls, but Jack is quite another animal.

The crowd are ecstatically applauding Cage. He lopes off stage, high fiving 'Veg' and 'Meat' — so named because of his carnivorous cravings, or some say, the meat he has dangling between his legs. I wouldn't know. Cage stops to talk to a table of mostly women at the front, and I feel suddenly jealous, imagining that he would make his way straight to our table.

"Goddamn that boy has talent," Courtney enthuses, all doe-eyed.

"Yeah, he sure does."

"These tights are giving me inner thigh rash." Courtney scratches her leggings, and it sounds like she's grating nutmeg.

"Give it a rest. People will talk".

"Let them talk — I'd *like* them to think I've got some kind of STD — at least they'd think I was gettin' some."

"I don't understand why you aren't getting any?"

"I know! I put myself in all kinds of compromisin' situations, but nobody seems willin' to take advantage of me..." Courtney catches me watching Cage: "Are ya sure ya don't still have a bit of a thing for Cage?"

"Nah!" The automatic delivery made it all feel very false.

"He still loves ya...ya know that don't cha?"

"Well, yes, I guess so."

"You know what he told me...shit, I shouldn't even be sayin' this..."

"What?" Suddenly interested. There's nothing like a secret to get the juices flowing.

"He said that one time when you were having sex you sang Billy Holiday's 'My Man', whilst you were still, ya know...engaged... he says it was one of the most movin' things he ever..." Cage is coming over. We both freeze, and our expressions must be a picture because Cage stops and looks down at us quizzically.

"You two alright?"

"Yeah, yeah...fine."

"You were great..."

"That's why they call me the fastest wrapper in the world..." When he sees neither of us respond in the usual manner, even struggling to break a smile, he looks rightly confused; he bravely continues: "as in wrap presents — rapper, get it?"

"Yeah, funny, wrap: I get it."

"No, uh, you were great up there, man"

"Yeah, really great." He lets a pause hang uncomfortably in the air, and then, never one to sit on uncertainty for long, moves on:

"Thanks, can I get you ladies some drinks?"

"Does a pope fuck his choir boys?"

"Make mine a rum and coke, please." Realising too late I shouldn't be drinking, but too embarrassed to change my order, and incite curiosity.

"I'll have a beer," Courtney struggles to find her normal setting: "you fucking twisted reindeer you..." she trails off sounding confused by her own words. Cage decides to leave us to our strangeness.

"Consider it done." And off he saunters with our eyes trailing after him. We wait till he is out of earshot.

"Oh, my God. I don't believe he said that…"

"Yeah, he's carryin' a fairly massive goddamn torch for ya. I'm surprised the poor bastard can stand up straight."

"I never realized…I'd forgotten about that…"

"Well, he sure as shit hasn't. You traumatized the poor guy. You pussy fucked him body and soul."

"It's just Billy Holiday: she gets you where you live."

"You could have been singin' Dexy's Midnight Runners and he'd a been a goner." That's when Tony walks in. He looks weighted down by his guitar case, and his trademark flea market clothing's as bedraggled as ever. His one concession to Christmas: a little tinsel on his hat.

"Oh, shit, here comes little boy blue." Courtney's spotted him too. "Oh, man, you gotta stop fuckin' guys — it's gettin' so's we can't go anywhere."

"A girl has needs."

"Yeah, but yours are just greedy. I mean half the reason I can't get me end away is that you've had it away with most of em', and dried em' out. There ain't any sperm left in this town for a five-mile radius."

"Thanks, girlfriend. I'll start practising that catch and release fishing philosophy you've been going on about."

"That's it girl — catch and release, catch and release — it should be your new mantra." Tony was at our table.

"Hey ladies."

"Hey." Together.

"Can I get you some drinks."

"Cage is getting' us some," Courtney enjoys telling him.

"Oh, OK," smarting, he turns to me: "How've you been?"

"Good thanks, you?"

"Yeah...OK. Well, I guess I'll get myself one then. See you ladies later." He doesn't look happy. Seeing me confirms his worst fears: that I hadn't fallen down a well but had just genuinely decided not to return his calls.

"But how could you have fucked *that*?!" I look over at Tony who is at the bar and try to reappraise through her eyes.

"What?! You think he's *that* bad?"

"Even if you put a bag over his head I wouldn't touch him with yours."

"Thanks."

"Ya see, this is what I'm talkin' about: you're just greedy and you don't care what ya shag! Leave some ugly men for the ugly girls!"

"He's not ugly. He has a certain old-fashioned charm."

"Honey, he just plain old." Cage was back with the drinks which was just as well because I didn't have a retort.

"Here you go." He dishes them out.

"Thank you"

"Thank you kindly."

"So, which one are you? Donner, Blitzen, Dasher, Comet, Dancer, Prancer, Cupid? — 'cause we've already got Vixen!" She doesn't need to look at me.

"I think I'll be Blitzen — 'cause I'll be fuckin' blitzed by the end of this evening!" Cage looks around the table, and leans in conspiratorially: "Which one of you ladies is gonna take a trip to Mount Rushmore with me? I've got some grade A ecstasy, but I've only got one tab. I'll split it with ya. I already had one."

"You two was made for each other: that's just greedy. Whatever happened to just havin' one?" Courtney is looking genuinely peeved.

"Ah, one doesn't do it for me anymore. I need that extra half…"

"Have you ever considered stoppin'?" The mothering angle doesn't suit her, or him.

"Why would I wanna do that?"

"I dunno — death maybe? That deterrent always works for me."

"Nah, death ain't lookin' for me. He likes 'em taller."

"Well you can count me out," I cut in. I find myself thinking about the other person who would be tripping if I dropped half a tab.

"What's up with you?" Cage eyes me, suddenly curious.

"Nothing, I'm just not in the mood."

"Since when did mood have anything to do with it?"

"Look, you two do it — I'm just not up for it, that's all." And that's when Jack walks in. Always late, but never absent. He doesn't waste time locating me in the crowd.

"Oh, shit," I watch him approach, a human cyclone.

"What's up?" Cage has no idea. I hope that Jack, at least, won't make a scene.

"Jack — my man!" Cage greets him warmly. Jack doesn't even look at him, his eyes burrow into mine.

"Cass, can I have a word?"

"Jack, I really think this can wait — it's Friday night..."

"Cass, if you don't speak to me I swear..." His eyes are bulging. I can feel Cage stiffen beside me, and Courtney put her drink down with more firmness than is necessary.

"Listen, my man, I don't know what's gettin' up ya, but chill and give the lady a little space." Sensing that this is all going to get very ugly, very quickly, I get up, putting a hand on Cage's shoulder, and push him back down in his chair.

"This better be quick," I say trying to sound like I'm not going to take any shit. Courtney and Cage watch me go. We weave our way to the door of the club, and I wink at Mack-the-knife, who lets us pass. In a corner, by the stairwell, he expels:

"Cass, you can't keep avoiding me!"

"Why not? We have nothing to say to each other!"

"That's my baby in there too!"

"It may be your baby, but it's my body."

"I don't want a fuckin' baby of mine out there!"

"Out where? I'm not gonna leave it out in the cold!"

"I'm not ready to have this baby." He says point blank.

"You may not be ready, but maybe I am! Maybe I want this baby."

"Don't you think that's pretty fuckin' selfish?"

"Don't you think it's pretty fuckin' selfish to ask me to kill something just because you're not ready for it yet?" He looks at me.

"This isn't about us — this is about the baby!"

"Yeah, and the baby has a right to live!" I was crying now. Just in time for Cage and Courtney to come out and see it. Cage looks like he's about to hit Jack. Jack's looking so angry he doesn't care who comes up behind us, and he doesn't look ready to let me off the hook just yet. I had said things I wasn't sure I had in me that I hadn't consciously considered. I was shaking from fear of a different kind.

"What the fuck's goin' on?" It's Cage, and he's standing very close to Jack.

"It's OK. We've finished talking. Let's go back inside." I steer Cage back into the club, Jack doesn't say anything, and watches us go. Courtney stares daggers at him right up until the point she goes through the door, daring him to come after us with her eyes. Courtney wouldn't hesitate to give him a piece of her mind, and it was some mind. She once gave a guy in the underground a piece of it when he tried to jump on the train before her. He never did get on that train.

"What was that all about?" Upset and anger work side by side on his face.

"Yeah, what the fuck was that?" Courtney always uses a swear word when a simple noun or verb will do.

"Nothing."

"It didn't look like nothing — what's goin' on Cass?"

"I don't really want to go into it — not here, not now. OK?" They both stare into me. "Now, who wants a drink?" I try to smile.

Neither of them is buying my diversion. Cage turns to me, the door to the club opens and Jack comes back in. Our eyes follow him as he heads to the bar.

"So..." Cage doesn't really know how to approach the situation. "If he ever hassles you again —ya know — I will beat him to a fuckin' pulp".

"Thank you. I appreciate it, Cage — I really do." I'm trying not to cry. I suddenly feel like I want to cry for England, Scotland, and Wales, and I'm not sure coming out was such a good idea any more. Cage, despite his best efforts, decides to move on:

"My round. Same as usual?" Realising baby might not be up for another rum, I counter:

"Wait, Cage, actually, could I just have a coke?"

"A coke?" He looks as puzzled as I feel.

"Yeah. I just feel a bit...um, like I want to stay sober, you know?"

"Hell no, but OK." Cage has never had such a confusing evening and coming up on ecstasy probably wasn't helping.

"Cass — what did he say?" Courtney turns to me as Cage lopes away.

"Court, please — not now. I will tell you everything, but not here. Let's just chill a bit, and then maybe go back to my place yeah?"

"OK, OK…" I could tell she was itching to know. Patience wasn't one of her virtues, although she had many. Up on stage, Blink is ho-ho-hoing her way into the next act, her big belly inching itself down her thighs. She hikes it up, and enthusiastically calls up the next act.

Tony lumbers up on stage. He's added to the pathetic hint of tinsel on his hat by tying a tawdry snot fall of tinsel from the head of his guitar; it bobs sadly along to his song.

"Oh, great, this is just like an evening dedicated to your love life. It shouldn't be a Christmas theme; it should be a Greek Tragedy."

"Sorry…" That's when we heard the noise over at the bar. A fight had broken out, and we didn't need a crystal ball to figure out who the sparring partners were.

Chapter 14
To the Sounds of 'Creep'
by Radiohead

I don't often pick up the The New Scientist, but I had a little time before visiting hours at the hospital, and it seemed to be calling to me from the top shelf in W.H. Smith. I'd wandered in looking for refreshment and found shelves of Baby magazines dribbling back at me; in an effort to erase thoughts of possible nomenclature; the admiring of pudgy nose and button eyes, I fished for a more sophisticated waste of my time.

The cover had a picture of love heart sweets; the kind you used to get when you were a kid, complete with those erudite declarations: Be Mine, Catch Me, Dream Boy, My All, and, my namesake — Hard Luck. This was set against a picture of a couple in bed which drew me like a moth to a blow torch.

It promised an article on the mating rhymes and rituals of the human adult, and I was eager to discover the latest statistics. I would be a willing guinea pig for their experiments if I thought I could be of any use, make my father proud, or simply give my bit back to science, but it seems they had already found a cornucopia of promiscuous humans to base their studies on.

Spreading my change on the counter and wondering if I looked the type to buy such a highbrow mag, the pimply cashier wordlessly processed my order, more concerned by his own existence than my purchase. I walked a little taller with my copy of The New Scientist under my arm. In a nearby café I unfurled it, ordered a tea, and read on.

According to Dr. Shmitt, who collected sexual data on men and women from 48 countries, whilst men's sociosexuality peaks in their late 20's, women are most likely to be unfaithful to their partners when in their early 30's. "That's exactly the point," says Herr Shmitt, "where the odds of conceiving start to drop at a bigger rate, and it's also the point where the odds of having a child with a genetic problem or birth defect start to go up."

The good doctor suggests that women's increased sociosexuality at around this time reflects an evolved reproductive strategy that maximises the chances of their conceiving and bearing a healthy child. Therefore, I can conclude, that my promiscuity, being barren to date at 30 plus, has nothing to do with wanton amorality but is simply based on my puritanical desire to conceive a healthy baby, and before I lose all my eggs! Albeit by a total fucking bastard, as the article goes on to prove:

Apparently the classically promiscuous man is characterised by high extroversion, low neuroticism, and fairly low "agreeableness"! In other words — a total wanker like Jack. "The extroversion gives you the desire to do it," says my now celebrated doctor, "the low neuroticism means you don't worry too much about doing it, and the low agreeableness means you don't really care if you mess someone around or cheat on your wife." The situation is apparently similar for women. So, I'm a wanker too.

I felt like calling my Dad to tell him about my discovery (leaving out the bit about my being pregnant). If anyone would share my enthusiasm for scientific/sociosexual knowledge it was him, but when I dialled his home number, I found only his answer machine in.

"Hello, sorry I can't take your message right now, but if you leave your name and number I promise to get back to you just as soon as humanly and scientifically possible...."

Suddenly I had an overwhelming feeling to see him. It wasn't every day that I felt like running round for a father-daughter session, but it had been happening more and more; I wondered if it had anything to do with the fact that I was now growing someone that *I* could be parenting? This was followed by the thought: What on God's earth am I doing?

I squashed the magazine into my small bag, which to all intents and purposes was only meant for frivolous girl things, not big, brainy magazines, and headed back towards the hospital.

Cage looked terrible. Holding the ceiling up, or so it appeared, was his leg, attached to pulleys, and a sling. He had a black eye, and when he smiled I could see that he was missing one of his front teeth.

"Well, well, well, look what the cat dragged in...."

"Oh, Cage," I leant by his bed, dragging the chair alongside with an angry scraping noise, "I'm so sorry!"

"Yeah, yeah...trouble saw you comin'"

"I think it saw you first!"

"So, what's the deal, sista? I'm tired of asking, and I think now I have a right to know. Don't you?"

"First, what's going on with you? How long are they keeping you in? Have you pressed charges?"

"Nah,"

"It's all my fault"

"You got that right." He was smiling. "So at least you have ta tell me what this is all about, yeah?" I look at the floor, and then at my hands, which were still holding the flowers I'd brought him.

"These are for you." The flowers' heads look bowed in shame.

"Thanks." I stand up and put them on the side table where they just look at me sideways now; their heads at a new, uncomfortable angle.

"Are you gonna tell me or do I have ta beat it outta ya?"

"Very funny..." I was beginning to realize that the longer you keep something inside the more difficult it is to let it out. The skin builds up around a secret. I didn't feel ready to tell anyone, but I owed the truth at least to Cage. He was suffering for my secrecy, for my stupidity, and for his love for me. I took a deep breath.

"I'm pregnant — it's Jack's — and he wants me to get an abortion." It took Cage a few moments to gather the information up into his brain, and then he looked at me long and hard.

"You know I'd stand by ya..."

"I know...."

"But you don't want that do ya?"

"I don't want anything from anyone right now except maybe some peace — inner and outer —you know?" He was quiet. We both chewed on the silence, which was suddenly broken by Courtney.

"CAGE! — Oh my God!" She flings herself into the room with the kind of drama reserved for widows in soap operas. She's at his bedside in two strides, and the pink roses look robust and delicious thrown across his chest as she hugs him as best she can with all the added apparatus getting in the way.

"That bastard! I will hog tie that ass hole just as soon as look at him! I hope you're gonna press charges? You know ya *have* to press charges don'tcha? — and right away — get that miserable piece of human excrement behind bars and outta our lives! Holy Jesus, Mary, Joseph, and little star of Bethlehem I don't believe what he's done to ya!"

"Well, actually, it was my fault — the leg — I fell over as I was leaving the club..."

"Yeah, but that's cause you was discombobulated! You just weren't yourself! Hell!" She was fussing over him like a mother hen, and suddenly I saw it — she loved him. She really, truly felt something deep and tender for him. All those times she'd watched him starry eyed on stage and made a big deal about how good he was she had been hiding her soft egg of love.

"Who wants a nice cuppa tea? There's a machine down the hall." I offer.

"Nah, ta…the nurses jus' brought me one."

"Well I…" Courtney stops her fussing, and looks from Cage to me, "OK — thanks." I leave before they can say another word. I imagine Courtney putting her head on his lap, telling him again how that son-of-a-bitch should rot in hell, and how he has to press charges. And then I felt something I hadn't expected: I felt alone. As the humdrum of people milled past me on their way up and down the corridor, in and out of their lives and doorways, I felt an overwhelming desire just to keep walking, past the tea machine, down the hall, past the bad mural of ships and sailing boats — and right out of there. At least one love story could end happily.

According to the latest data, love and the mating ritual give scientists a real headache. Apparently, there is no justifiable reason for us humans to spend the time and energy we do on attracting a mate.

The unbelievably colourful and decorous way in which we choose to song and dance our way into somebody's heart is really the most round-about way of self-replicating and makes no sound scientific sense at all. Most species just sub-divide, like our amorphic friend the amoeba; or achieve biblical status by virgin birth like the komodo dragon (mind you if you looked like the komodo dragon you'd have to do it yourself).

The fact is, however, that dear old komodo and her ilk have avoided the emotional and financial cost of wooing and schmoozing a date. She has saved a shit load on internet dating, high heels, and lipstick; achieving the goal of continuing her species with the least amount of energy spent.

And energy cannot be underplayed in our evolutionary process. Food was not always easy to come by, nor the strength with which to pursue it. They did not have endless supermarkets or corner shops in the dawn of our species. And so, any amount of fannying about in the name of foreplay was not evolutionarily sensible. $E = m(TL)c^2$ was not a working formula for the dawn of our species and would not have furthered our evolution. Too much TLC would have led to primordial extinction.

When our single celled ancestors evolved, crawled out of the mire, and started using oxygen they found that this was a valuable source of energy, and no doubt celebrated this fact with extra jogs around the muddy pool. However, with oxygen came the degenerative side effects of free radicals, and the resulting cell damage. Indeed, some scientists will tell you that sex grew out of a genetic response to death. So, we fuck to live beyond death! How's that for deep?

I have always found a dark poetry in the notion that sex and death are closely linked. We are told that men suffer "un petit mort" when they ejaculate. So why not go the whole hog and realize that our lives are not just an effort, as some have claimed, to climb back into the womb through sex for men, and for women to recreate life through childbirth, but also to realize that we are forever teetering on the edge of the abyss. With or without reproduction our lives are solitary, no matter how much we see ourselves in our children or try to pass on some semblance of ourselves. People say that they can happily shake off this mortal coil knowing that they have left something of themselves behind, but which part?

Whatever part of us goes on, we can only hope it is the better part. However, sexual reproduction only guarantees a 50% replication of our own genes, and God only knows which 50%. Probably the bits you would rather not pass on, halitosis and bad teeth, or in my case, morose tendencies.

And what of those unfortunate animals for whom sex actually does mean death? Take the humble chameleon, both male and female, which drop with the papery grace of autumn leaves as soon as they have successfully mated. Or the male marsupial Antechinus who dies of stress and exhaustion after non-stop fourteen-hour sex sessions. This certainly does not seem like a fair exchange for the time and energy that they have invested?

Many a case has been made for the alpha male in the trajectory of human evolution, and that may have been the case in the majority of species, but the day of the alfalfa may be on the rise. The female of the species will ultimately tire of the more flamboyant, like the peacock, or the biggest head-bangers, like the heavy antlered stag. These bozos may have bags of testosterone and have kick started many a species, keeping it fighting fit, but my prognosis is that one must never underestimate the under-dog. It is often the case that whilst these alpha males are battling it out for the love or lust of their lady, going at it hammer and tong like lions on the prairie, the female, growing bored of this show of male bravado, may wander off, and bump into a beta male with more sense than to clutter up his afternoon with jousts of male bonding. And the female would do well to tarry here where she will perhaps get more buck for her bounce as the lion is reported to have the shortest copulation time in the animal kingdom.

It has been said that the 'Meek shall inherit the earth' and like the tortoise and the hare, my monies on those playing the long game.

So why do we go to the endless extremes and complications of sexual congress? Even our friends the biologists scratch their heads and admit that there seems no rhyme or reason for the elaborate mating rituals of most mammals; the endless fanfare, the emotional and physical upheaval leading to the brief hiatus of sexual congress.

Sex, we are told, is the gene's way of ensuring, as my dear father has often told me, its evolution, and arm pit smelling aside, it would appear that the gene is simply shuffling its chromosomes like cards.

Amongst the busy bees of Radio Honey, the space-time continuum outside the glass partition window, it's like watching a hive without a heart. The worker bees seem automated, not one honey dance amongst them. The collective is trying to assimilate and disseminate; look busy whilst not really grasping the bigger picture; I long to inject a real pulse: a shock wave, a tidal wave that would build in intensity pushing them into a heightened state of reality. The hive was active, but the Queen was dead below the waist.

"Do we really do this for a livin'?" Courtney seems to be reading my thoughts again.

"Hell, we need to get a life."

"This is like the repressed leading the depressed."

"The bi-polar leading the psychotic."

"Quasimodo conducting a hunchback symphony of one-armed bandits."

"The lonely-hearts club leading the battered wives club."

"Gail's on her way in." Hell breaks in, no longer feigning enthusiasm.

"I better leave you to it." Courtney unscrews her eyes from the world outside the studio, "Hey," she turns the screws on me — "I'm takin' you out for a bite, or a coffee — or somethin' after the show, OK?"

"You got it". Gail and Courtney pirouette around each other. Gail takes her seat.

"So, Gail…how's it going?"

"Yeah, OK." Not looking up from her papers, she pulls the mike closer. I lean into my own:

"That was my all-time favourite singer-songwriter, Joni Mitchell, and 'Big, Yellow Taxi'—they've paved a few more paradises with parking lots since she wrote that 60's classic. It's still just as relevant today. Speaking of parking lots, we've got Gail with all the news and travel after these messages." Pulling down the fader I look over at Gail who still has her head down.

"You going home for Christmas?"

"Nah."

"Can't get the time off?"

"Nah. I just don't like them."

"Oh." There wasn't an answer for that one that didn't lead to a therapy lesson.

"So, you got any plans for tonight — you know, Friday night?"

"Nah, not really."

"What do you do for fun, Gail?"

"I like slasher movies...."

"Oh...uh-huh...you go out much?"

"To see slasher movies, yeah, or there's Club Slasher once a month, they do..."

"Don't tell me — they show slasher movies?"

"Well, yeah, but you can also go as your favourite slasher character, and there's a bar..."

"Sounds...yeah...very slasher..." Gail returns her head to the downward position, and we turn to the business of traffic: I line up Elvis Costello's "Accident's Will Happen" to lead us out of travel; it's not playlisted, but as far as I'm concerned, on some deep, psychological level that my listening public and I would respond to, it should be: suffering as we were our own car crashes.

Chapter 15

To the Sounds of 'Ebeneezer Goode'
by The Shamen

What happens when one object hits another? In molecular theory, when molecules collide, they gain, lose, or retain an equal amount of energy. Chemical reactions are at the core of everything that happens in the universe from thermonuclear fusion that powers the sun to the cells within our bodies. However, reactions require an initial input of energy, and molecules must collide in order to react.

When human bodies collide, it gets even more complicated. The force and impact of one life upon another can have huge consequences. Everything is in constant motion, and accidents, or collisions, I would wager, are inevitable. But surely it's how we deal with these incidents that mark the girls out from the women, the boys from the men? I mean many a 'collision' has gone on to lead full, significant lives, right?

I've got a full-on pile up going on in my womb, although both objects had been moving together, in rhythmic synchronicity when the accident occurred; and yet, here I am, cordoning off areas in my head to deal with the collision that is my conscious mind bumping up against my body clock:

doing a Scarlett O'Hara: she would always say "I'll worry about it tomorrow" in that southern-belle-drawl, and make herself a new dress out of curtains or whatever came to hand. I know I need to start dealing with it, with this collision, but short of another pile up, it's going to have to wait.

"We need to talk," Jack's phone message isn't subtle, and my ignoring him isn't either.

"We need to talk," says Hel as I get into the office. She's at her desk selecting a sheet of paper, and as she sits down her chair loses its grip, plunging her another six inches lower. "Shit", she exhales.

Her mini chair-a-thon in progress I have time to put down my bag, gather myself into work mode, sit down myself, and turn to face her; just as she manages to regain optimum level.

"Right, yes, there's a problem with today's show."

"No change there then."

"No, I mean a *real* problem, not our usual, we need to fill a slot, a guest is O.D'ing in the loo type of problem."

"Oh..."

"Yes, umm, the commercials system is down, Gail is off sick, Deborah is off sick, and I think I'm going to be sick..."

"Yeah, that doesn't sound good. How did breakfast cope?" Just then I catch sight of breakfast's answer to Genghis

Khan crossing the offices with Clare in tow, looking visibly upset.

"She beat Steve up on air, verbally and physically."

"Good tactics; I like it." Clare is putting a comradely arm around Angel, and I can't help thinking that theirs would be a fitting coupling. "So, what do you suggest we do?"

"Clare is telling everyone just to do the best they can, but she has also told us to get the presenters to read the news and travel themselves. The ads will have to wait, they can always run them later or overnight, or we'll double up tomorrow."

"Shit. Right, hand them over then."

"Ahh," she looked sheepish, "That's the other thing…"

"What?"

"The printer's down."

Headbanger FM seems the perfect antidote to the day. After a post work pub stop, and a tandoori, where Fay regales us with stories of her horny young stud's anatomy and prowess as opposed to her husband's lack of libido, we are ready to test the waters.

"So, which one are you doing?" I wanted to get the story straight before meeting one of the main players.

"Josh, he's the one with the really long hair," smiles Fay, unable to hide her delight.

"Haven't they all got long hair?"

"Yeah, but Josh's is really long."

"OK." Already feeling uncomfortably hairless.

"And whatever you do," counsels Courtney, "Don't look nervous."

"Why?" I whimper, looking nervous.

"They'll play with you like a mouse."

"Great, maybe I'll just get an early night; it has been a very long day." Wordlessly, and as if they had planned it, Fay and Courtney each grab one of my arms. Marching me towards the familiar surroundings of our radio lobby, things take a turn for the bizarre as we head upstairs instead of carrying on straight down the hall. Fay presses the intercom that reads 'Headbanger,' and without hesitation we are buzzed in. Courtney turns as Fay leads the way upstairs, and looks me in the eyes, raising her eyebrows and smiling a mischievous smile:

"Come on, slow poke."

"I'm coming." Fay presses another buzzer, and this one lets us in as neatly as the last. Inside the Head banger foyer the smell of marijuana hits you like cheap after shave. It's dark save for a floor light over in the corner by a low-slung sofa, and by its light I can just about make out a few classic heavy metal posters, and a reception desk. A hairy man pokes his head out of a studio door.

"Ladies, won't you enter the den of sin?" He smiles, showing a missing front tooth, and I'm even more sure that I don't want to be here. Following the hair, and the stench of strong reefer, from one darkened room to another, I find the studio houses three long haired youths. One has on earphones, the other is rolling a joint, and the third is leading us to a very long sofa at the back of the room.

"You ladies like Jack Daniels?" He's smiling that toothy smile again.

"Slap 'em up bartender," Courtney's ready to party. Fay slinks off to bend over the back of the DJ, her long dark hair falling over his, and plants a kiss on his neck. He turns around removing one side of the cans, and they kiss: long and hard. They look sweet together, and I find myself staring.

"Can you ladies drink a burnin' Sambucca?"

"No, but I can fuck start a Harley!" Courtney's all smiles, but Toothy doesn't quite know how to take her so he moves on.

"What about you?" Toothy is talking to me, and I have to do an embarrassing return-to-the-room-from-far-away-stammer:

"Uh, um, I'll, ahh..." I look around for support, but Courtney's up pouring out a massive bottle of Jack Daniels into three tiny shot glasses.

"Deal 'em out bartender!" says Toothy.

"Don't mind if I do," chirps Courtney. With Fay and the long-haired lover whispering in the corner, and Courtney and the toothy one clinking shot glasses, the one rolling the joint looks over at me.

He finishes the joint with a flourish — a lick along the seam, and one firm upward thumb movement. He turns to me: the spliff getting bigger and bigger as his arm outstretches to me.

"Umm..." Suddenly they were all looking at me. "Thanks." I had a bad feeling that this would be the first of many mistakes that evening. Whitesnake are singing, and the three hirsute ones join in, even with the air guitar middle eight. A lot of hair is spun around whipping the air and generally moving the heat and smoke around but changing only the ruddiness of their complexions. I take a very big drag on the joint: I figure I'm going to need it.

Courtney lopes over, and sits next to me on the settee, or what remains of it; there were large chunks of stuffing oozing out.

"So, what'ya think? They're two bales o' hay short of a hay ride, but worth the roll, eh?" Before I can answer, there is a chorus of, "Drink! Drink! Drink!" and we all watch as Fay downs three shots in quick succession. After the last one she leans over again, and deep throats her man.

Toothy is approaching us with a shot glass in each hand, smiling. Fay has moved away from the long-long haired lover and is doing a little dance in the middle of the room, arms dragging the air, head tilting on its stalk, a series of heavily scented Bedouin scarves would not have gone amiss, trailing in her wake; from where I'm sitting, she looks like she doesn't have a care or a husband in the world.

"So, what's yur name little lady?" Toothy's addressing me and holding a shot glass.

"Cass..."

"Cass, eh? Well, Cass, here at Headbanger ya gotta drink if ya wanna stick around so's get y'ar laughin' gear around this little beauty." I gingerly take the shot glass, and shooting Courtney a look, down it in one.

"Right — good — now let's see if you's can do that again...." He fills the shot glass with a bottle which is conveniently to hand. "Bottoms up..." I take the glass obediently and knock it back. The amber liquid doesn't burn so hard the second time. "Three's a charm..." And it was back in front of my face. "Good girl...now how about you tell me yur name again..." For a moment, I'm not sure I have one — that I can think of. And for those of you worrying about my unborn child: you're not the only one, but it was exactly these kinds of worries that were driving me to drink. That and a recent revelation:

"Dad?" I'd let myself in with my key. My Dad liked to have a back-up plan, and he was not the kind of guy to leave a key under the matt, or in some fake rock — No, you had your own key, and woe betide you lose it. In my Dad's world you didn't lose things. You could lose significant others, but not keys. Inanimate objects were to be cherished in a way that made it impossible to allow their mysterious disappearance. I remember the time I lost my school jumper. He came to the school with me and made me search through every classroom; we even put up posters and sent leaflets home with the other students. After that I was known simply as 'Sweater Girl.' It was humiliating, but it worked. I never lost that damn sweater again. It turned up eventually. Somebody had taken it home "by mistake." My dad loved to put the inverted commas around that phrase. He wasn't all that trusting of people; I believe he harboured simpering distrust which stemmed from his childhood. That sweater wasn't simply lost, it was waylaid, it was abandoned, it was stolen; there was a history of neglect that had echoes of his childhood wrapped in its woolly fibres.

"Dad?" The lights were off in the living room. I wandered into the kitchen and put my hand on the kettle: it was still warm. Back in the living room the only sound was coming from his bedroom where a few socks bled a white trail like large breadcrumbs. "Dad?" I knocked and opened the door.

The scars of that vision will remain with me for the rest of my life. Never have I wanted to see that much of him displayed with so much casual abandon. There was a feminine squeal accompanied by my father yelling something at me which was not so much words as angry sounds.

I threw apologies at them as I hurriedly closed the door and fled out of the house.

When he called me later that day, us both apologising and trying to justify our various misdemeanours, he came to a sudden halt and simply said, "So it seems as good a time as any to tell you I have a girlfriend."

"I told you already my name is not Jess it's Cass," I try to say this with as much pronunciation as my rubbery lips will allow, but already feeling far too happy to be angry with this silly looking boy with his missing front teeth, "It's Cass..." My lips feel like they are working to another agenda not specified by my brain; have been rented out to somebody else whilst I am still using them.

"As in Mama Cass?"

"If you like, but — No," I fight back, regaining my composure," — it's just Cass — as in Cassandra...."

"Oooo, very posh..."

"I'll give ya posh — hand me that bottle, bartender..." Courtney doesn't wait for it to be passed. She tears the bottle out of his hand, and meanders over to check out the one with the joint; leaving me alone with Jack Daniel.

"So, what do you do...'Not Mama Cass'?"

"I'm a DJ at Honey..." Still trying to sound posh and angry this only seems to spur him on, as if my squirming was some kind of foreplay.

"Ohh, you work at the girlie station..."

"It's not a *girlie* station — we are not all 12 — we are women — DJ's!"

"Yeah, well judging by your recent stats we are hammering you ladies!" More gum than tooth reveals itself.

"Where'd you hear that?"

"Don'tcha check your stats?"

"Well...yeah...of course, but I hadn't heard that."

"I'm not talking about hearsay; although the hearsay is that you're going down like a rat-infested ship — no offense. I'm talking cold hard statistics, girlie."

"Where'd you hear that pile of crap?!" The alcohol was now just making me angrier than normal. Courtney looks over and raises an eyebrow at me. She has a new joint in her hand and is coming over.

"It's not crap — it's bona fide, genuine statistics." His mirth is self-replicating.

"Hey, what's all the commotion?" Courtney says whilst still trying to hold the hit in her lungs.

"Jack Daniels here says our stats are shit, and word on the street is we're a sinking ship?!"

"Well, yeah, stat's aren't great, Cass." She exhales.

"When'd you hear this?"

"Well, today, but what with everything else I reckoned one nightmare at a time, right?"

"Shit." I take the joint she was passing my way, and let the information sink in.

"I didn't mean to upset you or nothing," says Jack Daniel, moving away slightly.

"Course ya didn't!" Courtney's giving the gift of joy, all smiles, and patting him on the back. "She's just not heard the news, that's all...." We all exchange silences.

"Hey, where's that joint?" Fay is dancing our way.

"Here," I offer it up, but give away the bonus, "Have you heard about our stats, Fay?"

"Aw, c'mon Cass — don't ruin the party." Courtney chokes on the hit.

"She may not have heard the good news."

"What difference does it make now — tonight — we've got enough shit on our plate. Can't we forget about it for just one night?"

"What stats?" asks Fay, innocently.

"Nuthin' darlin' — say, that was some jig you were givin' us there — care to spin me around the room some?" Courtney takes Fay's outstretched hand, and the two pirouette out into the centre of the studio, leaving a twirly trail of marijuana smoke.

"Hey, I didn't mean to upset ya..." Jack Daniels is doing his best to backtrack. A part of me wants to forgive him, but another part wants to lay into him some more. "Have another snort." The shot glass was back.

Chapter 16

To the Sounds of 'Do You Really Wanna Hurt Me?' by Culture Club

I'm playing vinyl not CD's, but they turn into paper in the shape of vinyl on the turntables.

Laying these limp sheets on the deck they spin silently; nothing but dead air playing out. Pulling more vinyl from their sleeves I put them on the turntable, but they turn into paper too. After a few failed attempts I feel solid vinyl in my hands, and throw it on the turntable, but now it won't fit: the hole won't line up in the slot, the nipple seems bendy, and the wrong size. Finally, as all hope evaporates, I hit gold, and Madonna sings a song I haven't heard before. I'm happy to hear any old song by then and don't care what the needle's found. But the needle goes down hard and slips loudly off the record.

There's a chorus in my head, but it's not Madonna. More of a cacophony of voices yelling, "Drink! Drink! Drink!". I sit up slowly, holding my head. My feet swing off the sofa, but instead of floor hit something soft and hard at the same time. Looking down I see Courtney curled in a foetal position. We are in the foyer of Headbanger FM.

The world slowly pulls back into focus. I kick Courtney gently. She lets out a low moan. I kick her again, "Wake up!" This time she gets verbal:

"What the fu...." As there are no windows in Headbanger FM it suddenly occurs to me that it could be morning. In fact, it could be show time.

"Get up! We've gotta get to work!"

"Wha..? What time izzit?"

"I dunno..." I look around me for anything resembling a phone or a clock or a gizmo of the modern age. The Motley Crew poster looks down at me, and the one low slung table lamp on the empty reception desk emits a paltry haze; too smoky to aid navigational purposes.

"Are you wearing a watch?"

"Dunno..." Courtney is failing miserably at pulling herself together, or even up off the floor. I have to poke her again with my foot.

"Stop fuckin' kickin me!"

"We could be late for work!"

"You'll be late for yur own goddamned funeral in a minute!" Realizing I can't even find my bag, I get up and make my way on unsteady stockinged feet across the worn expanse of carpet towards the one light. Picking up the phone on the reception desk, I dial the speaking clock. The incoming bleeps hit my sensitive eardrum like an onslaught of roadrunner beeps; I pull the phone away, but can still hear the lady pronounce:

"At the third stroke, the time from BT will be eleven fifty-seven, and thirty seconds..."

"Holy Fuck!! I'm on air in three seconds!!" I have never seen Courtney move so fast; in fact Roadrunner did spring to mind. All that was missing was a few little "Beep, Beep's" as she evaporated in a puff of smoke. I could hear her clattering down the stairs, three at a time, and then I hear a trip, a fall, a rush of expletives, then more running, and finally all is quiet.

Alone, I pick up my coat, and see my handbag, as my eyes grow accustomed to the light, in front of the studio door. Someone must have found it in the studio, and left it outside so I wouldn't have to enquire within — Like I would ever want to go back into that hellhole?

I sneak quietly down the stairs towards reception. The main aim is to avoid anyone seeing me emerge from Headbanger's premises. I get to the bottom of the stairs before my cover is blown:

"Where do you think you're going Ms. Up-All-Night? God, you look like you've been dragged through a combine harvester backwards. Bloody Hell!" It was Hel.

"Fuck off and get out of my way."

"Sorry, no rest for the wicked: Clare has called an all staff meeting, and if you could have heard your messages you would know that. Now come along, the meeting starts in five." She pirouettes on her mime feet, knowing I will have to follow.

"I gotta hit the bog first — where's it happenin'?" I mumble through woollen lips.

"Upstairs — in the conference room." I let out a moan, but she's gone. Finding the ladies gratefully uncluttered with human life, I manage to shoosh my hair, and reapply a little lippy — it's all I have in my bag.

Following the smell of panic Courtney left hightailing it into the studio, I wave at her through the window as I pass, but she is too deep in it; trying to claw back consciousness.

The conference room is mulling in an uncomfortable silence: everyone is seated; everyone is here, but an immersive hum sifts gently over their heads, whilst their composure has a sibilant reek, as if all the air is slowly but steadily leaking itself out from the pressure of working here. Courtney is the only one missing. I clock Jezebel over the other side of the room, and smile and wave, but she just shoots me a miserable look, which had been an attempt at a smile, but taken a turn for the worse and ends up a grimace. Sliding into a seat at the end of the table, I feel a wind behind me: Clare entering the room on a speed dial of adrenaline. Striding authoritatively to the head of the table, flanked by Angel and Gary, she puts down a sheath of papers, looks around the room to make sure everyone is there, and sits down; Angel and Gary follow through.

"Right..." we feel the pause like an ache in our hearts; we all know this is not going to be a happy meeting, a pat on the back for a job well done — No, this would be more in line with a meaningless blind date where you feel like you have wasted a portion of your life speaking absolute shit to an absolute stranger, and there will be no second date.

"I can't pretend that things are going well — they're not, and recent stats have proved it once again. Our overall rajar figures are down across the board, both morning and afternoon drive have dropped over 10% of their audience. Reach is down, hours are down, and our share is down." Her eyes flit across the room for effect. "The basic problem is our programmes are not hitting the target with our audience..." She picks up her biro, and pumps the nib in and out, rhythmically accentuating her assault on our senses and sensibilities, "...and our playlist is not being played in the requested order!" — At which she spins her head round like Linda Blair in The Exorcist and turns laser beams on me. Batting my eyes like a frog in a hail storm, as Courtney would say, her near wild gaze impales me; I feel her synapsis kick starting reserve chambers, those so diligently preserved in vats of corporate wine over the years, in order to maintain composure, and not spin off into No Man/Woman's Land. "Or indeed, sometimes not followed at all!" Again, her eyes hoover me up like land sweepers. "Suffice it to say that if the station is not turned around within the next couple of months our sponsors will no longer pay us to do our job, and our investors will no longer invest, and we will all be out on our arses."

"Speak for yourself," I heard someone whisper. I look around desperate to see what comrade in arms has spoken such delicious truth, but everyone appears poker faced. Have I spoken out loud?!

"I will be meeting with you all individually to look at the structure of your shows, and where improvements can be made. Meetings will start tomorrow so you will have to work overtime with your producers to make suggestions about how you can improve your show and submit these ideas to me starting tomorrow. So, make sure you are all ready — I do not want anyone to disappoint me. We are looking, at the very least, at lay-offs, so everyone must look to impress me." Angel angles her chin high, nodding anytime Clare says something with more than usual emphasis. The rest of us cower like dogs at obedience school. "Any questions?"

"Yes, Courtney." I hadn't notice her sneak in.

"Might I ask when or *if* the masts are due to be improved?"

"That is not for you to worry about. You must all simply concern yourself with your own show. Leave the running of the station to me!"

"The fuckin' transmitter is down...here's your problem! Hello!" I could see this was going to be one of those incidents where she was employing her usual candour. She blinked her eyes dumbfoundedly for effect. The hangover obviously hadn't hit yet; she was still working on Headbanger time. And she wasn't going down without a fight: "How *anything* the programming department does can make a blind bit of difference is beyond me. We can research, write and produce the most outstanding, award winning, jaw-droppingly compelling features the world has ever heard, and present them to our heart's content until our tongues fall out, *but I ask you* — what difference does it make if our spectacular sound bites can't be heard across 80% of our TSA because you haven't bothered to repair the transmitter and get the signal working properly?" As she pauses for breath all I can think about is the fact that she must have put on a bloody long track to cover herself, or that Radio Honey was playing out some major dead air. The silence in the room is exemplary; any school teacher would have been proud. I felt like high-fiving the air. Courtney is still blinking her way into her next tirade: "As long as our signal isn't serving the licensed TSA we never will unless some freak weather occurrence forces our entire area population to gather in the eastern corner of The Birchwood Industrial Estate's overflow carpark or under the Canning Town flyover, for the majority of our peak time over the next quarter and that's highly unlikely! In my humble opinion." Courtney adds as an afterthought, scanning the room for nods of approval. Everyone seems to have turned to pillars of salt; the silence is Biblical. The only movement is the pen, rotating around Clare's digits.

"Quite..." I hear myself utter: nobody more stunned than me. Everyone turns to look at me. I have the floor, or so it seems; the swarm turn their many, monstrous eyes on me. Never being one to back down from a challenge I then blurt out:

"Yeah, um, we don't really know how big an influence we could have until we actually get the opportunity to be heard by the majority of the population we were intended to hit..." I look to Courtney for help, and she doesn't disappoint. Picking up the baton:

"Big changes are occurring in radio broadcasting and big demands are being placed upon us. Big opportunities are ahead for those who are committed to rising to the occasion. One broadcast paradigm has not shifted: Radio is still the fast moving, highly competitive, low loyalty business it has always been.

"It's not about following an ill-managed playlist! It's about the responsibility of local radio to lead the community. We must be positive and proactive, not play listed and repetitive. If you want the general population to have a good attitude, project a positive attitude on the air. If you want the community to invest in itself, then invest in yourself. But remember at all times, capitalism is our ally, and we do not work for the Red Cross. These features have to be marketable; they have to be marketed, for fuck's sake! Where's the sales team? Where's the promotions department? We've barely got a news room, sorry Lily..." On behalf of news Lily nods her understanding.

I don't want to look over at Clare, but I have to. Her expression is one of pre-embolism. The pen rotating faster and faster around her fingers, but Courtney is on a role, and she isn't going to stop till her chin hits the dirt. "Owners pay too much for radio stations to allow programmers to become slower in their reaction times or complacent in the now-larger companies. Radio still only generates seven or eight percent of the advertising money pool and less than one fifth of the population is using radio in the average quarter hour. Broadcast companies are worth more than ever, and that just means that there's a lot more to lose should they fail to please their listeners and media buyers." She takes a breath, and continues, the room reduced to the pinhole of her open mouth:

"It's not easy, but it can be *fun* if you *specialize* in surprise, minimize negativity within the company, and you sell your product, i.e. *airtime.* Let's talk about Sales figures a while and leave programming changes and the running of playlists for a more appropriate time, eh? Heritage stations no longer have a monopoly on anything and certainly *not* on their users' *time*, and they can't afford to act as if they do. Why should we take a BBC approach to our programming? Tweakin' and alterin' and stealin' and re-repeatin' every single good idea and floggin' it until it gasps a bloated-Elvis sized sigh of release after its 7th year? We're not publicly funded! We have to do more! Don't you get it?" Courtney looks around the room for support but meets with fear. I smile weakly at her. Clare simply gets to her feet, and with a good deal of repressed rage manages,

"As I said, I will be meeting with you individually to look at the structure of your shows so be ready." Angel rises to meet her. The 'Honeys' file out slowly and quietly. Courtney and I wait till they have all left.

"Shit." she exhales.

"Wow!" I manage with admiration.

"I thought she was gonna fuckin' slug me one on the way out!"

"She'll deal us that blow in more insidious ways."

"Yeah, giant spiders in yar lunch box."

"Hair balls in your coffee." Courtney is quiet, and then all of a sudden lets out a yelp, "Shit!" I realise as she runs away from me that her show has become a mime fest.

I've got another syndrome to add to my list: Imposter Phenomenon or Fraud Syndrome. It's where you are unable to grasp your own accomplishments and believe yourself to be an imposter. Sufferers convince themselves that their success is just a matter of being in the right place at the right time, or common, good, old fashioned luck; that it's just a matter of time before they are discovered to be a fraud, or even worse, not good enough to service their own life. You find it in a lot of high-flying women, in careers normally associated with academia, and although Freud didn't discover it, and it's not officially recognized as a first-class psychological disorder, there have been a lot of books and articles written about it by psychologists. Sufferers believe they have hoodwinked others into thinking they were competent enough for the job. I *know* Clare now thinks there are others more worthy of my job, but the problem is I agree with her. I remember the day I came into the offices of Radio Honey and auditioned. I damn near peed my pants when Clare told me to make a live demo in the studio for her. My radio experience covered a spell as a roving reporter for a small radio station in Oxford, and a jock for Top Shop Radio. But she must have seen some errant spark in me, and before I knew it she'd moved me in the space of two months from the post breakfast slot — slow at the best of times — to drive time. Courtney's jocking lessons had a lot to do with it, and sadly her less than meteoric rise had a lot to do with the fact that she has an accent as thick as a rain cloud over Edinburgh. According to polls carried out by God-only-knows-who, people don't like to hear American accents in the morning or when they are driving home from work. Don't ask me why — I just work here. I've heard Brummies or Glaswegians with thicker accents than Courtney's host every damn show North to South, TV to radio, morning, noon, and night, and I can usually understand Courtney a hell of a lot better than I can them.

The smoking pit is full of Honey Bees after Clare's little 'Call to Arms' speech. There's a high ratio of nicotine pull to blow-release as everyone seems to be sucking the life out of their fags. Nobody dares say the word that's on everyone's mind: redundancies. Courtney, having switched to a pre-record out of bloody-mindedness, is coming down off her buzz:

"I'm so mad I could spit a ten-penny nail and chew a barbed wire fence!"

"I'm not sure how much more of this I can take," Courtney looks at me as if I've spoken the unspeakable.

"You can't leave before the rats, honey, that would just be damned bad manners. Wait till ya see the whites of their little ass holes runnin' away, and *then* think about it again." She has a point, whose tiny asses I couldn't help visualizing. "You might get a cushy pay out too."

I squish my fag out underfoot, mentally promising myself *again* that I was going to quit — for the sake of the baby — the who?! It still sounded strange to say that out loud; even out loud in my head.

"What say you we get ourselves a sandwich?" Courtney breaks into my nightmare with her usual precision timing. "C'mon happy," she pulls me with her, and her eyes inadvertently flit to my belly.

"So, what's the latest with Jack the Fucker?"

"I'm just back to avoiding his calls...."

"Well that can't go on forever. How 'bout I take a pop at him this time?"

"Nah, thanks. It's about time I grew up and faced him."

"Ya reckon y'ar grown up enough do ya? I'm still waitin' for my mammy ta fuckin' hurry up an powder my ass. I ain't growin' up anytime soon. Nah, ya gotta get on and just figure out for yarself whether y'ar havin' this baby or not...ya *have* figured that out haven't ya?" Her voice is hesitant, as if she is afraid of hearing the answer. I check her face for any signs I can work with; she is in mental lockdown over the morning's professional onslaught; I'm still studying her profile as we cross the road, hoping she's looking out for traffic, "What would you do?"

"Oh, hell, don't ask me, I've had so many abortions my womb looks like it got in a pile up with Edward Scissorhands."

"Do you ever wish you hadn't...you know...?"

"Sure, hell, I would have a brood fit to sing 'The Sound of Music' score by now...." We walk on, heads bowed in silence till we hit the front of the deli. How could I make my mind up about something as important as this when most days I couldn't even choose between two different sandwich fillings?

Louis always looks so bored when he sees me come in. I know this is his normal look, but he seems to anticipate my habitual uncertainty the minute he sees me at the door. He will disappear into the back room, and leave his wife, Rosa, to fill in my order. She has the same lacklustre attitude to my decision making but puts on a brave face. However, she always manages a smile when she sees Clive, our handsome studio engineer, but then I haven't seen a woman that didn't perk up when he entered a room. When he comes in ordering his double ham on rye with extra mustard you can literally see her bosom stand up at attention; he seems to make women flower whenever he is near: it's like spring arrives into any room that he enters; women break into blossom, breasts suddenly loosen their shirt buttons, cheeks become rosy, knees become weak as a baby giraffe, and he just smiles that warm, affable smile, and moves amongst the women like a harvester in August, reaping their emotions, sowing seeds of amorous intentions, even love. Sadly, all to no avail.

"What can I get you ladies?" Rosa is smiling. Clive must have been in earlier.

"A chicken mayonnaise on white, and a D'n'C..."

Chapter 17

To the Sounds of 'Praying for Time'
by George Michael

I'm not feeling it. The door looks back at me.

What if he invited *her?* — Smiling beside our poor excuse for a tree? Ready to be my new Mummy? Pouring salt on the wounds of the real missing person.

The wreath is blocking my shadow from falling into the front foyer through the thin, half-glass door; I have a bit more time to consider what I'm doing, standing in the simpering morning light, but not much: it's Christmas Day. I have a few hours before I need to be in the hot seat trawling out ready-made cheer. The Christmas spirit in the office has been about as heavy as a dead baby Jesus; nobody was in the mood to go to any particular effort or pull out any Christmas cheer. It was business as usual. Clare had bludgeoned the Christmas spirit just as surely as if she had cut off the stations gorgeous tits, and sexy ass with her negative feminine id.

Looking at my shoes inextricably for some hint of action, the door opens slowly:

"How long are you going to stand there looking at your shoes?" Oma's voice has a metallic, ground in quality that always makes me think of industrial machinery. Maybe it's the faint trace of the Germanic on her tongue. Moving to this country and raising my father here hasn't dampened that Teutonic patois. She stands holding the door, and looking at me with her steely, grey eyes.

"Merry Christmas Oma," I manage, passing over the threshold gingerly; looking right and left for an extra member who, to date, I have only seen hurtling under bed covers.

"There you are!" Dad wraps me in his arms; he looks like he has been at the spirits already: his eyes are merry in contrast to Oma's deadpan assault on the pupils. "Come and sit down! What can I get you? Oma has made her usual strudel for lunch, so we can eat anytime — what time do you have to leave?"

"Probably about two." Sitting across from Oma's industrial strength stare will wear me down quicker than usual under the existing circumstances; I'm liable to break under her search light glare if I stay too long. Images of blurting out my condition and whimpering with regret fall like enemy fire in my mind's eye.

"So..." Oma pats the sofa beside her, "Come and tell Oma what you have been up to..."

"Cup of tea or something stronger?" Dad calls from the kitchen. Seriously tempted by something stronger, I resist and call out for a cuppa. Oma hasn't moved an iota: her eyes are waiting for a response: they are glued on my face and seem to be performing a Nano exploration of my features:

"You look tired…" I try to avoid her piercing glare, and ferret around in my handbag for the presents I have brought. Their glittery wrapping temporarily assuages my panic, and I place them on the table in front of us hoping to shift her focus away from my face to the show of colour; like a crow entranced by glittery objects. Nothing gets past her, however, and she continues her assault:

"Your father tells me you've had some problems at work." Dad mercifully enters and puts my cup of tea down in front of me. I jump up, grabbing the presents:

"Shall I put these under the tree?"

"I'll do it — you spend some time with your Oma." Dad takes the glittery prizes from my clenched hands. Sitting back down, Oma is still waiting for a response.

"Um…it's under control, Oma. You know, just the usual work stuff. Nothing big…"

"Have you met any nice boys already?" The German knack for confusing 'yet' and 'already' is one of those little hiccups that Oma continues to make, despite years of conditioning. Her personal trademark, however, is finishing her own questions with an answer, which she now does without hesitation. I have lost track of the amount of times I have opened my mouth to respond to one of her insightful questions to find her cutting me off before I have even begun: "Although how could you possibly find a nice boy when you are working with all women? You might as well be working underground." She snorts to add emphasis.

"Yes, well..." She has positioned herself front and centre on the debating platform: tackling her is not an option; I have found ignoring her or changing the subject the only possible hope of escape. Thankfully Dad returns at this point, and the strains of Christmas cheer can be heard:

"That's better! Some seasonal music to get us in the mood." He is smiling, looking at us both with the kind of heart-warming glow that is reserved for this time of year. "So, Liebling, how have you been?"

"I was just telling Oma that I'm fine." I try to turn on my optimum watt smile.

"Good, good. No more nonsense from your horrible boss?"

"What is this? You didn't tell me about a horrible boss?" Oma looks hurt and disgruntled in equal measure; she is the only person I know who can carry both emotions in one facial expression. Perched on the end of the sofa I suddenly feel very nauseous and excuse myself. Hurtling down the small corridor that leads to the bathroom, I am struck with the bizarre realisation that I might not make it. The Christmas spirit was on my side, however, and I reach the bathroom sink just in time to relieve myself of breakfast.

When I return some minutes later, feeling worse and wobbly, Nana and Dad are waiting for me with their eyes.

"Are you OK?" Dad says. Oma scans my body head to toe for signs invisible to the average eye.

"Yes. Might be good to get a move on with the food though. I'm feeling quite peckish."

"Peckish?" Oma moves closer to me on the sofa and takes one of my hands in hers; they are warm and rough. She pats my hand. "You need more than a peck, you look like you need a good feeding, — and you're pale: what have you been doing to yourself? Why don't you come and see me sometimes? I could make you some food to take home and put in your fridge?"

"Thanks Oma. I'm OK really. I'm just a bit overworked at the moment that's all."

"At least you have a good job. It's not really a woman's job though, more like a man's job, but I suppose it pays well?"

"Yes, Oma, it pays well, and it *is* a woman's job. Anything can be a woman's job these days."

"This is the problem with *these* days: anything goes. Nobody knows anything or where they should be or who they should be because anything goes — *these* days." She adds for effect. Dad gets up, sensing a long discussion, or one of Oma's entrenched view-points.

"I'll put the strudel in to warm up shall I Mum?"

"Oh Lord, NO!" Oma lets go of my hand and gets up from the sofa. "I will do it: you will just mess it up. I have to put the vegetables on first." She hobbles off rolling from hip to hip. Dad takes her place, leaning back into the sofa. He turns on the TV and puts out his arm: I don't need any cajoling. 'It's a Wonderful Life' is half way through. Wordlessly we curl up to watch the last half.

We are immersed in the scene where George runs to the bridge to ask for his life back when the doorbell goes. Dad gets up and leaves me with his warm patch. I hear voices in the hallway and then *she* breaks the surface of my worldview.

The look on my face must have said so much more than the fact that I did not get up from the sofa, or wish her Merry Christmas as she did, weighted down with presents. She surreptitiously handed them to Dad who took them to the tree leaving us alone in the living room with George pleading for his old life.

Oma comes in wiping her hands on a tea towel, and Dad doesn't seem to need to introduce them. Oma wishes Elaine, which it turns out is her name, a Merry Christmas, and then disappears back into the kitchen. I'm tempted to follow her but felt stuck between a rock and a new, hard place.

"We didn't exactly meet under the best circumstances..." she's trying to make a joke, inching closer to the sofa: testing the water with words, and sensing the shackles where my shoulders should be. Dad lets her sit where he had been and takes the chair opposite. All the warmth evaporates from his patch of sofa as she positions herself a polite distance from me: "I hope you don't mind me joining you for your Christmas lunch?" I look at my Dad as if for the answers I feel sure should be coming or should have come before she entered the room and our lives and my Christmas (of which there was only a couple more hours; now ruined by her simpering smile). She seems to be wearing a kagool which she hands to my dad in one smooth operation, before sitting back into the sofa, in what could be a dance they have practised for eons in some mythical paradise of their own making; where Pan and faun display all the innocence of allegorical figures, but here none of the charm.

She's wearing a paisley skirt, and a blouse that must have rubbed shoulders at Woodstock with legends of some forgotten summertime. This is accented with chunky beads that should not have gone anywhere near this ensemble. Worse still was the fact that her long, wavy hair is trying to live side by side with a pair of feather earrings. She looks younger than my Dad should have been dating, and yet old enough to know better than to mix cheese cloth with feathers.

"Aren't you going to say 'hello'?" Dad is beginning to get upset, and anger is never far behind this emotion where he is concerned. I decide to do the right thing:

"Nice to meet you, uh — ," she comes to my aid:

"Elaine."

"Elaine." That painful moment over I am tensing myself for the remaining two hours-worth. Mercifully Oma breaks the silence:

"Lunch is served!"

I should have noticed the extra place setting. Dad pulls out a chair for *her* next to his at the head of the table. I am always on his other side, and happy to be his right-hand girl but today it just feels like we are two balls to his cock. Oma at the other end of the table smiles and performs grace: we all bow our heads. I look up through veiled lashes to peak at *Elaine*. She is playing it straight; head primly bent, and hands folded.

"So Merry Christmas one and all!" Dad smiles at his brood of women, and pulls the stopper out of a bottle of red: "Who would like some wine?"

"Oh, yes please," Elaine smiles at him and they hold the look longer than necessary. He fills her glass and then turns to me: "Cass?"

"No thanks." Oma raises her eyebrows one at a time; she can do that: I've never known anyone who could do that, but she can.

"No wine for you? My goodness child, what *is* wrong with you? You're not pregnant, are you?" She does a little laugh that does not spread around the table, but which means that everyone else has time to look at me. I'm not comfortable with Elaine being privy to such familial conversation and would have denied the very breath in my body if it meant keeping her out of my inner sanctum.

"Don't be silly, Oma." This brazen lie lights a little fire in my lacklustre loins, and I feel that old burning desire to build a hornet's nest under all and sundry. I will not go down without a fight. This is *my* home. *She* cannot saunter in here and take over with her cheese cloth smile, and bad perm.

Dad is looking less than enthusiastic with the conversation, and senses that tone in my voice which indicates a shift of intention. His eyebrows arch in my direction: he has learned some of this from Oma but is still no match for her individualistic magic trick.

"I hear you work at a women's radio station?" Elaine is gingerly cutting into the strudel; she has obviously never had this at Christmas, and nobody has explained what it is to her.

"Yes." I offer, tucking into mine.

"Cass has the drive-time slot which is the best slot at the radio station," Dad jumps in, sensing I am going to be difficult.

"Wow, that really is something." *Something?* Yes, it is something; you might like to clarify that with a modifier?

"Mmmm," I rejoinder.

"Tell her about your funny lady station," offers Oma.

"You make it sound like a tampon ad, Oma."

"I'm just trying to help: you are not explaining this thing," she quips between mouthfuls of strudel. "How is it?" She asks after the food.

"Lovely." Dad makes yummy noises as his mouth is full. Oma turns her steely gaze on Elaine who had better come up with something positive pronto or she will ruin any hopes she has of being a part of this family.

"Delicious," she manages, trying to smile through the crusty mouthful she has just inserted.

"So how did you lovebirds meet?" It's my turn to direct the questions; back in control I feel the couple squirm. Even

Oma looks curious. When was she made privy to this circus of doom I wonder?

"Well—," Elaine starts, but bumps into Dad starting his own explanation, and they both apologise and dance around each other with their little apologies until Dad takes the reins:

"I was brought in to organise the company's data systems where Elaine works…" They smile at each other, remembering.

"I thought it was through the small ads?" Oma looks confused.

"No, Mama, it's an ads firm that Elaine works for."

"Oh," Oma goes back to her strudel.

"Which ad firm?" I ask sensing blood.

"It's just a little ad agency that deals with council advertising and government incentives." Elaine tries to downsize her pitch.

"So, like, you work for the government?"

"We're linked to their services, but we outsource a lot of our regional content."

"So, you work within the political brief?"

"I suppose you could say that."

"Well, I guess you could." Oma and Dad are watching this with the kind of knowing exchange of eyebrows that indicates their little girl is about to chew on this newcomer's leg if they don't intervene:

"Elaine is a secretary for one of the commissioners, so her involvement has no direct political link," Dad puts down his fork and fixes me with one of his palliative stares.

"Would anyone like some more vegetables?" Oma holds up the bowl full of vegetables ready to throw them into the ring to loosen up the debate.

"Yes, thanks Oma," ferreting around in the vegetable bowl that she is holding out to me I can feel the Christmas spirit hyperventilate.

"Wait till you see what we have for dessert," Oma offers ominously. I pass the vegetables to Dad who offers them to Elaine who politely declines.

"Well I think it's ever so nice to have an extra guest at our Christmas feast," Dad looks around the table encouragingly, "It's been just the three of us for so long; it's nice to have a fresh face." He smiles, and Oma snorts into her strudel.

"How long has it been just the three of you?" Elaine asks innocently.

"You mean since Mum walked out?" I muse theatrically. "Let me think...Dad? What would you say? Since I was about three?" Dad looks uncomfortable with the direct time line. Strange as he has always been a stickler for a good time line.

"Your mother was never one for nappies," Oma adds, scraping the last of her strudel against the side of the plate; almost as clean as before it was food laden. This is an unusual comment from Oma who has rarely commented on Mum, or is it just that we have so rarely spoken of her? I am caught up in this revelation when it is rudely bludgeoned by Elaine's next remark:

"We have a woman at work who gave her child up for adoption." She looks clearly unabashed at throwing such a bombshell into the ring. "It was only a year old, but she admitted, and I admire her for her honesty that it just wasn't for her— mothering, that is." Dad smiles at her; rubber stamping her comment.

"You seem to be assuming that my mother, who you never met, simply decided that motherhood was not her cup of tea?" My tone leaves nothing to debate. Elaine stammers and looks to Oma and Dad for support, but finding none, attempts to cover her tracks:

"I'm not saying this is what your mother felt. Obviously, I didn't know her — "

"Obviously." I support her.

"I'm just saying that mothers don't always stay in the lives of their children for one reason or another."

"We haven't missed her," Oma ads with her inimitable *gemütlichkeit:* in German used to convey the idea of warmth and good cheer, but here used ironically.

"Speak for yourself." Oma looks surprised that I have not agreed with her, or furthermore, allowed her to drop her usual candour without comment; her lack of understanding has never impaled me so much as it has at this moment; it was always 'Just Oma being Oma', but here, in this fortress of doom, set around with plates, and the formality of cheer, her lack of sympathy for the empty chair at this table seems biblical.

"I'm sorry you just never seemed to comment on her absence as a child, or to ask after her." Oma seems struck by a moment's understanding. Why does it feel like this is the first time we have ever discussed Mum's absence?

"Well, maybe..." I'm stammering for some explanation in what suddenly feels like an unholy cavalcade of truth hailing down on us. "...maybe I was just too traumatised...or didn't feel I could talk about it...?"

"Don't be ridiculous. Your father and I were always there for you. You had a perfect childhood —," *and* she's back.

"I did *not* have a perfect childhood — I did not have a mother!" Shaken by my own words, I feel the tears puncture at their posts; Dad wades in sensing the unravelling is getting out of hand:

"Now Cass, come on, it can't have been all that bad?" But chooses his words unwisely.

"What do you know? I've never heard any of us talk about mum directly — until today. We've just talked around her absence as if she was a ghost that we're too afraid even to speak of —"

"I'm not afraid." Oma, ever the hard nut.

"And then you go bringing in this..." my words are tumbling over each other in my mouth, " — stranger — without so much as a discussion, on Christmas, and expect me to be all happy families for you?!" They are all sitting open-mouthed, even Oma.

"This is bullshit," I stand up, "I'm out of here."

"Cass! Wait a fucking minute! How dare you speak like that to Elaine, *or* to me?" Dad is angry now: never a good setting for him. You can get him to a slow boil, but don't ever inch that thermometer over the red line: it's not pretty.

"I can say whatever I want!" I glare at him. "I'm an adult — I can do what I want."

"You're acting like a fucking child. I have a right mind to take you over my knee."

"I'd like to see you try!" I push my chair back and leave the room. Dad catches up with me in the hallway and grabs my arm roughly.

"I want you to come back and apologise!"

"Let go of my arm!"

"Not until you come and apologise!"

"I'm *not* apologising. I'm *leaving!*" I yank my arm away and head for my coat and bag by the door. Dad grabs me again, firmer this time, and his eyes are bulging.

"How dare you treat me like this? You are just a spoiled little brat. What the fuck makes you think you can act like this in front of me, your family, and our guest?"

"This isn't a family. It's a fucking hole where a family should be." That's when he slaps me across the face. He seems just as surprise by his action as I am; in the hollow of our surprise, I open the door and leave.

Chapter 18

To the Sounds of 'Groove is in the Heart' by Deee-Lite

"So..." Hel has her self-important hat on, and sits down with particular gravitas, causing her breasts to jump, "...how shall we improve our show?"

"How do you improve the unimprovable?" She gives me a serious, no messing around look.

"Why don't we start by looking at our contributors, eh?"

"OK," I'm bored already; I hate being talked down to by a twelve-year old; somebody who had spent a year travelling after secondary school, came here for an internship, and ended up producing the drive time show: go figure.

"Now, Ruth is obviously brilliant at her job as a Theatre Critic..."

"Yeah, but she hates me, and thinks I know nothing about theatre."

"Yes, well, you're right — she does, and you don't — but the show must go on. You work best with her when you just relax and let her do the work. *She* is telling *you* all you need to know. You don't need to sound like you know anything about theatre — most people don't — she's here to educate us — and you!"

"OK, OK," my grumpiness expanding like a seeping tide. I've done my show; I just want to go home. Pye would be waiting with his own grumpy face on; the neck brace had caused his mood to deteriorate over the last few weeks. It was going to be another evening of his sorry face, and mine locked together in a small apartment on Christmas Eve. Come to think of it, can't imagine why I'm in a rush to get home?

"Why don't we think about having Ruth do a competition? You know, make it more interesting by imbedding in her interview a clue that could help you win tickets to see one of the shows?"

"We can't afford to buy tickets to give away." I felt sure Clare would balk at any pay out.

"We could send her to see things where they would give us tickets if we mentioned it?"

"Like Punch and Judy in the park?"

"No, silly — real theatre."

"Try it: if you can find anyone willing to give you a free ticket for a mention then go for it, but you're making a rod for your own back."

"Well, it's worth a try," she says huffily.

"Sure, OK. What's next?"

"Well, we've got our film reviewer, Jeremy…"

"Yes…" I was waiting for her next brainstorm.

"He's not very…"

"Good?"

"Well, I wouldn't say that, but…"

"It's OK — say it — he sucks as a film reviewer. I doubt if he watches the films. I think he just reads other people's reviews. He also has zero knowledge of mainstream and cult cinema. He's a total dork, frankly. No personality. Plus, he's a bloke. We should have a female! Why don't we find someone fresh and interesting?"

"Yeah, but he does it for free — who'll we find?" I pick up a pencil and start chewing on it: this is when Hel realizes I would rather eat lead than engage with her.

"OK, I'll just put that we would like a new film critic with more *oomph.*"

"Yes, that'll do." The ceiling tiles find their moment: when did that dark patch emerge?

Courtney sidles up at this point, following my gaze to the ceiling: "How's the remake goin'?"

"Fine if you like leftovers." Hel gives us a dirty look.

"Well, I'm off. See y'all tomorrow," Courtney turns to go, but not without putting a perfectly wrapped present on my desk. "Merry Fucking Christmas."

"Wait a minute —," confused by the appearance of this charming bombshell, and embarrassed because I'd left her present at home, "where are you going? What about your own make-over?"

"Ah, hell, I'll write somethin' crap up tonight while I'm drinkin' some Jack, put a spin on it, and hand it in to ma producer tomorra."

"That's not fair. Why can't I write some crap?" I turn accusingly to Hel.

"We are going to do this thing properly young lady!" She puts her best schoolmarm head on.

"Well good luck with that — see ya!" I watch incredulously as Court saunters out of the office, every bone in my body an envious one.

"What about Christmas?" I yell after her.

"What *about* Christmas?" She yells back; obviously unimpressed by the whole shebang. She disappears beyond the dividing line between earthly hell and illusory freedom.

"That's not fair!"

"You are drive time, honey — you have to make that extra effort, or you won't be drive time, and Radio Honey will be Radio Nothing!"

"OK already — what's next?" I was still looking at the door that Courtney sashayed out of, hoping she'd come back and save me.

"Well, then we have your regular feature with our horoscope lady…"

"Ugh — that witch! She's evil!"

"She is a bit strange, granted."

"Hel, that woman would voodoo you as soon as look at you! I'm sure she's put a hex on the station. Remember when she said she would get paranormal on our arses if we didn't pay her expenses?"

"Yes…"

"You did pay her expenses, right?"

"Well, it's on my desk…"

"Pay her goddamned expenses — we don't need any more bad blood around here!"

"OK, OK, but what do you think we should do, if anything, about our horoscope spot?"

"Well, it's a joke isn't it?"

"Why?" Looking hurt.

"Because she just comes in, reels of a list of signs, and goes out again."

"Well, what would you have her do? — It's about horoscopes?"

"Well, maybe we could combine it with Tarot or I-Ching or Runes or I don't know what —maybe each week it could be a different spiritual art?" Hel smiles. "Or even do it as a pre-record so that I don't have to talk to them; it just runs through the signs or the runes or whatever."

"I like it, I like it," she is noting things down on her little pad, the one she always keeps by her side. She has about ten in her bottom drawer which she nicked from the supply cabinet because she likes the size of them and wants to keep things uniform. Every time she turns over a new page she does it with a secretarial poise: all pushed out boobs, straight back, and self-importance; she could do with some bifocals, and a tight skirt to finish it off. "Great!' She finishes writing, and turns to me, "What else?"

The phone rings. Hel picks it up:

"Drive-time. Yes. One moment I'll see if I can find her." She puts her hand over the phone: "It's your dad."

"No!" My arms hurtling around my face and head she gets the message.

"I'm sorry she seems to have left for the day." Her tawny little head leans into the receiver as she pretends to listen intently, "I certainly will. Thank you. Goodbye." Replacing the phone, she looks at me: "He says to tell you he called."

"Thank you." Trying to push the afternoon out of my mind. "Your turn. What's next?"

"Well, there's live music — we have a lot of that in studio."

"Yeah, and it's a pain in the arse hooking it all up."

"A necessary evil."

"Yes, OK" the little minx was not going to let me off easy today; on the one day when I could have done with a break, or a bottle of wine drip fed, "What about if we get bands in who usually play loud aggressive stuff to play pretty, acoustic stuff, and bands that play pretty, acoustic stuff to play loud rock?" I smile, pleased with my own idea.

"Um, I'm not sure, that sounds a little dangerous…"

"Why?"

"Well, it might be too loud."

"We won't go over the top — it'll be soft rock."

"Tell me more…"

"Um, let me think," I get up out of my chair and start to pace the room, "we could call it Lullaby Rock Slot?"

"Mmmm — not sure." Hel is adopting the kind of thinking pose she must have seen in movies where executives harness the full power of a suit and tie. She looks Heavenwards as if for saints or certainty.

"What about Acoustic Bands Rock?"

"Getting warmer." Her pencil bounces gently off her chin which is ceiling angled.

"How 'bout ..." I stop and point at her: " — you think of an idea?!"

"OK, OK," she sits back in her chair, and looks around the room for inspiration. After what seems an eternity, I wade back in:

"What about 'Rock's Acoustic Sister'?"

"Let's just use 'Acoustic Bands Rock.'"

"I like 'Rock's Acoustic Sister' — it has that female tone, and it's unusual..." Hel was ignoring me. Jezebel walks by, her coat on and her bag over her shoulder.

"Are you leaving too?" She stops and smiles:

"Yes, I've got to get to my mum's before they start the big Christmas meal. They're all waiting for me." I imagine a room full of warmth and laughter; colourful wrapping paper littering the ground, jaunty paper hats...

"Have fun," I manage.

"Thanks. You too," and then she adds, as if an afterthought: "Merry Christmas."

"You too." We chorus.

"OK, so that's live acts. What about your guests?" Hel leaves no moment to the sanctity of space.

"Well, they're a pain in the arse — they just sit there waiting to plug their latest thing and get mad if you don't plug it throughout the whole interview."

"Yeah, but they have a right to want that up front — that's why they come on the show. The last person we had on you only mentioned their book at the top of the interview and didn't mention it again. You just got into some big, transcendental chat, and ran out of time, and straight into news."

"We were having a great chat — it was good radio."

"It was boring: two people patting each other on the back, sharing the same information."

"I thought it was interesting."

"*You* were talking — you love the sound of your own voice! It doesn't occur to you that you could be boring everyone else!"

"Wow! Thanks for your support. Anything else you'd like to unload?" Hel looks unsure for a moment, but then blurts out:

"You have bad breath!"

"What!"

"Yeah — you can't expect to share a small space with your guests, closed in that booth, and not brush your teeth in the morning!"

"I *do* brush my teeth!"

"Then get a mouth wash!"

"I don't believe we are having this conversation!" Hel keeps quiet.

"Has anyone else complained of this?"

"Just Ruth and Jeremy..."

"*Just* Ruth and Jeremy!"

"Yeah..." Hel's looking a bit scared.

"Ok — great! *Now* you tell me! I've spent months breathing halitosis on my guests and *now* you tell me?!"

"Sorry," she whispers sheepishly.

"Oh, this is just great...never mind the fucking show. The presenter is killing her guests with her rancid breath! Never mind the fucking ratings, I'm poisoning our contributors!"

"Now calm down, I just thought I would mention it whilst we were on the subject."

"We were *not* on the subject! We were talking about the show, not my personal hygiene!"

"Well, when is a good time to bring up personal hygiene?!"

"When people first start complaining about it!"

"OK, OK, I'm sorry. I'll mention it if it happens again."

"Well, it won't happen again will it — I'm gonna get the strongest mouth wash known to man! And if that doesn't work, I'll jock the show through a surgical mask!"

"Now, now, don't get all crazy about it. It's just a little problem..."

"A *little* problem?" I'm now squinting from the deafening octaves of my own voice." Sounds like a very *big* problem if everyone is complaining about it doesn't it?"

"Well, yes, it might sound like it, but really — it's not..." Hel's tiny forehead is wrinkling.

The phone rings again. Hel, relieved, picks it up:

"Hello, drive time," Hel looks at me nervously over the mouth piece, "No, I'm sorry she's not here like I said..." I grab the phone away from Hel:

"I do *not* want to talk to you! Get it!? Stop hounding me - just fucking leave me alone and go and shack up with the ad lady!" I listen to the voice at the other end of the line which is quite obviously *not* my dad. "Oh, I'm so sorry. I thought you were somebody else. Bye." I hang the phone up as if it were a cockroach, and physically recoil from the desk. Hel gives me that look:

"Well that's another listener we can say goodbye to."

"Everything alright?" It's Clare and she is deafeningly close. My heart jumps two floors, and then leaps off the building:

"Yes, Clare," I try to smile but it probably looks more like a grimace.

"Well, I'm going home now too." She looks from one of us to the other; confused but ill equipped to understand the situation and decides that the seasonal agenda can come first this once: "Well, Merry Christmas," she says, wandering harmlessly off.

"Merry Christmas," we both mumble after her.

"Oh, God…I don't believe this…" Sitting back in my chair with my bad breath and bad attitude it occurs to me that *I* am the problem.

Hel makes a tentative in road back onto the task at hand:

"Shall we, um…"

"No, I'm not sure I want to discuss the bloody show." I cup my hands in front of my mouth and breathe.

"I can't smell anything."

"Look, it's probably just them…I haven't noticed anything…much."

"What do you mean 'much'?"

"Well, nothing, I um'…"

"Look you can tell me — does my breath stink? I would rather know. Be honest." I try to sound calm, to coax out the truth: "C'mon. I won't be angry…I really won't"

"Well, it does a little bit…"

"Fucking great!" I fume.

"You said you wouldn't be angry!"

"Me and my bad breath lied! I mean if I've got bad breath being a liar isn't far off is it? They go hand in hand — bad breath — liar: they both emanate from my great big, ugly plug hole!" In fact liars, hence politicians are more likely to have bad breath according to the British Dental Association as apparently talking a lot makes your mouth dry out which in turn means that the saliva, which normally act as an on-site mouth wash, dries out leaving no opportunity to carry away the resulting bacteria; plus the movement of the tongue with all that yabbering wafts the smelly gases out into an unsuspecting audience. I blame my job for my halitosis.

I'm in good company: William Shakespeare, the bard himself, is purported to have suffered with bad breath as he made many a comment about it, and the 16th century was not known for its dental hygiene or orthodontists.

"Cass, calm down!" I was a poster ad for the un-calm.

"I will not — I'm going home…" I stand up: "Via a pharmacy…"

"Before you go..." Hel reaches into her drawer and pulls out a wrapped present. Now I feel not only smelly but stupid. I stammer:

"Hel...that's very kind...I'm afraid I don't...have anything for you — here..."

"That's OK." She smiles sweetly which unloads the full weight of my selfishness like garbage out on my front door, which, when I get to it, has the added 'bonus' of Jack sitting on it; complete with water dripping off his flat cap: looking like some sorry, bedraggled cat somebody has left out in the rain. The only light is the one he is standing in; switched on automatically by his presence in the firing line of electronic activation. Damn him. Why did he have to find the one area of haloed luminescence and go and stand in it? He's better than an actor at finding the light and hogging it. He looks sad, charming, and handsome all rolled up in one homogenous man packet; whimsical notions of our love rise like steam off a heat starved pavement.

"Merry Christmas," he tries. My arms loaded down with toiletries, I try to open the door without inviting him in. He holds the door open once the key does the work, and despite the evils I'm giving him, lets himself in.

"I'm not letting you up, Jack. What do you want?"

"I just want to talk." He looks calm, but I've never trusted that starter for ten. I know how quickly calm turns to choppy waters.

"We can't just pretend this isn't happening." He tries to take my bag of shopping, but I pull it away.

"I'm not pretending. I just don't agree with you, Jack."

"Cass," there it is: the irritable Jack; the one who is always sitting behind the smile, "you have to take my feelings into account. This is half mine!"

"What makes that half so important that you would ask me to kill for it?" He looks at me, his face burning: he's dying to say something.

"Cass," he's trying to stay calm, but his voice is loud at the best of times, "you have to see that this is unfair!" The door to the ground floor flat opens, and Steve pops his head out:

"Everything all right, Cass?" My knight in shining armour, he gives Jack the kind of look that lets him know he will have none of his crap. I look at Jack who turns and leaves slamming the door.

"Thanks Steve." Steve is wearing his pyjamas: he is often wearing his pyjamas. I don't really know what Steve does, but he is kind, and quiet, and doesn't make a mess. If he *is* a serial killer, he keeps it on the down low, and I have no ruck with him.

"No problem, love: happy to help." As he closes the door he adds, "Merry Christmas."

Chapter 19

To the Sounds of 'Walking in my Shoes'
by Depeche Mode

Just when you think you have mastered one cause of ill health another rears its ugly head: the single life, we are told, is bad for you. This from a new survey by a Professor Andrew Oswald who looked into the lifestyles of 10,000 adults across Britain over a ten-year period and found that being single is just as dangerous to men and women's lifespan as smoking.

Not only that, but the unhealthy effects of the single life seem to really kick in after 30. Our helpful researchers cannot tell us exactly why this is the case, but point to things like increased sociability, drinking, staying out late, eating more sporadically; plus, the lack of a lifelong confidant at your side to share the ins and outs with, literally and figuratively.

Add to this the possible stress of divorce, conflict with the x, the pressure of dating, the worry of that first wrinkle...all adds to the scale bending unhealthiness. The researchers found that men who had never married or who were separated or divorced at the start of the research were 10 percent more likely to die during the following eight years. Women who were single, separated or divorced at the start of the study had a 4.8 percent risk of dying. Proving that men have a more adverse effect on women's health than vice-versa.

This compares to the five percent extra risk of dying faced by smokers. I stub my cigarette out wondering if nicotine contributes to bad breath. Surely nicotine would mask it? — Burn up some of the less pleasing odours?

"Do I have bad breath?" Cage is trying to feed a reluctant Pye, who is still pushing his food bowl around the room with his head gear rather than managing to eat it.

"No! Why?"

"Hel said I had bad breath, and that other people had commented on it..." Cage picks Pye up and puts him in his lap; sitting cross-legged on the floor which is not easy with his foot in a cast.

"That's just plain nasty!" Cage spoons out some cat food from the can. Juggling the cat in one arm, and the spoon in the other.

"Well that's what she said!"

"She's got issues...damn this cat!" Pye's conical head bumps against his chest.

"He's depressed," I offer, " — I know how he feels."

"At least you aren't wearing an ugly neck brace."

"I might as well be — Apparently, I'm carrying around an ugly case of halitosis."

"That's just bull shit, and you know it." Pye is ignoring his best efforts.

"I don't. I licked my wrist, and it smelled…bad."

"What you smellin' yar wrist for?" Pye is walking away.

"It was in this article about halitosis — it said if you are in any doubt lick your wrist, wait five seconds for the saliva to dry, and then smell it."

"Gross. You read some weird shit." He gets up off the floor and throws himself onto the sofa. "If you ask me you just need to stop reading crap."

"You're probably right." Sitting together on the sofa it feels cosy with the rain outside. Cage has brought round the daily papers, and they sprawl beside us on the sofa. I want to ask him about Courtney but resist the temptation. It doesn't feel right to go nosing about in their business; although this hasn't stopped me in the past. Am I growing the beginnings of a conscience?

"So, what's new pussycat?" Moving some of the newspapers on to the table in front of the sofa the space between us dwindles. The ad sheets slip out of one of the papers and fall to the floor. Pye, who usually welcomes any opportunity to attack a moving object, walks past, and throws himself down on the floor by our feet like a cumbersome dog.

Cage starts to bend down, and pick up the ads, but I wave him away.

"Leave it — the maid will clear it up." We smile at the thought of my imaginary maid, and for a moment I am lost in the imaginary scenario. Cage leans back, still trying to get his cast comfortable. This easy camaraderie serves us both, but I know this is not enough for him. To me we are brother and sister; to him we are kissing cousins.

"So, how's the x girlfriend?"

"Still pregnant."

"Does she want you to be there for her?"

"Nah, she can cope. I don't see 'er much anymore." He thinks about it some more. "I don't think she wants me around. I think she's got another fella lined up to take the heat. Probably just as well. I don't love her."

"That's a shame." I mean it. There seems to be one too many kids getting made by people who don't care for each other. I think of Jack standing on my doorstep in the rain. The rain slinks down the windows; doing its best sexy dance, but there is nobody home. I feel about as sexy as a mongoose. A mongoose with halitosis.

"Ya know it's ok…she's a crazy bitch…"

"Well, you sure pick 'em…"

"Yeah, I sure do." He smiles, and looks at me for a moment, then we both look back at Pye; eyes closed, his fur moving up and down in rhythmic purring. Our errant child. Another pairing that went south. I'm about to spoil my five minute's worth of honourable consciousness by asking him about Courtney, when he butts in:

"So, what about you and Tony?"

"Nothing to tell." Cage absent mindedly reaches a finger down inside his cast to scratch. Suddenly the scene hits me: "You're a pair!"

"What d'ya mean?" Cage looks genuinely perplexed.

"You and Pye — both of you in your cast and head gear — what a pair!" Cage laughs. "Father and son!"

"Yeah, I guess ya could say that..." The rain is stopping, leaving a break of blue in the sky. The last droplets slide down the tall windows, a watery Morse code. There is peace in this silence. Just wish I could find it.

"What about the baby?" I don't want to look at Cage; the sky seems a better place to direct my attention when thinking about the baby.

"It's not a baby; it may never be a baby; it's just a foetus that nobody seems to want..."

"If *you* want it that's all 'dat matters..."

"I know, but I can't figure out if I want it..."

"Well, fair enough…" Now he's looking out at the rain and sky. Pye looks up at us all of a sudden and lets out a meow. Getting up, he pads back over to his food. We can hear the bowl scraping as it travels across the floor in front of his head gear.

I get up off the sofa, and go to his rescue, but he just gets irritated with me as I hold up the bowl under his mouth. We've been over this ground before; neither of us is buying into it.

"Put it down," counsels Cage from the sofa. I put the bowl down. "He'll get the hang of it." Pulling Pye's head gear down below the bowl line, he manages to get his head level with his food, but the food is too far into the centre of the plate for him to reach it; the head collar is keeping him at a distance. I push the food closer with my fingers. Pye licks them, and I bring them down to the food. Finally, he's eating.

"Eureka!" I go to the sink to wash my hands of cat food and throw myself back down on the sofa. We both watch Pye eat. The quiet doesn't feel awkward: we fit into it with our mismanaged lives, and poor judgements. Cage reaches out an arm, and it falls on my shoulder, brushing my collar bone; I twitch involuntarily.

"Y'ar not alone you know." My smile is more of a voluntary appeasement:

"I know." His hand moves up to my cheek and strokes it gently. My heart aches at the touch.

"You don't deserve this shit." My smile is real this time. He leans in, despite his cemented leg, and kisses me. He stops and looks at me.

"You don't have bad breath." I smile some more; wanting more. He plants his whole body on top of mine and the rest of the newspapers are brushed to the floor.

"I've found the most amazing psychic astrologer!" Hel's eyes are brimming with excitement.

"What's a psychic astrologer?" Hel hadn't expected me to ask, and her face displays all the confusion of the unprepared.

"It's, um, someone who does astrology, but is also psychic…"

"So how exactly does she do a reading? How would she read for everyone all at once?" Hel now looks truly stumped. I come to her rescue:

"It won't work — we need it to be general, not specific. Try to find somebody who can do something that will apply to a wider audience, or we'll be tied to one on one phone ins." I go back to what I was doing: trying to write my show with only half an hour to go.

A sudden breeze makes me pull my cardigan tighter around my chest with one hand, the other continues to finger type.

"How's it going?" That cold breeze is Clare.

"Oh!" I look around surprised.

"Great!" Chirps Hel, standing over me, looking for all intents and purposes to be overseeing this sinking ship. The rats keep their heads down all around us; sensing the mother ships great wave as she comes in to check the sails and kick the peg-legged amongst us.

"Good, then I'll see you both after your show to discuss the changes." And she walks on. Hel and I look at each other.

"Have you printed up the changes?" I ask accusingly.

"I'm still doing them!"

"Well you better finish them while I'm on air..."

"That's what I was going to do..." Hel's voice has that whiny overtone that ratchets like bicycle gears.

"What about somebody who does the I-Ching? That's really interesting — or Runes?"

"Runes?" Her little gopher face pinches inwards.

"Some old, Celtic thing — you throw stones and they tell you your fortune..."

"What's the I thing?"

"I-Ching," I correct. "It's a Chinese method of divination. You throw coins and the combinations spell out different predictions that reveal your destiny." Hel's eyes widen.

"Ok...I'll see what I can dig up..." She sounds uncertain.

"It could just be a one-off interview; an item in itself. But we still need a regular with a bit more umph — I really don't like that astrology witch..." I turned to see her come through the office door, "speak of the devil." Hel jumps to my rescue:

"Ah! Agatha! Have you come for your expenses?" The shrill nature of Hel's voice gives her away. Agatha keeps moving towards me, and I begin to recoil. She stops at the last moment, and turns to face Hel, like a tornado that spins in place:

"Yes. I was passing and thought I would drop in to remind you. You have them do you?"

"Um, yes, I have the receipts, but I need clearance from the boss."

"I can wait." Agatha looks for somewhere to sit.

"It will take longer than a few moments." Hel tries to smile. Agatha looks unimpressed.

"Well, how long will it take?" Trying to look uninvolved, I put my head down over my work, but was still privy to the unfortunate exchange. "Well, once my boss has OK'd it, it must go down to accounts, and then, well then it depends on what part of the month we're in, but usually it will take four weeks." Hel looks up to gauge Agatha's expression, her eyebrows cowed into submission. Agatha inhales to wind up like an air raid horn:

"Well, that's disgraceful! I can't believe I have already waited a month! Have the receipts even been OK'd by the boss?"

"Everything OK here?" That chill wind was back. Hel spins in her tiny shoes to face her; a small pebble between two boulders of simmering rock.

"Oh, Clare! Yes! Um, just sorting something out with one of our contributors..."

"Are you the boss here?" Agatha is not afraid to turn her stony face to Clare's. Clare seems to respect the lack of fear, and even smiles; a rare and disturbing occurrence; her mouth wasn't made for smiling; she lacks the contours of cheek and jowl; her face simply folds like a sheet, in two.

"I am. How can I help?" The firm tone creates a false assurity for those of us who have clung to that rock and been tossed against the crag. Agatha reels off her grievances, and

Clare, listening, paying particular attention to her eyes, and mouth, absent-mindedly rubs her inner thigh with her trusty biro.

"I will make sure it is dealt with straight away. Can I take your address to send it to? I will deal with it personally." Hel and I look at each other and raise our eyebrows in unison. Agatha, looking pleased, leans over the desk to take a piece of paper and pencil. Hel hurries to assist her whilst I try to look busy, and not part of this particular disaster. Agatha turns back to Clare, the white strip of paper a pristine tongue of understanding between them.

"Thank you. I appreciate your help in this matter." I'm not sure which of them has spoken; my back to the unfortunate scenario, they seem to have blended into one and the same person.

"It's not a problem. I'm sorry for the delay." I turn to see Clare smile as Agatha bids her goodbye. Clare watches her go, and turns to Hel:

"In future you make sure all receipts go in to accounts at the end of each week — without fail —do you understand?"

"Yes." Hel looks smaller than usual.

"If they are not being paid as contributors the least you can do is make sure their expenses are met on time."

"Yes, Clare. Sorry." Clare walks away, her hand rising to push her fingers through her hair. I snigger quietly to myself, but not quietly enough.

"Oh, shut up!"

"It's so nice not to be the one being told off for once!"

"Your time will come!"

"Oh, I know that — believe me — I know that!"

Chapter 20

To the Sounds of 'Mama Said Knock You Out' by LL Cool J

The courtyard is dark compared to the street. Spears of light fall in through the top of the buildings that huddle together against the grey sky: a Tupperware cover to this landscape of grey on grey: building on building, person on person, next to person, bumping into person. Just breathe.

Between finger and thumb a miraculous origami of paper comes together in a circle of calm; I lick and seal it, light and inhale it. Relaxation lifts up into the space between the buildings, kisses the grey, disappears; forms new waves of cloud, and lifts again. When the orange glow has burned down to cardboard, I let it fall to the ground, and my heel deals the last blow.

Looking furtively from side to side, I leave the safety of the courtyard, and join the street again. Swiftly now, and looking down at my watch, with minutes to spare, a left, and another left, and then a right.

Jeff nods as I pass the foyer and take the hallway almost at a run. I push open the heavy door, and Hel looks up:

"I thought I would have to start the bloody show for you!"

"I'm here aren't I?" I grab the headphones out of her hands, look up at the clock, steady my hands on the soft, plastic hub of the console, and lift up the fader as the second hand gently clicks around the face.

There had to be a way to silence this incessant music in my head. This soundtrack to our lives; this emotive dance of light and dark. I could still feel the electricity from last night coursing through my body; it felt good: then bad. How could I do this to my best friend? I knew she liked Cage; her eyes were on stalks every time she saw him. But I needed my fix; my fix of attention, and Cage was just in the wrong place at the right time.

"So, what have you got for me?" Clare sits back in her chair. Hel and I perch ourselves precariously on ours.

"Well," Hel begins, trying to sound authoritative, "we have some great new ideas for improving the show!" She pauses, flashing her favourite smile; it wasn't anyone else's.

"And they are?" Clare begins to agitate the pen in her hand. I can't keep my eyes off its motion. Fortunately, Hel is off at a gallop:

"We feel," she turns momentarily to me, pulling me in to her duplicity, "that our astrology section lacks involving the general population, and that we could do with maybe having someone with more pizzazz and..." Clare breaks in:

"You mean you want to get rid of Agatha?" Clare was not usually concerned by dismissals. I smelled a love rat. Hel stammers before beginning:

"Well, we were considering looking at some other astrologer type people — maybe not necessarily astrology, maybe..." and she looks to me for help, but I just smile sweetly at her, enjoying her discomfort, "maybe an I-Ping person, or a Rhumy, um..." again she looks at me for help, and again I simply smile.

"I-Ping?" Questions Clare.

"I think what Helena is trying to say, "I contribute in my smoothest voice, "is I-Ching, the Chinese art of divination."

"Oh, yes, I've heard of that."

"Or Runes — the Celtic form of divination using stones."

"Right." Clare obviously hasn't heard of either.

"Yes, and we thought," Hel was back; the baton clenched in her hand, "that we could have a slot that didn't necessarily just deal with the sort of hum-drum of astrology, but looked at all the different types of mystical divination out there so each week we could look at a different type..." She pauses to gauge effect. Clare stops agitating her pen long enough to deliver her point of view:

"As long as you keep the astrology slot. I think astrology is good because it quickly and easily sums up all our audience; allows everyone to get involved. I'm not so sure about all this other nonsense, however. What's next?"

"Well…" not sure if this means she has one in the bag, Hel pushes on with an air of desperation, "we would like to introduce a new slot called, 'Acoustic Bands Rock'!" Hel pauses for effect, but when she gets none, continues: "We thought that it would be a good idea to turn our live band slot into something that had an identity. So, when we had rock bands we'd ask them to play acoustic, and when we had acoustic bands we'd ask them to rock-it-up!" Hel looks pleased with herself. Clare doesn't share the same look of satisfaction.

"How would that work exactly?" Hel moves uncomfortably in her seat. Anyone who didn't know her better might assume she was itching her bum with the chair. It reminded me of when dogs drag their arses across the carpet to bring a moment's solace to a bad case of worms.

"Well, we'd have the acoustic bands maybe add some drum and bass…and…"

"I see where you're going with this, but I'm just not sure it will have the desired effect," Clare's pen was fidgeting again.

"It could be like a challenge," continues Hel, more desperate, "to see if they can make their songs successful in a new framework...?"

"It's about branding," I add, "finding a new formula that takes the show out of drive into hyper-drive, with new concepts feeding into the main frame, and challenging our previously held concepts of known bands — shaking up the content." I was talking, but I wasn't sure any of it was hitting the mark. Hel looks momentarily relieved; stopping her ass scratching.

"You can try it, but if it doesn't work I will pull it in its first week — OK?"

"OK," we chorus.

"And I want to be kept in the loop this time," she fixes us both with her death warp stare, "and I mean it. I want to know who is coming on and what songs they will perform and with what instruments — do you hear?"

"Yes," we chorus again.

"What's next?"

"Well, our last thought is that we want to re-vamp our TV and Film guy."

"How?"

"Replace him," I quip, smiling at my own joke. Clare looks at me, grim faced.

"He just hasn't got any *umph*. I don't even think he watches the movies. Plus, he's a guy!"

"Fine, OK, so replace him with a woman this time. Who hired him anyway?"

"You did," Hel says tentatively, afraid to utter the truth.

"Oh," Clare looks genuinely confused; it is not often that she has to face the truths of her own mismanagement. It seems to hit her hard. For a moment I see the child within the woman. Small, like a robin in tweeds: bespeckled, the brunt of jokes; that search for approval meant finding a big enough vantage point at which to look down on the world. She had found it. She peered at us over the top of her beakish nose. "Well, let me know who you find. Is that all?"

"Yes," Hel speaks for us both.

"Well, I can't say there are any big changes in there, but if you brand the acoustic rock thing properly you might get something good out of it, and let's talk tomorrow about moving the items around. I'm not happy with the running order. Think about that, and we'll talk more tomorrow."

We get up to leave.

"Oh, and Cass…"

"Yes."

"You and Court pulled the short straw on overnights for the next month of Saturdays."

Hel and I are walking silently back to our desks when Jeff comes down the hallway:

"Your Dad's in reception..."

His hound dog expression hits me the minute I step into the foyer; he waits for me to walk the distance towards him. Jeff watches us like cowboys sizing each other up.

"Wanna take a walk," he says first.

"I'm working, but I can give you five minutes outside." We push open the swing doors, and the fresh air soon wakes me up to the reality of this little talk I had been avoiding but was now about to have.

"I'm not here asking for apologies..." he looks like he's expecting one though, and this puts my back up straight away. My face probably says as much as my back does. "I just hope we can move on from this." I really don't feel like dancing to the usual tune; I know this little set like my face in the mirror. He makes it sound like he's sorry whilst all the while just setting me up for a pasting on a sociological, scientific basis backed up by fatherly know-how. He won't so much as take you by the hand and lead you to his point of view, as make you see it through a series of polite verbal gestures and background information that you will have ignored at the time, but he will dig up and present as justifiable evidence when you just thought it was happenstance. Lord forbid you live your life in any state of casual calm around this man; he will sweep it up and use it in evidence against you one day. You will think he is fine with you sharing a bite of his cake, and then ten years later he will bring up the fact that he has never been able to enjoy a dessert without you wading in with your fork. You'll think that it was a sunny day, and he'll tell you that a clear sky may look like there's an absence of cloud, but that doesn't mean there aren't cirrus or altostratus clouds grazing the horizon. He'll make you doubt your own mind; rewrite your own history, and he'll do it with such a sweet, calm voice that you will begin to question your own sanity and thank the Lord above that he is there to catch you when you fall. I let him talk his way through the usual justifications; I didn't stop him; I knew the drill. He explained how I had run off when things got difficult as I always do; how I had always been a complex child, unable to handle change, and how he and Oma were just trying to provide a stable environment in which for me to work out my issues. He adds the fact that Oma is particularly worried about me but didn't want him to say anything to me. Then he goes on to justify his new girlfriend's point of view, and how she is the innocent victim of a family feud, and really deserves an apology when she was invited for a nice Christmas meal and got a tsunami up the ass instead. How bravely she soldiered on after my exit is further explored, as is the gentle nature with which she handles all situations, and her appearance in his life being the very reason that Dad has taken this all so calmly, whereas usually he would have been a lot more upset with me. So really, I owed her an apology *and* *him* thanks for the graciousness and lack of gravitas with which he was viewing this set back.

When he's finished laying out his stall, he looks at me, suddenly aware that I haven't spoken or reacted to his symposium of reasoning.

I respond with a wry smile, and unable to draw any warmth up from the deep well of my bitter heart, thank him for dragging his way out to see me and leave him there in the street. There's a moments gentle euphoria as I walk down the hallway back towards my desk, but then I just feel a dark brooding which didn't lift but simply settles like dust.

"What are you wearing for Blink's this Friday?" Courtney is standing at my desk with one hand on her hip and the other hanging by her side holding a staple gun. At first I think my retribution has come, but she's smiling.

"Is that a gun in your pocket or are you just happy to see me?"

"I'm always happy to see you. Now what are you wearin'?" I was more interested in her hand gun:

"What or who are you stapling?"

"Can't a girl carry a staple gun around without everyone assuming she's usin?"

"OK, OK...well, I haven't given it much thought. What is the theme again?"

"It's a beach party — cool, huh?"

"But it's not even Spring."

"Exactly. There's gonna be outdoor heaters indoors, sand, it's gonna be hot and everyone should be in bikinis — well, the gals, and the gays anyhow."

"Cool, OK..." then I thought about my bump: "I might wear a one piece."

"I'm panickin' cause I look like Britain's answer to the Pillsbury Dough Boy."

"You'll be fine." I'm mindlessly gathering my stuff together to get out of the office.

"Easy for you to say, you turn sideways, and we can't fuckin' find ya..."

"Wear a grass skirt if you're so worried." I'm scanning the horizon to see if Hel has spotted my defection; if I don't leave before she sees me she might find something for me to read or do.

"I don't wanna look like a palm tree!" Courtney is following me out of the building; we both nod to Jeff.

"Night then girls," he waves and smiles from his circular booth, his head down on some newspaper.

"Hey, Jeff." Courtney stops, and turns, "how're we doin' on the ol' score board?"

"Headbanger two, Honey three," he says without looking up.

"Yes!" Court punches the air with her staple gun, and then slips it in her handbag.

"What's going on?" Court ignores me:

"Night, Jeff."

"Night, love."

"What's the score board for?"

"Just keepin' tabs on the loonies that come lookin' for autographs…"

"What from the station jocks?"

"Yeah, cool huh? We've got a lead on 'em."

"OK…and why don't we hear about it? Why aren't we signing those autographs?"

"You got any photos they can sign?"

"No."

"Well there you go then, and it's not station policy to promote it."

"Why?"

"Undermines the other jocks who aren't gettin' any..."

"That's a bit Marxist."

"Honey, you're always gettin' some — let the rest of us dream..." She seemed serious, on some level, so we let it drop.

"I could probably do with a grass skirt too." Courtney looks down at my stomach.

"Get out widcha! You ain't showin. You're like a bean pole on stilts *with* anorexia."

"Not at this rate..." Court stops and eyes me studiously: not a look I am used to from her.

"Have you made up your mind yet?" She winces as if she only half wants to hear the reply.

"I've made a few enquiries..."

"You know I'll come and hold yar hand, right?" Then adds, quickly: "Either way — before it comes out of yar vagina, or when it's comin' out yar vagina." The street is full of people walking both ways at us; I feel overwhelmed by the mass of them, and stop:

"I'm thinking about keeping it." She stops with me. She doesn't know what to say. I take this as a sign that she is not big on the idea. I push for a response:

"You look like you've seen a ghost."

"Nah, it's just that that is a whole other ball game. Wow. I'm just gettin' my head round the idea. You and a baby — Jack's baby." This image hangs in the air. A tiny baby with a peaked cap. I'm temporarily taken up by this image; disgustingly sewn into its mantle. Our hormones have a lot to answer for. How much are we a victim to them? How much of this is even my decision? How do I know if I am heading the call of the gene or my own decision making? How do I test the theory? I cannot clone myself; exist in an alternate universe where I test out these theories on a Cass with hormones and a Cass without.

Pregnancy is known to reduce the grey matter in a woman's brain in preparation for the mindless, repetitive tasks that must be performed in the name of baby. Endless diaper changes, reduced dialogue with adults, a narrowing of all activity that doesn't involve baby. If my brain cells are dying in preparation for this undertaking it goes to show that I will therefore have less brain cells with which to make an informed decision. I simply can't be trusted therefore to make the right decision. I need additional brain power.

"What would you do?" I practically wail.

"Nah — I can't be responsible for this life-changing decision. Sorry. You gotta make this one alone."

"But I'm scared!" Those words feel like the truest spoken since this whole episode began; a weight is lifted just letting them escape. Courtney looks worried now too; she searches the street behind me with her eyes.

"I don't know what ta tell ya kid. I'll support ya either way, but the decision has to be yars."

"It might not even be his." This latest thought is just a decoy to the overall problem; the puerile nature of my decision-making processes. The fact that Tony is oblivious to the possibility that he may be a father is neither here nor there: either way, there is a baby coming, and the father is A. Not somebody I want to raise it with me, or B. Doesn't want it to even be born. I've been so busy in my make-believe world of Jack that I've been ignoring the possibility that Tony's swimmers might have got their act together, and not been quite as useless as he thought?

The cavalcade of commuters dial up their intensity: the waves coming thick and fast.

"You need to let him know." Courtney says bluntly. I know she's right, but there's so much to consider. Too much. And I don't even have a family to lean on now that I've fallen out with Dad. Single motherhood tips her peaked cap at me. A mother with pushchair wheel past us, and Courtney and I both look at it and then at each other.

"That could be you in less than a year," she says speaking both our thoughts. "How far along are you now?" This too was a reality check that I needed to get my head around. Another month and it would be too late to pay the piper to wipe my womb clean.

"It's nearly decision-making time." We get to the corner where the main road buzzes with buses.

"Guess I'll see ya tomorrow."

"Yeah, have a good one."

"You too," Court turns to go, and then stops, "D'ya wanna go grass skirt shoppin' after work tomorra?"

"Sure." She tries to smile and joins the fray.

Chapter 21

To the Sounds of 'It Ain't Over Till it's Over' by Lenny Kravitz

One of the few memories I have of my mother is of a balmy day on Hampstead Heath; sunlight piercing foliage; bouncing off the white monolith of Kenwood House. Maybe it's just those sunny spectacles I wear every time I think of her that makes it all sit sun-lit in my mind; brilliant, colour-filled, preternatural. It's easy to be absent. You can be the biggest goddamned star when you are absent because you don't get to make any mistakes. In my imagination, she is this huge effervescent everything. She is the perfect mother; the perfect wife. She sits doing homework with me, always smiling, always something in the oven smelling good. She holds my hand and we walk together down the road to school, and she waves through the fence, and waits for me to go in before she turns to leave. She is there again at the end of the day, in the same space, with the same smile. We talk and laugh all the way home. Before turning out the light, she tickles me, but not before reading a long story that goes on for ages, and she plays out the different parts with different voices. When she stands up, she tucks me in, all the way around, and plants a kiss on my nose and on my forehead. At the light switch she blows me another kiss, and asks how I want the door left, A little ways open? Or closed all the way?

It was just the two of us; I don't know where Dad was that day. Her hand's in mine, some hard-won trophy. If I were to tell you that I always knew, even at a young age, that my time with her would be short, that I knew every moment was a temporary gift, would you believe me? The allotted time with her always seemed more precious, like a shooting star, gasping even as it's exploding with light. I always felt that her fragility was more than skin deep, but time deep too. Our moments together limited by her nature, which is, whether I like it or not, admit it or not, mine too. In some way damaged by her lack, I throw myself with greater urgency, and carelessness into life; daring her to turn up and save me. Save me from some horizon I have set for myself: blue and hazy: which doesn't exist. I tried to model myself on Dad, to get more balance in my life; to share his chromosomes not hers, but 50% must be hers; which 50% is anyone's guess, but I'm beginning to think the most wayward part. I can't escape my past, only embrace it with my clunky heart; it's created a few of its own add ons to compensate for the holes she made when she left. Even if she had the antidote, the glue to piece it back together, I don't believe it would make any difference. They say that knowing you have a problem is half the battle, but it can't be the cure. Knowing is just half the equation, then there's forgiving. Have I forgiven her for walking out? Not yet. Do I think I ever will? Uncertain.

We're standing in front of a painting. It towers above us, some six feet or more. We are in the orangery, a light and airy long gallery attached to the main house. 'Whistlejacket' rears up on his hind feet, alone against a backdrop without ground or sky, immortalized in a timeless space. Much like she will soon be. George Stubbs had grown up around the dead carcasses of animals, and studied their bones, their muscles, their fibres, and knew the making of a horse, made his name painting them. No rider to complicate the portrait; sitting haughtily astride; no medals and bows, whips and stirrups to hamper the line of the beautiful beast; just free and pure as nature had intended. Bristling sinews, bareback, unhampered, his strong head turns to face the gallery, rearing up above us all; letting us feel his supremacy.

There were tears on her face. Her cheeks were being assailed by them. At first I didn't understand. I remember feeling awkward, confused. There weren't many people in the gallery, and those that were there were not crying. They were stopping and moving on, stopping and moving on. We were standing still. Pulling her arm did not work: she carried on looking up at the painting that towered over us both. The nostrils and eyes bulged. I grabbed her hand, pinched it, and pulled it. The dark eyes of the beast stared down. I could feel its sharp breath, the weight of it bear down, the magma of its eye, as its head tossed up and back, witnessing us below. I gripped her hand more tightly, tried to pull her away from the painting, but she wouldn't move. Then my tears started, hot and angry, I pulled and pulled, but she was rooted, immoveable. My screams lit up the gallery, and she snapped shut like a box.

Under trees, sheltered from what begins as a light drizzle, and then a full-on downpour, the families gather. The tireless drip of rain on leaf, the tap, tap, tap; the onerous bellow of a thunder clap, and run for cover. Chosen for its stretch of branches, I am happy with my tree. It sees me through the small shower, its momentary anger. And when it passes, and the odd bird begins to sing again, it is like a gift. The worst has passed over; once again we are spared; simple sinners.

Emerging from the underbrush like the first animals from the ark, the families adjust themselves, and fan out across the Heath. The rain has sent them home, and I am happier to have the heath to myself.

The hill works back from Kenwood House, facing the Orangery. The dew turns my suede shoes black. I feel like I am not just approaching a stately home, mired in its own history, but approaching my own past that looms ever and ever larger.

To access the building, you must step through a small, curving overhang of passageway, tendril thick, and back out into the light, following the path that leads around the side of the house, and through the large, glass double doors into the foyer.

It has been a very long time, and I feel like an intruder on my own past. Did I have a right to trespass on my own memories? The opulent interior makes me feel smaller still. Like Alice, perhaps I shall shrink to the size of a thimble, and then? I tiptoe past the guard, leading left, away from the gift shop, and let my senses guide me. A mysterious stairway leads up to a 'no entry' sign, curving white against a royal blue wall, pure of painting, and up to a skylight that lets in the faintest hue. Hallways lead right and left, I choose right, and come to the library.

Cordoned off save for a pathway down the middle, if you follow the luxurious carpet, you can only stare at the backs of books. However, there are tall windows to tempt you to the view that gives out onto the vale of heath, all the way down to the lolloping pond and its bandstand sitting on an expanse of black water.

A succession of ever dwindling rooms brings me, finally, to the Orangery; it opens up before me — empty. My footsteps echo on the wooden floor, an odd urn containing flowers alternating between the floor to ceiling windows that run the breadth of one wall. Whistlejacket is gone. There is nothing to indicate that he had ever been here. Had I imagined it? Him? My mother? Everything?

My eyes scan the empty walls.

Footsteps make me turn. A man in uniform walks into the middle of the room and stops. Before he can address my concerns:

"Excuse me, but what happened to the painting that hung here? Whistlejacket? — the big horse…"

"That hasn't hung here since '71. It went back to its owner, Lady Juliet de Chair."

"Oh…" This news is startling; unable to identify my feelings, I forget even to thank him, and wander out of the room, my footsteps following after me: some sad echo.

The minute you decide your life must change is not the moment it changes. It's usually the moment when you cannot take any more of your own bullshit that it changes. When the sound of your own thoughts is such an incessant, insect drone that you would tear your own head off and throw it in the nearest river if you possessed the ability to separate pain from your own fiction. I sure as hell wanted to yank the damn thing off. I didn't want to think about Mum anymore. I'd had enough of memory lane, and mammary lane — both my breasts and my mother syndrome were tender.

My own mother would not be able to advise me on this most motherly of problems. My womb would remain my business. Her thoughts would remain her own.

In the world of science, creatures evolve; mankind evolves; so how was I meant to turn this situation into a positive evolution of my soul, my chromosomes, my being? Should the crime suit the punishment? Was I punishable? Was I going to perform an inhumane act? Should I be held accountable for a dodgy condom, a too big dick? Or a man who told me that he couldn't impregnate women? Was this a lesson in semantics or pedantic reasoning?

The meeting of sperm and egg is such a simple dance. So easily done. Too easily. So many runners in the race, the poor little egg doesn't stand a chance. There is bound to be one that can go the distance, stick his neck out, and stick his head in. If fairness was a biological component would the egg get more of a say? I mean it's a fucking gang bang. The poor little egg doesn't have a leg to stand on. What if she wants to spend the rest of her days travelling? Meandering down the fallopian tubes of life, admiring the rich, velvety landscape?

Doesn't want to be somebody's baby. Just wants some independence, and a good run. It's not like she gets much of a choice. The poor bitch is set upon by a million runners dead set on lassoing her into a Dr. Jekyll and Mr. Hyde dance of procreation. Her X, his Y. The odds are simply stacked against her.

Then she's at the mercy of simple multiplication: cells divide, and divide, and divide. She's caught in the loop. To think we came from single cell organisms — to this. Once upon a time the very simplest of organisms, and now a cosmos of the most intricate, multi-coloured, capable, complicated, miraculous, dastardly things. Who'd have thought?

Darwin made his points most conclusively: given enough time, and space, the single celled organism will divide, expand, evolve, move out of water, and grow into the many marvels that we see today, from flight to earth bound mobility. Too wonderful and terrifying for words.

And here was just another simple combination of chromosomes, trying out their stuff, turning over evolution in its little ball of possibilities, using me as the test tube for its experiment. Would I be a willing subjugate?

"It's 3.45am on a fine English morning with Cass Bates and Courtney Fiennes. We're getting you through the wee hours here on Radio Honey. What would you like to say on the subject of 'Boyfriends from Hell'?" The line went crackly, and then died.

"Well thank you for your call!" Courtney hollers, "You get a good night's sleep now ya hear! Some people lose the power of their limbs after midnight…"

"But not us! You have the pleasure of our company right until four a.m.!" I press the jingles button, and Clive's carefully crafted tune sings, "Cass and Court takin' you through the wee hours! They may be small but they're not man powered!" I press up another caller.

"Hey, good morning, you're on Radio Honey, what's your name?"

"Hi, I'm KD"

"Katy?"

"No-'K'-'D'" Court and I look at each other and shrug.

"Ok, honey, what would you like to say this fine mornin' — have you had a boyfriend from hell?"

"I sure have!"

"What he do — sell your engagement ring for beer? Shag your best friend on your wedding night?"

"Well, no, but I think it's up there with those ones....he...um, had sexual relations with my little sister, after he left me with my daughter whose now four, and my sister's so young and dumb she called me up to boast about it!"

"Well, honey, *she's* gonna get a wake up call from *you* when he dumps her ass with a bun in the oven, and takes up with your even littler sister..."

"I don't have one..."

"I'm talkin' hypothetically," Courtney was losing patience with the callers, "we're all sisters when it comes to men behaving like beasts!"

"Hail Mary!" My biblical tone brought the call to an end. I pressed up a fresh caller. "Good morning you're on Radio Honey. What stories have you got for us?"

"Hey there ladies!" This one sounded friendly and confident. "Can I just say how great it is to have you two on radio?"

"You certainly can."

"It's just so refreshing to hear two women who aren't afraid to tell it like it is and get away with it!"

"We haven't gotten away with it yet! We usually get ten shades panned out of us on Monday mornin' by our boss! And she's a woman!"

"Well she should understand?" Courtney and I look at each other, unwilling to spell out the truth.

"So, what have you got for us, honey?" Courtney's voice is warm.

"Well, you won't' believe it but my husband of twenty years, the man I've shared my life with, my children, all that I am, and all that I have — turns out has had another person in his life all this time — another family!"

"Oh, Holy mother of baby Jesus — hell, honey, that is tough!"

"Yeah, but the really tough thing is that this family is with another man and they have adopted two children!"

"Oh, my Lord!" It was my turn to sympathize. "How did you find out?"

"The new school he sent his kids to sent the application form to our house, not his other partner..."

"Well I'll be..."

"And when I opened it — 'cause I was curious — "

"Right on..."

"I saw this application, and it had the name of some child — not our kids' names! Not our kids' school!"

"Wow — did you never suspect anything? Did he like ever try and slip it in the back door?" I raised my eyes at

Courtney. She shrugged. I imagined Clare listening back to the show, and the swift summons to her office following it.

"No, but one time I got a nurse's uniform and stockings, you know, like to shake things up, and I came home one day to find him in them..."

"Some men do like to dress up in ladies' things I suppose..."

"No," the caller continued, "this is different: it was a rubber fetish nurse's outfit; and he used to want me to put it on sometimes, but then he'd want me to powder his bottom like a baby, and put these big baby diapers on him..."

"Well, I've heard some damn strange things on this show, but that's a corker!" Cries Courtney.

"Actually Court, I've heard about this: there are parties where overstressed business men go to unwind: places where matronly types treat them like babies and powder their bums, give them bottles, and all that baby stuff, and they say it relaxes them — all the stresses of being Mr. Tough, Mr. Can-Do can get on top of them, and this is how they unwind." Courtney picks her jaw up off the floor:

"I think they should just get on top of their wives and stop actin' like big babies! What is happenin' to the human race?! You can't turn around and there's some weirdo with a bottle in his mouth, and a dummy up his kazoo — 'scuse my French!"

"Thanks for your call, and good luck! I'd say you're better out of that one — let's face it — the guy can't make up his mind, or he wants the best of both worlds — either way you're not number one!"

"And a girl's gotta be number one!" Courtney and I chorus.

"Good mornin', you're on Radio Honey — have you had a boyfriend from hell?"

"Hi," the voice was timid.

"Hi, what's your name?"

"Jill."

"Hey, Jill, what's keepin' you up tonight?"

"Well, I've been seeing this guy and things...well...I thought things were going well..."

"We always do," I butt in, "we are such innocent, trusting creatures..." Courtney and I smile at each other, knowingly.

"Yeah," she ignores me, intent on managing to get her words out on live radio, "well we've been seeing each other for a few months now, and we finally, well, he — I mean — he spent the night last night, and then in the early hours of the morning said he had to go because he was expecting an important parcel in the morning and didn't want to miss it...should I be worried? It sounds like a pretty limp excuse."

"Well, as long as he ain't limp in the bedroom you should be saying a few Hail Mary's!"

"Hail Mary!" Courtney and I chorus.

"You know I wouldn't feel so bad, Jill," I offer, "I spent the night with this guy I really fancied, and had been working on for ages — this is going back a few years now —"

"Sure!" Courtney plays with me. I don't stop to play:

"And after we had shared our carnal knowledge..."

"The size of a small pocket book," Courtney cuts in. Again, I ignore her.

"...he told me he had to leave because he had to let his tortoise out of its shoe box before the light appeared in the sky as it would freak out otherwise!"

"And you said what?!" Courtney in disbelief this time; she hasn't heard this one. "Hey, I hope you said 'Now I know where that little tortoise you stuck in me came from!'?" Even our caller was laughing.

"I know, can you believe it?! Honest to God, they are the masters of crap when it comes to trying to winkle out of a situation."

"They'd rather chew off their arm than come clean with ya. Many a mornin' I've come to ta find a guy knawin' at his arm, his eyes wild as a skunk rat! He'd a left his whole body thar if he could'a!"

"So, Jill, you see: you're not alone. They just don't know how to use the English language. The melodious, honey'd tones that Shakespeare made famous turn to grunts and groans in their mouths, and worse, are left out completely when their legs can do the talking for them by running out the door. But don't get us wrong, we know that out there are decent, loving, upstanding men, who look after their wives and children..."

"Yeah, we just haven't met any yet!" cuts in Courtney.

"Right it's time to take one last call. Good morning, you're on Radio Honey, have you got a boyfriend from hell?" There's a silence, and then my blood runs cold as an all too familiar voice comes on the line:

"Cass you can't keep avoiding the fact that you're carrying my baby!"

"Well thank you caller," Courtney whips down the phone line fader as my mouth drops open, unable to speak, and carries the can for me, "God, some guys just think we're all walkin' around like big wombs carrying their babies. Get a life big boy! We'll be back after a word from our sponsors — and I don't mean Durex!" Courtney pulls down her own fader, and turns to me, knowing that I will not be taking this well.

"You OK?" I am still unable to talk. "Damn cheap radio with no interface switchboard to get us out of this kind of shit..."

"I'm OK," I manage, without feeling it, "It was just a bit of a shock."

"C'mon we've got two minutes on tampon ads, and one minute on car insurance, let's get us some fresh air."

Chapter 22

To the Sounds of 'I'd Do Anything for Love' by Meat Loaf

'Neophobic' rats, frightened by new things – different cheese, unfamiliar new rat faces — have a 60 percent greater chance of dying than their more confident brothers and sisters. Risk taking rats, 'neophilic', were found by a group of scientists at the University of Chicago to live longer than their shyer relatives.

When both rats were put in new environments with different objects, cones, bricks, food hoppers, etc., they were found to fall into two distinct categories: those who rose to the challenge of exploring the new, and those who hung like wall flowers to the corners of their new environment.

Scientists believe that similar effects have a bearing on us humans. They already know that people with a negative outlook on life are more likely to die early, now it's not just the shy rats who are succumbing to an early death; those shrinking violets amongst us are now decidedly more likely to die of cancers and other immune system weaknesses because of their timid ways.

The life span of a neophobic rat is 599 days, whilst his neophilic brothers die at an average of 701 days. Interestingly enough, the scientists found that both types of rats died of the same diseases, just later, producing the theory that neophobia made the animals more prone to disease; their raised hormone levels, due to the stress of new situations, undermining their immune systems sooner.

I have made a mental note to rise to new challenges. Aren't we just rats in bigger cages?

I have a theory of my own to check out, and it's unfamiliar territory, but I need to know; I need to see it for myself. I can't be blamed for feeling. I can't be blamed for being human, or rat-like. So, I'm testing my theory. I'm putting it to the test: bending the fear of my world to the granite of reality. It tasted dark, and bitter, but it was better to know. Ratty would have her day.

It felt good to be doing something. To be taking some kind of control. Some kind of vengeance on the stalking that had been done in my name. Let the prey become the aggressor. Turn the tables on the victimhood I'd been feeling. The club felt warm compared to the street. The hard-red innards of the walls and curtained coat-check area gave it the feeling of entering a womb (I'm aware of the familiar analogy.) Hugh didn't recognise me in my wig and dark glasses: he waived me in. I'd gone counter to my usual look all the way. Straight-up girl about town. No hillbilly or hint of patchouli. Wearing a tight skirt, tucked in shirt, and classic (almost office-wear) black heels. My wig was tied back in a big pony-tail. Tonight I was the blonde I'd always wanted to be; the girl that could have been; that might have been. I kept my coat on; I reckoned I wouldn't be staying long. Just long enough.

As I made my way down the small, dark stairwell the sweat, music, and heat rose to meet me. I was momentarily excited. Hang in there kid, I told my belly, this will be worth the ride. The stairway opened up into a hollow chamber lit badly by ceiling and floor lights that had long since been surplus to requirement. The real light was coming from the DJ booth. A mix of blinking neon strobes hugged the booth and spread its testy glow into the room. Bodies clung to each other or mixed it up on their own patch of darkness; spreading their arms to some invisible illuminati.

A fledgling hipster, sweating and wide-eyed, pivoted past me; I turned to watch her pitch toward the bathrooms: more horizontal than upright. Here in this seething mass I was hoping for answers; or more questions. But equally some move on the immoveable and the intractable. I scanned the crowd. There were a few faces I recognised, some who had been down to Blinks over the years, but there was one in particular that I had to find. Circling the room from the edges,

I wove between the bodies hurtling themselves around in the blackness. The bar, dimly lit by a series of small lampshades dangling from the ceiling, housed two lacklustre barmaids; young, pretty, and darkly moody. I wondered if the proprietor had fondled his way into their affections as part of their tenure. He had certainly fondled his way into mine, albeit not under duress, but under the influence of his clothes stripping charm. One of the young women was housing a particularly pert pair of breasts that heaved impetuously over her black top; I joined the men around the bar in ogling her for more time than was appropriate. She came over, preferring my ardent gaze than the herd of jackals.

"Sorry," I blurted, "I'm not drinking." She turned without a smile.

The walls moist with condensation; an aubergine hue sunk into the plasterwork, I cling to the perimeter, sensing my way through bodies, huddled on the floor and on the dance floor. That drink was actually beginning to sound good. I turned back around and went back to the bar. The girl with the great breasts ignores me this time: once smitten. Her accomplice finally comes to take my order. She simply sets her eyes on mine to let me know she is listening.

"A whiskey. Straight up." She turns to the wall, pumps and is back. Rummaging around in my pockets I fish out a fiver. As she comes back with the change, I hear a familiar voice:

"Kayley! Get a move on!" The figure passes into the crowd. Kayley, behind the bar, the one with the pert breasts, flashes a dark look in his direction. She has obviously tasted his valour first hand. I down my whisky and follow him into the mass.

Bodies fling themselves in front of me; irrespective of the music or real-time. A free for all of body parts and hips and heads. Despite this, the moment of truth inches closer. I can feel it.

Up ahead I see the DJ booth. A beautiful woman is on the decks, spinning with one hand on her headphones. Her lips pursed over the record, she slips it into the next groove and leans back, pleased with herself. Her naked arms wave in the air above her head, and her spandex top catches the lights from the desk console.

He moves in behind her, cupping each breast in his hands. She smiles and leans her head back into his chest, her arms still in a vortex of undulations above her head. His hands slip around her waist, and they move in unison. The dance we had once done together.

Momentarily stunned, I find my feet, and carry on forward; inching towards the DJ booth, the stage lights; the moment of inner truth.

"Hey," somebody spins me around. He's grinning, trying to engage me in the mating ritual. I push him away and keep trying to pitch between the bodies. "Don't I know you?" He's smiling: pushing his way in front of me. Turning my back to him, I push forward into the crowd.

That's when I stop, doubting my intentions. The club heaves around me; the music building. As the beat breaks over the top of its own volition, I regain my resolve, and push on through the crowd.

His face goes blank when he sees me; then the background information catches up with the current moment, and he is back in the room. Half surprise, half anger. It's a moment I will cherish. It's a moment I will use to kill his unborn child.

She's still dancing, lining up the next record: oblivious. He lets go of her waist. She doesn't notice. He stands his ground. I move in. Climb up onto the dais and approach them.

She sees me now. She's still smiling. He's still trying to process why I'm there. I take her hand and put it on my stomach; the one that moments ago was in the air; a free agent.

"I'm carrying his child," I tell her. She looks at me and takes her hand away; as if infected. Jack is yelling now and grabbing me by the arm I had used to show her that her boyfriend was inseminating women around the capitol and moving on to the next. I should have handed her some extra strong condoms. Her face is frozen in a look of sweet confusion as he drags me away. I can't hear what he's yelling: I don't want to hear his deadbeat bullshit, but he's dragging me at such an unholy angle that the guy who had previously tried to engage me butts up in his face and asks if I'm OK.

"No, I'm not!" I yell, looking wounded.

"Hey buddy, let the woman go!' My new man hollers.

"Get the fuck out of my way!" Jack, his usual charming self.

"Let her go and I will!" This young man is proving to be a worthy aggressor. Where are these guys when I'm in my right mind? Not that this mind set has been much in evidence of late, or of ever, but it is worth noting for the record, and here I take a moment to note, for the record; sizing him up: not bad, a bit short, a bit normal looking, nothing out of the ordinary, but he looks kind of tough when he is angry, and this could be construed as sexy when weighed in the balance with the rest. I wonder whether I will get his phone number or whether we will be separated in the ruckus.

"Fuck off buddy this is my club!" He tries to push past, dragging me.

"I don't care if it's your fucking planet — let her go!" There is a wide berth making itself apparent on the dance floor. People, sensing violence, are moving out to the edges to avoid the incident, but still carry on with their evening.

"I'm pregnant!" I wail, and that really gets my new man going. He throws a punch at Jack, who ducks, and in the process throws me to the floor. Next thing I know they are both on the floor scrabbling about on top of each other; to the side of each other, grabbing bits of each other, and generally trying to get in a punch. Jack's hat has come off showing his bald spot. It seems ages before Hugh pushes in and pulls them apart. Ages with their bodies tussling on the floor. I couldn't tear myself away. I don't know what I was expecting to happen once it was over, but I didn't want to stay around and find out. I fled out to the street and kept running till I had put several blocks between myself and the club.

Slowing my footsteps, the wind catches the hoody on my coat and flips it up over my head. I let it warm my ears; the loud music still ringing. His face still in front of me; angry. It feels like everyone is angry with me, and yet I don't know what I've done to create so much animosity in people. I had gone along for the ride, believing that we all had each other's best interests at heart. And here we were all undone.

The second hand clicks onto the four: I bring the fader up on the music:

"Welcome once again to the happiest hours on radio — your joy ride into pleasurable chaos, the music of the spheres, the melodies of modern music's favourite muses — yes, it's Cass Bates, and it's drive time on Radio Honey, five-fifty-four a.m." I sail in over the opening bars of Crowded House's, "Don't Dream it's Over." As I pull down the fader, I smile up at Hel who is waiting by the door, half expecting me to mess it up.

"Right, well, I'll leave you to it," she turns at the door, " —cup of tea?"

"Coffee, please, and don't forget to write up those ideas for the show."

"I know, I know." She leaves, a harassed wind. I smile to myself. My secret burning inside me, my private life, my private ills are mine alone, and at moments like this, high on my own stupidity, I can almost feel that I am in control. Sitting back in my chair, enjoying the song in the headphones, I turn to look round at the offices through the window. What am I doing here? The thought surprises me. I push it away. The money is good, I'm lucky to have this job; it's a great job, people would kill for this job. Thoughts of other worlds, other possibilities crowd my head. I push them away, putting it down to the smoke. Crowded House are building the dream back in.

Chapter 23

To the Sounds of 'Vogue'
by Madonna

"Aloha!" Blink's wild eyes welcome. I had *dared* to go bare. My bikini felt smaller than it actually was. Clutching my fake fur around me, I clunked past Blink in my wedgy sandals. Courtney and I hadn't found grass skirts, so she had opted for a sarong.

"If it's good enough for Jean Paul Gaultier's Spring/Summer collection it's good enough for me..."

"No, it looks good." Blink wreaths each one of us in a Hawaiian flower necklace as we come in. Tony's wearing a Hawaiian shirt, and a run of white sun cream marks out his nose.

"Ladies," he greets us, not being able to help his obvious appraisal of our semi-nude bodies, "you both look stunning..."

"Can it," snaps Court, "where's your bathing suit?"

"I'm wearing it," he pointed to his Hawaiian bathing trunks.

"Wearin' a shirt is just cheatin' — would ya wear that on a beach? — Oh, wait — yes you would!' Courtney answers her own question, sneeringly.

"Give a guy a break — I'm just warming up. I'll take it off later."

"You better or I'll tear it off ya," Courtney's semi-nakedness was doing nothing for her humour.

"Ooooh, that sounds promising!" Tony's eyes widen.

"Shut up pervert or I'll strangle ya with yar Hawaiian flower necklace." Courtney storms off to the bar.

"She doesn't like wearing a bikini," I offer.

"Sure, no problem," Tony tries not to look offended. "Can I get you a drink?" I think of the rats, and my usual tipple...something different, but what?

"I'll have a Shirley Temple." Tony looks surprised.

"What are you, pregnant?"

"Yes, and I think it's yours," I deadpan, surprised at the words that have just come out of my mouth. He laughs nervously, and turns, uncomfortable with the new tack the conversation has taken; he looks a sorry sight wandering away around semi-clad bodies under the orange glow of outdoor-now-indoor heaters. The multi colourful Hawaiian theme was not improving his bland body image; you would have thought after all those greys and blacks this would have been an improvement, but it just seems to highlight his physical frailties. Suddenly feeling more naked than I was, standing in the centre of the room, I'm relieved to see Courtney making her way back towards me with two drinks.

"Let's find somewhere to sit before this bikini bottom climbs up my ass and disappears for good..." I follow her and the icy glasses of coke.

Despite the weather outside, tonight's theme is creating a warm glow on the inside. Everyone looks sunny and has risen to the occasion: there are a plethora of sun hats and bikinis, and the smell of sun tan lotion melting under the electric light registers positive memories. Some have even brought beach towels and are sprawled on the ground on top of the un-seasonable sand, no doubt getting little grains between their bum cheeks. The laughter is contagious, and the little umbrellas in our drinks make us all the cheerier.

I'm sending up a silent prayer that Jack will not appear when Cage, hobbling on his one good leg, ambles in our direction. Several people stop him on his way over to our table, and it looks like, from the body language, that he's having to explain the cast on his leg. When he finally arrives, we both smile up at him, and he doesn't need to leer to let us know that he appreciates sitting with two of the smallest bikinis in the room. His emaciated frame, brandishing a few dark hairs makes him look child-like. His wide-legged swim shorts sport palm fronds, and he's wearing a wide-brimmed straw hat.

"Howdy!" He looks at me: gauging our current situation; knowing it could have been a "friends with benefits" gig.

"Howdy yurself!" Courtney gushes.

"Hey," I manage, my lips somehow stuck to the straw. I can see Tony making his way through the crowd with my Shirley Temple.

"You ladies need a tipple?" He tries.

"We're fine thanks."

"But I'll keep y'ar seat warm," Court sticks a foot on a chair for him: she had also seen Tony making his way through the crowd. Cage drags his leg off to the bar as Tony arrives; they nod their exchange in passing.

"One Shirley Temple for the lady!" He puts it down with some ceremony, and then sees that I already have a drink.

"Courtney got me one — I didn't realize," I explain.

"No problem. Hope you enjoy them both," he tries to look nonplussed, but I feel him dithering on the edge, unsure of whether to stay or go. Neither of us comes to his aid, and Courtney's glare certainly doesn't help. That's when I see Jack come through the door in a wet suit, carrying a surf board.

"Oh my God!" I can't help saying out loud. Courtney follows my gaze.

"Holy mother of God," Courtney assists. Tony turns to see what we are both looking at. He'd obviously heard about the fracas:

"I hope there won't be any more trouble tonight." We both ignore him, and watch Jack, who clocks us as he is talking to Blink. She wreaths him with much fanfare; she is an awful flirt. Good thing her husband doesn't often make it to the club.

Cage crosses the room with his drink, watching Jack as he does so. Courtney silently removes her foot from the chair, and he, equally silently, sits down. We are all staring at Jack, trying not to look obvious: which isn't working.

"Well, you guys take it easy tonight — no more punch ups!" Tony tries to make a joke but it falls on deaf ears. We ignore him as he walks off.

"Yeah, thanks Tony," I offer absent-mindedly. Cage lifts his drink to his lips. The seconds tick by.

"'E better not be thinkin' of starting anythin' tonight," says Cage, his eyes still fixed on Jack. Jack was still flirting with Blink.

"I'm sure it will be fine," I say, unconvinced. Blink breaks away from Jack to get up on the stage. Everyone whistles and cheers.

"You're in no state to take him on with your leg in a sling," Courtney sternly councils.

"Good evening!" she calls out in her biggest voice. "It's a great night tonight, and it's good to see you all looking so sexy in your bathing suits!" A big whistle goes up from the audience. Blink looks pubescent in her polka dot bikini, her white skin blinding. "Yeah! You look great! We will beat these winter blues!" More whooping from the audience. "And tonight, to kick us off we have Jack to start the proceedings — give him a warm hand!" Everyone did, and Jack climbs up on the stage with one grasshopper reach of his leg. He nearly touches the ceiling, and standing next to his surf board, which tickles it, he looks like a giant. For a moment I feel a stirring but quell it. Out of the corner of my eye I can feel Courtney looking at me.

"Hey — welcome — or 'E komo Mai' as they say in Hawaii!" A light suddenly lights up the corner of the room where DJ Danny was putting the needle down on The Beach Boys tune, 'Surfin' USA', which gently lifts under Jack's opener: "We are lucky enough tonight to have the singing talents of Blues Man, Tony," an appreciative cheer goes up from the crowd; Tony, standing in the corner of the room now, with his guitar propped beside him, bows from the middle, "...and we have the miraculous belly dancing miracle that is Miranda!" Jack seems particularly pleased about this, but we can't see a belly dancer anywhere, "...plus wicked sounds from...Cage..." the crowd really make some noise, whilst Jack looks less than happy to be saying his name, "...and the lovely Blink..." and here he turns, and smiles a sycophantic smile to our host, "...has promised to play one of her new songs..." Blink tries to bow with modesty, but fails, "...as for me I just want to say that you are all welcome next Saturday night at my new club, Jack's, on the Portobello Road, just outside the tube station, number one hundred and eleven: doors open at eight, and they'll be mixing some awesome Happy House and Trance for your pleasure — DJ Danny and DJ Spicer — be there crew!" There is some raucous noise from the audience that sounds more like animals escaping from the zoo than enthusiasm, but that's what passes for excitement these days, and Jack exits the stage, with another stretch of his legs.

"Well, we'll be givin' that one a miss!" Courtney says straight off the mark.

"Oh, I don't know," I say with a modicum of amusement, "sounds like fun!" Memories of last night's punch up still fresh in my mind; I enjoyed the playback on my own. Courtney and Cage both flash me a look but were otherwise innocent of recent events. Sometimes a girl just likes to keep her late-night manoeuvres private. I wasn't yet sure if I was proud or embarrassed by my nocturnal mission. Tony is ambling up on the stage, and I turn feeling eyes on me: Jack is eyeballing me from the side lines. I turn giving him a good view of the back of my head.

Tony sits down on a chair wreathed with fake flowers:

"I'd like to pay tribute tonight to The Beach Boys by playing my own rendition of 'California Dreamin''…hope you like what I've done to it…" He says humbly and launches into the sweetest rendition I've ever heard of this Beach Boy classic. The audience, soothed into a state of calm, relax into the heat and sand between their toes. When he finishes the applause is rapturous.

I stand up and Courtney looks at me as if I'm taking a limb with me:

"Where ya goin'?"

"To the loo." I don't want to entangle Court and Cage further; I need to lead the Lion away from the cubs.

"D'ya want me to come with ya?" She only half wants to: Cage is being called up on stage, and I could see she would rather watch him perform.

"I think I can manage to pee on my own," I reassure her with a smile. Jack is watching as I make my way out of the main door. I don't dare look behind me.

When I come out of the ladies room he has me up against the wall before I know what is happening. The hallway is empty, and he's using his height and strength to his advantage. I feel the cold, clamminess of his wet suit before I hear his words:

"You have a fucking nerve coming to my club and making such a scene!"

"Let go Jack — you're squashing me!" The smell of the rubber hits my nostrils, and I turn my head away. He holds one of my arms, and I feel a frisson of excitement course through me. I still have those feelings; he still does it for me. I realise I am a sick individual. I look up into his eyes, but they are hard.

"I'm so angry with you I could fucking kill you!"

"I think you just want to kill the baby by squashing me to death," I say only half able to breathe. I stop struggling and look him square in the face. His body pressed so close against mine, I feel his cock twitch. He pulls away just as the club door opens, and Mack the knife looks out on us:

"Everything alright out 'ere?" Jack lets my arm drop, and turns to Mack:

"Fine — just fine." Mack looks at me quizzically, and I reassure him with a smile. Jack pushes past me with his surf board under his arm. Mack looks at him, and then me, and we both shrug our shoulders.

Cage is bombarding his way through his song; "Meat" and "Veg" on backing track, feeding him the grooves. Cage's scrawny chest and minimal body hair make him look like an undernourished street kid, but he has the moves, and he has the animal energy. Courtney's eyes are fixed on the stage. She hardly acknowledges me as I sit down. He's singing his new song, 'Highway to Helluva Hit' and the crowd already had memorized the chorus. He was toking on an imaginary spliff, giving us the jist. It was catchy. It couldn't' be long before this one was storming it up the charts. But somehow, in this basement dive, all this talent just seemed to reside for us alone. Despite the fact that we were producing some of the freshest sounds of the time, the times just weren't catching on, and somewhere between living and breathing, we didn't have the time to care.

The applause is big and proud. Cage laps it up. He stops to talk to Meat and Veg, Courtney leans in:

"Lord, that fella has more talent in his little finger than a whole orchestra has on Prom Night."

"You need to get down on his talent girlfriend. Show some appreciation."

"Oh, stop it! He doesn't even know I exist. I could be naked tonight and he wouldn't bat an eyelid!"

"Well you *are* practically naked, and he *has* noticed!"

"I ain't got a hope in hell..."

"Have you actually tried?"

"I've been battin' my eyes like Miss Fuckin' Kansas — so much I've been makin' enough breeze ta blow me back thar!"

"Well, I think you need to take the bull by the horns..." We both look over at Cage, he's jumping down off the stage just as a crowd I hadn't seen before are getting on. Blink suddenly looks really excited, and jumps up onto the stage herself, grabbing the mike up off the floor:

"Ladies and Gentlemen, it is a big surprise and pleasure — I didn't know if they would be able to make it tonight, but they have, and they're here to play their new track from their new album, will you welcome, The Evil Knocky Men!" The crowd shows their appreciation, but this is a fairly closed group, and we don't always welcome outsiders. Blink's stamp of approval, however, sways us in their favour. Though what swayed me in their favour was the fact that all four of them were really easy on the eye. As they got themselves set up and settled on stage, I had time to look and admire.

"Well, who might this new strain of beast be?" Courtney is curious.

"I don't know, but I'm sure enjoying just watching them in motion." Cage comes and sits down, and after the congratulations I kick Court under the table, and nod towards Cage. She gives me daggers. I kick her again.

"So, Cage," she leans in towards him looking awkward as hell; I try to look the other way; to give her the space to try her luck. He's watching the stage. I kick her again, and she swipes me with her hand. "I like your shorts," Court touches the fabric tentatively. Cage turns to acknowledge her breaking into his space:

"Thanks," he manages.

"You look real sexy in 'em," her flirting is painful. I stand up and go to the bar with the excuse of buying another round. If anything is going to happen it stands a better chance with me out of the way.

"Hello!" Offers the lead singer from the stage. A gangly youth with short blond hair, glasses, and a pretty face. He quickly looks down at the ground belying a shyness that's out of place on a stage. "We are The Evil Knocky Men, and this is one we made earlier...." The bass player, another gangly youth with long hair, and a baby face, starts thumping out a bass line; the drummer picks up the beat, his curly, dirty blonde hair hanging down in his face; and the guitarist starts up a chord sequence that is syncopated sweetness.

The lead singer hangs back on the mike, teasing the audience, looking at the ground, and turning to look up sideways at the guitarist; sensing the right moment he lets his words flow into the mike.

There is something about them. It's obvious from the start. They have that chemistry between them, a feeling of taking sound to a new place. We, the audience know it, and they know it. Like when I first saw Madonna writhing around in the middle of the road with her fingerless gloves, and her twisted hair; her mouth inviting you to fuck her. There are moments of greatness glimpsed from the start; you are seeing a star in the making. These boys had something. It may not make them stars — (if they were in Blink's club it certainly wouldn't) — but they were damn good; good enough to make it.

Court was whispering in Cage's ear: she was working the rules of engagement. I would have high fived her if she didn't practically have her tongue in his ear. Putting the drinks down didn't shake them out either. I sat down, and continued lusting after the lead singer.

"There ain't one of 'em I wouldn't let tickle my fancy..." Courtney, back in the room, is reading my thoughts again.

"Yeah, what about all of them all at once?"

"Now y'ar talkin'."

"You two have a one-track mind," Cage looks genuinely hurt, and left out. Court fluffs his hair:

"They don't mean nuthin' to me," target engaged, he smiles. Maybe this has legs? Or a vagina?

"Wow..." I manage, to no one in particular. I study each member of the band in turn, flitting like a butterfly from one flower to another; each as sweet as the next, but there is something earthy about the drummer. He's working with a limited kit, and it focuses his intensity. He keeps the snare tight, and the hi hat light; he bends close to his kit, encircling it.

The lead singer is holding the mike as if it were the face of an angel he would kiss, and the longer the song goes on the more you want him — will him — to make that contact. Tortured and moved by his own words, he becomes the actor on the stage; half held in by his own shyness, half moved beyond his control by the music he has created. His glasses can't hide him, the music wants him there. The audience wants him there. Blink glows from the side lines, proud to have such a band on her stage.

Cage nods his head in appreciation. A shimmering heat bounces off the flat surfaces of stage and table tops, the heaters reabsorbing their own energy. The sand beneath our feet seems to hum with the snare drum, shuffling along the ground, grains dancing.

By the time they come shuddering to the end of the song we have all cum. The applause is instantaneous. With scant acknowledgment to the enthusiasm they launch into a second number. The lead singer intros it with a high, soaring vocal that arches over the crowd like a wave; melancholy, lonely, his voice isolated with the guitar, strumming a staccato rhythm. When the drums come in, insistent, churning up the emotion again, we aren't prepared for the velocity or contagiousness of the beat. This time the bass was last to join the melody, but when it does it becomes the central theme, and all the instruments follow after. The bass player is more his instrument than himself; I have never seen anyone perform with such zeal, or wind themselves around an instrument with such intensity. His long, black hair hangs down, caressing the strings; his look is almost Native American Indian. Small in stature, his playing makes up for his slender frame. He becomes his noise. The Evil Knocky Men have arrived.

Chapter 24

To the Sounds of 'Break it Down Again'
by Tears for Fears

"Why do I get the feeling that you don't even want to try this?" Hel is standing with one hand on her hip.

"Because I don't — it's stupid, and mediocre, and nobody is going to give a hair-brained shit about animal psychics!" Hel shifts her weight to the other hip, pouting with her baby lips. Monday mornings always suck, but especially after a week-end overnight. The office light is burning my eyes.

"Well why don't we ask Clare, and see what she says?"

"Fine! Ask her, but for God's sake don't make it a regular feature!" Hel looks at me, and tries her other morning artillery:

"And am I still telling your Dad that you are in Outer Mongolia when he calls?" Her tone is sarcastic; as well it should be. There was no getting around the fact that my life had turned into a merry-go-round. If I didn't step off soon I was going to get used to riding bad-tempered ponies all my life. My response is a well-honed glare.

"Suit yourself." Hel storms off in the direction of Clare's office, leaving the way free for Courtney to sidle up; she hates being near Hel, even for a brief chat.

"Hey sunshine!" Her voice sounds unseasonably loud; I wince up at her.

"Hey yourself."

"How ya feelin'?"

"Not so shiny."

"Ya shoulda come out with me and the Headbangers after the shift."

"Nah. I'm good."

"Ya woulda felt better…"

"What time you get in anyway?"

"Honey, I still haven't been home." My eyes widen.

"I thought those clothes looked familiar."

"It's alright, I'll have a good scrub tonight." She winks at me.

"You didn't do any of them did you?"

"Chance would be a fine fuckin' thing. Speakin' of chance: what about those Evil Knocky Men the other night? Pretty cute, eh? I could have fondled every last one of them, and still had room to fondle some more." She was cheering me up; I was smiling now.

"I coulda sucked each one of them in turn, and still drunk an ocean!"

"I could have mounted them all, and still rode a rodeo!"

"I could have rode a rodeo, mounted them all, and then sucked the living daylights out of them!"

"OK, OK— break it up!" Hel was back. "Clare is fine with it, as a one off."

"Oh, Jesus!"

"What?" Courtney is curious.

"Hel has gone and found this fucking pet psychic, and now Clare is happy for us to do a feature!"

"Well that's a damn disgrace! This is a radio station for human beings, not bloody animal farm! You'll be doing circus acts next! Mark my words!"

"I know!" We both look daggers at Hel.

"Well it's not easy finding new things to fill the show with each week," Hel is pouting.

"Well, hell, there's always the kinda normal stuff that radio stations fill their goddamn shows with every week like news, politics, current affairs, fashion, investments, travel — take y'ar pick!"

"You two should try producing a show for a week and see how you get on!" She huffs and puffs her way to her desk half a foot away, and sits down with a harrumph. Courtney turns back to me.

"As we were sayin'…"

"I want to know how you and Cage got on after I left." Courtney suddenly turns down cast:

"Oh, nuthin' happened…I bit my lip near off I was so nervous, and talked a bunch of crap about nuthin' and he looked real bored but tried ta keep his eye lids from fallin' in ta his drink…"

"I'm sure you're exaggerating, as usual."

"Nah, I'm tellin' ya, he has about as much interest in me as a man has in wearin' a condom."

"Well, I think you have no self-confidence when it comes to men."

"It's hardly surprisin'. Every man I ever dated preferred my sister, or only fucked twelve-year olds; they thought spankin' was a form of foreplay. Then when I got here they just plum ran a mile every time I opened ma mouth!"

"Maybe you should keep it closed more often?" I smile to show her I'm not serious. She returns the smile:

"Let's get some work done then 'cause we sure as hell ain't gettin' any dick just standin' around…"

Hel is suddenly standing in front of us with her attempt at a serious expression. She turns her stern little face to me:

"Please don't forget that we have to be at London Fashion Week tomorrow morning first thing." She hands me a sheath of papers, which appear to be in no particular order, and turns on her tiny heels.

"Yes, Ma'am," Courtney raises her eyebrows, and salutes at Hel's disappearing stodginess.

"You gotta get a muzzle for that one; she damn near bit y'ar head off: she'll be knawing on your leg next."

I look at the sheath of papers in my hand, that heavy feeling rolling back in. Court picks it back up:

"C'mon let's get the fuck outta here."

Courtney is at the back of the record store off the Portobello Road. She is engrossed in the 'C' section (no pun intended). Leafing through Crosby, Stills, Nash, and Young's back catalogue, she acknowledges my presence without looking up:

"I jus' don't know how the hell they managed to look so shit, and sing so sweet…"

"It's got to be a genetic thing: maybe when you can't get the girls with your looks you have to find other ways to lure them in, like music?"

"Mutation my ass — I'm beginning to wish I wasn't born so damn perfec'!" She picks out 'Déjà vu' and we walk up to the counter.

"That's got that great cover of Joni Mitchell's 'Woodstock' on it..."

"I know — I didn't buy it for the long-haired hippies."

Back outside the air feels cooler, and for a moment I think I can smell spring. Courtney hugs the record in its plastic bag to her chest, and we walk in silence. The market's in full swing, bright oranges and lemons, green bananas.

"Let's find a pew..."

The Portobello Travel Book Shop is not known for its fine food, but it actually does some mean home-made delicacies, and tucked away in the back you can get some 'me' time. We order two lasagnes and herbal teas.

"My Dad tore a strip off me..." She turns putting her jacket on the back of her chair:

"Why?"

"'Cause I walked out on Christmas and didn't embrace his new girlfriend like she was my long lost mother."

"So wearin' his usual goggles again?" Courtney has sampled some of my Dad's philosophical side lines and come up gasping for air.

"Yeah. I didn't argue with him; just let him reel off and then walked off."

"Well, that way you don't have to argue or try to understand each other: it's simpler." Courtney eyes up the waiter. "I've seen more of an arse on a cumquat." We watched the waiter's bum for a bit longer, and then with a mutual sigh drew ourselves back to the conversation.

"So, he's got himself a girlfriend…" Court purrs.

"Yes, and she's a cheesecloth wearing weirdo."

"Well, I guess he's managed more than we have." She had a point. "He's managed to find another weirdo to play with."

"Speaking of weirdos, have you seen Cage recently?"

"No, I already told ya, he's got about as much interest in me as a flea on a wooden horse."

"Well, I just got the feeling — at the hospital, all of a sudden — that maybe you guys —"

"Oh, get out widcha! He's my buddy!"

"Yeah, but you've gotta admit you've got an itty-bitty crush…"

"Aww, c'mon, who doesn't think he's hotter than July with those come-hither eyes?" She stops a moment to consider those eyes, "I mean y'ad have to be blind not to fall in'ta them — the guys got swamps for peepers! You could drown in those damn things!" Realising she's eulogising a bit much, she stops and glances at me nervously to see if I have caught a whiff of her mega-watt desire.

"He's scrawny as an alley cat," I counter.

"Ahh, that's just where he gets his musk from — it's par for the course, but hell, I ain't caught anything serious..." She bats her big blues at me, but I'm not fooled.

"Yeah, but what if it could be?"

"Hell, I'd jump him in a New York minute, but he's never looked more than once in my direction, and that was only 'cause I spilled some Jack Daniel's on me, and he was thirsty...."

"C'mon, you're not even trying!"

"Honey, nobody can compete with the ghost of Cassandra past..." It looks like she might have regretted the last statement as soon as she says it, but there it was — out in the open — bare naked as a new born.

"Oh, c'mon, that was ages ago — he's been out with other women since then...."

"He was jus' passin' time till you changed yur mind..."

"But I won't."

"And the poor guy looks half dead with hopin'..."

"You're really exaggerating; we're good friends, and I know he cares about me, but..."

"Hell, his eyes roll back in his head every time he sees ya!" Our lasagne arrives. We both look down at our food, considering. We thank the waiter and watch him walk away again.

"Such a shame — everything else is working for him except that ass." We silently agree, and move on:

"Court, if you like him you've got to at least have a go — let him know — go for it!" Her usual diamond studded eyes look forlorn:

"I've got more hope of catchin' the Easter bunny..." Her glum, downcast expression makes me feel similarly morose. It's a fact that women can naturally get in sync with each other's emotions — not just rag times — by reading facial expressions; responding to those non-verbal cues as much as the tone of voice or body language; and men are just as good at reading others, but I was surprised to read recently that although men have the reputation for being more stoic than women in the face of sentiment, they actually have stronger emotional reactions. Studies of men's faces show that the male brain's initial emotional reaction can be even stronger than the female! Sadly however, within 2.5 seconds they change their faces to hide the emotion, even reverse it. This repeated denial of their deeper feelings gives men that poker face; that monumental holding back that might well be a tidal wave of emotion. They will then go onto use their analytical rather than emotional hard wiring to solve problems that emotions have brought to the surface, completing the circle of denial.

A study was made at UCLA by two women scientists who, while talking one day at the lab were joking that when women were stressed they got together, had a tidy about the lab, shared a coffee, and bonded woman to woman, whereas when men got uptight they tended to withdraw into their cave. They found that this mechanical desire to clump together and share is what marks the girls from the boys, the de-stressed from the stressed. They discovered that not only do we enjoy valuable girlie time, full of shopping and gossip, but that this shared time is important because it shapes who we are, and who we are yet to become. These friendships with our women folk form a symbiotic stress inhibitor that counteracts the long-held belief that women, like men, respond to stress in the old 'fight or flight' manner. We now know that women because of the hormone oxytocin don't just respond to these old survival mechanisms like men, but rather respond by tending the young and gathering with other females — at last hours spent gabbing over coffee is no longer simply a waste of time. Now all we need is an excuse for shopping.

This calming response to stress, which men do not share as part of their make-up bag, is due to the fact that testosterone inhibits the effects of oxytocin. I have often marvelled at how women can start a conversation with someone they just met at a supermarket or at a bus stop and talk on the most intimate level about their lives and feelings.

"There's no doubt," concluded Dr. Klein, "that friends are helping us live."

I looked over at Court who was forking a competitively large portion of lasagne into her mouth and felt the first warm glow in days.

Chapter 25
To the Sounds of 'Fashion'
by David Bowie

London Fashion Week is the kind of pointless exercise in emaciated cool that makes everyone, including the stick-pin-thin models, feel inadequate. The designers attach their colours to the mast of these emaciated teenagers as if raising a flag.

Hel had been hammering on about it for a week. The moment of truth had arrived. I stroked my imperceptible bump unconsciously and caught myself: looking around the street as if to spot somebody who might know, by this sign, that I was with child, and would make comment. No familiar faces, however, jump out of the many bodies now strewn along the corner of the Cromwell Road and Exhibition Road; more pouring out of South Kensington tube every minute. The front lawn of the Natural History Museum has been transformed into a Saharan desert of white tents. Designer labels flatter every passing bag and signature cut. Sunglasses appear happiest on heads where they sail into an even bigger sea of heads, even in this greyest of weathers. Everyone is walking around trying to look incredibly important, busy, and in a rush. Chins tilted up, buttocks, and boobs pushed out, waists cinched in, hobbling on a fixed trajectory of self-importance. An unnatural perfection glazes over every walking specimen; they have been tucked and pinched, brow tweezered and skin buffed to an industrial sheen.

At the gates of the Natural History Museum I see her, lumbering under the girth of her own frame; winsome in a tiny Churchill sort of way; like a baby with boobs.

"Right," Hel is in authoritative mode, sunglasses high on her head, "we need to hit some of the stalls, and interview some of the designers, and then we've got seats reserved for Alexandre Hakaraia, Bell Monday, and French Detroit..."

"Oh, for fuck's sake..."

"What?"

"I've trodden in dog shit..." Eyeing the bottom of my shoe, I look for somewhere to scrape it off. Hopping over to a patch of grass, I unceremoniously drag my shoe along the ground like a dog with worms.

"Ugh," manages Hel, "make sure you get it all off — we don't want you to look unfashionable *and* smell bad."

"What do you mean 'unfashionable'?" I look up from dog scraping.

"Well, what season is that shirt?"

"Last summer!"

"What label?" She had me there; I paused.

"Um, Dorothy Perkins."

"Dorothy Perkins?!" Hel says this unmentionable name so loudly that people look around shocked.

"Shh! Yes, what's wrong with that?"

"Well, this is LONDON bloody FASHION WEEK! You could have made an effort."

"Listen, shut the hell up, and let's get this sorry excuse for a fashion item over with." Giving my shoe one last scrape, I push Hel in the direction of the main doors. Chanel number five could be smelt before we reach the main gangway. People were pushing in but trying to do it with decorum; their expensive handbags doing the pushing for them.

We pick up our badges and start perusing the ground floor stalls. Most of the clothes I would rather put on my cat than wear myself.

"How about this?" Hel is standing in front of Jane Llewellyn's bag collection.

"OK," I say looking over her shoulder at the other stalls in the vicinity. Hel excitedly pulls out the recording device in her shoulder bag. I watch her untangle herself, and then re-tangle herself in the wires. Waiting, I watch Jane Llewellyn notice that we have stopped in front of her stall, she moves closer, a smile pursing her miniscule lips. Hel has finally wrestled the technology into some order.

"Hi," I hold out my hand, "are you Jane Llewellyn?"

"Yes, I am," she says rather hesitantly, eyeing Hel as if she were a cheap import.

"We're from the all-female radio station, Radio Honey, and we were wondering if we could get a couple of sound bites about you and your bags for our piece on London Fashion Week?"

"Yeah, um, sure," she says rather uncertainly; even more so when Hel invades her space with an outstretched microphone. I too would have felt uncomfortable if a dwarf pushed a techno wand into my face.

"Don't mind her," I say nodding at Hel, "she won't bite." Hel gives me one of her best stern and unimpressed schoolmarm looks.

"What is your new season of handbags all about?" I take the opportunity to look down at the undersized, shrunken animal hides, and hideous, gory colours.

"Well, this season is all about colour, and texture. I wanted to mix contemporary animal hides with colours that were bright yet tonal and brought that Summery vibe. Last season was all about two tone. This season is the antithesis. It's mixing it up and making it bright. Statement colours."

"OK, great, um, and what does London Fashion Week mean to you as a designer?"

"It's a great chance to show off what you've got, meet other designers, see what they're up to, and meet the buyers of course!" She lets out a little giggle, which she quickly suppresses. I notice that Hel is perspiring along her top lip.

"Um, what other designers do you admire? Handbags or otherwise?"

"Well, I just love Judith Leiber. I mean she is just the forerunner at mixing art and fashion in handbags. Each one of her bags is a work of art; she uses luxurious suedes, hand-pleated fabrics, reptile skins, semiprecious stones — she is a leader."

"Great! Thanks for that. Have a good show."

"Thank you." Hel and I move away.

"You're sweating."

"What?"

"Your top lip — you're sweating — are you OK?"

"Yes, fine, I better just play that back and make sure I got it." Hel stops in the middle of the fray, and fiddles with the recorder.

"Why don't you come stand over here?" I pull her over to the wall and watch the young and the restless milling about. You could tell this season's must haves by this crowd — they were all wearing them: the arm candy handbag, statement shoes, midi-skirts, transparent shirts. The fashion merry-go-round is a predictable creature.

"Yes, that seems fine."

"Don't forget what happened last time."

"What? That was you!" How could I forget? Cringing at the memory of a recent interview with pop sensation, Guy Miller, that never got recorded because I got us high in my apartment which I'd somehow managed to lure him to, and then got myself into such an over excited state that I forgot to press 'play', only realising at the end of interview...I throw Hel off the scent of my own disaster by drawing attention to hers:

"What about the time you came to the interview without the recording device?!"

"I thought you had it!"

"I'm the presenter! *You* are the producer — the producer produces, and one of the things you should produce is a working recording device!"

"OK already!" We are attracting stares.

"Let's find another victim..." we look around the room. A cursory glance sends up dire signals of cultural lethargy. Moving things along seems the best alternative: "Let's try the next floor up." Hel follows with reduced enthusiasm as we wind our way up the stairs, at which point a familiar voice calls out:

"Cassandra! Dah-ling!" It was bloody Jane Harrison.

"Jane..." She arrives level with me on the stairs, towering over Hel who is already challenged by being one step below us.

"How is Radio-What's-It-Called?"

"Honey. Good thanks." She eyes my Dorothy Perkins top. "Didn't want to get dressed up today?"

"Didn't you know — dressed down is the new up?"

"Well, you do it very well, Dah-ling." She growls. "See you!" And she is off in a waft of Chanel number five.

"God, I hate that woman..."

The second floor looks very much like the first except there is a café at one end.

"Shall we stop for a coffee?" I suggest.

"Already? We only have one interview."

"Yes, but I desperately need a coffee..." The counter is full of enticing cream cakes: very un- anorexic fayre. I order two cappuccinos and two strawberry tarts. Hel is looking lost: a duck amongst swans, alone on a little table amongst a myriad of bespoke table gatherers.

"Here you go!" Her eyes light up as soon as she sees the strawberry tarts.

"Oooh, yummy!"

"Don't say I never do anything for you." Without answering she grabs a fork off the tray, and dives in.

"So why don't the other presenters have to cover this?" I was using the creamy cake to smoke screen and find answers to questions whilst she was high on sugar and animal fat.

"You're drive time," she says, her upper lip housing a dollop of cream, "we have to be topical and timely…"

"Did Clare say anything about my recent stats — performance — show?"

"No…" talking through the food, unable to stop, "she seems OK with it…"

"Do you think she's gay?" Hel chokes on her tart:

"What?"

"Gay — do you think Clare is gay?"

"Why?" The dollop of cream is now smeared along her top lip; a frothy moustache. She actually looks quite good with a moustache.

"Just some of the girls were talking, and well…you saw her with Agatha…"

"What do you mean?" Hel seems decidedly concerned and upset by this revelation. As if it hit her in some intimate place. This wasn't your average response to juicy gossip: it was positively motion-sensor disturbing.

"Oh, you are an innocent..." Getting an idea: "Haven't you noticed the way she looks at you?"

"No — what do you mean? How does she look at me?" Hel is spitting cream now, and it occurs to me that she may have gotten herself in deep without realising what she was up against. Had she promised to stay behind one too many nights to work up some editing clips? Taken a personal interest in Clare's haberdashery?

"She stares at your tits." Hel looks down at her tits, which now have flecks of cream on them. She holds them protectively.

"Does she?"

"Yeah, I think she fancies you."

"You can't be serious!"

"Don't you know anything? Why do you think she keeps calling you into her office? Why do you think she made you the producer of the drive time show when you have about as much experience with radio as *The Dukes of Hazzard*?"

"I don't know..." Hel's mouth is all but hanging open, showing little bits of tart crumb in the corners.

"Think about it...but don't fantasize..."

"I will not!" She manages indignantly. I try not to laugh.

"Just pay attention next time you see her...."

"What am I looking for?"

"Watch where her eyes go...." I insinuate, a vague, all knowing smile on my face. Hel doesn't know where to look. She stirs her coffee.

I can see Jane air kissing someone on the other side of the room.

"Right. Drink up, and let's get this show from Hades on the road." Hel gathers the recording equipment whilst wiping the last crumbs from her lips; she finishes with a whale of a tongue that whips up over her top lip. It was slightly unsettling as images go. I was still dealing with the cream fiasco.

'Peace Meal' is a designer tag with a difference: 'must have' is written all over it from its ecological hemp ingredients to its birth as a Nottinghill franchise. From bum bags with hip flasks, to T-shirts that scream cool, even I have to admit that I would welcome a goodie bag. Steering a cream filled, slightly dazed Hel, across the lobby floor to the shop front, I fix the man behind the counter with my most authoritative stare:

"Hi, I'd like to interview someone who represents Peace Meal. We're from Radio Honey, the all-female radio station?"

"Haven't heard of it..." he says, uninterested.

"Don't worry even we have trouble finding it sometimes, and I don't mean after a few beers!" He wasn't buying my joke. "Are you Peace Meal?"

"I'm one of the designers — yes." His dyed blonde hair was growing out at the roots and made his milky pallor scream 'Vitamin D deficient.'

"Would you mind giving us a few words about your collection — I'm a big fan by the way..." I elbow Hel who is still lost in some daydream or nightmare where Clare is eyeing her breasts. She teleports back into the room and hurriedly gets the recorder out.

"OK, what do you want to know?" He looks as interested as a beaver on Groundhog Day. Hel gets the recorder under his face just in time:

"So where do you come up with these highly original ideas?" I can tell he hates the question; a solemn wind sweeps across his face and stays throughout the interview.

"They are simply conceptual interpretations of our everyday uses and needs, packaged to wear...."

"I see," I don't, "and what are your expectations for London Fashion Week?"

"I never have expectations — "I am momentarily side lined by Hel sweeping her tongue over her upper lip in search of runaway cream.

"OK. Then, how important is London Fashion Week in the social diary of the fashion industry?"

"It is very important. It allows us to share our ideas with a wider audience, and to take our products to new markets."

"You have certainly set the British Fashion market on fire — where next?"

"We are branding for America now, and hope to have a buyer by the fall."

"Great, good luck with that." He turns without a second thought. We shuffle off; the uncool given their marching orders.

"What a wanker! To think I was going to buy something from them!"

"Well, we got some good quotes...can I do some interviewing?" Hel has recovered her composure and licked the cream clean.

"No. Why?"

"You never let me!"

"I do so. You do stuff all the time."

"But this is London Fashion Week! It's uber cool!"

"OK, OK. I tell you what, I'll let you do the next one, and if you do a good job, I'll let you do a few more...." Whilst I sneak off for another coffee, I thought to myself.

Our next victim was dress designer, Alice Evans. Her stuff was light, fluffy, exotic, and very, very flimsy. You had to be prepared to show everything, but your lady garden.

Hel clenches the recording device, her hand turning red.

"Hi," she ventures. The shop owner turns, and looks down to find Hel, the owner of the voice. I was going to enjoy this; settling back on my heels, I let my gaze wander as Hel performs her undersized interview:

"Hi," Alice Evans purrs, every millimetre the mistress of silky. I was captivated by 'Hi'; heaven only knew how Hel would get on.

"I'm Helena from Radio Honey, and I'd love to interview you for a piece we're doing on London Fashion Week?"

"OK, great," she even gets a silky smile. Hel clicks 'play'.

"Um, what do you think of London Fashion Week? Is it *the* place for a designer to show?" This was going to be painful. I was half tempted to peel off and find some real action. There was an attractive coterie of male models crowded round the Bick Sandler stand. Their lanky frames bent in towards each other as they shared a joke.

"Well, it's certainly one of them..." She isn't going to give any more. This throws Hel.

"Um, so, why do you make your dresses so...see-through?" There was a serious lack of vocabulary underpinning this unravelling. Thankfully Alice laughs before answering:

"Well, we like our clothing to have a diaphanous quality." I could see she had lost Hel at 'diaphanous." She helpfully continued: "We want our dresses to exude sensuality, and the fabrics are key to getting that right."

"Oh right, OK", the sweat was back on Hel's upper lip, and had found a sluice of cream, "and well, how important is London Fashion Week to you?"

"It's pretty important, and it's a great place to catch up with the local industry," she smiles: "Is that all?" — Hopeful.

"That's great, thank you." Hel pulls away, still holding the microphone stretched out in her hand: shell-shocked.

"Great, but remember, don't ever follow a question with another question."

"I didn't!"

"You did, you said, 'What do you think of London Fashion Week' and in the same breath, 'is it the place for a designer to show?'."

"Oh." Her arm is still held out, grasping the microphone; as if for dear life. Gently pushing her arm down:

"And 'Why are your dresses see through'?!" I pause for effect. "That is a little too blunt."

"Yeah, I know, that wasn't great." Hel's shoulders relax and hunch all at once.

"No, but hey, it was OK — it got a laugh. Why don't you go off and do a few more — on your own. I'll be at the coffee bar." Hel looks happy, then sad.

Holding a coffee between your hands, the warmth of it, is a good way to concentrate your thoughts; or at least give the impression of compression of thought. Jack's latest retaliation was still flopping around like a land lubbered fish in my mind. He had a little chat with Tony, didn't he? Put him in the picture about me being 'up the duff.' (What kind of expression is this anyway? It's like you have a duffle coat stuffed inside you.) Tony called last night sounding as panicked as a mother duck; I could literally hear the flapping of feathers, the clucking, and foot scraping down the phone. If he could have laid claim to my womb with his apron strings he would have been right in there. I tried to assure him that he had no reason to believe this was his, and that in any case there would soon be nothing to worry about as I was having it dealt with in the most final way possible; thus ending any possible thoughts about who owned what or whose chromosomes risked being brought forward into this increasingly dumbfounding world of ours. This only seemed to increase his distress, and this in turn served to annoy me further, and make me silently curse the name of Jack and all his sperm. I began to hatch a side conversation in my mind where retaliation could form a new plan; this latest offering with new scope for deeper depths of depravity and loathsome animosity. He would pay. Lord he would pay. Tony's plaintive voice was grating; I longed to be rid of him, but he pushed home the fact that it could well have been one of his little swimmers as there was still a small percentage of a possibility that his boys were still up to the job. And, therefore, he had a right (a right!) to be a part of the conversation. Another one laying claim to my womb. (It is always amazing to me how men lay claim to land that never was theirs, and only ever belonged to mother earth herself let alone a womb). This sent me into a spin of expletives; how dare he tell me this now? Wasn't it just like a man to use all the tools at his disposal to avoid using a condom?! He rallied to the defence of his kind. It wasn't the fact that he didn't like condoms. NO of course not. All men love dressing their dicks up in a raincoat so that they can't feel what little pleasure they are able to receive from the copulative experience. Especially when they figure out that the female of the species stands a better chance of enjoyment.

It is a proven fact that women have the ability to experience greater depth and longer duration of orgasm than the male. Tantra practitioners will tell you that men simply cannot match the intensity and length of the female orgasm. Plus, scientifically speaking, the vagina has more pleasure receptors than the male meaning that her ability to reach heights unknown by the male is endemic. The record is apparently one hundred and thirty-four orgasms in an hour (which is one orgasm every twenty-one seconds) for women. I don't have the physical data on that nor is it hearsay (or small talk around the kitchen sink) but I have read about the laboratory experiments. The most a man has managed in this scientific environment is sixteen, and boys don't go telling me he got shy. There are over eight thousand nerves of the clitoris which extend throughout the tissue beneath the surface inside the vagina and throughout the vulva and perineum. There are more nerve endings in the clitoris than in any other part of the human body, including the penis, which only has four thousand nerves in contrast. So, gentlemen, it just shows your lack of aptitude when so many women go un-pleasured; when they have such a propensity; your lack of invention in the face of all that possibility is frankly abysmal.

The fact that the male G-spot is in the ass begs other questions which will not be explored here, but could serve as the basis for an entire diatribe on how God is a class A joker, or a big fan of homosexual love.

Once more Jack had proved that he had more ways of ruining my life than I was previously aware of. Every nice guy in town wanted to be there for me, but him. The truly sad thing was that I was still in love with him.

By the time we sit down to our first fashion show of the day, Hel is perspiring heavily, pushing her grey, long sleeve Cacharel cardigan into black pockets under her arms; she blows her fringe up off her face, and flusters in the seat next to me. It isn't front row, but it isn't back so we have a half-decent view of the walking dead.

The music slam dunks us into catwalk mode with some one hundred and twenty beats per minute. Alexandre Hakaraia is known for his luminous, alien style attire, and he doesn't disappoint. The walking stick figures file out with luminous yellow and orange make-up marking their faces like jungle warriors; their clothes owing more to aluminium foil than cloth. I yawn and try to get comfortable on a seat not used to bum fat.

Jane, on the opposite isle, is jotting things down in a notebook on her lap. Flanked by blonde fashionistas, she is the dark, sticky centre. By the time Alexandre Hakaraiai fans out alongside his models I am ready to let blood, my blood, anyone's blood. It seems to mark a curious lack of faith in their own industry when the designers themselves, who make a living from selling us their strange and exotic couture, embellish themselves all in black. It doesn't bode well for the fashion business when its own bastions of cool prefer to shun the new designs that they and others create in favour of the blandest options. The Emperor's new clothes would be a welcome break.

"Why do you think Clare is gay?" It had obviously been playing on Hel's fragile mind. We dodge enormous handbags as we make our way out of the hooded, Ku Klux Klan tents that huddle on the lawn.

"Well, you know, gay is the new straight?"

"No." Bless her; she genuinely lives in a polystyrene world of make-believe.

"It is. It's hideously cool to be gay these days. If you're not at least bi you are not interesting."

"Really?" I can hear the little cogs turning gently in their sockets.

"Really." I dig in.

"I never knew that." She's letting the flavour of this coat the cogs.

"I mean you know how men love a little girl on girl action?"

"Yeah..." She genuinely doesn't sound clued up but is playing along.

"Well, now the girls are realizing they can enjoy it too..." I smile provocatively.

"Oh..." Hel looks like you've just stuck a finger up her ass for the first time. She is re-running those childhood memories of her and Anne in the playroom cupboard through her head; this time with a renewed frisson, and lack of guilt.

"Yeah, if you listen to the word on the street, go to any bar, club, whatever, and you get asked about your sexuality — for God's sake — don't just say you like dick. Say you like a little of everything."

"Are you pulling my leg?" Hel suddenly suspicious, regains her composure — that stick up her ass.

"I'm totally serious. I'm just trying to give you an education so you don't end up looking stupid. I mean come on — do you really think Clare likes dick looking like she owns one?"

"I don't know." The tiny cogs are working full tilt; trying to process; I can hear the hinges straining under the new knowledge.

"Listen, I've got a little idea..."

Chapter 26
To the Sounds of 'Basket Case'
by Green Day

New research says that helping others not only will give you that warm, fireside glow on the inside, but it can actually add years to your life. Psychologists now believe that helping out our fellow man can have as many health benefits as those accrued by a low cholesterol diet, stable body weight, and eating healthily. In fact, these simple acts of kindness, perfect in their simplicity, are now known to be worth more to our daily well-being than pots of money and worldly success. Even a six-pack of daily supplements.

I shall no doubt be down with the flu, at the very least, by Monday.

To add insult to ill health, you're more likely to feel positive health effects from somebody finding you an OK human being, than sexually attractive. There goes another past time. You also double your anti-ageing hormones when you're a do-gooder. Helping others is better than botox. At the Institute for HeartMath in Colorado they found that 'pro-social behaviours' — showing love and appreciation, to you and me, boosted levels of the important antibody, IgA. This secretory immunoglobulin is the body's first line of defence against invading pathogens: colds, flus, digestive and respiratory infections, and is lowered by anti-social behaviour: suspicion, anger, tension, aggression. My IgA must be bottoming out.

Lab tests in Atlanta found that playing classic laboratory games with human lab rats who chose empathy, and team work over selfish pursuits had MRI scans which showed the kind of pleasure normally seen when snorting up a couple of lines of cocaine or guzzling a chocolate bar. Being good has never felt so bad.

Based on these statistics, doing the right thing is not something we do out of a selfless desire; it is totally selfish, based on self-satisfying, greedy, feel good factors. Do gooders are just do badders by a sweeter name. Giving to charity no longer smacks of puritanical deeds, especially when it is tax deductible. The criminals amongst us at least work from a place of personal truth — honest greed — not self-pleasuring in the name of universal good. These days to connect to a feeling of greater good, bypass the meaningless trivialities of hardware, property, possessions; dig deeper than the odd habit of giving; embrace a bigger truth without personal reward. But how do you give without giving to yourself? Maybe that's just what we call unconditional love?

The sight of Hel sashaying off towards Clare's office, an A4 sheet of paper clutched in her grubby paw, fills me with a momentary, guilty feeling. It swiftly passes. We had spent the afternoon writing up a list of lesbian-friendly or bi features; clubs, zeitgeist, agony-aunt phone-ins. By the end, Hel was very much on board; excited to brush up on her *lesbianese*, and perhaps even read some clit-lit.

When she returned ten minutes later, I tried to read her facial expression as she walked towards me. Her arms hung lower and lower the nearer she got.

"What did she say?"

"She said there was no place for a lesbian spot on Radio Honey." Hel fell into her chair.

"A lesbian spot, eh? Is she referring to the clitoris?"

"Oh, shut up, it was embarrassing." Hel looks positively traumatised; like a cat that has just realised it has used up all nine lives as it's falling from a very high building.

"What else did she say? — Was she shocked?"

"She looked a little pale when I brought it up, and she didn't seem willing to even listen to the different ideas we had come up with…"

"She didn't like the 'Girls on Top' idea?"

"I didn't even get that far…doesn't she even realize gay is the new straight?" I laugh hearing my own words come out of Hel's mouth with such conviction. I had introduced her to a brave new world, and like Christopher Columbus she was ready to sail forth with the very flag I had made for her. Now, her boat roughly moored, she looks water logged.

"But," Hel pipes up, "she still loves the idea of a regular feature on pet psychics!"

"Oh, for God's sake!"

What is the point of stockings that ladder? A tyre that bursts? Tesla came up with an electricity conductor that you could stick in the ground in your back garden, and it would come up with limitless amounts of free electricity. He was mysteriously murdered. His laboratory ransacked, his papers missing. A tyre that would never break was invented, and the makers were bought out, their invention holed up in the vault of some tyre company with more money than future sense or humanity. I have the secret to universal happiness in my top pocket (or stomach drawer), and I can't even use it:

A global survey says that the secret to happiness is a loving family. I've got one growing in my belly but getting the man I want to share this joy with me seems like asking for universal peace and an end to global warming. Mice will walk on the moon, unaided by breathing apparatus before I gain the gift of a happy, fulfilled family life. Errant weather conditions will no longer affect frizzy hair, road rage will dissipate into thin air, and men will finally learn how to use a washing-machine and buy their own underwear before I will achieve my universal order. Bagpipes will replace elevator music, surgeons will no longer use knives but the power of positive thought, babies will be born without the need for belly buttons, gangsters will do good out of love not back handers, mothers and fathers will love each other for ever and never leave their children parentless. All this and more I promise if I am elected.

Fundamentally flawed, however, I am not without hope.

My toenail snags my second pair of stockings, and they are sent on a long volley across the bedroom. Shaving and shading with blusher seems the only alternative, short of an all-out screaming fit. My door buzzer sounds, and expecting Courtney, I press the door release. I can hear the spurs on her boots coming up the stairs.

"Aren't you ready yet?"

"Oh, don't you start! I'm having a major stocking problem." I look at her standing there, legs wide apart in a pair of leather chaps: I decide not to comment.

"I don't usually wear them, they give me thrush!" She says in answer to my silent survey.

"Everything gives you thrush."

"I only have to look at a guy and I get it." She walks into the flat; the very act of movement making the kind of uncomfortable noise that would explain chaffing.

"You need to get that itch scratched."

"I need a dick big enough to make an impression first. The last two were like being tickled by a baby's finger. "

"Hmmm…" I try to sound interested whilst I paint my legs with blusher.

"What are ya doin'?"

"Giving my legs a little colour. I've torn my last pair of flesh-coloured stockings."

"Why don't ya just wear trousers? It's nearly twenty below outside."

"Is it still raining?" Deciding to ignore the weather in favour of pulling options.

"No, but they're grittin' the road for snow."

"Ah, that won't happen…it's far too warm."

"You say that, but this is England. I've known it ta be sunny in tha morning, thunderin' in the afternoon, and snowin' by nightfall."

"Yeah, I guess…" absentmindedly sculpting knee cap and ankle.

"You English girls don't care what the weather is though; you're more interested in showin' off your crotch than saving yar self from pneumonia. I've never seen such short skirts in such cold weather. You shoulda perished as a race long ago from horniness and hypothermia." In the name of my people, I ignore her comments. "Why don'tcha just throw on some jeans? It's gettin' late."

"I'm wearing my costume." I point to a short, fringed leather shirt and tunic hanging up on the wardrobe.

"That's cool. Ya gotta big ol' belt ta go with it?"

"Check." Bent double over my legs, I stand up in my underwear, and I can feel Courtney's eyes on my belly.

"Not much of a bump yet...what's the latest on motherhood?"

"Jury's still out."

"They better get back in cause that'll be goin' ta college befoa y'all made up yar mind."

"OK, OK, very funny," I slip the dress over my head, push my feet into some moccasins, and strap on a belt pulled out of a drawer fit to bursting like the snake filled tomb of Indiana Jones. "Ready!"

"Thank God for that. I was gonna have an aneurism." The last thing I grab is my guitar in its world-weary case.

The boot snaps shut, the doors slam, and the little shit-coloured mini is on the move again. There's a huddle of people outside the club door which is unusual: usually everyone just piles in; it's too cold to stand out on the pavement, and smoking of all sorts is standard inside.

An unfamiliar bus is parked up on the sidewalk outside. As we came closer, we see the words 'The Evil Knocky Men' emblazoned on its side. We both look at each other wide eyed.

Down in the bowels where the club bubbles up, the strum of guitars can already be heard. The place is humming. The theme is Cowboys and Indians. The Evil Knocky Men are at the bar, all except the lead singer who's talking to Blink.

"Let's go up to the bar," Courtney winks. I hang back, shy.

"I don't know…"

"C'mon or do I have ta horse whip ya?" She starts to drag me, and I notice she actually has a horse whip wound into a hook on her belt. Deciding I don't want to look more of a fool, I submit so that she drops her hold.

"Hey, which one of ya's 'evil' and which one's 'knocky'?" Their eyes spell a blank. None of them have bothered to dress up which makes me feel incredibly stupid in my moccasins, and Haiwatha braids.

"We're all 'evil' and been known to be 'knocky,'" says the drummer suddenly. He doesn't so much look us up and down as absorb our presence. He has the kind of face that ships are named after, and wars are fought over. There is a gentleness to his gaze, but he holds it long enough to make you feel like he has x-ray vision; a cool undertone signifies resistance would be futile.

"That so," Courtney sizes him up, inching closer, "you don't look so evil to me."

"I'm having an off day..." his words woolly with sensuality; nobody says anything. It was Riley that broke through the smoke and mirrors:

"What'll it be?"

"Sorry, have you ordered?" Courtney asks the drummer.

"Yeah, I'm just cluttering up the bar,' he makes way for us, standing to the side; eyeing us from the side-lines.

"One beer and one coke, please." Then turning to the drummer, "So you guys were great last week." The bass player replies for them, "Thanks." He is smaller than the drummer, but once he emerges from behind his shadow cuts a decidedly dark and sexy figure. He has a kind of Native American look. Long, black hair, almost pale skin, dark eyes, and a wiriness to his limbs that implies gymnastic like manoeuvres. Courtney and I are summing this up in our minds as the seconds tick by between words.

"What might y'ar name be then?"

"I'm Theo, and this is Ben, and that shy one over there is Steve," the bassist points to the guitar player who is trying to blend into the shadows.

"Nice to meet ya's, I'm Courtney, and this here's my partner in crime, Cass — Cassandra if ya're angry with 'er." Acknowledging each other was the easy bit, knowing where to look after was the difficult part. Courtney picks up the ball, and just keeps running.

"So y'all playin' again tonight?"

"Yeah." Says drummer, Ben, who I can hardly look at; he has the kind of sunny countenance that makes you think of warm sheets with him in them. I wanted to get next to him without even knowing why. My body was responding quicker than my mind could catch up.

"That's some accent you've got there — where you from?" Theo is sizing Courtney up.

"I'm from Kansas…"

"You're a long way from home."

"This is my home now." Courtney meets his gaze.

"What about you," Ben is looking right at me, "you from the Deep South too?"

"Um, no..." I stammer.

"She's from half a mile up the road," Courtney helps.

"You play that thing?" Ben motions towards my guitar case which I had forgotten I was holding.

"Uh, yeah..."

"Cool. Look forward to hearing you play." My legs are feeling decidedly rubbery.

"S'cuse me," Theo, cuts in at the bar, and orders another drink, then turning to us says, "Either of you like a drink?"

"That's very hospitable of you," Courtney manages to sound touched and put out all at once, "but I'm just fine."

"Me too," I manage. Blink gets up on stage, dressed as an Indian Squaw with feather headdress, and fringed skirt; her war paint's particularly fetching: the red slashes across her cheeks matching her red hair.

"Good evening! Or should I say, HOW!?" She puts her hand up in mock native salute. The crowd was already with her, "Who wants to play cowboys and Indians?" A huge cheer goes up, and a few stray arrows fly through the air. One lands on the stage. Blink looks momentarily put out, but then smiles: "OK, let the festivities begin!"

"This place is crazy," Ben says to no one in particular. Theo stands next to him, beer in hand, "I kinda wish I'd dressed up." The singer joins them.

"We're on last," I hear him say to Ben and Theo.

"Nice to meet y'all," Courtney tips her hat.

"Likewise," says Ben; Theo smiles, and the singer just looks at us as if we are phantoms of his imagination.

"That singer's got a scary, half here look. Like he's seen a ghost — all the time."

"Yeah, but he's cute."

"Psycho cute, yeah." We find a table, and I prop my guitar up against an empty chair.

"Shit."

"What?" asks Courtney, ready for anything.

"I've got to get up and play in front of the Knocky Men..." We both inadvertently look their way.

"They's just people like everyone else," Courtney tries to sound convincing.

"Yeah, but they's cute people..." I say mimicking her way of speaking which is so inviting. I see Tony come in:

"Shit."

"What now?"

"Tony..."

"So?"

"He called me last night to say he'd spoken to Jack, and knows I'm pregnant, and asked if he was the father!"

"Shit."

"Exactly." We both watch Tony talking to Blink by the side of the stage.

"What did you say?"

"I said 'no'! I felt bad, but there's no way in God's little green acre that I want him sniffing around this baby too!"

"This is what you get for hooverin' up all the guys in town."

"I did not hoover them all up! There's plenty left — you just have to get up off your arse and get them."

"I would if I could borra' your tits and those long-assed-legs for a day or two!"

"It's not just about tits and ass..." at this point Cage, dressed entirely in cowboy finery, holster with gun, blue jeans (one side ripped open to reveal his cast), cowboy boots, plaid shirt, and cowboy hat, pulls out the empty chair; catching my guitar case as it begins to fall, and sits down.

"Cage —"

"Howdy." He tilts his hat.

"Let me ask you this," this was going to the vote, "what do men look for in a girl? Is it tits and ass or personality?"

"Tits and ass," he says without hesitation.

"Told ya!" Court loves winning an argument and pumps the air.

"Aw, c'mon!" I almost yell over Blink's sylph like voice as it makes headway into one of her new ballads. "You cannot be serious! You mean you would go for a girl with big tits rather than someone funny and cute?"

"That would be the first thing ta' hook me. Then I might stay a little longer if she had a good personality…" Cage looks completely unphased by the shallow words he has just spoken. He watches Blink sail into her ballad; her braids grazing the white flesh of her shoulders as she bends over her guitar.

"You men deserve what you get," I say putting my drink to my lips as a gag; fuming was too gentle a word for the emotions coursing through my veins.

"Told ya," says Courtney triumphantly.

"What's this all about?" Cage looks cute in his cowboy hat; he's even waxed his moustache and goatee.

"We were just arguing about whether men cared about brains or boobs most when they went for a woman, and you have just proved that all men are dick-heads." Courtney sums up for him.

"Wait a minute, I think that's a bit unfair," Cage is rising to the occasion. This is typical of him. He will say something brash and monumental, thinking this will seal whatever deal is on the table, using the male version of coercion to settle any disagreement, then, when it is clear this has not won the argument, he thinks it is perfectly fair and reasonable to wade back in with a whole suitcase full of alternative ideas and opinions. It was one of the reasons I found being with him truly annoying. You could never lay down your argument pitch and build up a store house of examples. He was always moving the goal posts and the argument around the pitch and telling you it was still in play. If he wasn't fundamentally a nice guy I would have just called him a wanker long ago and called it a day on our friendship, but underneath his inability to see he is straddling several fences with his argument in order to win is a good guy with genuine good intentions.

"Is it? I mean come on, Cage, if all you guys are looking for is a bloody great pair of tits then you haven't evolved from sucking your mummy's own!"

"Hey, look, we can't help it if we like tits! That's just the way it is. We like ass too." He looks happy with his argument. Courtney sits back smiling; her hat tilted back on her head, all that was missing was a wheat straw in her mouth.

"But once you've had the tits and ass, what are you left with? You've got to have a conversation?"

"Not always." Cage is smiling now, winding me up, "That's why we usually fall asleep." I was simmering. A small curl of his lip lets me know he is enjoying himself too much for it to be one hundred percent true: he is winding me up good and proper.

"You're such a dickhead." Blink has finished singing and is introducing the next act.

"Seriously tho'," Courtney's back in the game, "does a good personality ever make a man look twice at a woman?"

"Sure it does." Cage smiles at Courtney, Courtney smiles at Cage; I was almost relieved to hear my name called. From the safety of the stage, half my attention was drawn to the table where Courtney now had Cage's cast up on her leg and was signing it. From where I was standing, it looked like she was writing the Gettysburg address.

"Cass?" Blink was talking to me, but all I could concentrate on was the red of her lipstick, the red of her war paint, the red of her hair.

"Sorry…uh…" I was still expecting Courtney and Cage to look up at the stage, but they seemed engrossed in each other; two gay cowboys getting familiar. "Thanks Blink, yeah, uh…" I struggle to find my centre on the stage, in the room, in my slowly disintegrating world. Would I remember the words? The song: 'Butterlovers' was one I had written years ago, about a couple of friends of mine who got to know each other one night, better than they had ever known each other before, and it was all thanks to a tub of butter: a happy lubricant. As I looked into the audience, at my two dearest friends, I wondered if this was another such night. I launched into the song, revisiting the sky the way it was that week end down by the beach. Not quite spring, but the promise of it fussing with the tides. The freedom of being away from the city and having all that beach to discover: the million tiny rocks to turn over in search of fossils or treasures of the kind that made you want to take them home and watch their colour fade in the comfort of your own four walls. The salty cry of the sea birds circling over-head, sizing up your ground swell of stones, your tiny island paradise, where friendship was simple and only tides came and went.

We had rented an old cottage in Lyme Regis. There were five of us: Ted, Sarah, Andre, Stubbs, and me. It was obvious Sarah liked Stubbs — everyone liked Stubbs, but it was plain to see just how much one morning when I came downstairs and found the pair of them under a duvet on the living room floor, a tub of Flora conspicuously out of the fridge beside them. I didn't clock the connection at first — with the butter (its non-dietary uses, etc.,) but they were an item from that day forth; brought together by more than their love of Flora margarine. Where the butter was used, and how I didn't spend too much thought on, but it did turn into a song that I penned later that week. We'd brought a couple of guitars down with us, and I found a spot looking out onto the slowly greening vegetation of the valley, near our cottage, and wrote 'Butterlovers'.

As I relived that time, the Evil Knocky Men, Courtney, Cage, the baby growing in my belly, everything seemed to pale into some other dimension. My fingers found their place on the fretboard, strummed through the chord sequences, and time stretched far beyond and behind me in a never-ending line that I held to like a knot in the centre. The faces in the audience became unfamiliar, the room a void in a strange space, the sun a spoken of relic that once hung in a talked of sky. I was nobody, and this was my song. I furnished the room with sound, and a sense of rhythm that was primal, untapped. I would begin again. From a single cell.

An ache told me it was over. The corner of the guitar so deeply pressed into my rib cage with the fervour of my strumming that I didn't' feel it till I stopped; looking up, still dazed, not hearing applause, but noise, not seeing Cage and Courtney, just faces. Slowly it all came back into focus, and then hit hard. Reality fell back into place with such violence that it was all too much. The noise of faces, lights, talk. I left the stage and left the venue.

Chapter 27

To the Sounds of 'Stay Another Day'
by East 17

As a child I had this dream that all my teddies were lined up, and singing to me; a lullaby, to lull me to sleep, and there, amongst all my teddies was my mother, singing along, her face peaceful as one of the soft toys. When I woke up, I expected to find her there, on my bed, lodged between my line up of furry animals, with her frozen smile, still but present. I had that dream again last night, and when I woke I still expected, after all these years, to see her there, at the end of my bed. Pye jumped up onto the bed instead and scared the life out of me.

"What happened to you?" Courtney is pressing buttons on the console, preparing us for the next hour as the news runs in its groove.

"I just had a...a weird one.....kind of flipped out. I don't know. Couldn't take being there anymore. Just had to leave." Even thinking back to the evening turns my senses to jelly.

"OK..." Courtney gives me one of her looks, "you feelin' OK now?"

"Yeah — great." Unconvincing.

"Well, you nailed it! Shit. It was stonking!" She smiles, omitting the two conversations we should really be having.

"Really?" Revived by her praise, I smile a little; grateful that we can concentrate on this small moment of success rather than the unspoken issues up ahead.

"Yeah, even The Evil Knocky Men didn't have your magic that night."

"Get out of it!"

"Seriously, you were the magic number last night. And you only played one tune, and then done disappeared! It was fuckin' mysterious as shit!"

"Aw, well cool. Good to get it right once in your lifetime." We both pause, and she gives me the silent finger:

"You're listening to Radio Honey, 463 AM. Don'tcha just love those hemorrhoid ads? I can't sit down after I hear one! So, let's get you up and dancing with a little polka from the king of pop, Michael Jackson!" She hits the CD, and talks over the intro, "From his quadruple platinum selling album, Dangerous, it's 'Black or White.'"

"I don't know why ya don't play moa?" Courtney is back.

"I just had to get out of there. Can't explain it." Looking out at the squarely situated desks ranging beyond the glass partition window, empty at this time of night. "This place drains my soul."

"I hear ya," Courtney is fiddling with her jingles rack. "So, you're still wearin' those moccasins I see…" I look down at my feet; I hadn't noticed they were still attached to me. Had I slept in them? Suddenly I couldn't seem to remember anything between the club, and this evening. A panic rises in my chest, and I feel my cheeks burn.

"Do you want a cup of tea?" I manage, realising I need to keep moving.

"I'll have a coffee…you sure y'ar all right?" She gives me her wrinkled brow.

"Yeah. Stop asking." I clear the studio and make it to the kitchen where I lean against the counter as the kettle boils.

Who was I kidding? I was out of control. I try to remember what I'd done all day. I hadn't left the flat. Pye's the only one I'd spoken to. If you leave out yelling at the answering machine: Dad had left one of his messages. He was going away for the week end — with a friend; no awards for guessing who that friend was. This all felt very surreal as Dad doesn't do week ends away. I wanted to blurt out everything to him; tell him what was growing inside me, pushing my horizons in ways I had no control over, or didn't know how to respond to. Could he help? Would he have the magic words?

Could he solve my universal malfunction? Or would he just make me feel that I was a failure? Lumber me with more feelings that I couldn't cope with? When the time had come I couldn't talk to him, I couldn't speak the words I needed to say: just three words; those simple words that would have sounded like: "Help — I'm pregnant." Translatable in any language and spoken to many a father over the millennia, but mine was a not your average father — or was he? My translation was lost between larynx and tongue. If I wrote it in a Scientific Journal he might read it and understand:

"Scientists have today discovered a previously unknown link between Cassandra Bates' comprehension of her uterus and the real world. She previously had an unwritten belief that pregnancy was out of her realm. When, however, this was proved unfounded, and her womb was deemed fertile, her conscious mind was unable to deal with the reality. Despite the fact that women, throughout time and history have given birth to a stream of human kind she, invariably believed herself to be immune to this all-encompassing, human achievement. An achievement that has furthered the human race no end.

Scientists from The University of Life, London, now speculate that her inability to grasp this most basic of human conditions underlies a deeper disbelief in herself, and her abilities. It is a scientific fact that procreation is a fundamental norm, and the basis for all human life, however, Cassandra Bates seems to believe that it simply couldn't happen to her, and when it did she found herself in an emotional crisis. It is not uncommon for procreation to illicit deep feelings, but Cassandra, perhaps due to a lack of a bond with her true mother, seems unable to grasp the very real possibility of motherhood as part of her timeline. It is perhaps this deeper connection to her own mother that must be repaired in order for her to accept the reality of this truth in her own life. To connect with this part of herself will unlock her unspoken belief in her own life giving powers, and enable her to embrace the gift of life. As it stands, Cassandra is struggling with the very real biological process that has underpinned human existence and is making herself diametrically opposed to the very essence of life. She is unable to act with any certainty because of this dichotomy of thinking.

According to Dr. Mary Kimmel, medical director of Perinatal Psychiatry Inpatient Unit and an assistant professor of psychiatry at the University of North Carolina School of Medicine in Chapel Hill, 'Pregnancy is a huge transition in a woman's life, and it involves a complex mix of emotions, both good and bad.' As Cassandra Bates was beginning to realize, pregnancy can bring up all manner of emotionally charged issues, such as difficult family relationships, insecurities and unrealistic expectations; which may have been previously suppressed or ignored. Not to mention the emotional rollercoaster brought on by hormonal activity:

'At a biological level, the hormones oestrogen and progesterone are ramping up,' says Kimmel, and some women are more sensitive to these changes than others. This can account for mood swings, and an increase in irritability, all intensified by the very real issues going on in a woman's life: the changes to her status, her body, her relationships with the outside world, and the new world being created in her belly. The decisions that are being made by having a baby have a huge knock on effect, and these may underlie any day to day transitional feelings the mother-to-be may be undergoing."

"Two teas and some choccy biscuits." I put them down in front of Courtney on the console, trying to look pleased with myself. Courtney looks at me as if I have had a brain aneurism:

"I said coffee." When it looks like I will cry, she quickly changes tack:

"That's fine! I've probably had too much of the Mexican dancing bean anyway..." She keeps things moving, sensing my delicate frame of mind: "Great! You ready for our first caller?"

"Ready as I'll ever be!" I put on a brave face, and my headphones.

"Good evenin' you're on Radio Honey..." she breathes her brand of radio smooth down the line.

"What would you like to say about the human condition?" I cut in. Courtney looks at me but lets me lead. Our caller sounds tongue tied. I help her out:

"Tonight we've decided to talk about how things don't ever turn out the way you planned: you know the one, you planned to love some guy and he dumped you; you planned to show the boss how damn good you are at your job and he fires you; you planned that once you got out of university or school that you would take over the world, achieve your dreams, bring an end to world hunger...the reality..." I pause, and look at Courtney, but she can see I'm on a roll, and need to vent, so she doesn't say a word, "...is Sod's law. Did you know that there actually is a law that deals with the sodding best laid plans? Sod's law or Murphy's Law, as it is also called, is another way of looking at the second law of Thermodynamics, which is based on the observation that things, generally tend to become more disordered with time. The Third Law of Thermodynamics tells us that perfect order is actually nearly impossible!" I look to Courtney for confirmation of some sort, but she shrugs her shoulders. "After that it all comes down to probabilities, which is another way of saying that ideally, we all have our perfect outcome in our heads: we get the guy, the job, world peace. Whereas in reality there are many more possible outcomes, and less palatable. You've heard that saying by Burns, that Scottish sweetheart: 'The best laid schemes o' mice an' men'...?"

"You lost me at Thermodynamics..." Courtney finally joins in, "And who is this Murphy? Some Irish depressive?"

"...in fact it has been scientifically proven that if you let a piece of buttered toast drop, that in 50% of all cases, it will land butter side down."

"Don't ya just hate that?" Realizing Courtney is trying to move away from Science and back to any kind of basic human context, I press up our next caller who is still reeling from my diatribe:

"Good morning! You're on Radio Honey — what have you got to say for yourself at..." and I look at the clock, "one sixteen in the morning?"

"Hi Cass, hi Courtney, well I'm not sure what any scientific thing has to do with anything, but what I do know is shit happens, if you'll excuse my French..." it was too late to bleep the lady out so we just let it slide, hoping Clare wasn't listening, "I've seen a few things in my time, and what I do know is that even an old bird like myself…"

"How old are ya darlin?" Courtney cuts in.

"I'm fifty this year."

"Well, ya know fifty is the new forty?"

"That's good to know, thank you, well, what I do know is that young people today don't know how lucky they are. In my day you did what you were told and got on with it. You got pregnant, you dealt with it. You did an honest day's work, your boss was unpleasant to say the least, and you got on with it." Courtney looks at me, I was stony faced. "There's no problem big enough that the good Lord can't see through: it's all for a reason…"

"So why did he let his own son suffer on the cross — if we're going to go down the religious route — let's go down it!" I was ready for a fight now, and Courtney could see it in my eyes, and was eager to cut me off at the pass:

"Look ladies, whether there's a God or not is not the issue here. We wanted to talk about what happens when life throws you a curve ball, and — what's your name, honey?"

"Martha."

"And Martha here says stuff happens for a reason, now-"

"But what's the reason?" I cut in.

"To help us grow," Martha was ready with the answers.

"But how do we read the crap that happens to us as a time to grow? How do we know what to do?" I am seriously asking.

"It's not just a question of faith because some people just don't have that — although it helps —No, it's a question of seeing these things as a chance to grow…" Martha and I had taken over.

"What do you tell the mother whose little son has died?"

"That's for the good Lord not me."

"But that's too easy to say! He can't just take little children and get away with it!"

"We took his only son, and he forgave us."

"OK, OK," Courtney could see me gearing up for one, "as I said I don't want this turnin' all biblical on us — thank you Martha," she cuts the line, "I think what we want to talk about *tonight,* and let's put a positive spin on it, is things that go bump in our lives, and how you've dealt with them. We'll be back with more of your calls after these messages." Courtney slips us into ads, and turns to me, "What's goin' on?"

"Nothing," but the tears are millimetres from throwing themselves off the cliff edge.

"You're playin' the angry young woman card ta the hilt..."

"I'm going out for a spliff, want to join me?"

"Nah, I'll put us into some tracks back to back. You come back when ya're ready..." I nod, head low, and leave the studio.

The smoke takes away the pain of thought, but not the problem itself. If it is a short-term solution which has been getting me by for too long: it was time to find a longer-term solution. Silence, the perfect stranger, was the best friend a girl could have at this moment. Shifting from one foot to another to keep the cold from travelling up my shoes, the smoke clouds create further diversion. I just kept kicking the can further up the road in the hopes that somewhere down the line fate would intervene and show me the way: open a door, unveil a bridge, reveal a secret, previously undiscovered passage way. But that's not the way it works, and for as long as I kept numbing myself to the pain, the only reveal was going to be a brick wall.

Martha and the cosmos were trying to teach me something, and I was closing my ears, my eyes, and my mind. The universe was trying to cradle me in its wisdom, and I was swimming out towards a black hole, drunk on my own stupidity. It was like giving the key to the universe to a toddler. I was more likely to throw it down a man hole, than break out in a *Hallelujah!* of self-knowing. Whilst a miraculous maelstrom, the central nervous system, that myriad of intricate wonders, pumped and performed its majesty without my lightest concern; kept my own universe ticking over, what was I doing to support this universal good? Smoking a blunt.

"Feelin' better?"

"Yeah," I manage to smile; the drugs working.

"Good, cause we got a live one on the wire..."

"What do you mean?"

"Tom from Dickville is back..."

"Oh no..." Tom was a frequent caller. We only took his calls when we had nobody else to talk to and didn't want to make out that we were as unpopular as our lack of audience made out.

"Well, hey there Tom, what can we do for ya this fine mornin'?" Court was hedging her bets with an upbeat intro.

"You can start by telling me why you let all these religious freaks get air time?" He was starting on his high horse; no slow gallop in for us this morning.

"Well everyone has a right to their point of view Tom. Why do ya think we let *you* on?" Tom missed the non-veiled stab.

"I just wish you girls wouldn't talk down the male so much; where'd you think you'd be without us anyway?"

"According to statistics, Tom," I was back, "the female of the species is actually healthier and happier without a mate, and that's a scientific fact." It was a pretty gruesome statistic for the female of the species who was still pinning her hopes on a knight in white shining armour or a guy on foot, but according to study by data analysts, sixty-one percent of single women are happy being single versus forty-nine percent of single men. The proposed reason for this is that for women, being in a heterosexual relationship is actually a lot of hard work, and generally requires more effort and labour than for men. Professor Emily Grundy, talking in The Telegraph, picks up the discussion: "There's evidence that women spend longer on domestic tasks than men and I think they also do more emotional work — so they still do more housework and cooking and things as well as more emotional labour." What's more women are better at being single than men are. They're better at managing their social life, are more likely to have close friends, and get involved in a wider range of activities outside the home.

"Well I don't believe that for one minute! Mankind has been just fine for centuries without women getting on their high horse, and making it all sound so damn unfair, and unjust, and harping on about this and that..."

"Could it be that you just don't understand women? You seem so intent on pointing out what we're doing wrong, has it ever occurred to you that this might be stopping you from seeing what we actually get right each and every day?" I was trying to put a positive spin on what ordinarily spun out of line and got us in trouble with the boss the next day. This was a red-letter day: I was not trying to cause mayhem at every possible turn. I felt like patting myself on the back but knew deep down it had more to do with the palliative effects of the green than any particular change in my emotional make-up.

"I don't claim to be a saint, I just believe that men and women have a place, an order that has been in existence for millions of years, and along come you feminists —"

"Hold your horses there, bucko!" Courtney came cantering in. "This is not a feminist station. It's a station for women, run by women, serving ideas and music most suited to women."

"Well whatever you want call it, you are always going on about men this and men that and talking like we were the lowest form of life — it's not right."

"Well, Tom, if we didn't have a little bitch every now and then to let off steam there'd probably be a lot more of ya ten foot under!" Courtney was reaching her limit on tonight's dose of Tom.

"We like men just as much as the next hopelessly oppressed woman, Tom," I rejoinder, "we just have a right to voice opinions on our own station as a means of self-expression — you know—human rights. Why is it that women get paid less than men for doing the same job? Why weren't women allowed to vote? Why are women treated constantly as second-class citizens? Why do women still wear burkas in certain countries in the world?" My own roll frightens me, and I stop.

"It's worked perfectly well for millions of years, men are naturally more aggressive and leaders — "

"Just because they are more aggressive does not necessarily make them good leaders. An olive branch can be more effective than years of futile war," Courtney says sadly.

"Face it, ladies; you're just not up to the job. You never will be," he sneers.

"Well, I guess we'll never get the chance to find out because you and yours will always be cutting us out of the picture – "

"Ok ladies, I'm gonna have ta stop ya there! Thanks Tom for your views. We'll be back after these words from our sponsor!" Courtney turns to the switchboard which has lit up. "Well that certainly got the ladies callin'! That Tom is good foa somethin'!" Courtney turns to me, "We need to get ya to a nunnery – y'ar loosin' the will to talk nice ta people. Ya're like a real nasty Mary Poppins."

"Sorry..."

"Hell, I don't care, you can talk as dirty and mean as ya like on my time, but ya need to cut the freaks on air a little slack...they can't help that they're fuckin' bozos." Courtney bites down on a biscuit. Her crunching grates on me.

"We don't even have the excuse that y'ar premenstrual..." Courtney is between bites.

"Ha ha—no—we don't," lacking humour and stomach for anymore conversation, "but I am hormonal..."

"So have ya had any thoughts about – ya know – the baby?" Courtney slips us seamlessly into a track from the ads.

"No, but I think I'm beginning to feel a little protective of it – like, you know, protecting it from the world kind of thing."

"You need ta protect it from tobacco first…"

"Yeah, I know…guilty as charged."

"It's not like it's gettin' bullied or havin' it's rent hiked in thar…"

"I know, I know, it's just…I don't know — I'm just feelin' like it's me and it against the world — you know? Everyone seems dead set against it."

"You mean the asshole does." Courtney always one to bring things down to their most concise parts.

"Yeah, and I guess that counts for a lot."

"Yeah, but what if he ain't the Dad — what if Tony is?"

"Oh God — no — he can't be."

"Statistically, my little scientific rose, from what I understand — he can." She pops the last of the biscuit in her mouth.

"OK, so it's possible, but I don't want to even consider it — I mean can you imagine it?! A child of his? It would be part Blues man, part midget — it would probably be born in moth eaten, Oxfam clothing!"

"So what? It's a baby — your baby too — and I'm sure he was cute once…" Courtney looks unsure of her own words.

"Very funny. I guess…under all that hair, and bad accessories, a hobo chic is possible…"

"Totally. And anyway, what does it matter whose it is? It's in yar belly, and yar's to keep — if ya want it?" I was quiet, considering. "But do ya want it?" Courtney pauses again; brushing crumbs off her jeans, and fixes me with her laser stare.

The doorbell is ringing, and ringing in the dream and then, more real, it pulls me back from the warm ditch my body has created in the mattress, upsetting Pye who likes to nestle over my head like a furry hat.

"Who —?" Then I remembered the intercom doesn't work, and go over to the window, open it and look down. It's Jack, and he's yelling. I can't make out what he's saying at first, but he doesn't look happy. His words are bumping into each other, and then start to join up into sentences:

"Cass! You can't go on like this! I will be back and I will keep ringing this bell until you do the right thing!"

Chapter 28

To the Sounds of 'Ain't too Proud to Beg'
by TLC

Marilyn Monroe sings that a girl's best friend is diamonds, but I'd always thought a girl's best friend was her Daddy. My Dad had always said to me that he was there no matter what, and that if I ever had anything I needed to get off my chest, about him or anything else, I was to tell him straight. He promised me that there was no problem too big that he wouldn't listen, and he also led me to believe that he wouldn't take it personally if I needed to rag on him. Many moons ago, he had sat me down, and said that he understood that one day I would be angry about the things that had happened to me — Mum walking out, being raised by Dad alone, and that it would be my right to rant at him if that's what it took to put things right. I always held this comforting thought in the back of my head: that I could get it all off my chest one day, in Dad's understanding company, up close and personnel. And he wouldn't hold it against me.

The kettle's on, he's smiling in his chair, waiting for me to begin: it's our ritual. At least it used to be. I'm not really sure if we still have one after the Christmas debacle. He hasn't really apologised for bringing a stranger to Christmas lunch, for blaming me for the entire immolation of the festive event, or for slapping me across the face. Still…he's my dad, and I'm pregnant, and I'm freaking out so this is where we have to try again — right? — on the sofa, pretending we can still talk like the old days, about some possibly new days ahead.

"C'mon now, it's me…it can't be that bad?"

"It can…."

"I'm your Dad. I love you — no matter what. You know that — don't you?" I give him one of my deep, searching looks; all the while wondering if he knows this is my deep, searching look.

"Yeah, sure, it's just…"

"No 'justs' tell me what's going on…c'mon…" the kettle starts whistling.

"Hold that thought." He's up, and in the kitchen in a flash.

I try to comfort myself by looking at the familiar objects in his living room. A few more newspapers piled on the coffee table, different coffee cup marks, and two wine glass rings. He's smiling as he re-enters the room, carrying two mugs. He puts them down on the coffee table, hesitating over the two wine glass rings, and then gingerly covers them with the mugs.

"C'mon — out with it, girl."

"Oh, God, Dad...." I pick up the coffee mug; stare at the mixture of coffee and red wine rings, procrastinating.

"It can't be that bad, surely..." I look up at his face wondering if, in a minute, he wouldn't think of me in quite the same way.

"I'm pregnant, Dad..." He visibly pales.

"Oh...."

"Is that all you have to say?"

"Well, that is a bit of a shock..."

"*You* think it's a bit of a shock?" I'm trying to read his facial expression, but it's a mixture; not one I'm familiar with. "What is it?"

"Nothing, just...so...who's the father?"

"Oh, some absolute arse hole." My venom sits in the air like a bad smell.

"And he's not interested...?"

"No." His face looks pained.

"I see." He looks down at his coffee mug "So what are you going to do?" He knows he won't be ready for the answer whatever it is; he was not ready for the revelation.

"I don't know — I don't know what to do! That's why I've come to you!" I give him my best little-daughter-lost look. He seems unmoved.

"This is a big one, sweetheart, no doubt about it. The philosophers and scientists can't help us on this one. This is pure logic and reasoning..."

"What about feeling?"

"Well, yes, I suppose one must take that into account, but you really need to think about this carefully first....don't you....?"

"I suppose...." I'm not so sure.

"I mean this child won't have a father....and even a father that wants it to be in the world from the sounds of it..."

"You've got that right. He wants me to have an abortion. He keeps hassling me, calling me — he's driving me crazy!"

"Well, I suppose he has his rights too...I mean it is half his..." He's trying to choose his words carefully; half knowing it will never be careful enough.

"But he wants me to kill it!"

"Well, now, it's not a thinking, sentient being yet..."

"That's not true and you know it! It's alive, feeding, its heart is beating!"

"Its organs may be functioning, but it's like an automatic car without the driver...it wouldn't feel a thing..."

"How can you be so sure? What are you — God?" I feel a sudden pain as the words leave my mouth and hit home. He winces, but carries on, patiently.

"According to recent studies…" I groan, but he is ready for it, "no, hear me out, I was just reading about this the other day: the foetus cannot feel pain until at least the 28th week because they haven't formed the necessary nerve pathways; the wiring at the point where you feel the pain, for example the skin; doesn't reach the emotional part where you *register* the pain: the brain." I look at him numbly, and he continues. "The foetus does start to form pain receptors in the eighth week, but the part of the brain that sends the information to the other parts of the body, the thalamus, doesn't form for another 20 weeks". With statistics, numbers, evidence, scientists stacked against me, and even my Dad, I feel the weight of the universe pointing the finger at me. "Without the thalamus the information cannot be processed," he continues.

"OK! OK — enough already…" I can feel the tears popping inside my tear ducts. "But what if I just want to have it, eh?! No science, no studies, no statistics! I just plain want to have this baby?! For no good scientific reason! Just because it is growing inside me and I just might want to keep it!"

"All right, calm down a minute love; let's just take this one step at a time…" He takes a deep breath, "I can't help feeling that bringing a child into this world without a father is already a handicap." I turn to look at the wall rather than his face.

"Just because your own bloody father didn't want to know you, you think that no child should ever be born without one — I mean what's the big deal? As long as you have *one* parent — you had Oma?!"

"Yes, and I always resented her, deep down, for not giving me a father." This revelation stuns us both into silence for a moment. "I just don't want you to make the same mistake — to deny this kid one of the two people that will complete it. It's a tough way to start what by all accounts is a trying existence. You have all your life to get it right."

"But there is nothing *wrong* with this baby! It's perfect! It's only the circumstances that suck —it's not its fault! Why should it be penalized?!"

"You're not penalizing it. You have to stop thinking of it in such human terms. Whatever you say it is still relatively inanimate..."

"It is NOT inanimate! It is living and breathing as we speak!"

"OK, OK, calm down now..." he's looking at the wall now; one hand pushes hair off his brow.

"Look, you said that if I ever had any problems that I wanted to discuss with you that I could come and speak to you and get it off my chest, and well, tonight's the night..."

"Sure, I remember."

"I want to talk about our family — you and mum...your dad..."

"I don't know why you want to bring up the past: what's done is done. My father was part of another generation; they didn't understand the knock-on effect that illegitimacy engenders."

"We don't bandy that word around quite so much these days, Dad. It's just 'single mum' or 'single family' — you know?"

"I know, love, but it doesn't get away from the fact that you would be doing this all on your own..."

"'We are born alone, we live alone, we die alone. Only through our love and friendship can we create the illusion for the moment that we're not alone' — Orson Wells." Dad smiles his Buddha smile.

"That's nice...did you know that there was a recent study by scientists at the University of California..."

"Oh God — Dad! Can't you just talk, and not quote statistics?!" He ignores me.

"Listen, this is interesting, and it relates to what we are saying: they discovered that loneliness can be identified in the human gene!" He looks so excited by this fact. I roll my eyes. "The study shows for the first time how the impact of our daily lives can be felt at a genetic level. They found immune cells of people who are chronically lonely to be inflamed. One of the first signs of the immune system kicking into gear. Thereby linking social factors with heart disease, cancer and viral infections. We already know that the lonely and socially isolated die sooner than those who have full, active social environments..." He looks to me for some shared enthusiasm.

"Is this why you've started dating? You're worried that living alone is affecting your health."

"Look, my dating is hardly a study in socio-scientific phenomenon."

"Is it serious?"

"Yes." He tries to look defiant, this truth out in the open, but I can sense his nakedness, and it's this that I use to my own advantage.

"Dad, I'm angry — I'm angry that I never had anyone to go bra shopping with, or to teach me about girly things: teach me how to wear make-up, or cook a lamb stew, or...I'm angry that you let mum just walk out — just go and leave us both. I'm angry that you never tried to find her — to understand why she needed to go. Did you drive her away? I mean, did you ever think it was because of you...?" Afraid to voice the real thoughts that were only recently breaking the surface of my understanding, these questions hung lethally in the air.

"What do you mean?" He was quick to counter.

"I mean you never told me what your relationship was like? Did you argue?"

"No more than most couples..."

"What did she say before she left? She must have said something?"

"No...she just left..."

"People don't just leave, Dad!" The frustration visible on my face, he looks away.

"They do!" He counters, loudly. "They do just leave sometimes, Cass. Despite all your best efforts! You haven't lived and loved like I have — you don't know what it's like to love somebody so much that you want to hold them and never let them go; to be the only one they see, to be everything — above and beyond anybody or anything!"

"Even their own child?"

"Even that, yes," he looked me square in the eyes; defiantly.

"Did you suffocate her, Dad?" I deliver this question quietly, slipped under the door of his contemplation: he was reliving some moment; I could see it playing behind his eyes. "Did you ever hurt her like you hurt me?"

"I've never hurt you," he frowns, accusingly.

"Did you ever hit her?"

"Now wait just a minute." That fire is flickering in the black centre of his eyes. Any minute he might scrape the ground with his hoof. "You have no idea how hard it was to let her go! Have you any idea how difficult it is to let the woman you love — who means the whole world to you — walk out the door? Or what it means never to hear from her again — never? Do you know how badly I hurt inside? Do you?" I know better than to say anything, but "No" which comes out like a whimper. I'd never seen him so upset. "Have you any idea how hard it was to raise a little girl on my own? I didn't know the first thing, and I was scared — scared of doing it wrong, and messing up — she'd been scared too, but she chose to run away rather than face reality, and now you come here and tell me you're angry about the way things turned out? I'm not ready to sit here and take that kind of treatment because you know what? — I don't deserve it! I did the best I could, and if that's not good enough for you then maybe you should just take a moment to sit down and look inside and ask yourself why you're so goddamned angry because you're not angry with me you're angry with yourself for getting yourself in such a bloody state...with...well, you know — and I'm not going to sit here, and let you blame me!" He was standing now, pacing the room, and I felt even smaller than the words were making me, still sitting in the face to face chairs where he had left me. "And you're angry with *her* not me. 'Cause she's the one that walked out on you — not me!"

I had never expected, after all these years, to have the discussion thrown back in my face. The safe place I had always dreamed of, that he had promised me, was shattered. Maybe that was the day I grew up. Mum was gone, and Dad expected me to grow up, and get on with it. There was no place left to hide. So, I got up, and left. And he didn't stop me.

"Hi, you're on Radio Honey, what's your name, and your pet's name?"

"Hi, I'm Gabriella, and my dog is called Bella..."

"Hi Gabriella, I'm going to pass you over to our pet psychic, Megan, who's going to ask you some preliminary questions..." I sit back in disbelief: I was actually a party to this mockery. Megan sits upright, looking very self-important, her dayglo earrings swaying as she jerks her head forward, thrusting her throat rather than her mouth into the microphone. Her head tilted to the ceiling she seems to be preparing the animal spirits of her calling.

"Hi Gabriella, so how old is Bella?" She obviously believes every word she is saying otherwise she would not risk wearing those earrings. They do not scream pet professional.

"She's seven."

"And how long have you had her?"

"Since she was a puppy." Megan nods to her invisible client.

"And what seems to be the problem?"

"She is very aggressive towards my boyfriend." Megan nods at the microphone.

"Do you live with your boyfriend?" I'm thinking she's asking a lot of questions for somebody who's supposed to be psychic.

"No, he doesn't live here all the time."

"I see, so it's a relatively new relationship?" Gabriella moves one can half off her ear, allowing the dayglo earring to swing even more freely. I was hypnotized by its shape and colour.

"Yes, he usually stays over on the week-ends."

"I see, OK, um, is Bella in the room with you?" If you're so psychic, I'm thinking, you should know that!

"Yes, she's at my feet."

"Can you pick her up and put her on your lap, and start stroking her please?" I'm getting curious now.

"Yes, certainly…" we wait while the fumbling noises tell us that a dog is being picked up and put on a lap. Suddenly we hear a little whine, and a snuffle. I'm worrying about dead air time, but hell if Clare wants this shit then she's going to have to be prepared for the great conversationalists that are the animal kingdom

"OK, have you got her settled?" Megan intones softly.

"Yes."

"OK, I'm just going to tune into Bella…this won't take a moment," Megan seems to go stiff, and even more upright, her fingers play lightly with the hem of her gypsy skirt, its many Camden Town frills brushing the bottom of her calves, revealing flat pumps, in a merciful brown. Her sweater owed more to Marks and Spencer's, being a Granny cut, buttoned and bowed. "Now…I'm getting the feeling that Bella is not happy…" No shit Sherlock, why do you think she called?! "She's not happy sharing you with someone else…she's used to it being just the two of you…"

"Oh," Gabriella seems truly mystified, "I see…"

"Yes, she's not happy about the boyfriend…he takes her place in the bed — does she normally sleep with you?"

"Yes..."

"And when your boyfriend's round does she have to...oh, yes she's telling me that she has to sleep in the other room — is that correct?"

"Yes," there is a creeping embarrassment in Gabriella's voice: this is more detail than she had wanted to give.

"Well I think you are going to have to give her a lot of extra cuddles and affection when the boyfriend comes round and try not to exclude her where possible." Megan stops, she stiffens, "Oh...hold on...OK...yes, I don't think Bella feels your boyfriend likes her...is he affectionate with her?"

"Well, he's more of a cat person really," Gabriella sounds uncomfortable now, realizing the full extent of what she has let herself in for.

"Does he have cats?" You can feel Megan, like a dog with a bone (if you'll excuse the pun), homing in on her subject.

"Um, yes," Gabriella sounds positively tight lipped now.

"Ah, well, there's your other problem: she's feeling unloved by him, and she can smell the cats on him. You might ask him to bring a change of clothes that hasn't had contact with his cats when he comes round and also that he tries to be more tactile with her — can you do that?"

"Yes, thank you," it was obvious Gabriella wanted to end the call, and crawl back into her personal life.

"OK, was there anything else?"

"No, thank you."

"OK," I intervene, pulling the caller out of the mix, "thank you Gabriella and Bella. If you thought that was barking mad then stick around because we'll be taking more of your calls with Megan, the pet psychic, but first it's The Bangles, and 'Walk Like an Egyptian'." I try to act busy as the song runs: I have no intention of being drawn into a conversation with Megan: she gives me the creeps, and smells of Patchouli which always takes me back in memory to places in my mind I would rather not go: my Mum, for one, used to wear the stuff. Megan seems content with my insularity.

"Great show!" Hel pops her head around the door. I glare, and Megan smiles, but both of us say nothing. Hel continues, "It's sounding really good out there, and the switch board is chocka-block! Keep up the good work!" And she is gone. Even Megan seems relieved.

"Right, we're back with pet psychic, Megan, taking your calls, and who have we got on line one?" I press the lineup.

"Hi, my name's...Haley," the voice sounds familiar, that southern drawl, "and I've got a problem with my snake, Stevie Wonder..."

"I see, and what kind of snake is Stevie?"

"He's an African house snake." My mouth fell open — it was Courtney!

"How long have you had him?"

"Um, six month or so..."

"I see, OK, and what seems to be the problem..."

"I dunno, he just seems lethargic — not himself..."

"Have you got him with you?"

"No, he's at home..." I turn swiftly, and look out at the offices, scanning the desks for Courtney — there she was, the traitor; schooched down in her chair. Holding the phone close to her head, she tries to avoid looking at me when I spot her. I give her one of my better looks of displeasure and turn my back on her. How could she? She knows how much I hate this item! I don't care what kind of problems she's having with her pet snake: she was acting like one.

"OK, well, just concentrate on him a moment, really hard, thinking of his shape, his curve, what he looks like in his tank...."

"OK..." we all had to endure several moments of Courtney's imagining, and Megan's tuning in. Maybe she could be our new antenna?

"Right, I've got him," Megan says finally, "except it's not a him, it's a her!"

"Oh, Lord!" cries Courtney.

"Yes, and she's not happy...she's not happy with her environment, she will soon be ready to give birth..."

"Oh, my good God!" I'd never heard Courtney so enthralled.

"And she needs somewhere to give birth...yes...um, the water bowl..."

"Yes..." Courtney is hanging on her every word.

"It's not big enough she says..."

"OK."

"She needs a bigger one for birthing purposes..."

"Wow — OK."

"Right, that's all — good. Well, good luck with — well, you need perhaps to rename the snake now?"

"Ah, Stevie's a pretty good girls name too..." Courtney's voice is full of appreciative warmth: I had to break up this love fest:

"Right, well thank you *Haley*," the venom in my voice obvious at the mention of her pseudonym, "Megan will be

back next week with more of your pet psychic problems."
And into a song. I turn to Megan hand outstretched to shake.
She takes it, and holds it a moment too long.

"Your cat," she stiffens. I really don't want this and try
to pull my hand away. "He worries for you. He didn't like
that neck brace..." Now I was stiffening — with fear. "He
wants you to be happy..." Megan pulls her hand away
abruptly, still in a daze, not seeing me, then suddenly back in
the room. "Sorry...sorry. I didn't mean to...well, see you next
week then." And the patchouli smell is gone.

I fall back into my chair unable to move for some
moments. If my own damn cat knows I'm unhappy then I
really am a miserable git.

"That was great! Wow! I must ask her about my
cockatoo next time!" Hel enthuses.

"What cockatoo?"

"Oh, he's dead now, but she might be able to connect
with him?"

"Give me a bloody break! I've had enough pet psychics
to last a lifetime..." Gail comes in, ready to deliver.

"Hey Gail." She sits down unceremoniously.

"Hey," then she looks up, with a ray of enthusiasm on
her grey face, "that pet psychic was good. I asked her about

my tortoise. She said he needs more roughage." And back to the stony face.

"Great, this place is turning into a regular zoo. Why don't we have a bring your pet to work day?"

"I like that idea," Hel chirps, still in the doorway.

"You would. Pet psychics was your idea."

"And Clare's," she corrects.

"Need I say more," turning to Gail: "Cheer me up Gail — have we got any really horrendous traffic jams?"

"Nothing significant, just the usual snail trails."

"Please, no more animal references...." Hel slips out, and I bring up the travel bed.

"Gail's here with the latest bump and grind out on the roads..."

Chapter 29

To the Sounds of 'Wicked Game' by Chris Isaak

I almost expect to find Jack still on the doorstep after last night's most recent bell ringing service. He should try out at the local church: he's one hell of a bell-ringer. He's not particularly musical, but he's certainly rhythmic. That in itself could be our tale of woe summed up right there.

Isn't it amazing how love can turn to hate? How the deepest, most heart rendering emotions known to man can turn – in an instant – to darkest revulsion? How can we trust our emotions with anyone? How can we give our heart to anyone when at any point in the future they could take that most fragile of organs and stamp it into the ground? Love is Russian roulette.

It seems one of life's strangest conundrums: to give your most sensitive regions to another human being; to trust someone who perhaps you've only known for a few months to nurture the one most delicate part of yourself. And even after your love has been bludgeoned to death, to ask yourself to take that same heart, now covered with bruises and scars and entrust it to another unknown quantity: human being.

It's utter madness!

In my darkest hours I have often wished I could take out my heart and live a life free of love. No pain, no gain they say, but I say no pain, you live longer. In fact, studies prove that single women live longer than married women, and married men live longer than single men. What does that tell you?!

In the Journal of Epidemiology, they found that women who live alone had one third fewer mental health problems than women living with a partner or spouse. Thus, proving that men really do drive you round the bend.

The study, somewhat innocently, goes on to conjecture as to the reasoning behind the results, and comes up with the following assumptions: that although it is not clear why women living alone are thriving, they suppose that it may have something to do with the fact that living alone is less stressful than living with a man! Well, hello! Let's just state the bloody obvious – men are bad for our health! And yet the single among us spend our lives wishing for that someone. If they came with the same warnings as a cigarette packet we might think twice before asking them home for a coffee.

The sun's doing its best attempt at warmth as I close the front door behind me. Three, still creamy milk tops grace the doorstep. Up in the sky, a winsome blue is marked by just a few passing clouds. So white and fluffy on the outside it's hard to imagine that inside its diaphanous body it can harbour the cruellest storms, and if you were to open your eyes in the belly of the beast you would see nothing, not even your hand in front of your face. I shudder in the morning air and pull the gate behind me.

Turning left on to the Tavistock Road, now alone with the parked cars, I walk straight down to the square where the first few people of the day are grabbing coffees from Mario's. Sitting outside on plastic chairs, in front of rickety white tables, basking with the pigeons in the early morning sunlight; it feels like a good place to get my head straight.

As I focus on the people taking up the tables it becomes apparent that they are sitting, like animals on Noah's ark, two by two. Quietly reading the papers and drinking their frothy cappuccinos; hair slightly bedraggled after a mornings love making; casual clothing picked up off the floor to be worn again. There can't be a much better time to have sex than in the morning, if you leave out the morning breath. I mean you already have a captive audience: you only have to roll over; you bought the drinks the night before: paid the piper.

It's then that I recognise Cage's dark locks and feel my heart bounce. It stops mid-air when I notice Courtney sitting next to him, sharing some intimate body language; leaning in close over two steaming mugs. I try to double back before they see me, but it's too late: Cage looks up, he smiles, and then thinks better of it mid-smile; then realizes not smiling is even worse. His face is a battlefield of emotion. Courtney, registering these, turns and sees me. She does a similar don't know whether to smile or look like a cat with a bird in its mouth.

"Hey," I found myself waving.

"Hey," they both say in sorry unison. I walk over in the dawning silence that is our new-found friendship. Cage pulls out a chair for me.

"I won't stay," I offer, "I've got stuff to do…" It was an obvious lie, but one we all bought into.

"Aw, at least stay and have a coffee?" She's being too kind, and we all know it.

"No, really." The awkwardness was painful. Cage gives a weak smile. They look good together. "Listen, guys, enjoy the coffee — and this lovely Spring air — I really must run, but it's been great seeing you both…" They look guilty as hell. Guilty because I was alone, and with child. Guilty because they'd shared carnal fluids, and this was how I got to find out. Guilty because I look such a sorry sight alone on a Saturday morning on the Portobello Road. Guilty because they were happy.

"Take it easy — I'll call you later," Courtney calls after me.

"Laters," Cage sings out. I hold up an arm, with a wave attached and keep walking.

Any previous intentions are now bludgeoned to death. I walk without caring where. I make a left down the Portobello Road, and then another left onto Colville Terrace, clocking the Elgin where I had shared so many pints with Cage, circling slowly back.

"Honey buns," Hel's frisky voice is no palliative to afternoon fug," what on earth did you get up to on the overnight this week end?"

"Why?"

"Clare is doing the rumba, and it's not a pretty sight." She looks almost pleased.

"Well, we did veer off slightly..." To be fair, slightly is an understatement at best. Realising there was no way we were going to play 'Lady in Red' without self-immolating, we veered off course. "Well what choice do we have?" cried Courtney, "It's a long, hard, cold road to hell locked between Chris de Burgh and fuckin' Leonard Cohen. Give me a fuckin' break! I will personally take the fire!" I was on her side, but if we were going to do this we were going do this right. I'd been saving it for a special occasion: I pulled out my last weapon of choice in the free world; the diminishing world of my options as a woman in a dwindling world of choices. My nuclear arsenal of un-playlisted songs. I keep it on me at all times — don't' ask me why — my own mix tape of favourites. My musical Armageddon: the mix tape from my personal hell.

It starts with Jim Croce's 'Time in a Bottle' — the melodious strains of which could send any sound person towards the brink of suicidal melancholia, followed by, David Bowie's 'God Knows I'm Good'; a wonderful little ditty with Bowie's voice sounding like a half-child, half-breed imp praying at the corner of his bed one night; the Sex Pistol's 'God Save the Queen'; the Psychedelic Fur's 'India' a demented strain of punk memorabilia; X-Ray Spec's 'Warrior in Woolworth's, which is perfect Brit pop meets punk rock, and finished it off with the title track to 'Clockwork Orange' — the film — Mozart at his most synthesized.

When we were finished, we knew we had been very naughty indeed. As with any sort of ultimate enjoyment, it has a limited shelf life. You move from the orgasmic first bite into several stages of excitement and thrilling denial of the truth (calories), until you arrive at the end of said chocolate bar and sink into a sense of shame and impending calamity. You feel slightly dirty. The self-loathing creeps in; the sense of having sullied yourself somehow in unspeakable terms overcomes you: you have arrived at the bottom of the desire curve.

Studies suggest that pleasure peaks at the point when we anticipate a punishment but drops off dramatically afterwards. It would seem that the thrill of doing wrong is tied up with some fairly masochistic reality that we would all prefer to sweep delicately under the carpet. There was no getting away from the fact, however, that doing wrong had some fairly heavy dopamine hits inherent in its operative strategy.

"Clare's asked me to tell you to stick to your playlist like glue, or else. And I really don't think she's joking. She was too angry even to see you which, frankly, I think is rather an achievement."

"Well, thanks...I think." Courtney breezes in.

"Court!" I call her over with a nod.

"What's up?"

"Hel says Clare is having an epi over our overnight — even too angry to talk to us."

"Well, that'll be a first."

"And it'll be your last if you're not careful," sings Hel. Courtney shoots her a look. Deborah walks by with a dead plant that looks familiar.

"Where's that to?" Courtney asks.

"It's from the hallway. I'm taking it for a good watering," she doesn't stop.

"It'll need more than a good watering — try a good burial," I offer.

"So..." Courtney perches on the side of my desk.

"Yeah, that was not clever the other night..."

"No, it wasn't clever, but then sometimes you just have to live."

"Yeah, but sometimes you just have to eat, and with no job that'll be difficult."

"Shit, I can hunt and skin any wilder beast: stick with me and ya won't go hungry!" And she's off to prep her show. We don't mention the breakfast club.

"I think you'll need more than wilder beast to keep you warm," it was Hell — she was back.

"So," cutting her off, "what wonders have we got on the show today?"

"Well, we've got our restaurant critic, Pierre Avenport in with a roundup of the best new pub grubberies in town, and comedian, Ed Bay is in to talk about his new stand up tour, plus Ruth..." I groan.

"Yeah, well just avoid mixing social militant with theatre this time, OK?"

"Thanks for the advice."

"Oh, and…" why is it I always get nervous every time she begins her last "Oh, and"? — she always seems to save the worst for last.

"What?"

"You need to make some new trails with Clive." That wasn't bad news at all; time with Clive was always a bonus.

"And not so much of the comedy this time, OK? We want people to know what the show is about, not the contents of your fridge."

"OK already." I slink off to Clive's domain, Studio 2. Sure enough he is tinkering with his knobs and dials.

"Hey Clive."

"Well, hullo there, what can I do you for?" His smile is big as a Cadillac grill.

"You can do me…" I pause a moment longer than intended, "some new trails!" I save myself.

"Well, I can squeeze you in now if you're willing?"

"Oh, I'm willing and able, partner…"

"Then let's begin." He swivels round in his chair to face me, and my eyes inadvertently flit to his groin. Well, in my defence, he is sitting with his legs wide open! "So, what's your brief?" All I can think of is his underwear.

"Um…" I stumble, trying to rearrange my eyes, "Well, I think these next ones should be light and fun, talking up our regular guests as if we were all part of a big family, and trying to ignore the fact that I'll probably be excommunicated from said family within the week..." I try to make it sound funny, but it doesn't come out that way.

"What have you done now?" My misdemeanours were obviously a well-known fact not relegated to gossip or hearsay.

"Well I might have gone a little overboard on the overnight shift with Courtney the other night..."

"You two just spur each other on; you're like the two naughty kids in class who need to be separated because you just wind each other up."

"It's that obvious, huh?"

"To anybody with half a brain cell."

"Well, that — added up — would be the whole production crew of Radio Honey." He laughs.

"Oh, I think you're exaggerating — the whole production crew plus Headbanger FM". Now it was my turn to laugh.

"So, how's that damn girlfriend of yours?" I slip into that one seamlessly.

"She's good thanks. Still working over at Stock-Aitken as receptionist."

"Good for her..." I manage unconvincingly.

"So how about this for a bed? " Clive plays a piece of music that sounds upbeat and quirky whilst I think of other beds he could have laid down on.

"That'll do, yes, I like that."

"So, what were you planning to say?"

"Well, how about: 'Friends, Romans, Countrymen, lend me your ears!'?"

"That's snappy, and strangely familiar," he smiles, and turns round to face the console and start laying down the 'bed', gratefully relieving me of the view of his blue jeans cupping his admirable manliness. At this point the door opens, and it's Hel:

"Oh, hope I'm not disturbing," comedy smile, "but, Cass, Clare has asked for you and Courtney to meet her after your shows today at Babington House."

"Where in hell is that?"

"I don't know honey, I just work here. Look it up in your A to Z." And she's gone.

"Told you I was in deep shit."

"Wow."

"This trail could be my requiem."

"Shall I change the music?" That's when Court puts her head round the door.

"Hey, you — Cass, have you heard?"

"Yes, I've heard. I think it's curtains this time."

"Well, look Scarlett O'Hara made a damn fine dress outta her curtains so just hold fire — OK?"

"OK."

"We'll meet and go out after your show, OK?"

"Sure."

"Hey Clive," Courtney gives him her forty-watt smile, "Nice seein' ya — literally." She winks and is gone.

"Yeah, you better make that Mozart's Requiem Mass."

Chapter 30

To the Sounds of 'Nothing Compares to You' by Sinead O'Connor

Kevin's reading OK! Magazine behind reception.

"Kev, what's the score?"

"Headbanger nine, Honey eleven."

"Cool. Night, Kev".

"Night ladies." When we get out onto the street Courtney speaks:

"I can't believe we've gotta go across town to meet the bitch..."

"Yeah, what's the big deal?" I try bluffing: ignoring the reality of the situation was working for me so far.

"Well, it could be the fact we're fuckin' with her station."

"Ah, she's such a spoilsport." We cross the street in unison, right foot first stepping off the curb.

"Let's get a drink. A stiff drink. We've got a little time."

"Not a bad idea." Looking up ahead, The Crown seems as good a place as any.

"What'll you have?" Courtney leans on the bar, the bartender already waiting.

"A double rum and coke." Courtney gives me a look; *why*, suddenly dawns on me. "Oh, make it a single." Courtney doesn't ask any more questions.

"And a Fosters please." The bartender moves over to the glass case, we watch him bend and fetch, our minds half occupied with the infinite creases in his black trousers, and the other half contemplating the meeting we had coming up with the boss. We are both uncharacteristically silent. The drinks slip our way along the counter. Courtney pays, and I carry. The table by the window is fit for two. The drinks and our arses go down at the same time.

"So..."

"So, how are you and Cage?" I couldn't put off asking any longer. She holds her head in her glass after she finishes taking a long gulp, telling me she would rather not say. Finally, she emerges:

"Good. Yeah, good."

"So, are you guys an item now?"

"Oh hell, I don't know. I'm just grateful he didn't try to chew his arm off from under me in the mornin'..." We smile and say nothing.

"Well, I really hope you guys can be happy — I really do. I mean it would be nice to see somebody get some happiness."

"Don't go chasin' rainbows on me — could have been the beer talkin' that night, I dunno."

"He's a pretty sentimental guy; I don't think he'd be bluffing."

"Listen, just as soon as he realizes what he's done, and wakes up from his dope filled, alcoholic haze he'll do what they all do — double back like a rabbit. And I'll be left there smilin' like Ms. Kansas."

"You don't have much faith in yourself."

"Hey, I'm a realist." We suck on our drinks.

"What about you? You havin' this goddamned baby or what?"

"No..." head bowed, "I've got an appointment day after tomorrow."

"Shit. That's soon."

"Not if I don't want a fully developed foetus." We both look out the window. It was starting to rain; a fine spring drizzle — fake rain by London standards. The real thing would be back round soon enough.

A few coloured umbrellas sprung up like mushrooms outside. A taxi rounded the corner, diesel belching.

"I'm sorry Cass…"

"What for?"

"I just don't like to see ya this way."

"Well, that's just the way it is…" bright quips no longer seemed appropriate, or maybe we'd used up our quota. Our bright spark, our ascending star had hit its zenith, and was now coasting on back to earth. That message that we sent in a bottle, that hope that springs eternal had hit the shoreline unfounded. Time to park up, rest awhile, and maybe have the kind of internal monologue that suits the winter rain, not light spring drizzle.

"Shall we get goin'?"

"Yeah." It was time to face the music — or the lack of playlisted music. It was time to face Clare.

Babington House sits squarely on the corner of Westfield and Rye, which makes it sound like the perfect sandwich filler, and faces the towering edifice of Clarence House in Kensington. It's relevance to Radio Honey was beyond us, we simply assumed it was part of the syndicate, and when we entered the foyer found that it housed not one but four station outlets, and a chain of car parks.

The freckly faced, middle-aged man on reception (a contradiction in terms somehow) sent us up to the third floor.

"So, this is where all the budget is goin','" Courtney exhales as we get in the lift.

"They kept this quiet."

"Don't wanna let the natives know ya got collateral." The doors open on a long, quiet hallway with a brown and orange theme. We broker the beige carpet, marvelling at the wallpaper which was a cross between Art Deco and Art Don't Know.

"I'm having acid flashbacks." Courtney swoons.

"It's like a Biba nightmare."

"This must be what my insides look like after a night out on the town with too much curry and beer."

"I don't want to think about your insides — I'm having enough trouble keeping mine in place — I threw up this morning."

"No way?!" We were standing in front of a door marked Meeting 4. The freckly man with the middle-aged wrinkles said this was where we had to go. A door opened somewhere and shut. Courtney and I looked at each other.

"Well this is it," Courtney is upbeat.

"You knock."

"No, you knock!'

"Come in," the voice was unmistakeable. We both shiver, and Courtney puts her hand on the wisp of door handle, and pushes.

The boardroom is impressive. A long table takes up the majority of the space, made of polished wood, and shined to an unreal brilliance. You can still smell the wood polish. The chairs don't match, but they aren't cheap either; you can feel the weight of many meetings, many voices filling the empty room. This is a place where decisions are made, and people listen to the man at the top of the table. Which today is a woman, and she is twirling a pen between finger and thumb.

"Sit down," she says without hesitation, and then more softly, "won't you?" Courtney and I meander around the many choices of chair: should we go for the side nearest Clare? The side nearest the door? The opposite chair? The one next to Clare? After what seemed an interminable dalliance, we sit somewhere in the middle, near the door.

"Sorry to bring you both all the way across town." This is more a figure of speech.

"Yeah, I don't often sample Kensington's finer areas," Courtney is trying to sound relaxed, her usual banter echoes in the lofty room.

"We've had some better weeks, and months at Radio Honey," Clare begins, with a somewhat friendly air, "but as you know we cannot sustain the current drain on our ratings, or…" and she pauses not so much for effect, but it seems, for a woman rarely lost for words, more as if she really is looking for a way of explaining herself. Courtney and I take the opportunity of her pause to look at each other, and raise our eyebrows, "...or the current anarchy." The 'a' word hangs in the air like the sword of Damocles. I stiffen. Clare waits for the word to sink in and possibly to hear us comment; there isn't a whimper from our quarter. We knew the 'a' word was well and truly stitched on our pinafores. She continues when she sees we are not going to argue: "There are going to be sweeping changes which will radically change the direction of the station; we have some fresh investment, some new blood, and it is to such ends that I have the job of clearing the way for this next stage of development." She takes a breath and looks at us. We are both holding our breath. "I have spent a considerable amount of my time, and energy keeping an eye on you two, and reiterating, much to my displeasure, the same problems. Mainly the fact that you constantly choose to ignore the playlist and commandeer the station for your own whims. I don't believe 'God Knows I'm Good,' by David Bowie has ever been on a playlist nor ever will be. It's an album track, and that's where it should have stayed — in your album collection." She looks squarely into our souls, and an apology inadvertently squeaks out of me:

"Sorry."

"I don't need an apology. Frankly, it is far, far too late for that. I have had the apologies, and they mean nothing because you have repeatedly offended. I have a major job ahead turning this station around, and I do not need to consistently be stopping the running of the station to be handing out reprimands."

"We only had the stations best interests at heart," Courtney offers, blinking.

"If that were true you would be working with me and not against me. I'm sorry, Cassandra, Courtney, but I'm going to have to let you both go." The air hums with her words. "With immediate effect." We both sit stunned, unable to comment or move. Then realizing that she meant it, we rise, shakily, to the occasion.

"Well," Courtney begins, somewhat unsure, it was evident, where she was going to take it, "I think you're makin' a big mistake — we are the nucleus of this station."

"And that's precisely why you both need to go — anarchy aside — you have both been central to the station's identity, and as such, you must go." She was getting more blunt by the moment, sensing a fight. I, for one, just want to get out of there; wail to the heavens; scream injustice to the streets. I wasn't in the mood for her justifications, her pompous rendition of responsibility. I stood up, somewhat unsteadily.

"Right," I try to find other words, but failing, make my way to the door, turning for Courtney who is behind me, making her exit speech.

"You will regret this, Clare. This is not the way to run a station!" I watch Courtney close the door behind us — her mind momentarily frozen with the question — to slam or not to slam? In the end the door closes with a hollow click.

We stride speechlessly down the brown and orange hallway to the elevator, and then have to wait in silence, fuming, whilst the elevator idles between floors one and two, then sails all the way past us to five, and eventually settles on four. When the doors open, a solitary figure hugs the back wall, his glasses glazed over with a fine mist. His eyes dart uncertainly towards us, and then to the floor. We walk in and turn our backs to him. The doors seem to take forever to close.

"I don't fuckin' believe the goddamned nerve of that woman!"

"I'm in shock..."

"Let's bypass fuckin' shock and move swiftly on to fuckin' outrage!"

The doors open again, and we find ourselves back in the marble lobby. The little man hurries past us out the front doors; no doubt having had his share of four-letter words for the day. Courtney pushes against the door as it swings back towards us.

"I don't fuckin' believe it..."

"We've been fired." The word hangs in the air, heavy.

"We must have some rights or somethin'."

"No, Court, she just fired us, and she had ample reason to. All the un-playlisted songs for one."

"Yeah, sure there's that..."

We walk down the road, in no particular direction. People pass us in waves, their day an amalgamation of times and people and memories that we would never understand or share. All of us walking somewhere, to finish our chapter, our day; the story of our lives.

"Where are we going?" I venture. Courtney turns to me, and for the first time she actually looks lost.

"I don't know...I really don't know."

According to the laws of physics, when an irresistible force hits an immoveable object the effect is a classic paradox. On the one hand you can argue till the cows come home about the existence of an irresistible force or an immoveable object; it is logically impossible to have a force that cannot be resisted and an object that cannot be moved by any force in the same universe. Once you get past that, there are many possible solutions, including the supposition that they simply pass through each other, so that the force never stops, and the object never moves; or that neither ever stops moving, simply slowing exponentially in the fullness of space forever, and never meeting; or, simply, that the two objects contradict each other — since, by definition, an irresistible force is an immovable object, and that the event is a contradiction in terms. Others still may say that they will simply cancel each other out as both have equal physical power, or infinity.

The more poetic amongst us have chosen to view the paradox as, in the case of Jarvis Cocker's song 'Seductive Barry' from the classic album, 'This is Hardcore,' as a romantic conundrum: "When the immovable object meets the unstoppable force, there's nothing you can do about it."

In our situation, it seemed that the irresistible force — us — had been stopped by the immovable object — Clare. Standing in the middle of fashionable Kensington, the world and their mother swimming past with unnerving forward velocity, unending, infinite mass, our own inertia sent shock waves through our anarchic bones.

"C'mon, there's a pub over the road," breaks the ice. We brave the middle of the road, cars beeping their horns, taxi drivers leaning out on bent elbows, their faces contorted with angry insults, and find the opposite curb before a red bus can make mince-meat of us.

"What'll it be ladies," this genuine smiling face seems incongruous to us in the light of recent events.

"We just got fired so I think we should have a bottle of your finest champagne. What do you think, Cass?" The bartender doesn't know whether to apologize or start recommending the most expensive brands.

"Why not, it might be the last time I drink out in years." The bartender, now convinced that speaking is inappropriate, simply hands us the wine list.

"Right, let's have a look at these bad boys," Courtney scans the menu, "Oooh, nice prices..." Her eyes flick impressively over the list.

"C'mon, we've gotta go for the king of bubblies — like the king of beers — it's gotta be Moet an' Chandon!"

"Sold! — To the unemployed couple at the bar! Bartender!" He nearly jumps out of his pinny. "One bottle of Moet and Chandon if you please!"

"Coming up, ladies." We take a table in the middle of the room; it is relatively empty. There are two men at the next table, and as soon as we sit down I notice they are speaking French.

I inadvertently look at their socks: I have a theory about the French: the women always wear matching bra and undies (to their credit—there's nothing clever about the British mix 'n' match attitude), and the men match their Argyll socks with their Argyll sweaters. This time I am disappointed. There is no sock showing.

"I don't fuckin' believe it," Courtney is off again.

"How many more times are you going to say that?"

"I just can't get over it..." It doesn't seem like Courtney to be confused.

"Court, it's not that hard to understand. We didn't play by the rules. Plain and simple."

"But it wasn't harmin' the station none — it probably helped it! Our audience could do with an alternative to fuckin' Madonna and Britney!" The barman comes over with our bucket, the outside glistening, the bottle poking out of the top like a gold-coated-hard-on.

"Well, at least this should be good..." And it is. The pop of the cork is a beautiful sound, in a cruel world.

"Cheers," the happy clink more soulful still, the bubbles a friendly tickle up our nostrils, "Ohh — that's good! I feel better already." Courtney does look more cheerful.

We order food: olives and humus to start, steak and kidney pie with vegetables for afters. That's when I overhear the conversation at the next table. As we tuck in to our bottle of champagne, now on its last legs, and make in-roads into the pie, I can hear them talking about us:

"Look at them, the English — they have no idea — champagne and pie? It's so..." I can't translate the word they used, but I know it's less than flattering. The affair with my French teacher certainly payed off, maybe not in the full scheme of things, but in the short term it had been, how do you say? — an education. I relay to Courtney their conversation, and she's about to hit the roof. I calm her:

"Wait, I have a better way." Turning to the table of Frenchmen I tell them, in my most austere accent, perfected in a wild year abroad, that we have the right to drink Champagne with whatever we damn well chose, and to keep their noses out. The look of shock was enough to satisfy us both and make our sad little celebration a little rosier.

"So, what do we do now?"

"I'll try and get another job. Unless she's blacklisted our asses around town..."

"We'll never jock again..." My hand moves involuntarily to my stomach, and Courtney watches as I mindlessly stroke what is now a tiny roundness.

"Well ya certainly don't need an extra mouth to feed at a time like this."

"I guess."

"Why do I get the feelin' you ain't ready to say goodbye to that foetus of yars?"

"Oh, shut up, it's booked. That's it."

The waiter comes over, "Can I get you ladies anything else?"

"No thank you," I say, "I think that'll do us — unless," and I look to Courtney for confirmation. She shakes her head:

"No, thank you. We're done."

On Monday morning Courtney and I march up to the door of Radio Honey's reception, push them open with conviction, nod convivially to Jeff at his desk, and are continuing on our way when this old but sprightly gentleman is suddenly blocking our path.

"Sorry ladies, but you're not allowed in..."

"What do you mean?" we chorus, our faces an essay in 'gob smacked.'

"I'm sorry — orders. You're not allowed in." He tries to put on his sternest face, but it's difficult: we have a friendly history. I had spent over a year making idle banter with this gentleman, and now he's preventing me from taking one step in my intended direction.

"But I have to get my stuff!" I say, trying to hide the hurt behind the anger.

"That may be, but I can't let you in. I'm sure someone will send it on to you."

"This is outrageous," says Courtney in her poshest voice, "I've never heard of anythin' so ridiculous. What do they think we're gonna do — blow up the station?!"

"No, but..."

"How can you do this, Jeff?" I'm still trying to get over the fact that what pleasant exchanges had taken place over the year were nothing more than fake pleasantries and held no water or justice.

"For God's sake this is out of order!" Courtney's displaying all the signs of gearing up for a big one. I take her arm and steer her out before things get uglier.

Chapter 31

To the Sounds of 'If I Ever Lose My Faith in You' by Sting

It's a funny thing about endings, you can't imagine a new beginning, all you can see is the yellow brick road; you can't see how it could possibly ever take you to an Emerald City.

Hindsight may be a terrible thing, but no foresight is just as bad. Inertia rolled us into a ball, and there we stayed, all day; bodies on the sofa. Between cups of tea, and TV breaks we would remember. Watching old black and white movies where guy gets gal and gal looks overjoyed at getting guy in happily ever after scenario may not be perfect TV viewing in this state but served a simple source of feel good in a time where simple pleasures were needed; reminding us of when life was not so complicated, and right and wrong were clearly marked on the label. What does it mean to be a woman in the 20th century? It's not so clear. Do I get married and have babies or have a career or combine both? Do I find a man who can support me? Should he open the door for me? Should we go Dutch? Should I shag on the first date or will he think I'm easy, and if I'm easy is that a bad thing? Am I not simply taking what I want from life, or am I a slag?

If you look at the stereotypes we have been brought up with: Snow White, Goldilocks, Sleeping Beauty, it would seem that women are moon faced innocents with a gentleness verging on stupidity, in search of their prince, and apt to stumble into evil doers or large bears. Today's Hollywood versions have us still searching for Prince Charming. But who are we when we're not searching for a mate?

Jack was punctual. Of course. Courtney walked me to the door. I had told her a thousand times the night before that I would be just fine. The best I could offer her was to stay in my flat, keep Pye company, and wait for my return. I left her under the duvet on the sofa. She looked small and broken. For some reason I was trying to be strong for both of us; we had changed roles. I could be saviour and destroyer. I would do what was right for everyone. Surely this was what was required of me, now that life had shown me its true colours? I would roll with the punches.

They say that the trees that survive the storm are those that can bend with the wind; I will bend. I will welcome the breeze and the hurricane alike.

"Ready?" Jack tries to act like this was a trip to the zoo, and I was his baby cousin, except I was more likely the cousin carrying his baby.

A perfect Spring day was building up. It seemed unjust. There should be grey sky, clouds, thunderstorms, at least the tears of rain to mark the day. A band should play a mournful song, on foot, and follow, at a respectful distance. There should be women weeping, rending their clothes, grieving in black. I look down at my pink Dr. Martin boots, and feel the colour is all wrong for the day ahead.

"So," Jack starts again, but seeing I am in no mood to talk, gives up. We walk to the tube station in silence.

"What stop is it?" He asks. Standing in front of the tube map, I trace my finger along the Metropolitan line until I find what I am looking for:

"Ruislip."

"Oh...not far then." Bloody prick. Why had I said he could come? The sheer nearness of him made my body nauseous, or was that morning sickness? As the thought left my head, I felt my body respond with the feeling, and I stopped halfway to the escalator, desperately trying to still my belly. But it was no use: I ran to the nearest wall, beside the rolling arm of the escalator and let rip. Jack was not prepared for this reality and hung back. After the worst was done, I pushed about in my pocket for a tissue to wipe my mouth, just as the underground staff came over.

"You OK, love?" It was a big, buxom woman, and I just wanted her to fold me into those enormous bosoms of hers.

"I'm so sorry…I made a mess — I'm pregnant."

"Oh, love, don't worry. I'll get someone to clear it up. You get on and lie down."

"Thank you. Thank you so much."

"Take care now." I make my way on to the escalator, and only then feel Jack's presence a few steps behind.

"Has that been happening a lot?"

"Yeah."

"Wow. Well I guess you'll be glad to see the end of that, eh?" If I had to respond to him at that moment it would have been with violence.

Waiting for the train on the platform, as the wind brings the first sign of it, my coat blows open, and the gust brushes my belly, its touch intruding. I feel his eyes there; invading my skin. How could he do this? Go to his child's execution? What kind of man could do that? Why, more's the point, had I chosen such a man? Did I think that little of myself?

The long, slow ride across the network felt like an eternity, locked side by side with the executioner; the gallows a few more stops away.

"Name?" asks the lady at the clinic: the sweetly named Clare Bow Women's Clinic. And for a moment I think, "What would I have named it?"

"Just fill in this form."

How succinctly we all perform our parts in this sad ballet, this Swan Lake of loss. The receptionist pretends not to treat me as a murderer, and I pretend not to treat her like an accessory to murder. Jack hangs back, still not prepared to be affiliated with the reality of what he is a partner to.

I try not to think about the fact that in a moment I will have to take off all my clothes in an unfamiliar room and put on a gown that feels like stepping into a sandwich bag, and let somebody I don't know part my legs, stick a long device inside me, and suction out my baby.

Marigold walls, yellow curtains, doilies, and potted plants all in cahoots with this backdrop of normality. This was what we had come to. This backstreet abortion dressed up to be storefront. My insides felt as if they were all on the outside; naked, cold, ill conceived, shaking. And he's smiling.

"Won't you come this way?" She too is smiling. I turn to look at him one last time, to fix his complicity in my mind's eye. He gives me the thumbs up to accompany the smile. Never has a thumbs up been more inappropriate.

In the New Scientist this week, an article details the findings of the oldest female figurine dating back to 35,000 years ago. Discovered in caves in Germany it shows the grossly exaggerated form of the naked female, all bosom and gaping gash of a vagina. It's stumpy arms and legs an afterthought. But the most striking aspect is not the humungous proportions of its breasts that would put any surgically enhanced, mutated porn queen to shame, but the miniscule size of the head that looks like a pimple on top of the breasts. These figurines are said to be fertility symbols, though I can't understand why, surely conception was the one thing they had more than enough time for? These days, we don't even have enough time to get aroused.

It seems clear to me that women are still very much symbolised and abstracted. Baby doll figures of boobs to sell cars, exaggerated and pushed on to the cover of magazines, bent over for your viewing pleasure, and ultimately discarded once they have lost their immediate use, and perhaps grown a child in its voluptuous belly. Jill Cook of the British Museum says that these figurines,"...show that people at this time in Europe had reached a stage in brain development that enabled objects to be symbolised and abstracted." I think we are still abstracted; we are still trinkets, symbols of rather than living, breathing magical entities.

The waiting room. Surely it will be like any other waiting room? Why not? This is where you put the women, the figurines, the bellies, boobs, and gash of womanhood, before and after they have been emptied. This is where they go to wait, to be picked up by someone, anyone — won't someone buy?

The coffee and tea machine is on a low, small pine table. It has a little drawer in it. I wonder what's in it, but not enough to open it. I'm not that curious at this particular moment. The quiet in this room is ungodly. There are five of us: a girl who cannot be older than sixteen, with tracksuit bottoms, a T-shirt that says 'Angel', and a plastic bag at her feet from Next. She is chewing gum and looking at the opposite wall as if it is her salvation. I cannot catch her eye or see her eyes. The girl next to her has hair corn woven to her scalp, one leg crossed over the other, and a magazine in her lap that she is not reading. A big girl, braces, acne, holds her small handbag on her knees. She sits very still. Another, older, thinner, too thin, looks like her soul has been gouged out of her eyes and her body stuffed with cement to make her sit so upright. Another, professional, suited, with a cup of tea in its Styrofoam mug balanced on her knee; her attention is in the liquid. She is holding her centre there. She is holding. In. Another, thirties, in jeans, a sweater, a jacket, pink Doc

Martins — me, watches the other women hoping to share a smile, a roll of the eyes, anything to share this fucking awful moment, and give it some levity.

The door that we wait for opens. A woman calls a name. One of the women rises, and walks, slowly across the expanse of carpet: green carpet, so unlike the outside that we long to be in; just a shade off true life, and a whole world away from the reality we were hoping for when we thought we were making love, or thought we were having great sex, or thought we were going to be with them forever. Without looking at any of us, around the small, low table that holds outdated magazines, she does the gallows walk, and soon the door shuts behind her. That silence again.

I get up and go to the tea/coffee machine, sitting safe in its mystery in the corner of the room. It seems like the smallest of inanimate conundrums. With some pulling and pushing, not aided by anyone else in the room with tea/coffee that have obviously solved its riddle, I manage to get a tea out of it albeit not with the right amount of sugar.

Following the green road back, it seems to shift beneath me. The women shimmer and bend, shape shifting on their chairs. My reality re-adjusts, and I find my chair. My place to wait. I silently pray that I will not have to throw up again. If there were a clock in this room, we would sit and listen to its arm click seconds round the dial. We would listen to refracted moments in this space, count them off in our womb like eggs released and hopes dashed. The miracle of life countlessly lost in this place. Was there a big bin outside for all the lost lives that they had removed from us? Did they all jostle together for space in a wheelie bin; humanities unwanted rubbing undeveloped shoulders with each other?

The door opens, not my name. Another lifts, and slowly moves the grassy lime expanse. Then the other door opens, and another comes in, and joins us. She looks around the room only once and learns not to look again. After some time, she gets up the nerve to cross that vast no-mans-land of carpet and attempt to work the tea machine. Watching her crouch there, uncertain, I want to tell her how it works, but I am frozen, with the rest. I have sat here too long; I have become one of them.

I watch her break the inner code of the machine and take her tea back to her place. She holds it between both hands, leaning forward on her knees. Her bag has fallen on its side. She doesn't move.

The light that fills this room in not sunny. It is light pure and simple. It does not dapple, it does not slant in and alight, or dance across. It falls in. From a great height. Not curtains, not blinds, but a film covers the glass, and shades us from view. This is the room of shame; the vessel sits, and waits to be emptied.

And at the end, invariably, it is women who come for these women: mothers, sisters, and friends. Where are the men? What are they doing today?

The door opens; it is my turn to cross the great carpet. I feel I have advanced one step on a giant game board. But I won't win. I never win. I'm not lucky like that. I'm lucky in other ways. In strange ways. In ways you wouldn't expect, couldn't write, and wouldn't guess. No, I'm lucky in the way that is just this side of average. I get the lucky break that helps me avoid death, or full taxes. I'll get to spend my life skiving off with made-up excuses and make-believe jobs, and sunny days doing nothing. And even when I blow it, I'll be lucky enough not to starve. But not lucky enough to live happily ever after.

"You OK?" He asks, a little scared to hear the answer.

"Yeah." He looks relieved. We walk out of the door of that place, and I feel better. The sun starts to show through, and it warms us as we walk to the station.

"Do you feel OK?"

"I feel...yeah — OK." I try to keep a healthy distance as we walk side by side.

"You see — I told you you'd feel better. It's the relief."

"I think you're talking about yourself." He feels the anger and recoils.

"I'm not relieved. I'm sad this all had to happen. I really am." His look of sincerity is not attractive. Who *is* this man? I study the features, note to wrinkles bedding into his brow, the hair, brittle under his cap. The broken blood vessel on his cheek that reminds me of the blood vessels in a foetus' hand; the club like paw in amniotic fluid held aloft in its floaty world.

We walk on in silence across a street, and through a park. I stop on the pavement winding through the park.

"If you don't mind, I'm not going to take the tube back into town." He looks at me; unsure how to read my remark.

"Are you sure?"

"Yes." I stand firm. I want to be rid of him; this false chaperone. He has what he wanted.

"Well, if you're sure?"

"I am."

"What'll you do?"

"I really don't think that's any of your business, do you?" He seems stunned by my bluntness.

"Well, I just wanted to make sure you're OK..."

"I'm fine." I take a step back, pulling my bag tighter to me.

"OK, well I'll call you later to see how you are?"

"No. Don't." I turn. I can feel his eyes on me. I don't want any part of him to be near me, to look at me, to see me. Walking away from him, in the opposite direction — anywhere — I want to run. And then I want to laugh.

Chapter 32

To the Sounds of 'Finally'
by Ce Ce Penniston

In the New Scientist this week, underneath a picture of two gorillas, one leaning forward on his gigantic forearms, pushing up the muscles in his neck, another seated and looking off into the distance, her feminine jaw dropped and relaxed as if about to utter some monkey comment or simply relaxed to the point of idleness, there is an article entitled, 'Promiscuous males turn females on'. It relates the findings that female gorillas get hornier when their silverback man has sex with other females. Evolution has obviously made us less sharing; less inclined to find our partner's dick in another female a turn on.

Even when these frisky female gorillas weren't able to conceive they still wanted to get it on with the silverback prompting the experts, who spent two years watching a group of gorillas have sex — in the name of science — to surmise that these females were currying favour, preventing him from having any sperm left over to impregnate the others and, with less offspring around, increasing their own offspring's chances of survival. They didn't mention the fact that these females could simply like sex?

I saw the drummer of The Evil Knocky Men before he saw me but chose to discretely pretend I hadn't seen him: courting rituals being what they are: a hell-hole of deception. As Court and I entered the club, he called out my name. Both Court and I stop but summing the situation up with her forensic female aptitude, she wordlessly continues walking. I turn back, retracing my steps till I'm level with Ben.

"Y'alright?"

"Yeah — you?" Surprise lifting and undoing the creases in my face.

"I just wanted to say that you were really great the other night."

"Oh. Thanks." I'm not good with compliments.

"You sing alone?"

"Yeah, I guess. Never thought about it any further than that really. Hard enough to get me up on a stage as it is."

"Well you should do it more often." He pulls a hi-hat out of the open van door.

"Thanks. Can I give you a hand?"

"No, thanks, I've got it." He stops, and looks at me a moment; making me feel even more nervous than I already am. I notice his arm which is holding the high-hat, the muscle clenched, and the hair light against the faint tan of his skin. "Have you got many more songs?"

"Yeah. Loads." Spit was coagulating in my mouth, making conversation difficult; I was aware of my lips which seemed stuck to my teeth.

"Are you playing tonight?" Suddenly aware of the guitar case in my hand, brought back to reality by its weight I manage:

"Yeah...I thought I might try to play more than one song...especially since I just lost my job...got nothing but time..."

"Sorry to hear that," he smiles, and my legs feel warm and gooey.

"Well, see you later," I had to go, had to keep moving or I would be unable to string another sentence together. He makes me feel nervous. In a good way. His warm sensuality was more intoxicating than I could bear — his pheromones must be a match. I didn't trust myself.

Courtney's waiting for me:

"What was that all about?"

"Oh, I don't know, just wanted to say he liked my song the other week..." I say, blushing.

"Time to shave!" Courtney smiles, and walks into the club.

"What do you mean?" I know what she means, and follow her in. The club is resplendent in gothic banners that hang from the ceiling, low as it is, being in a basement. Candles stand in tall candelabras giving the place a moodier glow than usual, especially up on stage. Blink's husband is in full armour, clunking around the stage, moving a gothic chair into the centre, and lighting more candles.

"I'll get the drinks," I offer.

"I'll save ya a seat." Courtney disappears through the misty glow.

Riley was smiling through the corner of his mouth, watching me make my way over. Sometimes I feel he knows me better than I know myself; this was one of those times.

"Coca Cola for the lady?" He asks.

"Why not." I try to keep a steady hand on the conversation; he's looking at me; looking into my soul.

"And a beer please." So keen to stay cool I'd nearly forgotten the order. He comes back to the bar with the glasses and leans on the bar.

"So, how's life treating ya?"

"Oh, you know — OK...." I don't meet his stare. He goes back to filing the glasses, looking at me occasionally. Filing my glass with ice, he stops and looks down into the glass; if palmists read tea leaves, Riley read ice cubes.

"You're going away I hear." I'm unprepared for this.

"What do you mean?"

"Maybe it's too soon to tell?"

"Yeah, I've not got any plans..." He's confused me now; I'm flustered.

"Must be my mistake. Five pound and ten pence." He fixes me with his dark eyes as I rummage in my attempt at a gothic purse: a very old Hermes bag I'd found in a second-hand shop, the 'H's' I thought looked a bit like towers or bridges? I offer Riley a smile with the money; he takes the money.

"See ya," he almost yells as I scuttle away, the change he handed me still clenched in my fist.

"That Riley is weird sometimes!"

"Sometimes?" We make ourselves comfortable at our usual table, halfway up the room, and slightly to the right; the best position to see the stage, and the door, our backs to the bar.

Cage and Tony come in at the same time and stop to chat by the open door. The singer of The Evil Knocky Men stops Ben at the door with his bass drum in his hand. The main artery into the club is getting clogged, and all other entries are impassable. As Courtney downs her pint, I see the top of Blink's red mane behind them all and hear her shrill voice: this gets things moving.

"She's done it again." Courtney removes her head from her beer:

"Wha?" I indicate Blink's direction.

"Somebody give that girl a better reason to live than big dresses and big hair! It's little orphan Annie gets a dress up box!" We were just sore because we didn't have time, with all our sanctimonious moping around, to hit a dress up shop, and hire ourselves a costume.

"I wonder what she'd look like in sweats and a t-shirt."

"We'll never know…." We are still trying to imagine Blink dressed casually when Tony and Cage pitch up. It seems that neither of them could be bothered to dress up either.

"Hey ladies, what ya drinkin?" Cage's smile rests on Courtney.

"Sorted, thank you." Courtney looks genuinely sorted.

"Oh, OK." Cage looks almost sad.

"Is this seat taken?" Tony, always polite, indicates the seat next to mine.

"Be my guest," genuinely happy to see him, I pull the chair out.

"What will you have my good man?" Cage asks Tony.

"Oh, thanks, I'll have a beer." Cage hobbles off on his one good leg.

"So, what's new?" Tony asks innocently.

"We both got fired." I tell him. He looks suitably shocked.

"Well, she got fired — I just got an extended holiday." Even Courtney has gotten tired of being nasty to Tony. She could see, finally, that he wasn't a bad guy just a bad dresser.

"What happened?" He looks concerned for us both.

"We got fired," Courtney was toying with him. It was better than out and out abuse.

"Yeah, I know but, why? There's got to be a reason?"

"Seems we were naughty…" I smile.

"Weird, huh?" Courtney's eyebrows carry the joke.

"Not so strange really, no," Tony's getting on board, "I can imagine you two getting up to all kinds of…things." Bless him, he *was* trying.

"We didn't conform," I finish. Tony nods sagely, unsure what to say. Blink was bringing order to the room on stage:

"Quiet please!" Her husband is clunking around in his armour behind her on the stage, and you can see her perfect little red eyebrows narrow with annoyance. Turning around she glares at him, and he pulls to attention, flipping down his visor, and keeping stock still at the back of the stage like a proper empty suit of armour. The stage is set.

The candlelight throws strange patterns up on the makeshift banners. Castle walls had been haphazardly drawn onto paper and hung up as a backdrop. Blink stands resplendent in her floor length dress: sleeves cascading from elbow to floor, her red hair held aloft in thin, black netting, her tiny cleavage pressed back against her flesh and upwards, more bottom than bosom.

I find my eyes looking for Ben. They find him standing in the shadows, watching the stage from the side-lines. As my eyes grow accustomed to him, he finds mine. I quickly look away.

"Tonight!" Blink pauses for effect, and for the buzz in the room to calm under her auspicious gaze, "Tonight we have another action-packed show for you! Fresh from the days of yore, the knights of the round table are here, The Evil Knocky Men!" A roar of approval goes up from the audience, "and we have more blues magic from our very own court jester, Tony!" A reasonable cheer rises up — from our table in particular. Tony bows his head modestly. "Plus, Cassandra has agreed to play more than one song tonight!" The audience laughs, I blush, and my table of friends send up an encouraging cheer. "And we have Shamus O'Leary from Dublin to read some of his poetry!" A questionable hum of approval disperses amongst the audience.

"Who?" Courtney leans in to my ear.

"I don't know, some poet."

"And Halo and the Bats will be playing two new tracks!"

"Oh, I like them," whispers Courtney.

"I like Halo, but not the bats..." I reply.

"The bats are a bit...batty." Courtney's loss for words has something to do with the fact that Cage has his hand on her knee:

"Do ya want another?" He's eyeing her empty glass.

"I'd love one!" He turns to me.

"I'm fine thanks." Catching Tony's eye:

"Drink?"

"No, mate, it's my turn — what'll you have?" Tony takes everyone's orders as Shamus O'Leary ambles on to the stage, and adjusting the microphone, begins to read from a piece of paper he produces from his pocket which is more folded than anything I have ever seen before or since.

Ben is on the move: he's slowly making his way around the room, and I dare not look, but I can feel him. When he disappears behind me, the hairs on the back of my neck stand up. I imagine he must be heading to the bar. In a Nirvana t-shirt, and his hair looking longer and messier than last time, I found myself thinking about his chunky, firm arms, and the light hair that grows out of them. Are his eyes blue? I can't remember; I was unable to process all eye to brain visual data when he spoke to me.

My heart lurches into my throat as I recall that I had agreed to play tonight. I wonder if I'm next. Shamus is droning on, his Irish lilt a comforting backdrop; his words, in my state of anxiety, enter but do not register. Forgetting for a moment where I have put my guitar, I lurch in my chair, and regain composure, my hand reaching out to feel for the case beside me.

"You OK?" Courtney asks.

"Yeah...yeah". Then Tony is back, and glasses are being put down on the table in front of me. I can feel my insides turning to mush. The tell-tale sign of needing to urinate fills me with added dread, and I'm aware that I don't have time to go to the toilet and am not even sure if I really do need a pee, or whether it's just pre-stage nerves. Plus, I want to throw up for England. Shamus is folding his piece of paper and putting it back in his pocket. Courtney is laughing at something Cage has whispered in her ear. Blink is climbing on to the stage, grasping the sides of her enormous skirt. Her husband, in his armour, stops his frozen gag long enough to help her. Tony is touching my arm and giving me the thumbs up with the other. Blink is looking straight at me.

Tony is restringing my guitar. A soporific rain hangs in the air outside my apartment, barely touching the sides of the window glass. He looks very serious as he does it; his particularly bushy eyebrows seem to meet in the middle as he concentrates, getting the string through the eye of the nut on the head of the guitar. My 'Peach' and his bass are finally going to jam, and we really do mean music.

He tunes her up for me, enjoying the shape and the sound of this instrument that shares so much in common with his, and yet has two more strings, and a different melodic structure.

"That should keep you going..."

"Until I break another string..."

"I'm sure there'll be lads there that'll know how to help you..." The way he says it I can tell he doesn't like the idea of anybody else stringing my guitar.

"Here," he hands me a little, plastic box.

"What is it?"

"Open it." His head bowed, he appears sad, and proud all at once. Inside the plastic case is a mouth organ guitar tuner.

"Thank you." Genuinely touched, I lean forward and gave him a hug. It felt good. Bashful, he drops his head.

"So," he breathes heavily, "are you going to be OK?"

"Of course I am!" The bravado all mine. The door-bell saves me from further heroism. Buzzing them in, I turn to Tony:

"Sorry, they're early; we can still jam later…" Courtney and Cage stroll in all smiles, and flushed faces, their hands separating as they came through the door.

"Hey there!" Courtney's eyes tell me she's surprised to see Tony, and Cage simply sits down, never surprised by anything. Pye strolls out of the bedroom as if sensing his 'Dad' is here.

"Pye, you ol' dog — come 'ere!"

"He's a cat, honey — y'ar gonna give him a complex." Courtney's honeyed tones belie a new warmth between them.

"Tea, coffee anyone?" I offer.

"Haven'tcha got anything stronger?" Cage toys with me. He sits down on the floor next to Pye, who is now on his back, brandishing his stomach for Cage. I notice that Cage no longer had his cast on.

"When'd you get the cast off?"

"Courtney tore it off with 'er teeth!"

"Oh, get out 'widcha! I used a hacksaw!"

"Really?" They both look at me as if I'm mad.

"Naw! We just come from the hospital…"

"Oh…" I feel stupid and cover it up by moving into the kitchen to stick the kettle on. "I've got tea, coffee, or Ribena?"

"Tea please," says Tony, who everyone seems to have forgotten, sitting quietly, his bass now up on his knee; my 'Peach' propped against the sofa.

"Coffee please."

"Me too," Cage says climbing up off the floor.

"SO!" I nervously address the room, as the drinks go down on the table, "the reason I have gathered you all here today…" they are all looking up at me, and I suddenly feel very responsible, as if they are all my children. "Um, well, I don't quite know how to begin, but, I'm going away for a while…" There is a momentarily silence. Courtney, never quiet for long, is the first to pipe up:

"Whadya mean 'goin' away for a while'? How long? Where?!"

"Well, The Evil Knocky Men have invited me on tour with them…" I let this sink in.

"That's great, Cass." Cage at least can see the value of this recent success.

"Yeah," Courtney's trying, "but where ya goin'?"

"All over the country…" Tony looks up from the floor:

"When will you be back?"

"Well that depends..." I don't want to finish the sentence, but Courtney always has to know everything:

"On what goddamit?" Cage turns to her, surprised by her vehemence.

"Look, I need a change. This is a good opportunity for me to make that change, and I don't want to limit myself, or lie to you by saying I'll be back at a certain time or date because I just don't know. I want to be open to suggestion; I think one of the problems for me recently has been that I have stagnated here, and I need to see some new things. Maybe I'm more like my mother than I thought..." I let that big idea float out on its own, fermenting in the atmosphere; lost on Tony, but not on Cage or Courtney.

"So that's it, huh? Y'ar just gonna up and leave me?" I hadn't expected Courtney to be so upset; I can see tears welling in her eyes.

"I'm not leaving you! I'm just going on a journey..."

"A fuckin' long one by the sounds of it!" She isn't buying my payoff. I try to change the subject:

"Cage," he turns from Courtney to me, "I wondered if you would look after Pye..." Pye looks at me, "...since you're kind of his Dad..."

"Sure," Cage is uncharacteristically quiet.

"I'm letting the flat go at the end of the month, so any stuff I have will go to my Dad's till I get back…" Courtney's tears are flowing now, and she just sits there, letting them go. After all these months of holding it in, trying to be brave, fighting the system, Jack, what felt like 'everyone', having to finally grow up and make my own decisions — I crack too. I grab Courtney and we cry and hug each other whilst Cage and Tony sit feeling like real idiots.

"On the plus side I might bump into my mum…?" Court looks at me searchingly but says nothing.

"What about *the* bump?"

"It's coming too…"

Just like in the movie, 'Bel, Book, and Candle' my tears mark the end of my partnership with Pye. My powers of whatever persuasion — certainly not pure witch or I would have had greater success — no longer match the power of pure emotion: Pye takes his queue; he too is moving on. Taking one look at this sorry bunch of humans, he gets up, and jumps out the window: this time, having learnt how to land.

We all run to the window and look down.

ACKNOWLEDGEMENTS

My personal thanks go out to Judith A. Moose for her faith in my story. To the memory of my late father who celebrated both the spiritual <u>and</u> scientific worlds, and my mother, whose passion and zest for life is a constant inspiration. Also to Michele von Kaenel who will always be the 'Courtney' in my head. No dedication would be complete, nor my life, without my husband and kids. You three are the best part of me. Blessings, light, love , and sweet, sweet music to all.

ABOUT THE AUTHOR

Tara Newley Arkle comes from a long line of entertainers. Her parents, Anthony Newley and Joan Collins lit up stages and screens for decades. Her family heritage in entertainment traces back to Vaudeville during the Boer War. Tara's work was first published in Paris/Atlantic Magazine. She went on to study Literature at Boston University, and worked in London as a columnist and journalist, Radio DJ, and TV Presenter before starting her own contents company, NewleyDale Ltd. with television pilots made for Baby Cow, ITV, and Channel 4.

Radio Honey

Lightning Source UK Ltd.
Milton Keynes UK
UKHW020616090922
408591UK00008B/696